SILVER
CREEK
FIRE

SILVER CREEK FIRE

LINDSAY McKENNA

ZEBRA BOOKS
KENSINGTON PUBLISHING CORP.

www.kensingtonbooks.com

ZEBRA BOOKS are published by

Kensington Publishing Corp.
119 West 40th Street
New York, NY 10018

All Kensington titles, imprints, and distributed lines are available at special quantity discounts for bulk purchases for sales promotion, premiums, fund-raising, educational, or institutional use.

Special book excerpts or customized printings can also be created to fit specific needs. For details, write or phone the office of the Kensington Sales Manager: Attn.: Sales Department. Kensington Publishing Corp., 119 West 40th Street, New York, NY 10018. Phone: 1-800-221-2647.

Zebra and the Z logo Reg. U.S. Pat. & TM Off.

First Printing: November 2020
ISBN-13: 978-1-4201-5082-7
ISBN-10: 1-4201-5082-0

ISBN-13: 978-1-4201-5086-5 (eBook)
ISBN-10: 1-4201-5086-3 (eBook)

10 9 8 7 6 5 4 3 2 1

Printed in the United States of America

*To all my wonderful readers
who love romantic suspense!*

Chapter One

May 15

Did she have the courage to move to Wyoming?

Leanna Ryan ran her dusty fingers down the column of a piece of driftwood sculpture she had just finished creating for a client. She lived in Brookings, a small seacoast town in Oregon, and collecting driftwood during a meditative morning walk along the nearby beach was something Lea looked forward to, with her mug of coffee in hand. It was how she started her day: calm, quiet, and contemplative.

The velvety smoothness of the wood soothed her fractious inner state. Wood was alive, warm to the touch of her cold fingertips. She slid them with knowing experience as she followed the curve of the sperm whale she had fashioned. The wood soothed her, as it always had. It was another form of escape, Lea admitted to herself, but it was her passion: woodworking in all its various forms, and it was the world she chose to live within. Her father, Paddy, an Irishman from the Galway Bay area, was a master carpenter, known for his handmade, one-of-a-kind furniture.

He charged high prices and his clientele was more than eager to give him what he deserved.

He was seacoast Irish; his father—her grandfather, Connor—made his living as a trawler fisherman along the Oregon coast. Boutique grocery stores along the West Coast eagerly paid handsomely for his fresh catch. Paddy didn't want to be a fisherman, furniture was his passion, just as it was hers. Only, Lea had decided after that traumatic afternoon as a thirteen-year-old, to devote her life to woodworking. She didn't want to be a trawler fisherman, either. Paddy had often teased her that she had his woodworking genes, not the fishing ones. Her mother, Valerie, who was well known in North America for her art quilt creations, said Lea had not inherited any sewing genes, either, and they always laughed about that. Fabric didn't draw her. But wood always had.

Her red brows dipped, her hand smoothing the long flank of the whale she'd created, its golden-brown sides gleaming in the midmorning sunlight as it poured through the wood shop window. Sunlight was rare in Brookings. It was a tiny seacoast village that was usually hidden beneath the gray, scudding clouds over the Pacific Ocean. There was always lots of rain, too. Lea loved the rain and the moodiness of the Pacific Ocean here along the coast. It suited her own emotional nature.

Was she really ready to leave the only safety she'd ever known? Go east to Wyoming? Every time she thought about it, her stomach clenched in fear. She was twenty-nine years old. What woman stayed with her parents until that age? Single. Not interested in romance. Focused solely on her career and enhancing her master carpenter skills and wood sculpture skills.

She was such a coward. Oh, no one accused her of

being that, but inwardly, Lea knew that she was. And it shamed her in ways she couldn't give words to. Any man who flirted with her, or asked her out, she said no to. Luckily, she had plenty of women friends and she was more than grateful for them being a part of the fabric of her life. Her friends were her lifeblood. Full stop.

"Well," Paddy said, entering the wood shop, "looks like this will be the last sculpture you create here, colleen."

Warming to her father's Irish brogue, she turned, wiping her hands on her canvas apron she wore while working. Her goggles to protect her eyes were hanging around her neck. Lea smiled as her father wandered over to the table, his blue eyes twinkling as he halted opposite her. She saw him admiring her work and he looked very pleased with her efforts. "Looks like," she agreed.

"This is already sold," he said. "I'll box it up for you and make sure it's crated properly."

"Thanks," she murmured, loving the whale that she had created, rising in a breach, the tail in the water. Looking around, she whispered, "I'm really going to miss you and Mom . . . this place," and she gestured around the large, clean shop that had many windows to allow in plenty of light.

"Well," Paddy said gently, "it's time, Lea. I'm glad you're leaving to fulfill *your* dream."

She nodded. "Who knew when I was thirteen years old, that I'd read *My Friend Flicka* and *Green Grass of Wyoming* by Mary O'Hara, and want to live where she wrote those books."

"As children, we dream without inhibition," Paddy said, sitting down on a nearby stool, clasping his sixty-five-year-old gnarled hands. "And you've always wanted to go to Wyoming. It's a good thing to bring a lifelong dream to reality," he assured her.

Lea took another cloth, a clean, dry one, and began to wipe down her whale one last time. "Isn't it funny, Dad? How after I was beaten up by those boys as a girl, that I found Mary O'Hara's books? They were like an anchor to me, a homing beacon to overcome my shock and trauma, and focus on something good, beautiful. That was the beginning of my dream to go live in Wyoming."

"Your mother found them for you at the library," Paddy agreed, frowning.

Laughing softly, Lea continued to wipe the four-foot-high whale until the molten gold color of the driftwood gleamed. "I guess I didn't realize at that time how traumatized I was by that one incident."

"Hmph, it was more than an incident, Lea. Those boys broke your nose and fractured your left cheek. They meant to hurt you bad." He looked away, swallowing hard, then raised his chin and held her gaze. "It changed your life, colleen. Before? You'd been a loving, outgoing, carefree wild child. Afterward? And no one can blame you, you crawled deep inside yourself. Those boys couldn't take that you were blossoming into a young woman who was wild, carefree, and so full of life and hope."

"Some days, Dad? It seems like it was yesterday." Gently moving the cloth across the head of the whale, she added, "And other days? The incident doesn't bother me at all."

"Unless you run into strange men at the grocery store or any other public place," Paddy said, sadness in his tone. "And then it all comes back and you react."

"I can't help my reaction, Dad. I wish I could. And two

or more strange men nearby will send me into a panic that I can't control, either."

"Your brain sees these situations as a danger because of what happened to you," he agreed sadly.

Lea put the cloth down on the table. "I have to get on with my life. You and Mom have taken care of me long enough. Time for this baby bird to leave the nest."

"We'll miss you, but it's good that you're going," he agreed. "That letter from that rancher in Wyoming, Mr. Logan Anderson, wanting to hire you to come and do woodwork for him in the kitchen and living room, was your ticket to the life you've been dreaming about, Lea. It's a new door opening up for you. I'm glad you took the challenge and agreed to meet with him and look at the year-long project he has laid out for you."

Nodding, Lea pulled up a second wooden stool and sat down across from her father. "He'd wanted you, Dad. But you handed over the assignment to me. When I saw it was Wyoming, I wanted to go despite my issues with feeling unsafe out in the world. I'm glad you gave it to me. It's time for me to get on with my life and stop hiding from it."

"And when you talked to the rancher, you seemed settled."

"I asked him a lot of questions," she said, smiling a little. "He was patient. He seemed . . . well, nice . . ."

"But not a threat to you?" Paddy asked, prying.

"No." Lea shrugged. "For whatever reason, he didn't scare me like most male strangers do. I can't explain why not."

"Maybe the lure of Wyoming has dissolved some of this fear within you?" he asked her.

"I'm not sure, Dad. All I know is that while I'm battling

a fear of leaving the place I've lived my whole life, the yearning to go to Wyoming just got stronger because we talked to one another."

"Your mother and I think you should give Wyoming a try. It's a long-term project and it sounds like he's got the money to support your efforts. He's seen your work on our website, and he likes it. The unfamiliar is always scary for all of us." He gave her a soft smile, holding her unsure gaze.

"If he hires me, that will be the best, but if not, I can always get another job. Time to go," she agreed. "As I get older, I'm not as afraid as I used to be, and that's a good sign that the past isn't controlling me."

"You've made a lot of progress, Lea. Always pat yourself on the back for that. It takes courage to live, not just survive and breathe."

Grimacing, she folded the canvas apron, putting it away beneath the large, long table. "There's so much more to do." She straightened. "If you'd told me that *one* incident could wreck a person's life, I wouldn't have believed you. But"—her voice grew hoarse—"I do now."

Paddy stood and came around the table, giving his only daughter a strong, loving hug. "A day at a time, colleen, a day at a time." He released her, clasping her upper arms. "Just think, you're going to Wyoming, the place you've dreamed about. *That* has to excite you and make you happy. Everything is packed and we've put it in the back of your truck with a waterproof tarp over all of it. Your carpenter tools are in there, as well. Your sculpting tools are in your black nylon bag sitting on the front seat. You're ready to go."

Lea forced a smile for her dad's benefit. She hated being a wet blanket to her parents and often masked her reaction for their benefit. "You're right. Off on a new and glorious adventure." So why didn't she sound more enthusiastic?

May 24

Dread was replaced with excitement as Lea drove her Ford three-quarter blue and white truck closer to Silver Creek, Wyoming. The valley sat south of Thermopolis, below the archeological and dinosaur area of Wyoming. She'd just driven through Bighorn Canyon National Recreation Area and it was spectacular! There were plenty of mountains around the huge canyon area, but right now, the highway leveled out, descended several thousand feet to a huge plain below. Silver Creek Valley was filled with lush grass, ranches, and rolling hills dotted with stands of pine and deciduous trees here and there.

Her gaze was always on the types of trees in the area, most of them pines of the species she'd identified so far. The mountains were still clothed at the very top with white, gleaming snow.

It snowed often in May, she was told by a waitress when she'd stopped at a restaurant several hours ago. She'd seen several bighorn sheep, males and females, which had been thrilling. Lea had stopped and photographed them when-ever she could safely pull over and take the shots. She'd never seen bighorns before!

With every mile, her heart lifted with a carefully shielded and closeted joy. The southern half of Wyoming was plains, desert, and some gorgeous sedimentary buttes that looked like torte cakes created by soil, in white, red, and cream layers. She'd taken photos of them, too. Then, she'd rolled into central Wyoming where the Wind River mountains and Indian reservation inspired her. Her hometown of Brookings was surrounded with thick, green, old-growth forest; that part of Wyoming reminded her deeply of it, soothing some of her homesickness. She could see huge natural gas rigs dotting the area the farther north she drove. If she didn't miss her guess, they were fracking, which she disliked and didn't believe in. That bothered her because she was environmentally oriented. Each rig, and she lost count of how many dotted the landscape, reminded her that it was an oversized hypodermic needle slammed through the skin of the Earth, sucking life blood out of her, harming her. She knew not everyone looked at it like that. Natural gas was a cleaner fuel than oil or coal, no argument. But she'd heard about the many earthquakes created by fracking, breaking through the layers of sedimentary rock beneath the surface in Oklahoma, and the damage it was doing above and below ground to get to this natural resource. Oklahoma had more earthquake tremors than nearly anywhere else in the U.S.

As she approached the town of Silver Creek, the plain flattened out and she left the mountains behind. Now the hills were softly rounded, clothed in dark, thick, green grass, ranches to her right and left off the highway. This was a lush, verdant valley. To her artist's eye, it reminded her of a dark green emerald, faceted into the earth, full of life, vigor, and vitality. She saw many herds of Herefords in different pastures along the way, all heartily eating the nutritious fare. There were some patches of snow here and there, but the green grass had the say and Lea was sure the cows were very, very happy with their lives at the moment.

Traffic increased as she drove past the SILVER CREEK sign at the right side of the two-lane asphalt highway. It said: POPULATION 10,000. Below it, the sign said that the town was incorporated in 1905. She'd seen photos of this magical place that reminded her of a gypsy-like, Bohemian hideaway. But photos she'd seen online couldn't match what she saw in person as she slowed to twenty-five miles per hour in midmorning traffic. There were bright wooden crests on nearly every business, looking like a colorful hat for each one. Some had silver or gold outlining the color of the wooden building's headdress. She saw a light blue hardware store, the crest darker blue and outlined in silver. There were narrow alleys in between these 1900s-era buildings. The donut shop was painted a fuchsia color with a pink crest outlined in gold, flashing in the morning sunlight across the clear blue sky. On the other side was a bright red Dairy Queen, with a white crest outlined in red, the company colors, with a flash of gold.

She didn't see many major corporate businesses along the half mile of buildings packed on either side of the four-lane highway. Most looked owned by individuals, not megacorporations, the main street of the town looking like a fabulous collection of Easter eggs bracketing the street. Huge pots of brightly colored flowers were hanging on antique brass lamps on both sides of the street for a good half mile or more. May was still a snow month, so Lea figured they would be filled with cold-loving colorful blooms until June first.

In the center of town, there were three major traffic lights. Most of the vehicles were either pickup trucks, ranch flatbed trucks, or muddy SUVs. She saw few other types of cars, but they all had out-of-state license plates and most likely were tourists just like herself. At ten a.m., the town was waking up. To her delight, she saw a large bookstore, The Unicorn, to her left, and it was painted a pale lavender color with a dark purple crest outlined in shiny silver paint. Below it was painted, in silver lettering: 1905, the year it was built. Next to it was a large restaurant that took up half a block, Olive Oyle's. It was a two-story brick building; the crest painted a bright yellow, orange highlights with gold trim. She saw a sign that said: LUNCH AND DINNER. There were lots of pickups parked in front of The Unicorn bookstore. That was a good sign! She saw a sheriff's black-and-white Tahoe cruiser parked in the mix, as well. Hungry, Lea decided to stop at The Unicorn bookstore because it had a large sign out front that said: COFFEE, PASTRIES and BREAKFAST/LUNCH. She never ate breakfast, per se, but coffee was her saving grace.

Parking in a space in front of the bookstore, she took the large black nylon bag holding her carving tools off the passenger seat and placed them out of sight, down on the floor of the cab. Climbing out, the chill of the thirty-degrees-Fahrenheit temperature made her glad she'd pulled on her trusty purple goose-down nylon jacket that fell to her hips. Taking a purple, white, and pink knit hat her mother had made for her last Christmas, she pulled it over her cap of short red hair and looped the muffler of the same colors, around her neck. Picking up her small knapsack, Lea hitched it across her left shoulder and locked the pickup. Patrons were coming and going, with large cups of coffee and sacks of pastries in their hands, wearing big smiles.

Lea stopped and peered through the large plate glass window. It showed aisle after aisle of books that were arranged nicely so that people passing by might be tempted to come in and check them out. Lacy white curtains were arranged around the top and sides of the window, giving it a decidedly feminine look.

Walking into the bookstore it smelled welcoming, and automatically, Lea inhaled the scent of thousands of old leather-bound books. It was a dizzying fragrance to her and she stepped aside so other patrons could come and go, just looking around, admiring the two-story building. This place reminded her of the ancient library of Alexandria, Egypt, thousands of books crowded perilously on very old, stout, wooden shelves that had to be made of a hardwood or they would have bent and bowed under the weight a long time ago.

Laughter and chatting filled the air and it was satisfying to hear sounds of happiness, ratcheting down the tension within her. She smelled the coffee, lifting her nose, inhaling the scent deeply and with appreciation. There was a full service restaurant on the right side of the huge area, a cash register and L-shaped counter on her left. She could smell bacon frying, the scent of vanilla pancakes, and her mouth watered. The door was polished gold brass with a window from top to bottom. No one was at the cash register. She looked and saw that the coffee bar was down on the right. There was an entrance to the busy restaurant for those who wanted a sit-down meal. The aisles opposite that area were filled with books, all neatly labeled: astrology, astronomy, environment, numerology, tarot, and on and on, in alphabetical order.

Lea loved the old, highly polished oak wooden floor. It pleasantly creaked beneath her boots, the sound telling her the wood was not only well cared for, but also, in very good shape despite its age. More than likely this floor had been placed in 1905. The golden color of it brought light into the aisles. There were plenty of antique lights above her as well, probably from the 1900s, all brass, all carefully polished, with the latest bright lightbulbs, which threw a lot of light. A person could spend hours in this place, Lea decided. She saw lots of short wooden stools, all oak, in every aisle, so patrons might sit down on one and open up a book to check it out. There were also some porch swings that had been recreated to become like sofas with soft, colorful cushions upon them, where readers could sit in one of the many alcoves to enjoy the book they'd chosen to peruse and while away a few minutes or an hour.

She was in love with this place.

Arriving at the coffee bar, a tiger-maple counter, twenty-five feet long, caught Lea's knowing gaze. It was beautiful, with golden horizontal bars against a reddish darker wood, well cared for, too. Behind it, she saw a woman in her late twenties, blond hair, flashing green eyes, her lips in a smile as she served her customers, who waited patiently in line for their coffee orders. They were farmers, ranchers, and white collar types, a mix of women and men. Two girls in their late teens, the baristas, were making up the coffee orders as fast as possible for their eager clients.

Lea stood back and studied the overhead menu. She could see three waitresses delivering breakfast to the patrons in the restaurant. The glass bakery case up front had cinnamon-laced rolls drizzled with white frosting, and so many other yummy pastries. She leaned down, her stomach growling. There was an orange and pineapple pound cake, by the slice, for sale. Deciding on her order, Lea walked to the back of the line, glad that there was time to just absorb this wonderful old place with all its eccentricities. She spotted a man in his late twenties or early thirties in the restaurant and he looked like the manager in charge of running it.

Four customers ahead of her, Lea noticed the sheriff in a dark green khaki uniform, his black Stetson on his head, broad shoulders. He wasn't that old, maybe in his early thirties, dark brown military-short hair and green eyes. She wasn't immune to good-looking men and from an artist's perspective, this law enforcement officer was very handsome in an interesting way. When he picked up his coffee and ambled down past the line, she read SEABERT, D. on his gold brass name plate across the left pocket of his jacket. He had green eyes like her, but they were a darker jade color, and he gave her a quick perusal. Not feeling threatened, she was sure the county sheriff made it his business to know who was new in his town and jurisdiction. Lea knew she posed no threat to him and he nodded, smiled a little, as he ambled past her, heading for the door. Dressed in a pair of worn blue jeans, her light tan hiking boots and a violet-colored jacket, Lea thought he might be wondering if she was a New Ager like this bookstore was.

Hiding her smile, she focused on the rest of the people in line, curious about who lived in this Bohemian dream that was clearly out of Queen Victoria's nineteenth-century rule. This bookstore and its owner just never caught on to the twenty-first century, and Lea found it delightful.

Turning her attention to who she thought might be the owner of The Unicorn, it didn't take a detective to spot her among the other hardworking employees. The woman was dressed in gypsy-like clothes: bright red, orange, and yellow flowers on her ankle-length skirt, a white blouse, and a colorful blue scarf around her shoulders. Her blond hair was held up with an orange scarf, and she wore long, dangling gold earrings and at least ten or fifteen multicolored bangles on each arm. The rings she wore on her small, slender hands were many and flashed with green, blue, and pink gems in each of them. The bright Kelly-green sash she wore around her waist had tiny gold bells stitched onto one edge of it, and every time she moved, they tinkled pleasantly.

Lea loved this woman's audacity to be herself. She looked like the wild child Lea used to be, and sadness moved through her. From the time she'd started school as a six-year-old, she'd worn colorful skirts, blouses, and scarves, just like this woman. Her choice of clothing had drawn a lot of attention, but as a young girl, she didn't care. It was her artist's eye, her appreciation of all colors, that had decided what she wanted to wear. And her mother, who was a wonderful seamstress as well, would take the fabric they'd pick out at a quilting store in Brookings, and make her the big, swirling skirts she loved so much. Those were happy days for Lea and she left it at that, enjoying watching the owner chat warmly and sincerely with each customer as they came up to the counter to order. Many of them also bought egg and ham sandwiches along with some baked goods. Just about every man in front of her left with a sack of food, bakery items, and the largest cup of coffee they could order, in hand.

"Hi!" she said, greeting Lea. "I'm Poppy. What can I get you this morning?"

Smiling, Lea said, "One of everything?"

Laughing, Poppy said, "You're new to town, aren't you? I haven't seen you in here before."

"I am new. My name's Lea Ryan. Could I have a large mocha latte? And I'd love a slice of your orange and pineapple pound cake."

"Sure," she said, calling out the coffee order to her busy baristas. Grabbing a bakery tissue, she hurried over to the bakery case and placed the slice into a paper sack. Coming back, she took Lea's money and ran the order through her cash register.

"I see you have tarot readings here?" Lea asked.

"Yes, I'm the tarot reader." Poppy's eyes gleamed. "Are you in need of a reading?"

"I'd like one, yes. Could I get an appointment?"

Poppy saw her line of waiting customers was slowing. "Why don't you go over there." She pointed across the way toward an open door. "That's my office. Go sit down on the couch and have your coffee and pound cake. I'll be done here in another fifteen minutes. We're about finished with the morning rush." She gestured toward the line.

"How much do you charge?" Lea asked, taking the coffee brought up by one of the employees.

"On the house," Poppy said. "You're new. I'll bet you're looking for answers and information."

Lea grinned and stepped aside for the next customer. "You got that right. Thanks, Poppy." She turned and headed for the open doorway that was about six aisles away.

Poppy closed the door to her office and sat down at her messy desk, clearing a space for the tarot reading. "My husband, Brad, will take over for me now. Have you ever had a reading before, Lea?" She quickly shuffled the oversized cards.

"I have a friend in Brookings, Oregon, who is a tarot reader," she explained. "I never got a reading from her."

"Oh?" Poppy smiled and tilted her head. "And why not?"

Shrugging, Lea said, "I liked my life the way it was. I didn't want to know about any changes that were ahead."

Laughing, Poppy said, "There is nothing *but* change in our lives, Lea. That's the only thing we can honestly count on."

"Well, mine's been pretty quiet until just recently."

"What are you doing in Wyoming? That's a long ways from Brookings, Oregon."

A grin edged her lips. "Touché. I'm meeting a potential employer about a job later on this morning."

"Great!" She held up the deck. "I'm going to do a three-card reading. The first card will represent your recent past. The second, the present. And the third, your future." She held out the deck across the desk to Lea. "You can shuffle them as you like. Mentally, as you shuffle the cards, ask them: What are the energies surrounding me presently?"

Lea had finished her pound cake, which had been delicious, and half her coffee was already gone. She wiped her fingers on the sides of her jeans and took the deck. "Okay," she murmured.

Poppy sat back, remaining silent while Lea did as she instructed.

"There," Lea said, laying the cards on the desk.

"Well done." She separated the cards into three different piles and then picked them up in no particular order.

Lea watched, fascinated. What would her future hold?

Poppy picked up the first card, stared at it, and then turned it around and flipped it over. "This is the four of Pentacles," she said. "It shows a woman standing in her beautiful garden, dressed regally, and she's holding the pentacle, which is the symbol for money. This is your recent past. This represents who you are: a woman who loves being alone, with her garden and making good money at whatever career she's chosen. You are happy and content. Life is good." She tapped the Rider-Waite tarot card with her fingertip. "This is a card that says you have everything you want."

Lea nodded. "Wow, this is accurate! I live in a small seacoast town and I'm a master carpenter and wood sculpture artist. I make a very good living and I'm working at getting established."

"Well, you certainly had a wonderful world in your past. Why would you want to leave it? Or, perhaps you're wanting to set up your own business here in Silver Creek? We have an artist's colony here, you know? But no one who is a wood artist. You'd fit right in!"

Holding up her hands, Lea said, "I'm here to see if I get a one-year job that involves a lot of carpentry, along with some sculpture."

"Oh?" Poppy queried, her gaze thoughtful looking. "Which ranch?"

Lea smiled a little. "Are you psychic, too?"

"Oh, just a little," she admitted with a smile. "The main economy here in the valley is based on farming and ranching, although that's changing, and Silver Creek has become a highly popular tourist destination. It's the ranchers who have the kind of money it would take to hire your kind of specialized services, not the farmers. Not really psychic, just logical."

"I like your style," Lea said. "Yes, it's for a ranch owner."

"Hmmmm, there's only one rancher in the valley who I think has probably hired you. That would be Logan Anderson, owner of the Wild Goose Ranch."

Shocked, Lea sat back, staring at Poppy. "And you know this how?"

Tittering, Poppy shook her head. "Logic, again. Logan usually comes in here a couple mornings a week for his large Americano and a sit-down breakfast. In fact, he was in here yesterday and was talking about hiring a master carpenter to do work for his kitchen." Her eyes gleamed. "That *has* to be you, Lea. Am I right?" She gave a giggle.

Laughing, Lea said, "Yes, it is me. I haven't taken the job yet. We've talked on the phone, but I wanted to see his home in person and do an assessment, to see if it's something I really want to do or not."

"Ohhhhh," Poppy purred, giving her a sly look, picking up a second card. "I have a feeling this is a done deal. You just don't know it yet." She flipped it over. "My goodness," Poppy said, frowning, "that's the Tower."

Lea stared over at the card. The illustration on it was a huge tower and the triangular top of the castle was being struck by a bolt of lightning, people falling out of the windows. Even she knew it didn't bode well. *Great.* "What's it mean?"

Sitting up, Poppy said, "Expect the unexpected. Things to occur to you out of the blue. You don't see them coming. Look, this isn't always a bad thing. You can have a nice surprise that you didn't expect, also."

"Then why are you frowning like that?"

Grinning, Poppy said, "Your parents didn't raise a dumb kid, did they?"

"No, they didn't." Lea pushed the card with her finger. "So, my present, being here, is like a bolt out of the blue?"

"Yes. But understand that even bad things or un-expected things that happen can turn out to have a silver lining; something you never saw coming. But it does mean stressful moments when you least expect it, at a minimum. I hope you're adaptable and flexible?"

"I've lived with stress most of my life. I'm pretty used to it."

"If you're a flexible, adaptable person," Poppy said, "you will have a far better chance of negotiating these sit-uations than people who are stuck and unbendable by nature. Are you really adaptable?"

"Yes, I'm pretty flexible," Lea agreed.

"Good! Then no problem. You'll have ups and downs by being here, but hey, that's Life 101. Your future card will tell us how it's all going to turn out." She flipped the card up from the deck. "Ah," she murmured wryly, "the Fool."

Lea stared at the young man with a staff, standing on the edge of a mountain cliff with his dog, off on some kind of journey. It looked like he was taking a step into thin air off the cliff, not worried at all about it. Was this good or bad? She gave Poppy a questioning look.

"The Fool is about taking a new journey, Lea. You're off on a brand-new track, a new lane or a chapter in your life you've never had before. This is a good card, one that means you are free of any worries, stresses, or demands from your earlier life. It's a risk-taking card. But not all risks are bad," she counseled. "We all go through times when our lives are steady and calm and the same, day in and day out. But then, life has cycles, and so the Fool is the person who entrusts herself or himself, to a new road that they are challenged to take."

"But 'fool' means just that," Lea muttered, worried. "Someone who does something without thinking or caring what the consequences of their decisions might be." She pointed at the card. "This guy is standing on the edge of a cliff and he looks like he's going to step right off it and into thin air. Who in their right mind would do that?"

Poppy smiled. "Risks come in many forms. And the beauty of the Fool card is about trusting our spirit, our faith in ourselves and others, our heart, and following our passion, no matter where it might lead us. The Fool has faith in whatever develops through the synchronicities life reveals, finding everyday magic, doors opening without struggle, and moving forward toward a new life, regardless. He has the faith that as he steps off the cliff into thin air, he will not drop and fall to the ground below. That sounds pretty good to me."

Frowning, Lea said, "You really hit the nail on the head when you said my life has been very quiet, very same, day in and day out. It's the way I needed it to be."

Gently, Poppy laid her hand on the cards. "I guess the tarot has decided you're ready for your next adventure, Lea. It's nothing to be afraid of. It can mean another chapter has begun to open up in your life, is all."

"I liked the last chapter I was in," she hesitantly admitted.

Giving her a long, studied look, Poppy wrote down the three cards in a nearby notebook along with Lea's name. "Tell you what? After you get done with your interview with Logan Anderson, come back and see me. Let me know what happened. We can always do a full tarot spread for you and it will give me a lot more information that may be of help to you."

"A new chapter. Okay, I can try to adjust. I can't go back to my home because I've more than worn out my welcome with my very tolerant, loving parents. It's past time I flew the nest and started standing on my own two feet."

"There you go," Poppy encouraged, smiling warmly. "You have what it takes, Lea. Logan is well respected around here. He started a wonderful midsummer festival for the town, and now it's so popular we get tourists coming from overseas for it. He's a really nice guy. No one speaks ill of him here in Silver Creek. He and his family have been on this land for four generations. I'd be hard-pressed to hear you say you didn't like him."

Lea stood up. "Well, I'm about to find out."

"Just take the road north, out of town. Logan's ranch, the Wild Goose, is four miles out of town and on the left. You can't miss it. His great-great-grandfather, Cyrus Anderson, was a metal worker and sculptor. He settled into the valley, trying to make a living at it, but he couldn't. So, he turned to cattle ranching, which he became very successful at. The Wild Goose is forty thousand acres of wonderful, lush grassland, woodlands, and it's the biggest spread in the valley."

"Which explains why he's willing to ask someone like me to do some one-of-a-kind woodworking for his home."

"Oh, that!" Poppy stood up and smoothed down her skirt. "The Andersons have a long history here in the valley. It was cattle ranching and selling lumber to the silver mines in the mountains west of us. When Logan was born, things started to change. He wanted to transform the Wild Goose into something other than just a cattle ranch. He'll tell you himself about the changes he's already made, and I'm sure he'll share some of his dreams for the future of his family's ranch. He's very innovative. I think you'll like him."

Lea hoped so. "Thanks for the free reading, Poppy. I will let you know how the interview went."

Chapter Two

May 27

Driving out of Silver Creek and onto the flat plain of Silver Creek Valley, Lea saw nothing but either huge farming operations or large, rambling green pastures filled with brown and white Hereford cattle. Wild Goose Ranch was four miles down on the two-lane asphalt highway that spanned north to south across the long valley.

To the west, she could see the backbone of a mountain range beyond it, but didn't know its name. On her right, to the east, was the Bighorn Recreation Area. Up ahead of her were rolling plains for as far as she could see.

Poppy had told her that this particular valley, where mid-1800s silver mining had gone on in the mountain range to the west, had a special microclimate. In western Wyoming it was nine months of winter and blizzards. Even worse, as a result there was no ninety-day window to grow fruits and vegetables. But here, in Silver Valley, it was a Garden of Eden, as Poppy had termed it. They could grow fruits, vegetables, and farming crops, with ease. The winters were always mild and temperatures never below zero. They had six months of spring and summer, and six months of fall and winter; much better than the western edge of Wyoming, where Yellowstone and Grand Teton National Park had been cheated by Old Man Winter. Yes, this was a very special valley, Lea realized.

She replayed the phone call she'd had previously with Logan Anderson. His voice was low, modulated, and she liked his easygoing nature, reminding her of a type B, not a gung-ho, aggressive type A. Men who were aggressive scared her into having flashbacks, much to her consternation, which she could not control. Logan seemed, well, safe, from what she could tell from that one thirty-minute discussion they'd had. He'd sounded excited to meet her, telling her that her wood sculptures were incredible and beautiful. Her entire portfolio was online and she was glad her dad had talked her into displaying her work. Everything seemed positive, and her heart lifted because she desperately needed something good to happen for her on this new journey.

The four miles unwound quickly. She'd entered Wild Goose Ranch property a mile back. The fence line was made of rusted, round pipe, welded together. The rust color contrasted with the lush green grass in the pastures, with the blue sky a canopy above her. In some pastures, there were cattle. In others, there were no animals; it looked like the grass had been eaten down. She had no idea how big each pasture was, but in the center of each one was a circular grove of big, old trees that would give shade as well as protection against weather. That was good planning in her mind, plus the owner cared about his livestock. A north-south creek ran through each pasture, giving the animals a place to drink their fill. From a cow's point of view, this must be heaven. She saw lots of newborn calves in one particularly large pasture, at least thirty mothers with their frolicking, playful babies. She smiled as she saw some of the calves racing around, tails up in the air like flags, galloping madly with a group of other youngsters, having fun. In another one, she saw men and women wranglers on horseback, herding cattle between the pastures to an unknown destination.

Up ahead, she saw a huge gate made of metal piping. A metal banner across the top showed three geese flying, one after another. Below the sculptures was a sign: Wild Goose Ranch. She braked a little, putting the blinker on for a turn left. The two long, huge gates were open, the dirt and gravel road was wide, welcoming her. About half a mile down the road, she saw a cowboy on a horse. There were more wranglers in the field next to the road. It looked so peaceful and inviting; just like the books she'd read.

Her heart beginning to pound with anticipation, Lea started her turn since there was so little traffic on the highway.

BAM!

A scream lurched out of Lea's mouth. She was slammed forward as she made the turn. Something big and dark, a large pickup, slammed full force into her left fender. Color flashed before her. The airbags deployed, blinding her. It was like a fist hitting her. She was airborne! Her fingers were wrapped in a death grip around the wheel as her pickup sailed up, twisting as if in slow motion through the air, falling with a crash. The tearing of metal hurt her ears as they plunged into a nearby ditch at the side of the entrance. In seconds, her truck had been struck, did a 360 in the air, and landed upright on all four tires, all of them blowing with explosive bangs. Her neck was jerked hard. Sobbing for breath, stunned, Lea couldn't see for the damned airbags! Fighting them with her hands, she smelled steam and heard it escaping like a Yellowstone geyser up in front of her. The radiator had cracked open. Someone had hit her! The entire front window was gone!

Vaguely, she heard a horse galloping at high speed nearby. She was incased in deflating airbags, frustrated that she couldn't see anything or get out. Angry, stunned, and hands shaking as she tried to find the release on her seat belt, Lea jerked at it until it opened. Before she could open the door on her left, someone yanked it open.

"Ma'am? Are you all right?"

Blinking, Lea angrily shoved aside the airbag that had deployed out of her steering wheel. The man standing on the edge of the ditch, leaning down, peering into the cab, looked just as shocked as Lea felt. "Y-yes, I'm fine!" she snapped, her voice wobbling.

"Are you hurt?"

His voice was low and calming. Lea pushed her long legs out into the ditch weeds, next to where he stood. "I'm okay," she said, anger bleeding out of her voice.

"Here, let me help you. This ditch has no water in it, but the snow has left the grass slippery."

He thrust his elk-skin-gloved hand toward her, offering assistance.

Lea grabbed his hand. He was strong, but he didn't yank her out of the cab. Instead, he kept a firm grip around her hand and slowly eased her upright, into a standing position. The cowboy was right: The grass was slippery because the soil beneath it was muddy. He offered his other hand and she gratefully took it, unbalanced by the sharp incline of the ditch. To her left, standing calmly above the wide ditch, was a big buckskin quarter horse. Her mind whirled as the cowboy helped her negotiate the wet grass and guided her to flat, bare ground above the truck. He released her one hand, but held the other, giving her an assessing look.

"Ma'am? Can you stand on your own or do you want help?"

Her knees felt like so much jelly, but Lea tried to look strong and capable. She didn't want anyone thinking she was a wilting lily. "N-no . . . I'm okay. You can let go. Thanks for helping me." A part of her cried inwardly when he reluctantly released her hand. He took a step back, touching the front rim of his Stetson. "You must be Lea Ryan?"

Giving him a look of surprise, she absorbed his deeply tanned face, the crow's feet at the corners of his gray eyes, which were focused on her. "Yes . . . I am." Her mind felt jostled and disconnected, but then she realized who he was. "You're Logan Anderson?"

He gave her a slight smile. "Yes, ma'am, I am. You look pale. Are you *sure* you are all right? Do you want to sit down?"

Touching her brow, her hair tousled by the accident, she said, "I'm feeling pretty shaken." She twisted toward her truck, feeling a pang of urgency. "My truck . . ." She gestured toward it.

"We'll take care of that," he assured her, taking a radio out of his pocket. "I'm going to call my foreman, Barry, and get the truck out of the ditch. Do you want me to take you to the emergency room of our hospital?"

Frowning, Lea turned, her knees feeling a bit stronger. She liked Logan's quiet air of confidence, that mellow voice that soothed her distressed state. "No, I think I'm okay. Nothing's broken, thank goodness. Just . . . shaken up . . ."

"Did you hit your head?" he asked, after calling for his foreman to meet them at the main gate.

"Uh," she said, frowning, touching her brow, "I don't think so . . ."

He tucked the radio away in a pocket. "You've got a nosebleed," he said, and pulled off one glove, searched and found a white linen handkerchief in his back pocket, and handed it to her.

"Oh . . ." Lea pressed it to her nose. Sure enough, it was leaking blood. She hadn't even felt it!

"Here," Logan said, pulling off the denim jacket he wore and laying it on the ground. "Why don't you sit down? You're going even more pale on me."

Sitting sounded good. Lea sat on his denim jacket before she fell. Pulling her knees toward her body, wrapping her arms around them, she pressed her brow against her knees, closing her eyes, feeling suddenly emotional and unstable. "Thanks," she whispered hoarsely, even her voice sounding weak and trembly to her. Her brain felt like it was a bowling ball, loose and rolling crazily all over the place. She felt him come and sit nearby, his closeness giving her a sense of stability. He said nothing, simply remained beside her. After five minutes, she felt a bit better. Lifting the handkerchief away from her nose, she saw the bleeding had stopped. Out of the corner of her eye, she studied his profile. It was one of strength. "This isn't a very good way to meet," she heard herself mumble in apology to him.

"Don't worry about that," he said, cocking his head, meeting her gaze. "Let's worry about you, first, okay?"

"Did you see it?"

"What? The crash? No. I was riding up to the corral next to the gate and was opening the pasture entrance when it happened. I heard the crash and it startled my horse. I was trying to get him under control before I looked your way. I saw the truck spin around in midair and land in the ditch."

Lea looked at her truck. "It's totaled. Did you see who hit me? I know it was a pickup. I got a brief flash of it after he struck the left rear fender."

"No, I didn't. I had my hands full with my horse. The noise spooked him and I was trying to calm him down, at the same time watching your truck fly through the air."

"Whoever it was, he didn't care. Wouldn't you think his truck is pretty damaged, too?"

"Should be," Logan agreed. "I'm going to make a call to the sheriff. We need to report this. I'll handle everything here, so don't worry." He pulled out his cell phone and made a call. Afterward, he twisted his head in the direction of the ranch road. "Here comes my foreman, Barry Craig." He slowly unwound from his sitting position and stood. "Why don't you just sit there for a moment?"

"I'm not going anywhere," Lea promised him darkly, staring unhappily at her truck. What was she going to do now?

"Good to know," he jested. "Stay put."

Lea watched him walk to where the white pickup truck had pulled over and stopped. A pewter-colored sign was painted on the door: WILD GOOSE RANCH, with three geese flying below the words. She saw two other people emerge from the truck, both wearing cowboy hats. One was a woman. They talked briefly with Logan and then he led them over to where she sat.

Logan knelt down on one knee, facing her. "Lea? This is Jody Constance. She's one of my wranglers, but she's also a paramedic. Jody, meet Lea Ryan. I've asked her to check you over."

Jody came around to the other side of her with her medical bag in one hand. "Hi, Lea. I'm sorry this happened," she said, kneeling down in front of her, opening the bag.

"Makes two of us," Lea said, glad to see a woman. Logan calmed her, but he was her potential boss and it was tough to think right now, her brain addled. Women, she automatically trusted.

"Let me give you a quick, painless exam?" she asked, looping the stethoscope around her neck and donning a pair of latex gloves.

"Sure," Lea said. "I'm just more shook-up than anything else, Jody. Nothing feels broken."

"Good to know. I'm going to do a gentle physical exam with you. You tell me if something feels tender or hurts." She started at Lea's ankles, gently squeezing them, moving them carefully to make sure they were mobile, and asking if Lea felt any pain. In five minutes, she was almost done.

"Is she okay?" Logan asked, standing nearby.

Jody carefully examined Lea's neck and shoulders.

Lea flinched. "My neck is tender," she offered.

Jody nodded and lightened her touch. "I'll know in a minute, Logan," she said. Jody returned her attention to Lea. "Did that hurt, or is it tender, or something else?"

"Yes," she muttered, frowning. "My neck feels really stiff, and it and my upper shoulders are really tightening up."

"Probably whiplash," Jody said, moving her fingers knowingly around the base of Lea's neck. She pulled a small penlight from her shirt pocket. "I need to check out your eyes," she said. "Just look at my nose." She pointed to it as she moved the light slowly from right to left across Lea's field of vision.

Jody put the light away, tucking it back into a portion of her emergency medical bag and then lightly palpated Lea's brow and then her nose.

"Ouch," Lea said.

Jody lifted her fingers away. "You've got some swelling at the base of your nose."

"Hence, my nosebleed. Right?" Lea asked, looking up at the woman's serious expression. Jody had short blond hair, blue eyes, and fair skin. She looked to be in her late twenties. She saw the woman nod.

"I think you're going to have a really nice-looking shiner under your left eye."

Making a face, Lea muttered, "Great. I hope it doesn't swell shut."

Jody grinned. "It probably won't." She looked up at Logan. "I don't think she needs to go to the ER, but she definitely needs to go to the ranch house and stand down. It's shock more than anything else. She needs quiet, some-place warm where she can lie down when she wants to." Jody shifted her attention to Lea. "A good hot tub of water and soaking your neck and shoulders should help more circulation get in there and work on that whiplash you got. How does that sound?"

"Sounds like a good prescription, Doc," Lea said, giving her a grateful look of thanks for her help.

Logan peered down at her. "Lea? Are you okay with staying with us? I've got three bedrooms in my ranch house, and you can have any one of them. My housekeeper, Maddy Long, is there and she'll make you comfortable."

Jody said, "I'll go with her, Boss. Make sure Maddy knows what she needs."

"Good," Logan said, giving her a nod.

"That sounds great," Lea said, gazing up at the rancher, "but are you sure?" She wasn't even an employee and he hadn't hired her. She had heard about Westerners being kind to strangers, but this was shocking to her—in a good way.

"Positive," Logan murmured. He moved his chin toward the highway. "Here comes the sheriff. Barry? Why don't you and Jody take Lea to the house? I'll stay out here with the deputy and give her the details on what happened. If he wants to talk with her later, I'll ask him to drive to the ranch house."

"But, what about all my tools?" She pointed to the large silver galvanized toolbox located in the bed of the truck. "I also have my wood-sculpting tools down in front of the passenger-side seat. I can't have any of those things taken away."

He cut Lea a glance. "I'll get a couple of my wranglers to salvage all of it so you have it with you here at the ranch. You want to talk to the sheriff later? Or maybe tomorrow morning?"

She slowly stood up and appreciated Jody's hand on her upper arm. Her knees were still wobbly. "Thanks for doing that. My tools are my livelihood. I'm feeling really tired, Logan. All I want to do is lie down right now. I'll talk to him later."

"Understood. Shock does that to a person," he agreed. "I'll let the deputy know you're feeling exhausted. Depending upon how you are tomorrow morning, I'll drive you into town, where you can give them the details of the crash."

"I need to call my insurance company, too," she said.

"I'll do it. Just give me the card with the name and

phone number. I'll tell the representative you're wanting rest and you'll call them tomorrow."

"Sounds good," she said. "I have to call my parents, too. They need to know what happened . . ."

"Or? Maddy will get you to a phone in my office and you can talk with them, and save some money on a cell phone call," he assured her. He picked up the reins to his buckskin and walked to where the sheriff's cruiser was parking.

As Jody guided her to the company truck, Lea asked her, "Is Logan always like this?"

"Like what?" she asked, opening the door for Lea.

"So . . . efficient?"

She laughed. "Yeah, he's overly responsible, if you didn't already get that. It's bred in the bones of him via his family."

Lea slowly climbed in. Barry had gotten in, shutting his door. The sound hurt her ears and she felt supersensitive to the world around her right now. It had to be from the accident. Jody scooted in and shut the other door.

"Don't worry about seat belts," Barry told her. "It's just a mile to Logan's home. We aren't gonna get into any accidents between here and there."

"Good to hear," Lea joked weakly, closing her eyes and resting against the cushy headrest.

"Logan will take care of you," Jody promised. "He's the cosmic mother hen around here."

Laughter burbled up Lea's throat, and opening her eyes, she saw Jody grinning. "A cosmic mother hen? A man? I've never heard that saying before."

"He's just that way," Jody said, her eyes gleaming. "He loves this ranch and he understands that he's entrusted with over a hundred years of Andersons creating and then developing it. He's very responsible."

Barry drove slowly and Lea was grateful because every jolt and jostle pained her stiffened neck. The mile was nothing but pipe fence on both sides, and different pastures with cattle in them. Ahead, she saw a huge U-shaped two-story log home. It was the kind that settlers had built, with white seams of mortar between each thick, weathered log. The place was huge and had a circular gravel driveway. She was especially interested in all the bushes and trees of varying sizes, ages, and types along the way. It reminded her of the Portland, Oregon, botanical gardens. She'd spent endless hours wandering trails and admiring the many species of trees. Perhaps, because she worked with wood, trees held special meaning for her.

"We're here," Barry announced, opening the door. "I'll go talk to Maddy. Jody? You want to help Ms. Ryan in?"

"Sure," Jody said.

Barry was gone and up the stairs of the wide wrap-around porch that led to a huge door that Lea thought might have been made out of pine a long time ago. It looked pretty ancient and she obliquely wondered as she and Jody took the steps up to it, if Logan wanted something done with it. Of course, he hadn't hired her yet, so why was she thinking about replacing the door? Grimacing, she thanked Jody as she walked into the foyer. Jody closed the door behind her and Lea was grateful for the warmth that met her.

"Maddy will most likely be in the kitchen," Jody said, pointing to the first door to the right. "Let's go into the living room and wait for her and Barry."

Lea saw the soaring river-rock fireplace that went floor to ceiling. A fire snapped and crackled behind the glass and brass screen, sunlight pouring into the huge eastern window. Beneath her feet, to her surprise, was flooring made entirely of beautiful, ribbed tiger maple wood. The gold of the wood-grain had horizontal ribs of a lighter cream color wood, the "stripes" and why it was referred to as "tiger" maple were the reddish colored ribs.

The living room was at least six hundred square feet and semi-rounded. All that was missing was the Round Table from the King Arthur legend! Whoever had built this must have needed an architect and other craftsmen, because even the windows were slightly rounded, and that took a specialist. In fact, she loved the bright panels of stained glass around the top of the windows, the sunlight making them glow with rainbow colors. Two huge, light tan leather couches faced one another, a round antique oak coffee table with a stained glass top between them. Half of the living room ceiling was made of tiger maple, the other half was open, displaying a lovely, curved staircase that led up to the second floor. While wood was the main design element, she saw drywall that had been painted a cream color, so that the eye had breaks between the logs that comprised the outer framed structure.

In some ways, Lea felt as if she were in an antiquities museum from the late nineteenth century. There were massive elk antlers on one wall, and woven Navajo rugs on another, and glass-encased plants that had been carefully dried and presented in what looked like a colorful meadow of flowers. She wondered, since the family had been here for generations, if each one had chosen something to dress up the empty walls. There were daguerreotypes on a lace-covered table in one corner, the lace reminding her of the Victorian era. Had one of Logan's grandmothers crocheted it?

"Ms. Ryan?"

Turning, Lea saw a woman with black, shoulder-length hair and brown eyes, smiling as she entered the living room. "I'm Maddy Long, Mr. Anderson's housekeeper." Maddy clasped Lea's extended hand warmly within hers. "I'll take care of all your needs."

"Thank you," she said, releasing the woman's hand.

Barry sauntered up. "Jody, let's get moseying on down the road. We got cattle to move."

Jody nodded. She turned to Lea. "Try and get some rest. And if you need me? Maddy, here, will get on the radio and call me."

"I think I'll be fine," Lea said, reaching out and touching her shoulder. "Thanks for everything."

"You bet. Let's go, Barry."

Barry, who had his dark tan Stetson in his gnarled hand, threw it on his head and tipped the edge toward Maddy and Lea, turned and walked quickly out into the hall. Jody was on his heels.

"What an awful thing to happen to you," Maddy said, taking Lea's hand and pulling her along. "Come with me. Logan was concerned about you and he said to give you the pick of one of the guest bedrooms down the hall from his office."

Maddy wore tan slacks, a neatly ironed blouse, and an orange apron around her waist. Lea followed. There were four doors down the long, wide hall.

"I think this one would be best for you, Ms. Ryan." Maddy opened the door to the one on the right, after passing the open office door.

"Call me Lea, please?"

Maddy smiled. "That's a pretty name." She pushed the door open further. "This bedroom has a bathroom across the hall, and the other two are farther away. I think you'd find this one a better match. What do you think?"

Lea stepped into the room. It was bright, with west-side windows, two of them with white, gauzy curtains that allowed a lot of light into the room. "Looks fine, Maddy. You don't mind if I call you by your first name, do you?"

"Of course not. That's a queen-size bed, and the quilt on top of it was made by Logan's grandmother, Miss Trudy."

Lea recognized right away that it was a colorful patchwork quilt. Her own mother made quilts from time to time. There was a deep red mahogany rolltop desk in one corner, a landline phone, a printer, and a desktop computer. For all of its antiques, the desk presented her with everything she might need to communicate with.

"This is fabulous," she murmured, gazing around at the dark oak rocker in another corner, a blue crocheted cushion on the seat.

"Logan had all the electric replaced. It was so old and out-of-date." Maddy turned on the switch near the entrance. The whole room became bright, but not glaring.

"I like lots of light," Lea said, pleased.

"Well, Logan was thinking that you'd like this particular room. He was telling me to get it fixed up for you, and he just had all the equipment on your rolltop desk brought in last week for you."

"But," Lea stumbled, "he hasn't hired me yet . . . I mean . . . we just talked on the phone about his carpentry needs."

Making a snorting sound, Maddy said, "Young lady, you're hired. You're the only one that doesn't know it," and she patted Lea on the shoulder. "So, no worries, okay? I'm sure he'll let you know that, by the end of the day. Your

crash out there has kind of upset the plans he had for you,
but it's nothing that can't be done tomorrow or the next
day. He just wants you to rest. He's *such* a worrywart. He
makes a settin' hen look undisturbed in comparison."

Lea nodded, feeling a lot of angst dissolving within her.
"He is going to hire me?"

"Sure." Maddy opened up a roomy closet where she
could hang all her clothes. On the other side of the bed
was another closet. It was for large things like suitcases.

Maddy turned and said, "What do you feel like doing?"

"I'm going to call my parents. They need to know what
happened. I don't want them worrying."

"There's a landline there on the desk, or you can use
your cell phone. Whichever suits. Are you hungry, Lea?"

"No . . . not really."

"Want a bath? Jody said you had whiplash. Hot water
will really help relax those muscles."

"That sounds like a good idea. I am feeling really tired."

Maddy gave her a sympathetic look. "I'm sure. Logan
said your truck was totaled. It has a broken rear axle."

Groaning, Lea said, "I'm glad Logan is going to call
my insurance company. What a mess."

"Naw, nothin' that can't be sorted out," Maddy assured
her gently. "Might you like some coffee or tea? I can bring
it up to you."

"Oh, coffee . . . yes . . . that sounds wonderful. I could
come down and get it—"

"Nope! You do what you need to do. I'll just put everything on a tray and bring it up in a hot minute."

So many worries had slid off Lea's tightened shoulders.
First, call her parents, enjoy her coffee, and then, a hot
bath. And best of all? She had this job! Feeling as if she
were in the middle of a tornado, she walked over to the

rolltop desk. A bright red phone sat on the highly polished desk. Sliding her fingertips over the very old mahogany wood, it felt like satin. This was a very well cared-for piece of furniture, no question. She knew that wood dried out over time, and where it was sitting—in or out of sunlight—had a lot to do with the dehydration of the material.

As she sat down on the rolling chair that was ergonomically comfortable, she knew she would fall in love with this home that had held at least four generations of Andersons. A family home, kept in the family. That appealed strongly to her. She was homesick, but pushed it away. Too much was happening and she needed to stay focused.

A soft knock on the open bedroom door made her turn.

"Well, I cheated," Maddy confessed. She brought in a delicately carved, black lacquered wooden tray. "I not only brought you a pint of freshly made coffee, but some of my to-die-for almond-cinnamon coffee cake that I made yesterday. I think a shot of sugar just might be good for you." She smiled, placing the tray on one side of the desk. She'd added a porcelain sugar bowl and creamer, decorated with hand-painted roses, along with a delicately crafted silver spoon. A dark blue linen napkin was neatly folded next to a plate bearing several slices of the coffee cake.

Lea gave her a look of thank-you. "You're priceless, Maddy. Thanks."

"Well, now, you can sip your coffee and relax while calling your parents. Tell them that you're in the *best* of hands. Logan's a mother hen and so am I." She chortled, turned, and left. She closed the door quietly behind her.

The coffee smelled heavenly and Lea poured cream and sugar into the cup. Just getting to taste it after stirring it, made her groan with appreciation and lean back in the chair. Everything was going to be all right. She sagged against it and continued to savor and sip the coffee. The scent of cinnamon and almonds wafted pleasantly into the air. Maddy was wonderful. So was Logan. And Barry, although very weathered appearing and somewhat gruff, was still sensitive and thoughtful. It felt good that Jody, a woman, was here on the ranch, too. Not that she distrusted Logan. No, his care of her had been genuine. He was tall, broad shouldered, and was easily two-hundred pounds, but it was muscle, not fat.

Through the last hour or so, she kept re-hearing his low, mellow-toned voice. It was like a blanket of calm surrounding her. He was not a man who got rattled easily, that was for sure. The kindness in his gray eyes had startled her, if for no other reason than she never expected a man to behave in that way. Her father was like that, of course. But she had no male friends and wanted to keep it that way. To find that sincerity and concern in Logan's eyes startled her, but it had also reached deeply inside her, affecting her immediately. Even her heart rate had slowed down, simply because he was nearby, offering her support if she wanted it right after the crash. So why did her heart, of all things, swell a little with a euphoric joy every time she visualized Logan Anderson's strong, tanned face? That kind of reaction to a man had *never* happened to her. *Ever.* Why now?

Chapter Three

May 27

It was near noon when Logan made it back to his ranch house. He could smell an array of lunch goodies that Maddy had made for him. His heart, however, was centered on Lea Ryan. How was she? Taking off his Stetson and hooking it over a wooden peg on the wall near the door, he pushed his fingers through his flattened short black hair. The day was beautiful, a welcome change from the winter, for sure. He made his way down the hall. To his surprise, he saw Lea in the kitchen helping Maddy. They didn't see him as they chatted amiably with one another, laughing now and then. He smiled, relief flowing through him.

"Hey, ladies," he announced, sauntering in, "anything I can do to help?"

Lea looked up, surprised, her hands frozen over a salad she was making for lunch.

Maddy tittered. "Just come and sit down, Logan. We girls will handle the serious stuff."

"Yes, ma'am," he said, grinning. As he walked over to

the kitchen table at one end of the L-shaped kitchen, he asked, "How are you doing, Lea?" He pulled out two chairs and sat down in one of them.

"Better," Lea said, bringing the bowl of salad over to the table. "I got some good sleep. I feel more like my old self. I'm assuming my truck has been hauled off to a shop?"

"Yes," he said, "I've had it taken to a garage in Silver Creek. I talked to the local insurance agent and she's going over to examine it." He shook his head. "It's a scrap heap, Lea. Sorry to tell you that, but whoever hit you, meant business."

She wiped her hands on the pink apron around her waist that Maddy had given her earlier. "I want to know what the sheriff is doing about it."

"Lea?" Maddy called. "Go sit down. I'm bringing the sandwiches."

Taking off the apron, Lea placed it on the counter and did as she was told. The housekeeper brought over four huge beef sandwiches. Surely, three of them must belong to Logan. She doubted she could finish eating one of them!

"Maddy? Don't you want to join us?" Logan asked, pointing to another chair.

"Naw, you two go ahead. Lea's dying to hear about her truck and who hit it. I've got to run to the grocery store for you. I'll be back in about an hour."

"Okay, but did you eat?" Logan pressed her.

"Of course, I did. You're *such* a mother hen, Logan. I swear . . ." She turned, shaking her head, smiling, waving good-bye to them.

"Oops," he told Lea, "now you know my nickname."

"There's worse ones," Lea said, taking the salad from him and putting some into her bowl.

"I suppose," Logan groused, a grin edging his mouth as he took the first beef sandwich onto his plate and slathered some creamy horseradish on it. "How are you doing?"

"I'm okay." She pointed to the base of her nose. "There's swelling over it, but not much. I'm hoping Jody was wrong about me having a shiner."

Passing the plate of sandwiches to her, he said, "It will be temporary. No headache?"

"No, thank goodness."

"How about your whiplash?"

"Much better after taking a hot soak in the tub. I went to sleep after that."

"Good."

Lea munched on the sandwich. "What did the sheriff say?"

"Deputy Emma Harris took the report. If you feel up to it? I'll take you in tomorrow morning and you can talk with her about it. She's not ready to say much at this point. She did contact all regional garages to be on a lookout for a pickup with front or side damage. Where your pickup got hit, there's a lot of blue paint scraped off and she's hoping someone will come in with the vehicle and they can look for blue paint, which could tie them to the scene of the crash."

"That's smart," Lea said. "My parents are worried sick, but I tried to downplay it. I don't want to think that some-one wanted to kill me."

He frowned. "Emma said the jury is out at this point. It could have been a hit-and-run, where the driver panicked after he hit you and took off. Sometimes that happens."

She picked up the paper napkin, wiping her lips. "I'm sorry to land on your doorstep like this. I was looking forward to the job interview."

"So was I. We still can," Logan said. "If you're up to it, I'd like to spend about an hour with you on the projects I'd like you to work on and you can tour our wood shop."

"Okay, that would be fine."

"Sure you're up to it?"

"The nap really helped me. I don't feel shocky anymore, Mr. Anderson."

"Call me Logan. Okay if I call you Lea?"

"Sure. Where did you put my tools you took out of my truck?"

"I've had them put into my wood shop." He hooked a thumb over his left shoulder. Finishing one sandwich, he reached for a second one. "I looked at the chisels you use for wood sculpting, and they're really expensive, good ones."

"Phew, that's good news! My father, Paddy, helped me collect my chisels over the years. They are birthday and Christmas presents." She smiled fondly in remembrance of those times.

He warmed to her reaction. "I know you mentioned your father was responsible for you getting into his craft. Looking on your joint website, I really thought your work was incredible, Lea. I'm excited about hiring you." He saw her cheeks grow pink, and her willow-green eyes sparkle. "I know we've talked on the phone, but I think you seeing what I'm going to show you, will persuade you to take on this long-term project."

"I'm excited about it," she said, eating her salad daintily after pouring a bit of Maddy's special blue cheese and peppercorn dressing on it. "This is the first time I've ventured out of Oregon, and it's scary and exciting all at once."

"I was impressed that since reading those books you told me about, you wanted to come to Wyoming. Most people like to visit in the summer and then run home because our winters are pretty harsh. Around here in Silver Valley? Not so much winter. We live in a perfect spot between mountain ranges, and the weather is much milder. It's a mini-climate, of sorts."

He liked her short red hair that gleamed with copper, gold, and sienna highlights. The tendrils were soft around her temples. Logan felt like a giddy, excited teen. Something magical was occurring between them and he swore he could see it in her green eyes. Logan had a lot of personal questions for her, but didn't want to go there, if at all, right now. Still, he found himself far more curious about Lea's personal life than he could have ever imagined. Logan had decided she was Irish fey magic. Since meeting her, he couldn't erase her from his daily demands and he couldn't figure out why.

"Wyoming has been a dream for me," she admitted, finishing off the salad and now focusing on the beef sandwich.

"Do you miss the ocean, though? I know Brookings sits right on the Pacific."

"Very much. Where we live, we are surrounded by a dense forest of evergreens that grow almost down to the beaches of Brookings. Those trees always made me feel like a child among them, that in my wild imagination, they were like doting grandparents surrounding me, always there."

"They made you feel safe?" Logan wondered, seeing her eyes go a darker jade color for a moment. She had beautiful lips and she tucked the lower one between her teeth for a moment.

"Yes . . . I guess you could say that. I honestly never thought about it in that way, but I always felt like I was being lovingly watched over."

So, safety was an important quality to Lea? Damn, more questions, but no answers. Lea struck him as being shy and reserved, plus she felt fragile to him. Anyone would, of course, after a major crash like the one she'd just survived, so Logan wrote it off to that awful incident.

"As soon as we're done eating, I'd like to start driving you around the ranch so you can get a feel for the land. There's something you need to see and know about," he suggested. Instantly, he saw her perk up, eyes bright and shining once more with burning curiosity.

"That sounds interesting," she said.

"But fun," he amended. "Something good is about to happen to you . . ."

Taking one of the white ranch trucks, Logan drove them down a long dirt road between major corrals. Lea had a small Canon camera with her that she held in her lap, wanting to take photos once they arrived at wherever they were going. Logan had promised that she'd want to get out and explore.

As he drove, he said, "I'm fourth generation Anderson. My family is from Scotland. We still have relatives in the Highlands and they continue to raise Highland cattle. My mother's side of the family arrived here in Silver Creek right when silver was discovered in the mountains, west of the valley. That was a hundred and thirty years ago. My pioneering relative, Horace Anderson, was a miner and had heard about the strike. He was one of two brothers, and he took his family to America, while the other brother remained behind to continue the raising of Scottish cattle. Horace had just married Evangeline and they were in their late teens when they headed West. Once out here in Wyoming, Horace found out that mining wasn't for him. He turned in the silver he'd found, sold the mine, and used the money to buy the Wild Goose Ranch. At that time, it was just ten thousand acres without anything on it except dense forest, good water sources, and plenty of grass. They turned from mining to a lumber business because everyone needed wood to build their mine shafts. He is the one who did something amazing that's become a part of our ranching history." Logan took a side road that led up to a series of gentle, rounded hills. Parking, he got out and Lea followed him.

"In this grove, there's a thousand acres of tiger maple that Horace and Evangeline planted." He moved his index finger from right to left.

Lea's mouth fell open as she saw the trees were just leafing out. And yes, no question, they were maple. "They *planted* all of these?" she asked, stunned.

"Yes." Logan smiled and turned, watching her amazed expression as she absorbed the grove. "The hardwoods like maple, oak, Greene's mountain ash, quaking aspen, and paper birch were needed for mine shafts. There was already lodgepole pine and blue spruce on other areas of the ranch property. They're softwoods and not designed to take the weight a hardwood can in a mine. There was already mountain maple here, and a lot of it, enough to supply the miners. It was Evangeline who got the tiger maple seeds and she spent ten years planting these hills, which became a grove by itself. Tiger maple was in huge demand by furniture makers everywhere on the East Coast because of the beauty of the grain. There was already a quaking aspen grove"—he pointed to the south—"and Greene's mountain ash, to the southeast, local trees that grew well here. Horace later created a huge five-thousand-acre quaking aspen grove, and to the southwest, paper birch, which is a hardwood in high demand for furniture making, as well."

Lea whispered, "Wow . . . this is a wood carver and carpenter's dream come true." She smiled over at him.

"That's why I wanted to bring you out here. We're going to visit each of these groves this afternoon. It was Evangeline who, after twenty years when the trees matured, made connections with some of the finest furniture makers in the East for all of this lumber. Horace had a sawmill built, hired good people, and pretty soon, it was a booming business that made them richer than any silver mine would have. As a result, he bought thirty thousand more acres of land to add to what they'd begun with. It became the largest property in Silver Valley."

"But what a lot of hard work."

Nodding, Logan said, "No question."

"Then, when did the cattle enter the picture?"

"Horace and Evangeline had one son, Abner. He married a local girl, Abigail, whose father had a big cattle ranch. Together, they kept the lumber business, but expanded another part of the forty thousand acres. Abigail was a cowgirl and knew everything about raising beef, creating pipe fencing because it withstood winters here in Wyoming and was less labor intensive than constantly repairing wooden fences. They are the ones who built the three huge barns you now see at the main ranch area, down below the hill where the ranch house sits. Their son, Frank, my grandfather, learned the lumber and cattle business. Each successive generation has enriched the family ranch in one way or another."

"Do you still sell the lumber to the East Coast furniture makers?"

"Yes. I've split up the two. You've seen two other buildings about half a mile from the main ranch house: One is for my lumber employees and the other is for our cattle employees. Barry, my foreman, oversees it all and he's a good manager. His father was a lumberjack in Washington State, so he grew up around sawmills, cutting down trees, and knows the lumber business. His mother was a ranch girl, and they lived on a small spread in the Cascade mountains of Washington. He got to know both businesses and luckily, my grandfather Frank found him, hired him, and the rest is history."

"But you have to know the businesses as well," Lea said, gazing at the magnificent stands of tiger maple.

"Oh," he said, scratching his hair and then settling his Stetson back on his head. "My father, Mike, took me out riding with him at three years old. My mother, Jessica, is an artist. She is not only a painter, but a wood sculptor, which led her to teach me about the lumber business. I got good training." He grinned fondly.

"Is this what you wanted to do?" she wondered.

"Yeah. My mother says I have more of her genes than my dad's. She taught me woodworking and furniture-making when I was a kid, and I love it to this day. Most of the things that I've made, when I have the time, are utilitarian, like furniture." He gave her a warm look. "Your portfolio of wood art reminds me a lot of my mother's work. I'd like to show you a book that was written about her talents."

"Oh," Lea said, "I'd love to see it!"

"She's very famous," he said proudly. "And every once in a while, my parents will fly up from Phoenix, where they live now, and she'll take a truck and visit the different tree groves, collecting limbs that have fallen, for future art pieces. She'll send it by UPS and she'll have enough wood of various grains and colors to last her another six months."

"What a wonderful background you have."

"I'm proud of my family," he said, "because they have been environmentalists from the time they set foot onto the Wild Goose land. We work with the federal government and we now have a pack of timber wolves running free and wild on the property. Our creeks are cold, clear, and unpolluted. We have an annual trout fisherman's championship here on the ranch in early September. It draws trout fishermen from around the world."

"Wow," Lea murmured, impressed. "Your family does so much, and yet they were all sensitive to feeding the land, not just taking from it or ravaging it. That should be known."

"We are well-known," he assured her. "The only fly in the ointment is there, to the south." He pointed to the area. "A guy by the name of Harvey Polcyn, who owns Polcyn Natural Gas Drilling. He's been in central Wyoming for the last ten years, fracking."

Scowling, Lea muttered, "Fracking? That's bad for everyone."

Snorting, he put his arms across his chest, staring darkly to the south. "The bad news is that a lot of these ranchers do not own mineral or water rights to their land. And if they don't, Polcyn comes in and buys the mineral rights and starts fracking, tearing up their land, destroying it, and then moves on."

"Did those ranchers willingly sell Polcyn the rights to do that?"

"Hell no. We're a pretty tight lot in the valley. We have an association and no one wants fracking in this area. Especially me. Geologically the valley is built on sedimentary rock, which is porous, consisting of limestone and old ocean beds from millions of years ago. There is natural gas trapped in the seams, but as they push charged water down into these holes, they destroy the strata and that causes earthquakes. And the water they use gets into the ground water, putting dangerous chemicals into it, poisoning the people who drink it. We have ten wells on our land and I don't want them poisoned, or our cattle or our groves of trees, destroyed."

"You said you had mineral and water rights, though."

"Yes, we do." He shook his head. "Polcyn's a snake and manipulative as hell. He won't stop at anything to buy up a ranch and take it for fracking if it owns the mineral and water rights. We've seen him doing it south of us in another county. He's like a cancer spreading across the land, and it's frightening because he's very rich and powerful. Most of the ranchers and farmers in this valley make a living, but they aren't rich. We're watching him and his progress. I've already had six different Realtors want to buy my ranch, but I'm not selling. We've found Polcyn hires these Realtors and they go to ranchers with a song and dance about having someone who wants to buy their property for good money. And after the rancher sells, then the seller finds out it was Polcyn who was the buyer behind the scenes, and that his land will be nothing more than fracked and destroyed belowground. Another thing he does is buy up the mineral rights on any property, even if the rancher doesn't want him on his land. He fracks it anyway. It's not right, but the laws are not on the side of the property owner."

"Thank goodness your family does own them, though," she said, hearing the anger and frustration in his tone.

"Come on," he said, "let's get to the other groves. I don't want to tire you out on your first day here."

"Oh," she said, keeping in stride with him, "this invigorates me. Being out in Nature, being with the trees, is like the best medicine for my soul."

Startled, Logan halted, staring at her. "What did you say?"

Lea repeated it, wondering if she'd said something wrong. The look on Logan's face was one of stunned amazement.

"I'll be," he muttered, looking away and then staring at her hard for a moment. "My mother has said those very same words."

Laughing a little, Lea said, "I've got to meet her, then. We sound like kindred souls."

"What are the chances, though?" Logan asked, turning and beginning to walk toward the truck once again. "That's just not what you hear people say every day."

"I was raised in the woods. I grew up with old-growth forests, Logan. They were my teachers. My mother and I used to walk through them because she said it was good for my soul. That it was healing. I could feel it, Logan. Just like, well"—she turned on her heel, gesturing toward the tiger maple grove—"being here, with all of them. It feels so good to be among them!"

"A tree soul is what my mother said we have as a family."

"That's nice," she said, catching up to him. "Tree soul. I like the sound of it. And it's true. Your family started with the trees on the land, gave back to them, and always cared for them so your land wasn't denuded and then degraded by rain and snow cutting into the soil of those hills."

He shrugged and opened the truck door for her. "Your family has a tree soul, too."

"My father told me that you'd contacted him about the work you needed done."

Shutting the door, starting the truck, Logan drove slowly and turned it around. "I didn't even know that his daughter was a wood artist," he admitted, "until I talked at length with him. He is very proud of your art, Lea, and urged me to look at your work on the website. When I saw it, I called him back. He didn't want the job for a lot of reasons, but he said you were available." He looked over at her as he drew the truck to a stop where the road intersected with the highway. "He told me you are a master carpenter as well, and I saw some of the furniture you'd made for several of his clients. I was very impressed."

"Thanks," she said. "That means a lot coming from a family like yours. How proud you must be of your heritage, Logan. I'd be busting my buttons over what you're caretaking for this generation."

"Oh," he chuckled, "you've only seen some of it."

"You mean there's more than just these groves?" she gasped.

"Oh, yes. As we drive back toward the ranch house later, we'll take a side road to another place, one that was created by Trudy and Frank Anderson, my grandparents. They're gone now, but they left us an amazing legacy. I'll show it to you pretty soon."

"No hints?" she teased, grinning.

"No. Surprises, nice ones, are always worth keeping that way. I want to see the look on your face."

"Ohhh, sounds exciting!"

For the next hour, Logan felt a level of happiness that had evaporated at age twenty-three. He absorbed Lea's excitement as he showed her each grove, five thousand acres of a specific type of tree. He felt proud of his forebears and all their hard work because it was his generation that was truly reaping profits from them as never before. There were no longer silver mines, nor was there a demand for hardwood to create the adits—tunnels—in order to hunt for the metal. The lumber was now considered top grade and furniture makers were still buying, but now, it was shipped around the world.

As they rounded a long, flat curve, he pointed ahead. "There's the surprise." He parked beside a group of trees that lay in neat rows. "This is our fruit orchard, Lea. My great-grandparents, Abigail and Abner, are responsible for it. And Abigail was the one who conceived the idea and was mostly responsible for planting the first fruit trees. With so much of Wyoming buried in long, hard winters, a lot of places in the state don't have the ninety-day growing season fruits and vegetables need in order to ripen."

"But they do here." Lea nodded. "What kind of fruit?"

"Montmorency sour cherry and sweet cherry. Both are hardwoods, and Abigail did a lot of research and talking to experts about what were the best cherry trees for the area. And because they are both hardwoods? When their fruiting time was waning, the trees would be brought down and taken to the saw mill, their hardwood in high demand."

"I love cherries," Lea sighed. "My mom makes the best sour cherry pie."

"Grab the recipe. Maddy is crazy about fruit pies and she makes them when the fruit is in season."

Smiling, Lea looked at the many trees and the different flowering blossoms on them. "What other fruit?"

"We have Contender and Reliance peach trees, McIntosh apples, Parker pears, Stanley plums, and Sungold apricots. We have a special foreman who runs the place and the employees. We mainly sell the fruit to local and regional grocery stores. My grandmother used to sell jams and jellies, as well. We took fruit for ourselves and our employees, but sold the rest. If the fruit is bruised, we work with a regional volunteer kitchen out of Thermopolis, to the north of us, and it's distributed to poor families throughout the area. Nothing, and I mean nothing, goes to waste around here. If we have fruit that is too bruised, then we compost it along with other vegetables in our huge compost bins behind each barn. Makes great, nutritious soil and it gets used and put back into our orchard or vegetable gardens."

"This is an amazing place, it truly is," she said, sitting back, enjoying the pink and white blossoms for as far as the eye could see.

"It was my idea to bring in local honey with local bees." He put the truck in gear and he drove down the side road.

Lea saw at least a hundred beehives all in neat, clean rows off to one side of the road.

Parking, Logan said, "A lot of hives are collapsing around the world, but we have an excellent beekeeper, and she knows her business. You'll probably meet her at some point. We use the honey in lieu of white sugar or chemical sugars here on the spread. The rest of our honey is sold regionally. We also donate twenty percent of it to poor families, so that they get some, too."

"I love honey," Lea said. "My mom cooks and bakes with it. Funny, how our two families are so much alike."

"Indeed," Logan agreed, giving her a wry look. "Let's go home. I want to show you where you'll be working if you decide you want the job."

"I can hardly wait to see it," she admitted.

Logan led her to the double-car garage. It stood off to one side of the ranch house. He watched Lea's jaw drop as he led her through a side door and into the wood shop. The concrete floor was painted a cream color to take advantage of the four skylights above, which allowed more light into the cavernous area. There were two long, wide tables with different types of saws on them, and other tools to make anything from a wood sculpture to an elegant piece of furniture.

In one corner, his wranglers had brought in her huge metal tool box, having taken it out of her damaged vehicle earlier. Beside it, on a stout metal table, was her black nylon bag that contained all her professional wood-sculpting tools. She immediately went over to each of them, opening them up, making sure nothing had been broken or bent during that crash.

Seeing her expression go from tension to happiness made Logan smile to himself as he stood off to one side, allowing her to take in the enormity of this shop.

"This," Lea said, slowly turning around, taking it all in, "is an incredible, thoughtful, and well laid-out shop. It's woodworking heaven to someone like me."

"Sure is," he murmured. Motioning to the metal shelves along three of the walls, he said, "There's plenty of work space in here for you, as well. And there's a specially made desk with good light, plus an architect's desk that you can raise and lower when you're working on a design."

Lea wandered over to the corner. The huge desk was U-shaped, and a comfortable chair sat in the middle of it. She could work and look out across the entire clean facility. She ran her hand lightly across the blond-oak desk. "This is old, an antique."

"It was Horace Anderson's desk and it's over a hundred years old," he said. "He used wood from an oak tree that had recently died of old age, took the inner lumber, which was still good, and he made that U-shaped desk. No one had thought to design a desk quite like that and it was the talk of the valley. People would drive over on Sunday, after church services, in their buggies, just to look at it and admire its design." He grinned. "I've got photos of it from one of our family albums. He also made the drawers on the right and left of it. You'll see the quality of his dovetails on each corner."

Gently removing one of the drawers, Lea turned it and saw the exquisitely created dovetails. "He was a master carpenter and he paid attention to all the details," she agreed, running the tip of her finger over several of them, which were sanded down to perfection and smooth as a baby's butt.

Logan wandered over. "Do you think you would be happy working out here, Lea?"

She eased the drawer back into place and looked around. "Very much so. It's warm in the wood shop, too. That's pretty unusual."

"There's a gas heater in every room of the house, this shop, and the garage. In the wood shop, I did a renovation on it when I took over running the ranch from my parents. We insulated the attic and all four walls, and put drywall over it. It's a lot warmer now, and it's especially comfortable in the winter. You can keep it at a temperature that's good for you while you create out here."

Shaking her head, she gave him a grin. "My dad's workplace has no heat. I grew up working out there with him, no matter how cold and damp it got in the winter, but it never snowed like it does here. This place is like a dream come true for me: heat, lots of wonderful light, and plenty of space to move around, not to mention the work tables, which are to die for."

"Did you see the coffee dispenser over there?" He pointed to the end of one long shelf where a coffeemaker sat, with all the fixings.

"No, but that looks great. I drink a lot of coffee when I'm in my design mode."

"You can have all you want." He pointed to the wall next to the desk. "There's a phone, a landline, that you can use. And there's a desktop computer and printer for you to use as well. I have a special printer over there." He pointed to the other side, where a large printer that was three feet wide, stood. "I've modernized what I do out here. I'm not a master carpenter like you, but I like building furniture when I want some quiet time. You can draw a design using some special software that's in the desktop computer, send it to this large, wide printer, and you'll have a working map that you can use in building or creating whatever you want."

She walked over to the printer. It had a clear plastic

cover to protect it from sawdust. The desktop computer did, as well. Anything electronic was wisely protected. "This is going to make my life a lot easier," she admitted.

Cocking his head, hands in his pockets, he said, "So? Would you like the job? Creating one-of-a-kind cabinets in the kitchen? Reworking that staircase and rail? It's going to be a minimum of six months to do all of that, maybe up to nine months, depending upon how it goes." Never had Logan wanted something more than what was standing in front of him right now. He didn't try to dig and find out why he felt that way. "Will you allow me to hire you and your artistry?"

Lea looked around the large space one more time. "I'd love nothing more than to work in here. You have a wonderful family history and this workshop is a testament to that. Yes, I'd love to work for you, Logan."

His heart swelled and he tamed his emotional reaction of joy, trying to remain serious and unreadable. "That's great."

"Where would I live? I saw some rooms for rent in Silver Creek."

"Oh, no," he said quickly. "You'll have your bedroom in the main house on the first floor. You'll eat with me, and Maddy will take care of the rest. I want you comfortable. I know from trying to do artistic pieces, how much the surrounding environment plays on your senses. I want you happy, feeling at home, and looking forward to coming out here five days a week. You'll have your weekends off. You do whatever you want to do. Don't worry about using the landline phone to call your parents or talk to your friends. There's no overhead for you, Lea. You'll be treated by us as a member of our big family here on the Wild Goose. How does that sound?"

"That's such a generous offer, Logan. I'll take you up on it, but I promise not to abuse the privileges you've given me, either."

"You don't strike me as that type," he offered quietly. "You'll have a ranch truck of your own to use while you're here. I'm sure you'll want to go explore those groves for the wood color or grain that you'll be looking for."

She grimaced. "I'm going to need a vehicle for sure. Mine is totaled. I have to wait to hear from my insurance agent about a replacement vehicle."

"Barry will assign a ranch truck to you today. You can use it on and off the property."

"I'm hoping that in less than a month," Lea said grimly, "the insurance company will reimburse me for my loss and I can buy another one."

"For right now, you have wheels."

"Thanks, Logan. I . . . well . . . this is my first foray out into the real world and I didn't expect such kindness from an employer."

"Stick around," he teased. "Ask the people who work for the ranch. They're treated like family, Lea, not employees. The Anderson clan has always had good hearts, and were kind and thoughtful people."

"I can see that. I think the first thing I need to do is listen to what you want for those kitchen cabinet doors."

"We'll do that tomorrow after breakfast," he said. Trying to still his inner happiness over her taking the long-term job, he added, "I'll leave you now. Dinner's at dusk. That's how we do it around here: up at dawn, dinner at dusk, and night is bedtime."

"I can handle that," she said, giving him a grateful look.

"If there's anything you want to eat? Let Maddy know. She'll want to know your favorite foods and meals, too, as well as what you hate to eat."

Laughing a little, Lea said, "I'll eat just about anything, Logan, so don't worry about me." She looked at the watch on her wrist. "I'll see you at dusk for dinner. Both start with a D." She met his smile. Her heart did a little bounce and she tried to ignore how blatantly good-looking he was in a rough, cowboy kind of way. Now, he was her boss.

Chapter Four

May 30

Logan tried to quell his excitement at seeing Lea once again. His news wasn't all good, but a mix.

Taking the steps to the ranch house, he took off his Stetson as he went inside. Maddy was in the kitchen preparing dinner for tonight. She gave him a wave hello and then returned to what she was doing at the counter.

At ten a.m. the chill was off the valley and welcome May warmth was starting to come in to replace it. He wore a rust-colored goose-down vest over his long-sleeved chambray shirt, stuffing his elk-skin gloves into the back pocket of his Levi's.

"Is Lea in the shop?" he asked.

"No, in her bedroom office. She's working on finalizing those drawings she's been making for the kitchen cabinets," Maddy replied.

"Okay, thanks." He headed toward the hall. Her bedroom door was open and he called her name as he stood in front of it. No answer. Something told him she'd left her office and gone down to the wood shop.

"Hey," he called, entering the shop from the side door, seeing Lea at one of the long tables, many pieces of paper spread out from one end to the other. "Maddy said you were finishing up the drawings. Can I look?" Even though they were living in the same house, he rarely saw her unless it was at meals. She had been hard at work drawing up designs for the doors to the cabinets in the kitchen. He was curious about the designs, but didn't make a pest of himself by leaning over her shoulder to see what she was working on. She wore a loose pair of jeans, dark blue tennis shoes, and a long-sleeved, gold waffle tee, setting off the color of her shining hair, bringing out the coppery freckles across her nose and cheeks. She looked up, surprised.

"I didn't expect to see you until supper," she murmured, straightening, giving him a smile of welcome. Lea pushed away several tendrils from her cheek.

"I had some news about who hit your truck," he said. Closing the door, he added, "I didn't want to wait until tonight to tell you." He saw Lea's brows pull into a frown and she lost her smile. He knew she had been worrying about who had done this to her. Unfortunately, his answer wasn't going to satisfy her much, or him.

"Oh?" She wiped off her hands on a nearby terry cloth towel. "Did Sheriff Seabert call you?"

"Yes." He halted at the other side of the table, wanting to look at all her charcoal drawings for the cabinets, but resisted, holding her concerned gaze, her eyes turning a darker green. "They found the truck that hit you, and it belongs to Polcyn, the fracker. It was discovered by a hunter on a back road about forty miles from here, and he called it in. A day before your truck was hit, Polcyn's office called in to the sheriff's office and reported one of their white trucks was missing. It had been stolen and no one had seen who had taken it."

"Then I was hit by a guy who stole their truck?"

He shrugged, giving her a grim look. "Maybe. Polcyn would do anything to buy this ranch out from under me. He's worth a billion dollars, with fracking companies all across the Midwest, and now, in Wyoming. I don't like saying this, but I think Polcyn hired someone to pretend to steal one of their trucks, in order to do his dirty work."

Her frown grew deeper as she absorbed his explanation. "He hired a hit on *me*?"

"It probably wasn't meant to be you specifically, would be my guess," Logan said heavily. "Just anyone driving in through the front gate was the target for that morning. Another harassment warning shot over my bow that I need to let Polcyn buy our ranch."

"Damn," she muttered, rubbing her brow. "What other 'warning shots' has he done to you, Logan?"

"Many of our herds of beef cattle are in very remote pastures, far from the main hub here at the ranch house. The watering tanks are located in each pasture for the cattle. Last year, one of the tanks was purposely poisoned by an unknown person, and it killed twenty of my cattle."

Gasping, Lea made a sad sound. "That's horrible! Were you able to prove that he'd done it?"

"Unfortunately, no. Polcyn has money to hire the thugs who do his bidding and keep him out of the picture, even though he's an accessory to the act. I just can't prove it, and it's driving me crazy."

"That's horrible! Oh, those poor animals, dying in such a way."

"It really upset me. The sheriff came out and dusted the water tank, but found nothing. Not even shoe prints."

"What about tire tracks? If it was an out-of-the-way pasture, wouldn't they have to drive to reach it?"

"Yes, but we have a decent dirt road around the entire acreage. The sheriff did find tire tracks leading across and between some rolling hills that they'd taken to reach the main road. But despite a lot of footwork on their part, they couldn't match them with a specific truck in the area. They did go over to Polcyn's maintenance area and look at every truck's tires, but none of them matched the tread they found on my property."

"Could you put video cameras in each of those areas to protect your cattle?"

He scratched his head and sighed. "I've thought about it. But that's a lot of money and time to install something on that scale. I may have to, though."

"What else has he done that you know of?" she demanded.

"Oh, we'd find the tires on our ranch trucks with nails in them. We'd go to the maintenance area to pick the vehicles up, and when we'd drive them for the day, they'd go flat. Again, no one saw it happen. Our maintenance yard is always open. I don't lock it up. Never had to, until this started happening. Now we have lights and the place is locked up with concertina wire on the top of the fencing around the entire area."

"But if you'd had video cameras there? You might have caught them or him, in the act."

"You're right," he admitted tiredly. "This is Polcyn's doing and I know it, even if I can't prove it. When I took over the ranch, my parents showed me the geology report that they'd had made years earlier, because we own the mineral rights. It showed a lot of potential for natural gas beneath the ranch. They were worried about fracking, which had just started when they left the ranch in my hands. I've been watching Polcyn and his thugs slowly moving from southern Wyoming, northward. This area"—he gestured around the shop—"is one of the richest untouched natural gas areas in the state. That's why he's after it."

"That's why he wants your ranch so badly," she said, anger in her tone.

"Yes." He moved his shoulders, lessening the tension he carried in them. "So, Polcyn has his truck back. The sheriff put forensics on it to check it out, but they found nothing. Whoever had been driving it was wearing gloves, so no one could lift his fingerprints. They found no DNA evidence either."

"Maybe if you'd had video cameras at the front gate area, we might have seen who it was," she said.

"Yeah, it's time to do something like that," Logan admitted. "There's a small company in town who does this kind of thing. I think I'll mosey on into Silver Creek tomorrow sometime, and talk with them."

"It's going to be a big expense," Lea agreed, "but I think it will be a big help."

"I'll write it off as a business expense," he said. "Hey, Maddy said you were done with your drawings. Can I see them?" He wanted to talk about something that was positive.

Lea nodded. "Yes, come around the table. These are just rough-draft charcoal sketches, something I did quickly, to give you an idea of where I'm going with the themes we talked about earlier."

She had rubbed her palms down the sides of her jeans, telling Logan that she was nervous about showing them to him. "That's fine," he said, wanting her to relax. He walked around the table.

"It's best to start here," she said, pointing to different sketches on butcher paper at one end of the table. She gestured down the length of it. "Each square has the left and right doors to the cabinet," Lea explained. "I started near the kitchen entrance door and worked my way around the L-shaped kitchen to give you a feel for what I was doing."

He marveled at her quick, clean, and concise drawings. They were the size of the cabinet doors. "Wow," he murmured, leaning over the first set of doors, "this is incredible." And it was. It showed a pond with cattails and three ducks, a drake and two hens, taking off from it. "That afternoon we spent talking about the scenes on each set of doors," he said, twisting a look in her direction, "you have translated the idea beautifully, Lea."

"Oh, good," she said, placing her hand against her chest. "I was worried that my interpretation of your concept, the stories you told about each set of doors, might not be what you wanted."

"No," he murmured, studying the pictures, "it's perfect, Lea." Just like she was perfect for him, but Logan refused to go there.

Her face lost some tension, a little hope showed in her expression, instead. He moved to the second set. It was the same pond, but now there were two Canadian geese coming in for a landing, one on each door. "This is perfect. You've used the pond as a center point. I like that a lot."

"Well, your first three cabinets were about that pond. I loved the stories you told about it and I've been out to it twice, getting it right so the wood sculpture repeats what is out there in real life."

He grinned, studying the drawing of the third set of doors. It showed two trumpeter swans, which came to

Wyoming to have their young. "These trumpeters look great," he murmured. "I especially like the babies tucked up under the mother's wings, and dad is on the other door, keeping watch. Well done."

"Thanks. I didn't realize the trumpeter swan is the largest swan in the world. It has at least a six-foot wingspan."

"They are huge," he agreed. "We get what Wyoming Fish and Game call the stragglers. But we get them every year, and I always enjoy when they have their cygnets on our big pond. You've captured them wonderfully. Truly, you're an artist."

"Thank you."

They moved to the fourth set of doors. Logan saw that the scene had now switched to the rolling hills that comprised half of the ranch. There was an incredible tiger maple, the oldest one, and they called her the grandmother of that grove. Lea had drawn the tree with the gnarled trunk on half of the left door, her spreading arms and leaves extending to the right door. At the bottom of the right door was a mother raccoon and six of her kits following her. It was an unexpected but touching scene and he smiled. "I know you've spent quite a bit of time out on the land. Did you see this mama coon and her kits?"

"Yes, and I got them on my camera, too." Lea turned around to another table, picking up her Canon camera. She turned it on and flipped through a number of photos she'd taken around the ranch property. "Ah, here they are." She brought it over, their shoulders touching as she showed him the photo.

"That's really nice," he murmured, her face inches from his own, his eyes meeting and holding her green gaze. Logan could smell the fresh air, the wood scent that came from being in the shop, in her hair. Wanting to lose himself in her gaze, he straightened and took a step away from her. If he didn't, he was going to do something really stupid and it would have ruined the trust she was building with him. Logan didn't know why she was skittish around men, but he knew something had happened to Lea at some point. More than anything, he wanted her trust. And he was sure that she wasn't attracted to him as he was to her. The unexpected moment where their heads were bowed and almost touching as they studied the photo she was showing him, created a driving need within him.

"That's a great scene," he complimented her, purposely walking back to her other sketches on the table. He moved to the next set of drawings. Again, Lea had captured a mother with her newborn fawn lying in the grass, the mother licking it, the pine trees surrounding them.

Lea had turned and set the camera on the desk and then she came and stood next to him. "Are you all right with this one?" she asked, not sure.

"Do you have a photo of this?"

"Well," she hedged, "not of here, but in Brookings, when I was hiking, I came upon them at the edge of a small clearing." She gave him a questioning look. "What do you think? Is this something you could look at every time you're in the kitchen?"

"Of course," he said. "I've seen fawns romping around here, both deer and elk. I know Maddy will go bonkers over it. She loves babies of all kinds, too."

"It's a woman thing," she intoned drily.

Grinning, he chuckled. "You could say that, yes."

"I decided to sketch it up because even though you're male, you're very much the mother hen that everyone refers to you as around here." She saw his eyes sparkle with laughter.

"My nickname," he deadpanned, shaking his head. "Yes, I love all the babies around here, too. And that mama raccoon likes bringing her young down to the fishing pond because there's mussels in the mud along the banks. It's easy eating for her and her brood to dig and find them."

She moved to the next set. "I wanted to do a montage of the deer and elk, so on these two panels I have four white-tailed deer—females with their fawns. In the next one, I have the elk, and I wanted to show the bull with his herd of girls." She grinned.

"That's quite a set of antlers on that dude," Logan agreed, impressed. "Come fall around here, you'll hear the elks bugling back and forth with one another. It's a sound I love."

"Sure is," she agreed. Walking to the next sketch, she said, "I wanted a winter scene with elk—cows, yearlings, and a bull. And this last grouping will round out all the cabinets." She walked back to the first set of doors, leaning down and drawing out a smaller box from a shelf, setting it next to the sketch. "I'm going to use tiger maple to represent the pond because it has that natural gold ribbing, that if placed right, will look like rivulets being created by a breeze across the surface of the pond." She laid out a piece she'd already cut to size over the sketch. "Then, I have various other woods here, based upon color and grain, to create the rest of the scene." She laid the pieces around, filling it in so that it took on the sketch in a more meaningful way. Logan stood there, watching her as she set the cut pieces into the drawing.

"Even unpolished or using your sculpting tools," Logan said admiringly, "this feels like it's full of life, like it's breathing." He ran his fingertips across the perfectly smooth surface. Each piece fit tightly into the next so there was no space between them. Logan knew the kind of skill it took to do that. He saw that she had gone and collected wood branches from the different groves and they were sitting in boxes with the name of each tree species on the front of it.

"So? You like the idea?"

"Sure do. I like the choices of wood you've made and the different grains to give it not only texture, but almost a three-dimensional effect. I'm no good at things like this, so I'm sure I'll learn a lot from you as I watch you create each of these masterpieces."

Her cheeks grew red over his sincerely spoken compliment. In some ways, Lea was so damned confident in her skills when it came to woodworking. And yet, she was incredibly shy around him, especially if he gave her a compliment.

"I'm glad you like my idea and my choice of woods. As I make the pieces for each diorama, I want you to come and see it and approve of it before I put it together."

"I trust your concept," Logan said. "Surprise me."

Laughing, Lea said, "Oh, no. That's not how this goes down. I learned a lesson from my first customer, who said the same thing. He said he trusted my vision and had approved the door I was going to make for him without approving the sketch or the woods I had chosen. Then, when it was done, he was shocked and he didn't like it. Ever since then, I get people to write off every stage of my job so I never go through that again."

"Hmmm," he said, rocking back on the heels of his cowboy boots, hands in his pockets. "I don't blame you with what happened. But if it makes you happy, I'm all for it."

"That will make me very happy, Logan."

"You said that you carve doors, too?"

"Sure do. Why?"

"Well, you've seen the front door, and it's pretty rugged looking, and very aged after too many winters around here. Would you like to create a new door for the front entrance of the house?"

"You keep this up, Logan, and I'll be here a full year. I'll be underfoot."

"Nah, not you. I enjoy your artist's eye and you have an incredible sense with wood grains and colors. I've never seen anything quite like what you're doing. That fascinates me." He wanted to add, *you fascinate me*, but he sensed Lea wouldn't want to hear that from him. *Patience . . .*

"Do you want a particular motif or scene on your front door?" she asked.

"Sure do."

"Like?" she baited, waiting for him to give her some ideas.

Shrugging, Logan said, "Tell you what. I can see by the way you're driving around the ranch with your camera, you'll find some remarkable moments with the animals that live here with us. How about *you* come up with three different design ideas for the door?" He saw her jaw drop and then she promptly compressed her lips, studying him.

"Seriously?"

"Sure, seriously. Why not?"

"Because I'm a stranger in your home, that's why. I haven't been here that long to honestly grapple with everything that goes on here. This place is gigantic."

"Sometimes it takes a stranger to come in and see things that we locals miss because we're so used to the place. Take your time on this. Do it when it feels right. I'm in no hurry." He saw the frustration glitter in her eyes, as if she wanted to say something but withheld it. "I know I'm probably not the kind of client you're used to working with, Lea."

"That's for sure," she muttered, shaking her head.

"But we get along, don't we?"

"Yes," she admitted grudgingly, going back to the box and carefully laying each hand-cut piece of wood back into it.

"Why are you looking so concerned?"

"I guess I wasn't expecting a job quite like this."

"Can you be more specific?" He leaned his hips against the table, watching her.

Placing the box on the shelf below the table, she said, "I was prepared to rent a room or a small apartment in Silver Creek if I did get this job. I didn't know how long it would take." She took a damp washcloth from a glass bowl, wiping her fingers off. "I wasn't expecting to be living in a home, a wonderful, beautiful home. Or have someone like Maddy and you, who are incredibly kind and caring."

"What? Are all employers dragons?" he teased, chuckling, liking the faint blush staining her cheeks once again. She placed the washcloth back into the bowl and slid her palms against her jeans. A creeping grin edged the corners of her lips as she lifted her chin, looking him in the eyes.

"I've had the good, the bad, and the ugly."

"There be no dragons here," he said, smiling into her sparkling gaze.

"Phew. Good to know."

"Have you got a few minutes?" he asked, not wanting to leave her company.

"Sure."

"According to Maddy, you rarely leave the shop. I want you to take breaks, go outside, and enjoy Nature. That's always good for one's soul."

"I guess I'm obsessive," Lea hesitantly admitted, following him out of the shop and closing the door. "I get lost in what I'm doing and I forget everything else. Time doesn't exist when I'm in that lane."

"Spoken like a true artist," he said. Halting in the kitchen, he saw Maddy at the stove. "I'm taking Lea into town with me, and giving her a well-deserved break."

"Well!" Maddy chirped. "About time!"

"Geez Louise," Lea griped good-naturedly. "I give up. I surrender."

Maddy and Logan laughed, giving one another knowing looks.

"You need to get out more often," Maddy said, shaking her finger in Lea's direction as Logan opened the kitchen door for her.

"Anything you want from town?" Logan asked his housekeeper.

"No . . . not that I can think of."

He gave her a sly look. "Sure?"

"Well," Maddy sputtered, "if you put it that way, I always enjoy a caramel macchiato from The Unicorn bookstore. Poppy just makes the best! Tell her it's for me? She always gives me extra caramel."

Lifting his hand, Logan murmured, "I thought so. And yes, I'll let Poppy know your druthers."

Lea waited for him out on the porch after pulling on her denim jacket. She was finding that even now, nighttime temperatures dropped to around forty degrees. In Brookings, that was a wintertime temperature, and her body had not adjusted to her new digs yet.

Logan was so tall. His shoulders broad, carrying the proud lineage of his family through the generations. Most of all, she liked his weathered face, partly roughened by the elements, his gaze always showing his emotions, which she could easily read, and she found that remarkable. Most men never broadcasted how they felt. As he pushed the screen door open, he gave her a warm look and she felt it sizzle throughout her body and her heart blossomed with hope. Something that just didn't come that often to her. But around Logan? It happened every day, without fail.

"Come on," he urged, "hop in. We'll drop in and see Poppy first, grab some of her good coffee, and then I'll show you some of Silver Creek you probably haven't seen yet."

She climbed into the white ranch pickup. "Lead on," she said.

It took all of ten minutes to get into town. The pastures were green, grass growing fast, and some wildflowers sticking their heads up, blooming even in this cold weather. Lea was impressed by the strength of the plants and trees against winter. "In Brookings, we don't get snow," she said, turning her head, looking at him. Logan drove with two hands on the wheel and she noticed he wasn't a distracted driver, even though he had all the up-to-the-minute electronics in his vehicle. In fact, every ranch pickup had not only a two-way radio, but a cell phone that was charged and ready to be used in case of emergency.

"No snow," Logan said, "but you folks get a lot of rain

out there. I lived in Portland, Oregon, for a couple of years and I couldn't handle the constant rain and gray, gloomy days. I pined for Wyoming." He gave her an elfish grin.

"I understand."

"How are you able to take weeks of dreary rain throughout the year?" He shook his head. "I got depressed. I hungered for the sun to peek through those low-hanging gray clouds."

"Maybe it doesn't rain as much in Wyoming?" she wondered, watching the town of Silver Creek appear over a slight hill.

"Depends upon where you live in the state," he said. "We get twenty inches here in this valley. North of us, Thermopolis, only gets twelve inches. There are weather differences all over the state. In the winter, we'll get fifty inches of snow. Thermopolis gets around fifty-three inches."

"Wow," she murmured, "that's a *lot* of snow!"

Smiling, Logan slowed down as traffic increased. "Our snow melts sooner because we're in a very special weather pattern, a rare microclimate in the state, which is good. Still, snow converts to water, and water in Wyoming is always needed because so much of the state is bone-dry desert, especially through the center of it."

"And yet, this valley is so unbelievably lush."

"Special place," he murmured, pulling into a parking spot near The Unicorn bookstore. "Ready for a mocha latte, yourself?" He climbed out of the truck.

"Anytime." Lea beat him to the door, the traffic always coming and going from the busy hot spot in town. She noticed more people out on the sidewalks. As she opened the door for Logan, who nodded his thanks, she asked, "Tourist season is starting?"

"Yep," he said, "it sure is. Our time of plenty around here for our small business owners. In the winter, we don't have any snow sports, so it's our lean time, economically speaking."

Lea moved inside and stepped away from the door. Lots of the traffic was at the rear, at the coffee station. There were clumps of people at tables in the restaurant area, where she spotted Brad, Poppy's husband. "I'm more than ready for that mocha latte. It will be good to see Poppy again. Did I tell you she gave me a tarot reading?" She fell into step with Logan in the wide book aisles.

"No, you didn't." His eyes glimmered. "You know, Poppy's *very* accurate. She's dangerous with those card readings."

"And you would know this how?"

"Oh, when things are slow and I drop in at times, she'll offer me a quickie read."

"And you believe in her readings?"

"Well," he said, "she's been darned accurate with me over the years. Not that I go around asking her to read for me."

"Of course not," she teased.

"You don't believe in tarot?" he asked, his boots thunking along the wooden floor. Up ahead, four people just left the coffee station with happy smiles on their faces, clutching their lattes or whatever they had ordered.

"I don't know . . . I've never had a reading before."

"Well, did Poppy tell you to say nothing about what she read for you? She's a stickler on privacy."

"Yes, she did."

"So? Your lips are sealed, eh?" He made a turn, gesturing for her to step up to the counter.

"You could say that," she said, waving her hand at Poppy, who had just come out of the back, her arms full of paper napkins to put into dispensers. "When she did the reading for me when I first came to town, she told me to expect the unexpected, that events could suddenly happen to me. And no sooner had she told me that? Ten minutes later I got slammed into by that truck at your ranch entrance."

"Phew," Logan muttered. "She was right on the money."

"She warned me to be careful and stay alert." Lea shrugged. "I never thought about a car crash like that happening."

"OMG!" Poppy called, placing the napkins on the counter. "If it isn't Logan the Ghost!"

Tittering over the nickname as they came to a halt at the ordering area, Lea asked, "Why do you refer to him as a ghost, Poppy?"

She was wearing a bright red and yellow scarf in her hair and she pushed tendrils of escaping curls away with her forearm. "Because we rarely see hide nor hair of him, Lea. And you, too!! I haven't seen you since you walked in my bookstore."

"I've been keeping her busy," Logan said, grinning.

Poppy hurried to the cash register to take their order. "Well, Logan, you should let Lea out of your cabin every so often. I've missed her. What would you like, Lea?"

Lea gave her and Maddy's order.

"Oh, Maddy loves *lots* of caramel," Poppy laughed. "And you, Logan? Your usual? Americano?"

"You bet," Logan said.

"You don't like lattes?" Lea asked.

"Nah, I'm a simple kind of wrangler," he demurred.

Poppy managed a snort. "Oh, sure. Lea? He's the master of understatement, humble and unassuming. He's been having an Americano since I came and bought this store ten years ago."

Shrugging, Logan watched Poppy start to create the three orders. "Hey, Lea, you shoulda heard him protest when I put a tiny dollop on his Americano to gussy it up a little."

"Not a great whipped cream lover, are you?" Lea teased, grinning over at Logan.

"Like I said, I'm a simple kind of guy."

"You're the lord of understatement, Logan," Poppy warned, bringing him the Americano. She went back to work, finishing off the rest of the order. One of her helpers was stuffing dispensers with napkins. "Hey, Lea, do you find him to be simple?" she hollered over her shoulder.

Laughing, Lea said, "He seems to know a lot about a lot of things, Poppy. I don't find him to be simple at all."

Logan rolled his eyes at her. "Simple as in foods. Maddy is the best cook in the valley."

"Yeah, you ranchers are all alike," Poppy hooted, bringing over the two cups and putting them in a cardboard carrier for Lea. "Meat and potatoes."

"Well," Logan hedged, sipping his hot coffee, "that's probably true, Miss Poppy."

Lifting her pert nose, Poppy's fingers flashed over the cash register. "Indeed, it is. So? You gonna let Lea off the property to come see me some afternoon? Huh?"

Chuckling, Logan said, "She's free to come and go anytime she wants."

"What are you, Lea? A workaholic?" Poppy nudged, grinning.

"I really am," she said lamely. "Logan tries to shoo me out of his wood shop, but I love what I'm doing. I get lost in it and then I lose track of time. Before I know it? It's dinnertime."

"Sounds like a disease to me," Poppy opined, her smile huge.

"Okay, I'll get up here and visit you."

"Soon?"

"Yes."

"What's soon mean to you?"

Now it was Lea's turn to roll her eyes. "How about next week?"

Throwing a thumbs-up, Poppy said, "Roger that. Because I heard about that truck ramming you from behind less than an hour after I did that tarot reading. I started to worry about you. I called Logan to find out how you were."

Lea gave her boss an eyebrow-raised look. "You never told me that Poppy called."

"Sorry, just forgot. I told Poppy you were shaken up, but all right."

"Yes," Poppy said, "and that your truck was totaled."

"That's the truth." Lea grumbled unhappily.

"But Logan has given you one of his ranch trucks as wheels to get around?"

Lea nodded in Poppy's direction. "Yes, he did. I never expected that."

Giving her a cocky look, Poppy said, "Now you know why I told you Logan was one of the most eligible bachelors in the county. You see how nice he is."

Heat instantly shot into Lea's cheeks and she stopped

the urge to rub her burning skin, because Logan was watching her through half-closed eyes as he sipped his coffee, interest in his expression. Scrambling, Lea didn't know what to say and then added lamely as she picked up the cardboard carrier, "I'll be sure to see you within a week, Poppy. That's a promise."

Chapter Five

May 30

"Now that we're tanked up and topped off," Logan said, slanting her a glance as he parked the truck near a group of buildings, "I wanted you to see the center of Silver Creek when it comes to the folks who live around here."

"It's a fairgrounds," she said, climbing out of the cab.

"The heart and pride of our community," he assured her, settling his Stetson on his head, meeting her at the entrance from the parking area. He resisted the urge to cup her elbow. Since #MeToo, he'd been aware that a lot of things men did were *not* seen as positive or invited or wanted, as he'd assumed. *Hands off.* That was it. Logan was trying to put himself in a woman's world. Men were taking unconscious, unthinking advantage of them. It was a whole new world for both genders. No more uninvited physical contact. Not touching her hand, no touching her shoulder. *Nothing.* And yet, that's exactly what he wanted to do, but he curbed his desire.

Lea seemed to have ramped down and appeared less stressed. Maybe the ranch had lulled her with its own unique magic, its ephemeral beauty, the wildlife, or perhaps she had dived fully into the job and was comfortable being there. He liked having her around. Even more, he made more stops at the house at lunchtime than before she had arrived. And dinner was something he eagerly looked forward to every night, whereas before, it had been lonely and like one hand clapping. Now he was feeling positive in ways he hadn't been for a long time. And he knew it was because there was a woman under his roof. But not just any woman. A highly intelligent, creative woman with common sense for a soul. Never mind he found her beautiful in every possible way, but those words weren't coming out of his lips. At least not yet, probably never.

"Over here, my grandfather and his wife had the 4-H building built." He pointed to the one-story, warehouse-like structure. "My mother and father had a livestock arena and pens built next to it. That allowed 4-H kids who were raising animals to compete."

"I like the copper rooster on the steeple," Lea said, appreciating the huge, long, wide building. Turning, she looked up into his eyes. "What are you going to build for the town?"

He smiled a little, gesturing to another huge building. "My mother was old-fashioned. She gardened, raised everything we had on our dinner plates at night, and created beautiful flower gardens, which you've seen around the property. She wanted a place where people who had gardens like hers, of which there are many to this day, as well as people who owned fruit trees and grew flowers, could compete for prizes, too. When I was younger, I worked with my father on blueprints, along with my mother, to create such a building. My mother wanted lots of classrooms built within it, too, where people could go to learn best agriculture and gardening techniques, or, if someone wanted to raise irises, for example, what it took to do that."

"Wow, you just about own everything at this fairgrounds, Logan. You and your family. What a gift to the people of this valley." She saw his cheeks redden a little, a bit of shyness in his eyes.

"I grew up learning one thing is very important," he murmured, "and that is, we all need one another. My family provided timber for the silver mines. When they turned to raising livestock and continued to expand the wood business, they worked in the valley in partnership with other ranchers. When we became prosperous, so did everyone else. I like that idea. It's an 'all for one, one for all' sort of idealism, but we manifested it by actually doing it here in Silver Creek Valley."

"I'm a dyed-in-the-wool idealist, too," Lea said quietly, standing and welcoming the warmth of the sun to cut the chill of the breeze, which was much colder. "I love that your family wasn't selfish, self-centered, or greedy. They spread their wealth to others. That's so commendable, especially in today's environment where you see big business and lobbying groups buying and running our government instead of the votes of the people."

He nodded. "It's not right. There are other models, better business models, than turning into a greedy, selfish company or corporation. Right now, I'm leading the charge with our city council and our county to keep fracking out of it. I'm also working with the state legislators, but that's tough because they want to be paid for their vote, and I don't have that kind of money. No one in Silver Creek does." He scowled.

"All we can do is get people registered and then get them to vote. It sounds simple enough, but it's complex.

And it takes everyone's attention on the problem in order to fix it," Lea said quietly.

"That's what my family has done here in the valley," Logan said. "We saw a problem, we came together, chawed it over, came up with ideas on how to fix it. Those weren't county or town board meetings, either. The ranchers would invite townspeople to a ranch barbecue, a barn dance, and together, they'd solve a problem over a good meal and dancing with their families."

"Well, it sounds like the real problem confronting this valley right now is with that fracking corporation that you mentioned to me early on. They fall into the rich, powerful, greedy, and *I don't give a damn about any other human beings other than my own family*, kind of mentality."

"Harvey Polcyn is sixty years old, worth one billion dollars," Logan growled. "He's got three children, two boys and a girl, and he's got them on his board. He refuses to be on the stock market, keeping the company from going public, wanting to make his own rules rather than go by the ones that are already in place. He's been destroying the geologic substructure in the county to the south of us. He's tried to bribe our town officials, but they turned him down cold. The whole valley wants nothing to do with him, but there's loopholes."

"What kind of loopholes?"

"Some of the ranchers in the county don't own the mineral rights to their own land. Polcyn can come in, pay them, set up his fracking equipment, and start destroying the geologic substructure of our valley, legally."

"Isn't there anything you can do about it, Logan? This sounds heartbreaking."

"It is heartbreaking." He sighed. "But, a glimmer of hope. Oregon's legislature created House Bill 2623, which imposes a five-year moratorium on hydraulic fracturing for oil or gas in your state. Did you know about it, since you live there?"

"Yes, my family and I followed it. We were relieved when it passed. Oregonians are ecologically minded, first and foremost. We want clean water, breathable air, and as little or no pesticides or herbicides used on crops. There's an awful lot of organic farmers in the state. We hate genetically altered anything. We won't buy it."

"That's why Silver Creek will be good for you," he noted. "We're into fighting climate change, supporting the environment, and eating clean food that is organic."

"I got really lucky."

"Have you been to Mama's Market yet?"

Lea shook her head. "Not yet. You're feeding me too well, Logan. And I'm rarely in the kitchen except to offer a hand to Maddy, which she usually turns down."

"Next time Maddy goes grocery shopping for the ranch? Go with her. You'll love Mama's Market. It's actually owned by a good friend of mine, Chase Bishop of the Three Bars Ranch. His family has been in this valley almost as long as mine has. They own a thirty-thousand-acre ranch and he's turned part of it into an organic farm, and has plans for more ecologically friendly commodities. Mama Mary Bishop is the matriarch of the valley, and the one who started the supermarket here in Silver Creek. Over time, it has become the only grocery store in town because everything is fresh, organic, and non-GMO. She's been responsible for just about everyone having a garden. Matter of fact, Mama gives classes at the fair on how to start one. We have a huge knitting group here, which, by the way, comprises women and men."

"Do you knit, Logan?"

He chuckled. "No. My interests are more in building infrastructure in the valley to serve the people who live here, not wrestling with yarn."

She laughed, and then became serious. "I find that admirable. I wish we could clone you and have you in every town and village in this country."

Logan felt his cheeks growing warm over her husky, emotional comment. "When you live out away from cities and suburbs, you learn to rely on your neighbors." He removed his Stetson, running his fingers through his short, dark hair and then settling it back on his head. He motioned her toward the exit. "I want to give you the layout of our town."

"Sounds good to me. I feel like it's a bus woman's holiday," she teased, grinning over at him.

He smiled and opened the door to the outside of the building. "You need to take more breaks, Lea."

"I just get lost in my work. And it's not really work at all, to me," she amended, walking with him toward the truck.

"You're passion driven."

"Good way of putting it."

He opened the door to the truck before she could reach for the handle. There was humor in her eyes as she nodded her thanks and climbed in.

"Silver Creek, the town, is a strip kind of place," Logan said as they drove slowly down the mostly deserted highway. "We have photos in my family album of buckboards drawn by horses coming into this town." He gestured ahead of them. "It was a muddy, rutted main drag."

"I can imagine it," she murmured, wanting to always know more about the man, not the owner of the largest spread in the valley.

"The fairgrounds sit outside the town for a reason. My grandfather, and the other ranchers of that era, got together a long time ago and drew up a kind of map of what the town should be and should have. They were pretty farsighted."

"Your grandfather fight in World War Two?"

"He did. For four years. Like so many other young American men of that era did." Logan's voice dropped. "Nowadays, we know that a lot of military men and women come out of combat with PTSD. Back then, it was called battle fatigue, but everyone who had it either drank heavily upon their return or just buried it and tried to hide it and adjust to civilian life the best they could."

"What did your grandfather do?" Lea wondered. She saw Logan's dark brows dip momentarily. He had one hand draped over the top of the steering wheel and he opened his hand in response.

"I grew up remembering he was a pretty closed-up gent. I didn't know why at the time. I just accepted him like that. And no one talked about the war. So, I didn't understand until I went into the army why he was so inward and untalkative. I was a software mechanic on the Apache gunship helicopters and was stationed over in Afghanistan, in Helmand Province, one of the worst combat areas in that godforsaken sandbox of a country. We'd routinely get mortared or have hand grenades thrown over the fence around the perimeter of our base. I didn't see combat like my grandfather did in Europe. He survived the Battle of the Bulge in Belgium, near the end of the war. I found out from my grandmother and mother about some of his heroism in combat. He had a Silver Star and a Bronze Star with a V for valor. He'd been in the thick of the army move to drive the Germans out of Europe. I began to understand from my own four years in the army, what he must have gone through. I wish—" He sighed. "I wish I'd known then, at eighteen through twenty-two, when I served my country, and realized how much pain and suffering my grandfather endured daily. By the time I left the army, he'd passed on. It's one of my great heartaches, not getting to speak with him, understand some of what he went through. I wonder if he talked to anyone about it. My grams knew some of it because she would tell me he'd wake up screaming at night, scaring the hell out of her."

Shaking her head and giving Logan a sad look, she said softly, "I think war should be the *last* option any country thinks about, not the first. I see so many vets returning, and their spirits are shattered and broken."

"Yes," he said. Taking a deep breath, he glanced at her. "We're coming up on The Unicorn bookstore where Poppy and her husband, Brad, own it. It's here on the left and I know you said Poppy was one of the first people you met when you came here."

"Yes, she's wonderful. I met her husband, Brad, and he's just as nice as she is. He runs the restaurant portion for her in the back of the bookstore."

"Sometimes, Brad wrangles at our ranch. We often need more help in the summer when we're vaccinating our calves and such. He's a hard worker, honest as the day is long."

"Like everyone else you employ, I'm sure."

He smiled . "I think you draw what you are. Don't you?"

"Most certainly." She pointed toward the bookstore. "There's a hair salon on the other street behind it." She touched her hair. "I'm going to have to get a trim pretty soon."

"We only have one hair salon, too," he said. "Mariposa was the name given it by Helen Dinkens. She's the owner.

Everyone loves her. She's in her fifties now, but came here thirty years ago, worked hard, saved her money, and had her salon built."

"Are a lot of the people here from other parts of the country? Are they drawn here for a reason?"

Nodding, he said, "Pretty much the story. Most of them were from cities or suburbs. All of 'em wanting a country or rural lifestyle." He pointed to the right. "There's our only school, and it has all grades. The school was originally built in the 1920s, but has been added on to over the decades as the population grew. I spent my twelve years there."

"It's a huge, gray, stone kind of looking building," she said, pointing to the year it opened: 1922.

"At least from what you can see from here," Logan said. "Behind it are far more recent buildings to house the growing student population."

"What is the population here?"

"Forty thousand, now."

"I see you have a pancake restaurant." She pointed off to the right.

"It's a diner," he said. "Good food, day or night."

For as far as Lea could see, the town was definitely built around the straight-ahead four-lane highway. "Is there something here that you're really proud of?"

"Yes," he said, "and I got involved in it because of my grandfather's PTSD. About half a mile up on the right, I'll take a turn and you'll see a number of tiny houses. This has been in my heart for a long time because a lot of the ranchers around here went into the military and then came home. Silver Creek is a mecca of sorts in the summer months. A lot of homeless vets come into our valley. I wanted to have a place for them to live, not on

the street, and so did the other ranching families." He
slowed the truck and made a right turn, driving down two
blocks and then pulling over on the berm. "You see these
tiny homes?"

"Yes." They were all brightly painted, reminding her of
Easter eggs, each small home with a yard and white picket
fence around it. She saw a number of men and women out
and about around each home or on the porches, where
rockers sat.

"Last summer, we got wrangling crews from all the
ranches in the valley, and the town paid for everything we
needed. We spent three months putting up these small
rows of homes for the vets. Now, they all have a place to
stay. It's warm in the winter, air-conditioned in the
summer. We don't have a Veterans Administration hospital
here, but our own social network for the town helps them
with mental and emotional issues, any drinking or drug
problems. We've gotten the county to put money into
social services for them." He grimaced. "That wasn't easy.
Wyoming is not a highly populated state, so we don't have
tons of taxpayer money around to pay for things we all
might want for others."

"How did you get it then?" she wondered.

"Writing grants. It's not my forte, but there's a number
of ranchers here who sent sons and daughters off to college, and they did the work. We supplied most of the
lumber for their homes. It was time to thin the groves and
we'd done that two years earlier. Took the wood to our
local sawmill and had the lumber made and donated it to
the project."

"You could have sold that lumber for a lot of money,"
Lea said, her heart opening even more to this man.

Shrugging, Logan said, "What's money if you can't do

something good with it? Why have it? My parents were fully behind this project, and I'd talked it over with them beforehand. Our ranch is unique in that we've got many streams of income. No one else has groves of hard- and softwood like we do. But it was my relatives who planted them and now, it's paying off in many ways." He smiled slightly. "I would like to think my forebears would approve of the use of this wood to help the homeless."

"I think," Lea said, touched by his family's generosity, "that they would celebrate your kindness toward others."

"Most do, some don't. We have our detractors here on the city council. We almost didn't get enough votes to build these homes for the vets. Everything, nowadays, is a battle of one sort or another, to hold a dream and make it come to fruition."

"You live in a world I honestly don't know much about. My parents never got invested in their city council."

"Well," he warned, putting the truck in gear and easing out onto the road once more, "if you don't? Your voice and needs aren't going to be met or heard. I had civics classes in high school, teaching us how democracy works. Voting is a privilege. I was over in Afghanistan, where no woman could vote. No man can, either. It's all about the tribe and the facilities within it, and they all have an authoritarian leader. Some of them were good men with good hearts, but others were not like that at all. I understood our democracy as never before while I was over there. I came home realizing if I didn't take part in what was going on in the town I lived in, that I was shirking my duty as a citizen."

"Nowadays," Lea said darkly, "schools don't teach civics. Mine did, but I know it is an anomaly to what's going on with our education system right now. Kids can't count money, they rely on a computer to do everything. I often wonder if the electric grid ever collapsed across our country, how many of them would know how to survive without technology."

"Exactly," he said, pulling over to the curb. He pointed to the left. "Here's another undertaking we're proud of, Lea. This is our homeless shelter. Right next to it is a medical and dental outreach clinic which charges nothing, or next to nothing, to help homeless people or low income families."

"Did grants pick up that cost?" she wondered.

He grinned. "Sure did. We're a town full of grant money, and the people who write them are always scouring for ways to find more. Not all grants are forever, and many have to be renewed or we have to go through the entire process yearly, which is a lot of work on our part." He pointed to another building. "And right next to them is our women's shelter."

She saw the large two-story white building with green trim. "It's so nice to see a town taking care of those who have difficult lives. I rarely have seen something like this."

"Part of it is that we have a woman mayor," he said, chuckling. "She's been voted in every three years for the last couple of decades. Daisy Woods is now sixty, silver hair, blue eyes, and a real hands-on mayor. She has made huge changes, including the building of the women's shelter during her tenure. And like every city council, she has her detractors that try and stop her vision for Silver Creek from coming true, but she's a very smooth, diplomatic politician. Most of the people here love her. She worked tirelessly with all of us ranchers to get the tiny homes built for the homeless vets."

"Women see the world differently," Lea said. "We are the nurturers, the caregivers, and the ones who bring life into this world. I'm afraid I see a lot of men who all they want to do is to chase greed, money, and power. They don't care if they destroy our water, our air, our animals or way of life. They just care about money, position, and power over all of us."

"Well," he growled, "that's not happening here. Not in our county, our valley, or in our town. The only rat we have like that is Polcyn and the money that his company has for fracking their way from the Gulf, northward. And now, he's at our county's doorstep."

"That's such an awful thing, this fracking. They're destroying the rock and geology beneath an area, polluting the water so people can't drink it." Lea shook her head, feeling as grim as Logan looked. "Is Mayor Woods in this fight to stop him from coming into the county?"

"Better believe it," he said, pulling out of the parking zone. "But we're in a fight of our lives with the state, too. There's men like Polcyn in power at the governor's office, as well as in the state legislature, who want him to frack all the counties where there's natural gas."

"Do you have to lobby, then? That takes a lot of money."

He drove the speed limit, heading out of town. "Yes, to both. Like I shared with you before, our biggest worry is Polcyn being able to frack in our county where some of the ranchers don't own the mineral rights to their property. We've got a team of lawyers working on that side of this battle, already."

"I hope they can help you stave off that greedy monster."

"I think they'll do it. But it involves years of holding that vision, and stopping Polcyn from ever setting foot in our county. It's a daily, constant threat to all of us."

As they sped out of town, about half a mile from the

entrance to the ranch, Lea saw a dark blue truck pulled over on their side of the road. A cowboy climbed out.

"That's Chase Bishop," Logan said. "I'm pulling over to see if he needs some help."

Lea nodded. "He doesn't look happy." Chase was easily six-foot-four-inches tall, the light blue chambray shirt outlining his massive shoulders and chest. He wore a white straw Stetson on his military-short black hair, well-worn Levi's, and scuffed, well-used dark brown cowboy boots.

"No, he doesn't. Probably an issue with his vehicle." He put his truck in park and climbed out.

"Hey, Chase," he called, shutting the door to his truck, "what's going on with your Bronco? Do you need some help?"

Chase gave him a one-sided grimace. "Yeah, my beloved 1992 Ford Bronco here, had an oil light come on. I pulled over immediately and turned off the engine." He got down on his hands and knees, staring hard at the underside of the engine. There was a slow oil leak dripping onto the asphalt shoulder.

Logan got down beside him, spotting the leak. "Did you pull over in time?"

"I think so. Otherwise, I'd have blown the engine on my girl." He sat up, leaning back on the heels of his boots, wiping his large hands on his thighs. "It's got two-hundred-thousand miles on it, and you know I care for this baby."

"I do," Logan said, standing up, brushing off his hands. "I hope you can patch that oil pan or replace the oil line to it."

"Oh, no worries, I will. Can I hitch a ride to Three Bars?"

"Sure, come on. Lea, the woman who is a master wood carver, is with me."

Bishop grinned elfishly. "I don't bite and I'll leave her alone."

Chuckling, Logan waited while he locked up his white Bronco with gray trim. "I don't think either of us need to worry. Come on."

Lea scooted over as Chase introduced himself after opening the passenger-side door. He tipped his hat and was all manners, asking permission to come and sit next to her when Logan took him to the Three Bars Ranch.

"Of course, you can," Lea said. She didn't say anything about the opportunity to sit close to Logan. Literally, she could feel the heat from his body despite the clothing he wore. Deciding that he was a magnet to her, Lea smiled over at Chase as he edged in with his height and bulk.

"Three Bars is about five miles down the road," Logan said. "Do you want me to drop you off at the ranch house first, Lea?"

"No, thanks. I've not seen any other ranches, so this will be part of my reconnoitering around Silver Creek."

Chase took off his hat, placing it in his lap and pulling on the seat belt. "Logan has the nicest-looking ranch in the valley," he said. "But ours isn't far behind."

Driving out onto the highway, Logan hooted. "Three Bars is a model ranch. You've been leading the way to different types of ecology for the valley." He turned his attention to Lea. "He owns thirty-thousand acres and our ranches butt up against one another. We've been good neighbors forever."

"Our families are like kissing kin," Chase told Lea. "But when you live out in the middle of nowhere, you learn to appreciate your neighbors and overlook some of their other more eccentric qualities."

Snickering, Logan added, "Chase can be diplomatic when he wants to be."

"Better to be neighbors," Lea agreed.

"I'm glad to meet you, Lea. There's word buzzing around the valley that you're the real deal. I don't know how long you're going to be in our valley, but I'd sure like to get your thoughts on some kitchen remodeling."

"I didn't know you were a man of the kitchen," Logan jabbed, grinning even more.

"Well," Chase admitted, "I'm not. But you know? My mother, Lea, was on me just a month ago to make some much needed changes to our kitchen."

"Mary Bishop is Chase's mom. She owns Mama's Market," Logan reminded her. "She runs it to this day."

"Oh, I see," she said. "And your mother lives with you, Chase?"

"Well, she lives nearby. The house I'm occupying now was her home when my dad was alive. After he passed, she didn't want to care for such a large house and we built her a much smaller one, about two hundred feet from the main ranch house."

"But she wants you to update your kitchen?" Lea asked.

"Yes. The cupboards are really worn. They've been there for a hundred years and she thinks it's about time they got replaced with something better."

"How do you feel about it?" Lea wondered.

"I'm fine with it. We had a good last year, and I have money enough to do it, but hearing what you're doing with

Logan's kitchen got around. Mary wanted me to contact you, and here you are."

Laughing, Lea said, "I'd be happy to come over and look at your cabinets. Would Mary be there? I'm sure she'd like some input, or to give me suggestions."

"Sure, she'd be there in a heartbeat. She's all excited about you. Logan, here, has been bragging all over the county about your incredible artistry. Mary and I would like to come over and see it, if Logan will let us in the front door."

Snickering, Logan said, "Chase knows he and his family are welcome anytime at the Wild Goose. And seeing Lea's incredible gift for woodworking will make you salivate, pardner."

"I'm sure it will. Once I get my Bronco back in order, I'll give you a call or email you and find out when's a good time to come over. Mary will be beside herself."

Five miles wasn't that far and too soon, Lea saw their threesome go down to a twosome once more. The Three Bars Ranch was huge, had a two-story log ranch head-quarters with plenty of wranglers either riding horses or on ATVs, doing a lot of daily work that the sprawling ranch demanded. After dropping off Chase, Lea reluctantly moved back to her original spot in the cab.

"That Bronco is a 1992 model, and it's still running?"

Backing around in the large circular driveway, Logan said, "Chase is the kind of man that doesn't let go of anything. His father, Tom, died at forty-five of a heart attack and it was his car. Chase took it over, has babied it over the years, drives it everywhere, and I think it keeps him close to his dad, even though he's gone."

"That's so bittersweet," Lea said, sad for Chase.

"They were close, although Chase was very young when his dad died."

"So, he grew up without a father?"

"Yes. Mary never remarried. It was well-known in the valley that she and Tom were deeply and forever in love with one another. She started Mama's Market about a year later because she and Tom had dreamed of having an organic grocery store. In a way," Logan murmured, his voice lowering with emotion, "I think Mary having her grocery store was like Chase having Tom's Bronco. Each of them had a piece of Tom to hold on to."

"That's such a beautiful tribute to Tom," she whispered, giving him a warm look, wanting to put her hand on his shoulder, seeing the pain in his expression, wanting to comfort him. But she didn't. It would have been unseemly. She was an employee. Nothing more. But how she wished there was so much more between them.

"It is. They have a family graveyard on the Three Bars, just as we have our family plot on the Wild Goose. Mary, I think, found a lot of solace in starting up the grocery store, following her and Tom's dreams. They had literally a three-inch binder of notes, ideas, and so much more, for the grocery store before he died. She calls it her bible to this day. And it's always in her office there at the store. For her, Tom is still alive, still a part of her life as she walks the aisles of their store. I know it gives her closure, but also, comfort. Tom might be gone, but he's not forgotten. He's well loved by his wife and son to this day."

"That's something that people like Polcyn will *never* understand or value," Lea murmured. "And I cherish that kind of warm relationship and connections, like you do."

"Well, luckily," Logan said, turning into the driveway

of the Wild Goose, "my parents are both alive, and happy to be in Arizona, where there's no four seasons."

"We're both lucky," Lea agreed. "I hope my folks live to be a hundred like yours."

"I learned a long time ago, Lea, to just live the day that's in front of me. I don't normally look past that because being in Afghanistan taught me that a person you love can be erased in a nanosecond. They won't have any tomorrow."

Chapter Six

June 1

Skimming off the bark from a piece of oak limb, Lea kept up a steady, gentle rhythm to remove the dark pieces, which flew all around her feet. Working with wood was working with a living being in her mind and imagination. She had always loved trees. Her father had taught her that everything in Nature was alive, and therefore was accorded respect and considered a member of the greater Earth family. He showed her how to talk with a tree if she wanted to take one of its "arms" to be used in carving it later. If the tree said yes, she would take the limb. If it said no, she would move on to the next possible tree candidate.

The morning sunlight lanced in the windows, the first day of June upon them, and it was filled with a light blue sky. Outside the shop, she could hear occasional calls from one of the wranglers as they worked nearby. The scent of the hardwood entered her nostrils and she inhaled it as if it were a perfume. In a few minutes, the bark was removed. This was a small limb, the size of her forearm, and she had chosen this blond wood for one of the scenes that would eventually go on one of the cabinet doors she was making. Running her fingers down the wood, it was dry, not green. If green wood were used it would take a long time to dry out. Worse, it would crack over time. She'd purposely gathered old, dead limbs for the dioramas she was going to create. The wood had a velvety feel, a tight grain, and a slight yellow appearance to it.

Her heart, if she acknowledged it, settled on Logan in quiet moments like this. The man was fair, generous, sensitive toward others, and yet, she sensed a deep sadness within him.

Poppy had told her about Logan losing his wife, Elizabeth, a year after they were married. That could be it. She took the wood over to her saw, making sure a very small-toothed blade was in it so that it would make a clean cut to the wood. After sawing it in half, she took her final sketch and placed the paper pattern on the branch. It fit perfectly and she quickly outlined it with a special pencil that would not leave a stain on the wood.

She measured the piece and took it back to the saw, settling her safety glasses over her eyes. She wore earplugs as well. Every time she used the saw, there were automatic safety checks. She did not want to lose a finger, or worse, a part of her hand, by being negligent or distracted around such equipment.

Once the piece was cut very thin, about one-quarter of an inch wide with her jigsaw, she laid it aside after numbering it on the back. The number would never be seen by anyone. There was the cabinet number to put on it, the piece number that she could look up on her master drawing sheet for that particular cabinet, the right or left side of the door, and that it was blond oak. She had a large plastic basket nearby and she laid the piece gently in there for later steps to be taken. For these first two cabinet doors, the basket would have all the pieces contained within it. After they were all cut, she would start with the left door and make sure all the pieces for it were present and accounted for. The last step was assembling the puzzle pieces of wood into the actual scene on the door itself.

Logan gently intruded into her focus once more. He seemed to be like fog stealing silently into her heart, making her feel warm, stoking longing that she'd never experienced before this. How strange was that? How magical? Lea knew it wasn't her imagination. In her mind's eye, she pictured him smiling, because that is when the sadness she saw in his eyes would go away, and then his gaze glittered with pure pleasure over the moment shared with her.

How Lea wanted more of those moments! Logan rarely came into her shop when she was working. She did see him at lunch and always looked forward to that. In some ways, he seemed to be avoiding her, but she was hesitant to call it that. More like giving her room and freedom to be herself; whatever that meant. Dinners were the times she loved the most with him. Maddy was gone for the day, back home with her hubby, Alvin, and they were alone. It was a time she looked forward to, more than anything else. Logan was usually tired at the end of the day. She knew he worked hard with his wranglers and often was on his buckskin horse. He didn't like using ATVs, wanting nothing to do with them. It went against his particular code of the West, where cowboys rode horses, not four-wheel vehicles.

During every dinner, Logan, whether he meant to or not, revealed more about himself as a human being. These were like nuggets of gold to Lea. She also tried to unveil and share who she was, too. Their evening meals were always spirited, exciting, and evolving as far as she was concerned. Every day was a feast to her and her silly, yearning heart that pined for Logan's nearness, what he thought and how he saw life. She needed to talk to her mother about this, never having experienced this kind of longing before. Her mother had never laughed at any of her serious questions. Would she now? She wasn't an innocent teen girl or an inexperienced young adult anymore.

Taking a piece of maple, an old piece of branch she'd found in that grove, she began the task all over again of relieving the wood of the outer, crusty bark. In no time, she had the white wood that would replicate the white breasts of the Canadian geese that she was going to eventually create. The maple color would serve well as a foreground in another door diorama. As she cut more wood, shaving the bark from each one, shaping it, categorizing it, Lea decided to call her mother an hour before the dinner hour. She had to talk to someone.

Lea picked up the phone to call her mother. There wasn't anything sacred that Lea couldn't tell her mother, who was like the Rock of Gibraltar to the family. Nothing fazed her.

"Have you ever heard of this feeling before, Mom?" Lea asked, describing it to her. She sat in her bedroom, the door closed, after taking a shower earlier and changing into comfortable clothes—tan slacks, a three-quarter-sleeve flowery print top, and comfy tennis shoes.

"Sure have, darling girl. So, you've never felt like this before about any man, eh?"

Smiling a little, Lea said, "No . . . not like this. Is it a virus?" she asked with a laugh.

Valerie laughed heartily with her. "Of course not! But I'd say you're *very* interested personally, in Logan. What I wonder is this: Is he just as infatuated with you as you are with him?"

Pondering her mother's question, she sighed. "I honestly don't know, Mom. We have these wonderful nightly dinners with one another. We're alone and it feels as if we are each giving the other information about ourselves."

"This is called the *getting to know you* stage," her mother counseled, sounding more serious. "What you have to make sure of here, Lea, is that it isn't just one way. You are interested in him, but there's no sense falling for someone who doesn't reciprocate or let you know how they feel about you. It has to be a two-way street. If you are falling for him and he's not interested, you will be hurt, and I'd hate to see that happen."

"I don't know if it is or isn't, Mom. How can you tell?"

"It's a feeling. You sense when a man is interested in you whether he ever touches you or not. And I don't imagine Logan is touching you at this stage."

"No, there's no inappropriate touching. How can I tell, then?"

"Have you watched him around other people? How does he act and react with them? How does he act and react toward you? If there is a difference, look at it realistically. Good grief, back in Victorian times men and women were cloaked in this other very subtle language that would telegraph that they were interested in one another without ever touching or kissing. It's a silent, nonverbal language, Lea. And not everyone has been schooled in it, there's no manual for it; rather it's about revealing secretive or little-known things to one another. In other words, you are entrusting that person with things that most people would not reveal to others. That is how you tell."

"Logan has been very open with me."

"Men, typically are *not* open, darlin'."

"He is with me."

"Then maybe that's his way of letting you know that you're special to him, that he's seriously interested or is entrusting you with secrets or sacred parts of himself that he'd rarely share with anyone. Does that make sense?"

"Yes . . . yes, it does. And it helps me understand this cloak-and-dagger dance that the Victorian era lovers had with one another."

Her mother laughed. "I like that he's not crowding you, or pressuring you in any way. That's smart of him. He must have learned it from somewhere."

"Maybe his life experience has been much fuller and robust than mine," Lea said, smiling a little.

"Well, just be the observer," her mom said. "If there is really something between the two of you, something good, positive and healthy? It doesn't hurt to take the time to find out who he is, but also, that he knows who you are, too. True love isn't about sex and a toss in the bedroom. It's so much more than that, Lea. And I hope, whatever happens, that you take it slow with Logan."

"I will," she promised, grateful for her mother's always keen, common-sense eye on human nature.

* * *

Logan sat with Lea at the dinner table. Maddy had made them spaghetti with all the trimmings. He'd come in half an hour ago, six p.m., took a quick shower, and changed into clean Levi's and a long-sleeved dark blue cotton shirt. Lea had retrieved the salads from the refrigerator and he plucked the spaghetti from the oven and the garlic bread slathered with butter from the overhead warmer.

"How did your day go?" he asked, passing her the toasted French bread.

"Progress. I got a lot of wood cut for the first cupboard door, done today. They look like jigsaw puzzle pieces." She smiled, taking the platter of bread, the scent of garlic divine to her.

"Did you pick up these branches out at the groves?" He took the platter back from her, adding four pieces to the outer rim of his plate.

"Yes. From the ground, because I wanted to make sure the wood was already dry."

"Did you absolutely have to go back out there to get anything else you needed?"

"Are you really asking if I should have someone with me?" She saw one corner of his mouth quirk. Logan's hair was sleek from the recent shower, blue highlights in its short length. His beard shadowed his lower face and it emphasized the strength she always saw in him.

"Yes, I guess I am."

"Are you worried about me going out there by myself?"

"Caught me." He gave her a slight grin.

"My dad speaks in mysterious tongues, too, and I've watched my mother translate what he was really saying or asking. It's man-speak." She poured some Italian dressing on her salad, capping the bottle. "I have a good teacher."

"Hmmm," he said, taking the bottle as she extended it to him, "is that how a male talks? Women can be very diplomatic or very subtle when they talk."

"True," she acknowledged, "but we don't like to hide what we really want to say. My mother has always been direct with my father and I like it that way." She tasted the spaghetti and made an appreciative sound. "Maddy is just the best," she murmured, grateful that she didn't have to do the cooking.

"You tend to speak directly, I've discovered. I need to thank your mother." He teased her lightly.

Tossing him a grin, she said, "It doesn't leave people any room to guess where I stand on a topic."

"My father is like that and so is my mother. I guess I'm a Neanderthal throwback, eh?" He gave her an amused look.

Chuckling, Lea murmured between bites, "You might be many things, Logan, but one of them is not a Neanderthal, thank goodness."

"I think we have good communication skills with one another, over all. Don't you?"

"Yes. It's the only way to be, I discovered as I grew out of my dumb teen years and into my early twenties."

He took a bite of the fragrant spaghetti. "I've seen a lot of relationships go on the rocks because of this very thing: poor communication between the two people."

"Never were truer words spoken."

He gave her a studied look, mopping up some marinara sauce on his plate with the French bread. "Do you have any sisters or brothers?"

"No, but I wish I'd had a big brother."

"Why?"

Lea gave a one-shouldered shrug. "When I was fourteen, I got beat up by three boys in school." She saw his brows dip and he froze momentarily over her admittance. "I could have used a big brother then, but I fought back. They were bigger and stronger than I was, so in the end, I lost. No one came to help me, either, which was just as big a blow to me as getting beat up."

"I'm sorry to hear this. If I'd have been there, I'd have waded in and fought right alongside you."

"So why didn't the other boys, who stood around and watched it happen? Some of them were my friends . . . or, I thought they were."

"Were you injured?"

His voice was barely a growl and she saw real anger in his eyes. "A black eye, a broken nose, fractured cheekbone and very hurt feelings. One of the boys? I broke his nose with my fist. The others got black eyes from me, too." She set her utensils down, wiping her mouth with the napkin. "This probably was the wrong time to talk about this. At the dinner table . . ."

"I like our discussions at night," he rasped. "I guess I wasn't expecting any girl of fourteen to be ganged up on by a bunch of boys."

"Oh," she muttered, "they were trying to 'teach me a lesson,' that girls were weak, and I didn't accept that crap at all. Back then? I had a real mouth on me. My parents called me an Amazon warrior, like Wonder Woman. And actually, this face-off had been brewing for a while. One of my girlfriends, Chelsie, was bullied by these three about two weeks earlier. I'd been with her when they started attacking us verbally. Then they threw spit wads at us and that's when I cut loose and charged them. They weren't expecting it. And luckily, there was a teacher who saw it all happen and she called for the security guard.

The three boys were kicked out of school for two weeks and had to do their schoolwork at home. I thought it was over, Logan. But the day they got back, they caught me coming out of the girl's bathroom and got even." She grimaced. "At least they didn't have guns on them or I'd be dead. I should be thankful for that."

"That's not even funny," he said, scowling heavily. "What happened next?"

"I was a bloody mess, my nose took a beating. I ran to the principal's area where there was a security guard usually around, found him and screamed for help. He took one look at me and ran toward me. The three boys skidded to a halt, turned and ran away. The guard got me to the office. I told him the names of the three involved, and eventually he rounded them up. My parents pressed assault and battery charges on them. When it was all over, those three went to juvenile hall for the rest of the year. We were rid of three bullies at school. I became a folk hero of sorts for a lot of other girls who were being mercilessly stalked, harassed, and bullied by them. I didn't want the acclaim, fame, or whatever it was called when I was that age. I just wanted to hide. It scared me in ways that I didn't even realize. Their attack hurt me psychologically and physically, too." She touched her left cheek. "The fracture healed and so did all my other bruises and scratches, but it left a mark on me to this day and I'm not very proud to admit that."

"Is that why you more or less remain here in the ranch or shop? I notice you don't usually go off the spread."

His voice was low with concern, the anger replaced with compassion. Lea shook her head. "I turned into a fraidy cat after that ruckus. I was grateful that those three boys never came back to our school. I didn't like being singled out as a hero of sorts. My parents taught me to stand up and fight for what was right. To not lie down, ignore it, or walk away from a confrontation."

"That was a price to pay, too," he said softly.

"You're right. One that I wrestle with every day, whether I like to admit it or not. It's my Achilles' heel. I never dreamed that something like that would stain the rest of my life, but it has."

"In what ways, Lea?"

She gave him a frown. "I don't trust men until I get to know them for a reasonable amount of time. I question their motives when they look at me, which makes my gut clench, and I automatically go on guard because some looks are threatening to me." She saw him glance away for a moment, move his mouth as if to say something, and then think better of it. "I'm not saying you are this way with me, because you aren't. Some men don't realize a pinch on the butt, rubbing up against a woman, touching her without her permission, scares us and makes us wary of that type of male. It's a threat to us. My mother's a feminist and so am I. My body is my own. It's not out there to be bullied, touched, raped, or to entertain a man sexually for his own personal gratification and never mind my gratification. I grew up being very confident until that fight occurred."

"That age is a crucial stage of development," Logan agreed quietly, absorbing her impassioned response. "My parents were like yours in many ways. My mother is a feminist, too."

"I thought that might be the case," Lea said, finishing off her spaghetti.

"Oh?"

"I've watched you, Logan. You don't assume you can reach out and touch me. I appreciate that."

"It's terrible that many men expect that they can touch a woman anytime they want," he agreed. "On my end? Going through school, I watched most of the boys my age doing exactly that to the girls. My mother told me to watch a girl's face when she was touched inappropriately. I started doing that, and that's when I got it."

"Welcome to the male-dominated world. They certainly don't see women as equals or to be respected. It always comes down to sex with most men. They want what they want. I had a number of run-ins with teen boys in high school over this very thing. I ended up wanting to be homeschooled so that I could breathe and just be myself. In the end, my parents didn't have the money to send me to an all-girls school or stay home to homeschool me." She placed her dinner plate aside, clasped her hands on the table in front of her. "I just became a shadow of my former self. Luckily, I had wonderful girlfriends and we would go off and do things together at the school or go hiking in the surrounding area, or just spend time with one another. We also helped one another with our classwork, as well."

He shook his head. "I don't know what it's like to live like that, with that threat, that sense of being hunted all the time by boys or men."

"No man does. But with the #MeToo movement, those days of pawing us, chasing us down for sex, touching us inappropriately, are over and done with."

"Of course. The current generation wants what they had before," Logan agreed. "With each succeeding generation ahead of them, mothers are teaching their boys to behave differently toward women. To see them as human beings, not a body that they own. I got plenty of training about that growing up. I watched how my father related to my mother. He's always treated her as smarter than he ever could be, and he told me that many times over. I saw my mother's intelligence in and out of the home. She was the one whose ideas I've shown you around the ranch, that were incorporated. All my father did was have them built." He grinned. "Men are good for something."

She smiled thinly. "That's true. And not all men are like the ones that have hit on me. I recognize that, Logan. But there's a lot more of them out there than your kind of twenty-first-century man that all women are yearning to have in their lives. We want an equal partner, not be treated as less than."

He put his empty plate aside. "I hope I've shown you the respect and equality you deserve?" He held her gaze.

"Every day, and I'm deeply appreciative."

"Are you wary of me, I wonder?"

"Of you? No. But whoever is trying to chase you off your land and force you to sell it, I'm very much on guard about that. Being hit from behind brought that home to me."

"I don't think you have to be a woman to be on guard about that," he said, standing, picking up the plates and flatware. "I'm just as jumpy about it as you are. I keep wondering what Polcyn has up his sleeve next."

She stood and picked up the napkins and two bowls, following him into the kitchen. "I'm on guard, too. But you know him better than I do."

"He's so damned rich that he can afford to hire hit men

and leave no trail that law enforcement can track back to him after the destruction happens," he muttered, rinsing off the plates in the kitchen sink.

"I need to go back out to the Maplewood grove tomorrow," she said. "Could you have one of your wranglers go with me, since you're worried about me being alone out there?"

"I'll send Jody Constance, one of my women wranglers, with you."

"She's the one who helped me after I got hit from behind when turning into the driveway of your ranch."

He took the bowl from her, their fingers touching. "Yes. She's a licensed paramedic. On her days off, she's over at the women's shelter, where she does health checks and examinations for them and their children. She's also working on her nurse practitioner license right now. In about another six months, she'll have it."

"That's great. Silver Creek seems a long way from a major hospital if something awful happened."

"Well," he said, putting the dishes in the dishwasher, "we have a rural hospital, but we don't have a gynecologist medical doctor on staff. We're just too small for a doctor to come and live in this rural area. Jody's focus on her NP is obstetrics and delivery. Another woman, Cathy Lovell, is an NP and has been helping Jody to take over her position at the hospital. Cathy is sixty-five years old and she's leaving at the end of this year. With Jody as a replacement I'll lose a great wrangler, but the entire region will be under her skilled care, especially pregnant women who are worried about delivery and not having proper medical support. Now, they will. The changeover will be seamless and that will take a huge worry and stress off the women in our valley."

She leaned her hips against the counter, watching him work. There was a grace to Logan she'd always appreciated and admired. "Jody is a lifesaver, then."

"Yes, and she'll have her own department in the hospital, which is great. All the women's medical services will be under her care. I'm really proud of her." He straightened and punched a couple of buttons, the dishwasher quietly whirring to life. "Jody, if you recall, was a medic in the military for four years. She was twenty-two when I hired her after coming out of the service. Since I was a vet, and we both served in Afghanistan in combat, we've been good friends. I've paid for her to get her NP training, because our family has always made decisions for the good of all the people who live in this valley."

"Wow, what a generous thing to do," Lea said, giving him a warm look. "It's so refreshing to meet someone like you. Hearing so much fake news, that lies are in and truth is out in our country, has been hard on everyone and made America look a lot less welcoming than it usually has been."

"Norms have been busted," he agreed, wiping his hands on a towel. "You get out of Washington, D.C., and you meet people, it still gives me hope."

"Yes, but Silver Creek *is* a special place," she said.

"For you as well?" He cocked his head, giving her a teasing look.

"Absolutely. I love working in your wood shop. It's candy land to me, Logan. I love waking up in the morning, looking forward to my day, excited and focused." She saw his face grow softer; his eyes, if she read him accurately, had a wistful look in them. His expression was new to her, but it also made her feel warm and fuzzy around her heart at the same time. Why that look? What was he thinking but not saying? Lea wished she knew. Tomorrow was a new day. Jody would escort her out to the elm grove to pick up more branches that she needed for her first set of cupboards. She looked forward to a girls' day out, but in her heart, she wished it would be Logan at her side.

Chapter Seven

June 2

"How are you feeling about going back out in the groves, Lea?"

Lea gave Jody, the twenty-nine-year-old woman who was dressed in Levi's and a long-sleeved white canvas shirt, plus cowboy boots and a straw Stetson on her short blond hair, a frown. "Uh-oh, I think Logan's been telling you that I don't feel safe out there by myself?"

It was nine a.m. and the sky was blue, the sun bright. It was a beautiful day in the valley.

"Yes, he mentioned it. Do you feel unsafe out there working alone?" Jody asked, driving the company truck down a twisting road that led to a high elevation where the maple grove was located.

"Men scare me, and I admitted it to Logan one day. I guess he took what I said seriously and thought I might like a buddy out there while collecting wood, is all."

Jody's lips curved and she slanted a quick look in Lea's direction. "Being wary of males in general is number two on my list, so I'm not far behind you."

"A lot of women are leery of men. Most everyone I know, is. A man has done something awful to them, and their trust is broken with all men as a result." Lea held on as Jody slowly drove the truck up and around on the bumpy, deeply rutted gravel road that had a hairpin curve to it.

"The #MeToo movement erupted like an ancient, simmering volcano," Jody agreed, easing the truck around the tight, narrow turn. "Like you, I haven't met one woman in my life who hasn't been harassed, touched when she did not want to be touched, raped, or sexually assaulted. It's a silent epidemic, and thank goodness women are speaking out about it now. It's time males realize what they're doing to us as a gender. We women need to put a stop to it."

"I would imagine you've found that to be true in the military, too?" Lea was wearing a black baseball cap and pushed some errant strands away from her face. They were now within the huge grove where most of the trees were at least a hundred years old.

Her lips twisted. "To say the least. I've just never met any woman who didn't have a story to tell me about unwanted sexual attention, assault, or worse. And rape is not about sex," she reminded Lea. "It's an act of power over a woman, domination and violence. It's hatred of women— misogyny."

"I hate to ask this, but have you experienced it too, Jody?"

"Yep, I'm one of the many." She glanced over at Lea, turning down a smaller, narrower dirt road that led into the heart of the maple grove. "What about you?"

"I've got my own sad story, but nothing close to rape. But it was enough to make me wary of men in general." Lea told her about her assault as a young teen.

"This behavior has been normalized by societies around the world over the last ten thousand years," Jody grumped. She brought the truck to a halt, looking around the grove. "I feel the most important thing women can do together is vote. Vote for candidates who are women. There's a low percentage of twenty-first-century males who are with us on this badly needed societal change, but it's on our shoulders as women to make this happen via our political clout." She looked around the deeply shaded grove, sun dappling golden spots on the earth beneath the trees, changing and dancing around with a light breeze.

"Oh, no question. At least women are banding to-gether."

Jody rested her hand on the top of the steering wheel. "Change of topics. I'm checking the area out before we get out of the cab, per Logan's request. Looking for any-thing out of place or different than I recall." She tapped the leather holster at her waist that carried a .45 pistol. "I know how to use this, too. Years in the military, plus combat, I always carry my pistol on me. Logan agreed with the idea, and most of us do carry, and we have a permit to open carry here in the state."

Lea gazed around. "Did he ask you to carry a weapon for this trip, too? I don't feel vulnerable out in the groves."

"I should give you some time on our shooting range. Logan had it created for all of us so we would keep up our skills with the weapon we carry. Are you interested?"

"I don't know if I could pull the trigger, Jody. Maybe I'm a coward?"

"No, you aren't. A lot of people just can't kill even if they're threatened with death by another person."

"I hate to ask you this, and tell me if it's none of my business, but have you been in a firefight?"

"Yes," she answered grimly, unsnapping the safety on the holster. Pulling out the .45, she efficiently placed a bullet in the chamber, leaving the safety off. Sliding it back into the holster, she said, "That's where my PTSD came from. I get flashbacks, but they're less now than before. And," she said, opening the door, "nightmares, which are at least a couple of times a week. Come on, the coast looks clear. Let's look for those special branches you need for Logan's cupboards."

"Just having you help me is wonderful," Lea admitted as they placed the last of the five branches in the back of the truck. It had been an enjoyable hour with the other woman. She saw Jody preen.

"Good to know. As long as I'm here at the ranch and you need a hired gun at your side, I'm available. Just ask me to escort you, okay?"

Laughing, Lea said, "I doubt I'll be asking you to be with me, although it was fun having company out there." She climbed into the truck. Jody was pure athlete, and boneless in the way she walked, always a telltale sign of being in very good physical shape. She herself was still clunky and awkward in comparison, not used to the demands of being a wrangler, which were many.

Once in the truck, they belted up and Jody backed around, taking them out of the grove and down the hill.

"Since you're wary of men," Jody said, "how is it, working in close proximity with Logan?"

Lea knew that Logan treated Jody as if she were like the younger sister he'd never had. She felt comfortable saying, "Logan is what I call a twenty-first-century man. I see him struggling at times when we're in conversation, but he always manages to think before he speaks. I like him a lot. He's a visionary for this beautiful valley, with solid roots in common sense and practicality."

"He got that from his parents. I sure miss them, but I know they're happy down in Arizona. They've worked all their lives for this ranch. They deserve retirement. I don't think Logan will retire." She drove around the hairpin curve at a crawl.

"No?"

"He's married to the land." Jody chuckled. "He's the kind of guy that loves hard, daily work. Loves the challenge. And I don't think he sleeps more than five or six hours a night. He's enthused about what needs to be done at the ranch. And, on top of that, he's a great manager. His wranglers dote on him. They brag to other ranch hands when they get a chance, on how fair and caring he is of them and their families."

"He's got a lot of great attributes, no question." Lea frowned and then said, "He was married at one time, from what Poppy told me."

Jody slowed and braked as they left the hill and turned toward a more major dirt road that would lead them back to the main ranch house. "Yes," she offered, sadness in her tone, "and his daughter, three days later, after the birth. It devastated him to his core." Jody whispered softly, "I was hired on to the ranch about three months before it happened. I didn't know Logan that well at the time, but Elizabeth was a bright, beautiful light in his and everyone else's life. She was the type of person who was just naturally warm, nurturing, kind, and softhearted. Logan loved her fiercely. And you can understand why." She opened her hand resting on the steering wheel. "I've just never seen two people more in love than them, Lea. They were made for one another. They had grown up together here in the valley, met in the first grade and became the best of friends. And I think that's what made what they had so special. They had a long buddy relationship, and then in middle school, they became best pals. By high school, they had puppy love from what Elizabeth told me. By the time they were eighteen, they were engaged once they gradu-ated. Logan went off to the army for four years. On his return, they married. She got pregnant three months later with Jessica. Logan was twenty-three when everything suddenly went to hell in a handbasket when she died in a car accident. They saved the baby, but she died three days later from complications. That's why Logan has been single, I think. He still loves the two women in his life who died too soon."

"Grief has its way with us, no question," Lea murmured, seeing the main ranch complex coming into view, her heart aching for Logan.

Jody gave a sharp laugh. "Seriously, yes. I don't know why people think if you grieved a year, that it's long enough and you should be over it. From what I can see? Grief over a major loss is more like five to seven years long. Logan is now thirty, and I see signs in him that he's finally allowing Elizabeth and his baby daughter to rest gently in his heart instead of ripping him up daily, like it had before." She gave Lea an evil, teasing glance. "In fact? Ever since you've come here, I've seen a *real* change in Logan."

"What does that mean?" Lea asked warily, watching as two wranglers rode by toward a corral filled with Here-fords. Her heart beat a little harder because Jody was giving her a look she couldn't read.

"He's more upbeat, outgoing, and I've never seen him

smile or laugh as much as he does since you arrived." She drove into the gravel driveway and parked. "I think he's sweet on you, Lea. Are you aware he's interested in you?"

Gulping, Lea sat there, feeling the shock roll through her. "Well . . . uh . . ."

"Come on," Jody goaded, turning off the engine. "You can't tell me he's not handsome, he's intelligent, kind, and every single woman in the county has him in her sights."

Opening her hands, Lea looked at the calluses on her palms. "I like Logan a lot, Jody. I've been drawn to him since I first saw and spoke to him. I knew he'd lost so much, and I've tried to keep my distance from him partly because I was sure he might be grieving the losses."

"Well"—she chuckled—"how'd that go?"

Laughing nervously, Lea said, "Not very well."

Jody stared at the ranch house. "I've never seen him interested in any woman except you, Lea. That's the truth." Glancing in her direction, she added humorously, "I keep hoping you two will let down your walls and really get to know one another. Logan already likes you, but you pretty much stay in the shop all day long. We don't see you very often. I wondered if you were hiding from him."

"No," Lea answered sadly. "I'm hiding from the world. After I got bullied and beat up by three boys, and I became a total introvert. I know I'm not very social, or very outgoing."

"Well, an experience like that would make you become a shadow of your former self. Bullying is horrible. It does terrible things to people for the rest of their lives."

"I'm a good example of it," she admitted, clearing her throat. "I wish I wasn't such a scaredy-cat. I used to be much more extroverted, but after that, I ran and hid. I'm not very proud of myself. I know where my weaknesses are. And I am trying to stop the past from controlling me so I get out more, and become more social."

Reaching out, Jody squeezed her forearm. "Listen, we all hide in some way. I know I do. I just shove it so far down in myself it will never see the light of day again."

"Because of the sexual assault? Was that when you started doing that?"

Jody nodded. "Exactly. Like I said, we all run and hide. The how is different, but the outcome is the same . . . quiet shadows who don't want to be seen by men who harass women."

"That's heartbreaking for all of us," Lea whispered, shaking her head. "Why don't men realize that their actions against us brand us for the rest of our lives? We're never the same after that. I know I'm not. Are you?" She looked at Jody's serious expression, her blue eyes dark.

"No one is," she admitted, frowning. "Hey, let's go do something happy. Let me help you carry those branches into the shop?"

"Thank you," Lea said, opening the door. "I appreciate your help."

"Next time," Jody said, joining her at the rear of the truck and releasing the tailgate so they could reach the wood, "if you need help, why not reach out to Logan? He's not dumb. He'll pick up on that subtle signal. Maybe what the two of you need is to start working together where and when you can. It's a good way to ease into a relationship and see if it's going to work or not."

Jody's radio, which she wore in her shirt pocket, went off.

"Hey, Jody, this is Barry. Got an emergency out at barn two. Logan was on a ladder coming off the second floor when the step busted on him. He's either got a broken ankle or it's badly sprained. Can you get out here with your ER bag?"

"Roger that," Jody said tersely, giving Lea a glance as she signed off. "Do you want to go with me—"

"Absolutely," Lea said, throwing the branches back into the rear of the pickup. "Where's your ER bag?"

Jody pointed to the aluminum metal locker up at the front of the bed. "It's always with me. Hop in!"

Heart pounding, Lea jerked the door open and hopped in. Barn two was three miles away. Jody turned on the truck engine and they raced out of the driveway, kicking up a rooster tail of dust in their wake.

"He doesn't need this right now," Jody growled, both hands gripping the steering wheel.

"Isn't the fair happening pretty soon?" Lea asked.

"Yeah, he heads it up and everyone counts on him to take care of all the details. If he's broken his ankle, that's really going to stress him out because the demands are huge, beginning next week."

They arrived at barn two, a group of wranglers standing in the maw of the huge red building. Jody leaped out and climbed into the back, opening the locker. She hoisted a red canvas bag out and threw it over the side of the truck into Lea's waiting hands.

Leaping off the bed, Jody took it, throwing the strap up and over her head, the bag large and unwieldy. Lea followed at almost a trot, trying to remain calm, but that was impossible.

"In there," one of the wranglers told Jody, pointing toward the side of the barn. "He took a really bad fall . . ."

"Thanks, Larry," she said, hurrying by the knot of cowboys who were all frowning.

The lights were on, high above them, and Lea saw

Logan sitting down, scowling darkly, his foreman, Barry, squatting at his side.

"Hey," Jody said, unloading the bag and setting it nearby as she knelt down on one knee next to Logan. "Tell me what's going on."

"A step broke," Logan growled, pointing above. "I fell, slammed into a rusty nail that went through my boot, and I landed on my right foot. It buckled and I went down."

Jody nodded, quickly looking at his right cowboy boot. She saw a four-inch nail, only the head and one inch protruding out the side. The other part had gone into his foot. "Pain?"

"Yes," he muttered, teeth clenched, giving Lea a glance as she halted nearby.

Gently, Jody ran her hand, now encased in a latex glove, above the top of his boot. "When was the last time you had a tetanus booster, Logan?"

"Don't remember," he gritted out, his gloved hand going to just below the knee.

Frowning, she leaned over and with both hands, gently pulled up the hem of his jeans to expose the top of the boot.

Logan stiffened. "That hurt."

Jody placed his foot on the barn floor. "I have to see if there's blood coming up and out of that boot of yours, Logan."

"That nail is making my foot ache like fire itself," he mumbled.

Jody looked up at the foreman. "Barry? Call 911. Get an ambulance down here, stat."

Barry nodded and quickly pulled his cell phone out, punching in 911.

Lea swallowed her gasp, arms across her chest, her

gaze riveted on Logan's face. Even though Jody was being very careful, her movements designed not to cause him more discomfort, she could see pain reflected in Logan's darkened eyes. His mouth was a slash and she knew that meant he was in agony, his one leather-gloved hand flat against the aged floor. Watching Jody ease the hem upward, she gasped as blood poured out of the opening, dripping onto the wooden floor. Clapping her hand against her mouth, Lea hadn't meant to make a sound. Logan saw the blood.

"Well, hell," he snarled, "this isn't good."

"No, but we'll find out once we get to the hospital. They're going to have to x-ray through your boot to see where that blood is coming from. Could be the nail puncture."

"Just drive me to the hospital," Logan demanded as Jody worked, wrapping the boot, and the bleeding stopped.

"No way," Jody said. "Logan, I hate to say this, but you may have an open fracture, and if it is, that means the broken bone could have cut into an artery. We need to keep this boot around it in order to support your bones as well as to slow the bleeding."

"Awwww, come on, Jody!"

She gave him a one-eyebrow-raised look, and finished off the wrapping with an elastic bandage. "No griping, Logan. This is serious." She looked up at Barry. "Tell the hospital to have their ortho surgeon standing by, just in case. Have a tetanus booster ready. Antibiotics, too. And I also want two pints of blood type A on standby." She glanced over at Logan. ". . . Just in case, Logan. I don't know if an artery has been nicked by one or both of your bones breaking, or it's cut clean through. We won't know

now, but we'll know at the hospital. Are you feeling light-headed or dizzy?"

"No, just absolutely, certifiably pissed off. I got too much to do, Jody, without something like this happening." He jabbed his index finger down at his injury.

"I know, I know," she soothed, watching the top of his boot for blood to well up in it.

"Ambulance will be here in seven minutes," Barry told them. "Jody? The ortho is in surgery right now, but she's ordered up everything you said."

"Good," she whispered, relieved. "It's going to be all right, Logan."

He glared around the barn and then back at Jody. "Any *good* news?"

Laughing, Jody said, "You're still alive, aren't you? And you *are* breathing. Right?"

The wranglers in the barn, who had crowded in a semi-circle around them, laughed. Jody was a fixture at the ranch, Lea realized, and the men treated her like a beloved sister. She had been at the ranch a lot longer than most of them, except for Barry, the foreman.

"Very funny," Logan groused. "Give me your para-medic opinion. What do you think about this?" He jabbed down at his ankle once more.

"I'm hoping that the bone, when it broke on impact, nicked the artery. If that's the case, then that's easy enough to repair with surgery. A bone takes six weeks to heal, Logan. A sprain can take two or three months, depending. And I'm also hoping that the MRI won't show any of your muscles or your ligaments torn. That's another thing to consider here. That means six months before you're off medical help and devices. And let's not forget this nail in your foot. That has to be removed, too, and, hopefully, it hasn't done damage except for a nasty puncture wound."

"I'll take the broken bone," he muttered, shaking his head. "Six weeks is a helluva lot better than six friggin' months."

Lea forced herself not to smile over Logan's rough language. She'd never heard him curse, much less raise his voice, until now. But he had good cause under the circumstances. Even though he had the beginning of a good tan from being outdoors, she could see he was pale. And his brow was sweaty, as well as wrinkled. She understood pain could do both.

"I hear the ambulance," one cowboy called from the door.

Barry looked at one of his wranglers. "Charlie? Go meet them. Take Jody's truck and bring them down here. They may not know where barn two is located, and we don't wanna waste time getting Logan into the ER."

Jody stood and tossed Charlie the keys to the truck. The wrangler nodded, turned, and trotted quickly out the door.

Jody knelt down again, warily watching his boot.

"What are you looking at so intently?" Logan demanded.

"See if the blood starts oozing up and out of the top."

"And if it does?"

"It probably means an artery is involved, instead of maybe something lesser, like a small vein."

"Hmph."

"You aren't a very good patient," Jody teased, giving him a warm look, trying to get him to relax a little.

"I know," Logan said, giving her a look of apology. "This isn't your fault. I shouldn't be grousing at you."

"No," she said lightly, smiling, "but I have a wide set of shoulders and I can take anything you dish out."

The siren got louder. Lea stepped aside. "Can I do anything to help you, Logan?" Her heart melted when he gave her a little boy look. The expression happened so fast, she wondered the next moment if she had imagined it. She could see something in his eyes, too, but couldn't translate it.

"Would you drive the ranch truck to the hospital? I don't intend to stay there any longer than I have to. You can hitch a ride back with Charlie."

Jody snorted. "Logan, that isn't gonna happen. This is a serious injury. I'm sure the doctor will keep you a lot longer than you think she will. In fact, the bleeding will probably put you in a hospital room under observation for at least a night. Why don't you let Lea stay with you? That way, she can give Barry, here, updates on your condition because everyone will want to know how you're doing. You need someone from the ranch to be there for you, for us."

Lea could have hugged Jody in that moment. She saw Logan hesitate. Why? She *wanted* to be there with him and didn't try to ignore why. "I'd be happy to do that, Logan. Besides, if after the examination the doctor tells you that you can go home, I can drive you back to the ranch." She saw his brows draw downward, his gaze left hers, and he looked torn. It was time to stand up and be counted. "Logan, I'm going to drive to the hospital. If you want me to stay for a while, I'd like to be there for you." Fear hit her and she fought it back. She was really stepping outside her safety zone, but it was past time. She was tired of being a meek, scared mouse, little more than a shadow stepping quietly through life. Lea didn't care anymore. Logan was wrestling with real pain, trying to remain levelheaded and acting as if he were in charge. But he wasn't.

"Yes," Logan said, holding her gaze, "I'd like that."

"I'm the most expendable around here," Lea added. "Everyone else here at the ranch has a lot to do."

He gave her a mirthless look, managed a tight, one-sided smile, and then nodded. "Okay, it's done. Come along and be with me."

The ambulance pulled up outside. Jody stood. "I'll be back with them and the gurney. Don't move, Logan." She shook her index finger in his direction, sounding more like a mother scolding a recalcitrant child who might misbehave in her absence.

Logan looked up at Barry. "You ever get the feeling that I'm really not in charge around here?"

Chuckling, the foreman said, "You'll always be the boss."

In a few minutes, the two firefighters, a woman and a man, brought in the gurney. Lea stood back and Jody calmly directed everything. Logan didn't like being carried over to the gurney to be strapped in. It took four wranglers to manage him. Most important, Jody kept an eye on his leg, making sure all was well for the transit. Lea decided to ask Charlie to take her to the main ranch house, where she could unload the branches at the shop. Then, she could follow the ambulance to the hospital. She didn't know that much about trauma, aside from her own run-in with bullies, but understood Jody's concern over an artery that might have been involved in Logan's injury. Inwardly, she felt scared for him. Who knew a wooden ladder step could give way? Had the wood rotted out? Had there been an unseen crack in the wood and Logan's weight, at the right time and right place, made it fall apart? So many questions and no answers.

Charlie was more than happy to take her back to the ranch house. There, he helped her with the wood she'd selected and he carried it to the shop for her. Thanking him, she quickly grabbed her purse and the keys to the personal truck that Logan had assigned to her. As she walked to the truck, the ambulance passed nearby, its lights flashing, but no siren. She thought she glimpsed Jody in the back with Logan, sitting nearby. That made her feel good because Jody, being a paramedic, knew what to tell the ortho surgeon once Logan arrived at the emergency room for examination. She hoped his injury wasn't life-threatening, but it nagged at her anyway. He'd already lost his wife, Elizabeth. Could someone die from falling off a ladder? Yes, they could.

Her hands wrapped tightly about the steering wheel and it was easy to catch up to the ambulance, which was taking its time on the dirt road. Once they got on the highway, it would be about ten minutes to the hospital by Lea's guess. Her emotions skewed one way and then the other as she drove a good distance behind the ambulance. The midday June sun was bright and unrelenting, the temperature easily in the eighties, she would guess. How bad was Logan's injury? Would it require surgery? She hoped not, having a bad taste in her mouth for anything in general having to do with hospitals. No one ever wanted to be *that* sick, to be forced to go to one for help. Logan was only thirty years old, in the prime of his life, and then this had to happen.

By the time she got to the hospital, found a parking spot

and walked quickly into the ER department, Logan and Jody were nowhere to be seen. She went to the nurses' station and gave her name and asked if she could see Logan. The clock on the wall said it was 12:15 p.m. The day had flown by.

"Are you his wife?" the woman asked.

"Uh . . . no, but I work for him." Lea saw the young nurse grimace. "He told me to come along. I'm here and I'd like to see him." Again, she was pushing out of her comfort zone, but Logan was too important to her to let this nurse tell her no.

"You're not kin," the nurse said.

"I don't care. He asked that I come along and be with him. Can I talk to your supervisor about this?" She turned, seeing five closed doors, each a room for someone who had an emergency. The hall was empty.

The nurse said, "No, I'll go ask him myself. What's your name?"

Lea gave her name, keeping her voice respectful, but firm.

"Wait here," the nurse instructed.

Lea watched the woman, dressed in what looked like blue surgery scrubs, go to door three, enter and disappear. So, Logan was in there. At least she knew something about his location.

Jody came flying out the door, heading straight for her. "Hey," she called, "come on in, Lea."

Relieved, Lea saw the young reception nurse frowning, but she said nothing, bypassing her and heading back to the desk.

"Thanks, Jody."

"No problem." She hooked a thumb over her shoulder. "They have rules they have to follow. Logan was asking for you and he made it clear to the nurse that you were to be in the room with him."

"Really?"

"Yes. The orthopedic surgeon just got out of surgery and she's in there with him, as well as two other nurses. He's in good hands, so don't worry."

Walking quickly to keep up with Jody, she asked breathlessly, "But . . . what about his bleeding?"

"Don't know yet." Jody opened the door. "Go on in . . ."

Chapter Eight

June 2

Logan closed his eyes, wishing the fall he'd taken had never happened. Dr. Sonja Ribas, the orthopedic surgeon, had instructed the nurse to cut away one side of his boot. When she did, blood burst out, splattering both of them and the floor. But the pressure . . . God, the pressure was relieved. Glancing down, he saw his ankle swell to the size of a cantaloupe in a few minutes and turn a bright purple-blue. They had given him a powerful pain medication in the IV. In the other arm, whole blood was waiting to be infused into him, should he need it. The throbbing of his ankle was horrendous, and he gritted his teeth.

Dr. Ribas ordered the brunette nurse to up the pain meds for him. In moments, the throbbing reduced and Logan tried to relax, but it was impossible. The blood wasn't coming from his ankle. It was leaking out of the top of the cut-away boot. He wasn't sure which felt worse: the break of one or two of his bones in his leg, or that damned nail that had buried itself deep inside his foot. Dr. Ribas, fifty years old, short red hair and large green eyes, gave orders to carefully cut away the rest of the boot just above the sole. She kept her hand on the bottom of his boot as the nurse slowly cut through the thick, worn leather, so the nail wasn't jiggled around.

When Jody reappeared, and he saw Lea come in, something cracked open in his heart. Lea looked frazzled, worried, and then their eyes met. For all the quiet murmurings going on around him as Dr. Ribas had the top of the boot removed, and then the sock cut away, Logan suddenly felt peaceful. It was because of Lea's presence. He saw her strength, but also, how shaken she was as she stared down at his exposed foot. He'd taken off his work gloves on the way in and he lifted his left hand, signaling Lea to come around to the left side of the gurney. Jody remained with Dr. Ribas; they talked in low voices and he couldn't hear what they were saying.

Lea's eyes were warm with welcome and it moved through his shock, making him relax even more. Maybe she was another form, a better one, of pain medication. Right now, Logan was sure it was Lea. He understood her shadowy presence in the cubical, being seen but not heard. Luckily, everyone in the room was female, and that made her feel more comfortable. He opened his hand, palm up, reaching toward her. Seeing her shock at his gesture, Logan continued to hold his hand out toward her. He needed Lea to know she meant something good and hopeful to him. When he persisted, and after she looked down at his hand and then into his eyes, he saw the shock leave and something wonderful replace it. Whatever it was, it was good. Her long, cool, roughened fingers slid across his sweaty palm, wrapping gently around his long, thick fingers that were as callused as her own.

And then, she stepped closer. Logan deeply inhaled her scent as a woman—not the sterile, bleached scent that hung in the room, but that sweet aphrodisiac scent. Closing his eyes, he sank against the gurney that supported him in a partial sitting position. Jody had called it the Fowler's position. *Whatever.* He wrapped his fingers around Lea's, felt her lean her body against the gurney, brushing lightly against his left shoulder, as if to tell him everything would be all right. It felt wonderful and so damned welcoming. He wanted to tell her how beautiful she was to him, how she made him feel hope that had been destroyed when Elizabeth and his baby daughter had suddenly died. She represented the sun to him, but he was afraid to tell her that, for fear that she would think he was stalking her. Women were stalked routinely by male jerks, and he felt a brief anger over it until the nurse lifted his left leg, placing a pillow beneath his knee to his heel, to stabilize the entire area.

Opening his eyes, he saw Dr. Ribas instruct a nurse to hold the sole of his boot in place. She then took some tape and carefully wrapped it over his toes and around the sole. As they took him to X-ray, he gave Lea an apologetic look of farewell and released her hand.

"To be continued," he promised her roughly, giving her one last look as they pushed him out of the cubicle. He saw her barely nod, worry settling into her eyes once again. He would be fine. He was young and healthy. All this was going to be was a damned inconvenience, with the fair coming up. He was the chairman of it, and now he was going to be hobbled for at least six weeks.

In X-ray they took quick photos and then he was

wheeled back into his cube, where Lea was standing and waiting for him.

"Hey," he said, his voice gravelly, "where's Jody?"

"Oh, Dr. Ribas asked her to come and look at your X-rays with her."

"Betcha they find a nail in my foot," he joked weakly. "This med they gave me is making me feel silly and woozy."

The two nurses placed the gurney in park.

"Am I supposed to be woozy?" Logan asked one of them.

"I'll tell the doctor," the older woman said. "I'll be back in a minute."

The other nurse hooked him back up to the machinery.

"If you need anything," she said, opening the door, "just come and get me. I'll be out at the desk."

"Alone, at last," Logan joked, giving Lea an amused look.

"You must be feeling no pain," she said, coming over, standing on the left side, facing him.

"I liked holding your hand, if you want the truth," he said, opening his hand, inviting her to hold it once more. "Maybe I can blame it on the opioid concoction they gave me in this IV." He gave her a hopeful look and grinned.

Lifting her hand, she slid it back into his. "Maybe this med is making you silly and bold," she countered, giving him a slight smile, holding his gaze.

"Probably," he admitted with a sigh. "At least, I'm not in a lot of pain. It feels cranky, like a toothache off and on. I can handle that." He studied his injured foot. "That doesn't look good, does it?"

"No," Lea said, "it doesn't. Can I get you anything, Logan? Are you thirsty?"

"No . . . I'm fine now." He squeezed her fingers gently. "I wish I could do more for you . . ."

"Me, too." The corner of his mouth hitched into a slight curve upward. "One nice thing to come out of this? I get to hold your hand every once in a while."

She leaned against the gurney, wanting that contact with him, even if it was just his gowned shoulder. "I like holding your hand, too."

He preened inwardly over her hushed comment. "Doing it of your own free will," he reminded her, giving her a teasing look.

"Completely," she said, the corners of her mouth lifting.

"I wish they'd come back. I want to know how bad this break is," he muttered. "I'm worried that I won't be able to do the work I need to oversee the fair."

"Do you have an assistant?" she wondered.

"Yes, Poppy is my backup. She knows everyone, and is well loved and respected. They'd listen to her if I couldn't be present. She's a whirlwind and she gets things done and done right."

"I would think," Lea ventured, "that this accident is going to lay you up for a while. Well past the fair, Logan. I'm not a doctor, but your ankle and foot look awful."

"I'll be okay," he reassured her, giving her a concerned look. "This isn't the first time I've broken a bone."

"Or stepped on a nail?"

"Well," he amended, "that is new."

"Did they give you the tetanus booster?"

"Right away."

"Good," she said, relieved.

"How long has it been since I've had one?" he asked archly. "It's not like I put down on my yearly calendar that I need a booster."

She grinned. "I can't remember how long it's been for me."

"I'll bet this will spur you into getting one, huh?"

"Yes," she agreed, squeezing his fingers.

The warmth rippled up Logan's hand and he absorbed the dancing humor in Lea's eyes. She was beginning to relax, to be the woman he had gotten to know in his wood shop and his home. "I can't begin to tell you how much I like having you at the ranch with me." Lifting his chin, he met her gaze. "And I hope what I'm going to say doesn't scare you off or make you want to leave. I really enjoy your company, Lea." He lifted his hand, placing it over his gowned chest. "For whatever the reason, you fill a hole in me I didn't know I had until after you arrived. I really enjoy coming in for lunch and sharing the time and space with you. I like following your woodwork artistry because you are incredibly skilled and talented. And at night? Dinner? You have no idea how I look forward to spending that time with you. It fulfills me, Lea, and I hope it does you, too?"

Logan held his breath, afraid he'd said way too much. The drugs were doing it. The expression on Lea's face staggered him. Her eyes softened and he felt that same warmth stealing through him, feeding his heart, his soul. It was a look that said so much without a word ever being uttered. Briefly, her fingers tightened around his and then relaxed.

"Maybe there's a silver lining in your accident," Lea

began haltingly. "I've always prided myself on being honest with everyone, so I'm not going to dodge what you've just shared with me, Logan." She took a deep breath and released it. "Since coming here, I've felt so at home that it's scared me. I've hidden in my parents' home and my dad's workshop up until I pulled together enough guts to drive out here and take the job at your ranch. I scared myself doing it. I wondered why I was doing it. I was happy at home. I love my parents very much. I wasn't sure I was making the right decision to take the job you were offering me."

"But then, that truck hit you as you were turning into the ranch driveway," he muttered, shaking his head.

"You were right there, Logan. I was so shaken and you were so solid and unflappable. I was amazed at your steadiness because that hit from behind shattered me. I was so scared." She tilted her head, giving him a half smile. "You took away my fear, my shock. You were so gentle with me, quiet, and built my confidence back up. No man has ever affected me like that before. I just didn't know, at that time, what to think about it and how you were affecting me."

"That's a good start," he said. "I felt the same about you. Even in the midst of that accident, I could look into your deep green eyes, and felt nothing but peace and calm. It was a crazy reaction to have," he admitted, shaking his head.

"Then we really had an impact on one another, and it was the accident that caused it," she said wonderingly. "Your presence calmed me, Logan."

"And yours calmed my terror that you were dying. I saw that truck hit your truck. I was grateful you were okay," he added, holding the tender look swimming in her eyes.

"And yet, we've never really had a chance to sit down and say this to one another," Lea admitted quietly, giving him a look of apology.

"I was afraid to admit what I felt toward you, Lea." He shrugged. "I guess I didn't want to find out you weren't interested in me, and, maybe, the beginning of some kind of relationship with me."

"I was chicken, too," she whispered, her mouth quirking. "I thought if you knew how I really was beginning to feel toward you, that you might fire me. I didn't want to lose this job. I love what I'm doing. I love the Wild Goose Ranch and everyone who works there." She gave him a jaded look. "And I certainly did not want to tell you the personal side of my feelings, because of my fears."

"We're a pair," he muttered, lying back, staring up at her. "I was afraid of rejection. You were afraid of being fired. Two peas from the same pod?"

She managed a slight laugh. "I think so. And it took your accident to tear away our fears and be honest about one another. I used to be so brave, and took so many risks, before that one, darned, bullying attack," she admitted hoarsely. "I've lost that part of myself and I miss it so much."

"Maybe we're good for one another in different ways, Lea. Maybe just being in close proximity with one another, learning to be friends, is the best thing that has happened to both of us in a long, long time?" He searched her troubled gaze.

"I feel you're right," she said, sadness in her tone. "I want my old self back."

"When I lost Elizabeth," he admitted in a choked tone, "I felt like I'd died in the process, too. She was my light, my reason for all the dreams I had for us, shared dreams we'd created out of being friends throughout our school years."

"I can't imagine your loss. And I'm so sorry it happened to you."

"I should be over it, and for the most part, I am. She died when I was twenty-three, and now I'm thirty. For the past couple of years, I've felt like I've been coming out of some kind of vacuum, or suspended animation of a sort. When she suddenly passed, I went numb. Completely numb. I could feel nothing. I couldn't even cry about her loss for years." His eyes darkened. "I was lucky to know what love is, Lea. Not everyone gets that chance. I realize that now. I guess I'm old enough, gone through the grief, and it started subsiding a couple of years ago. I went from being numb to feeling as if something important was missing from my life and I couldn't define what the hell it was." He didn't want to add, 'Until you came along,' because Logan knew it would probably scare Lea into leaving. It was hopeful to know they had something good, a foundation of liking one another, but that wasn't enough to build dreams on. At least, not yet. Maybe never. He really didn't know, and he could see the confusion or possible consternation in her eyes, reflecting how he felt right now about all these unexpected admissions.

At that moment, Dr. Ribas, Jody, and the two nurses returned. Logan didn't like the look on the doctor's face. He tried to inwardly steel himself for the bad news, whatever it might be. He felt Lea's hand tighten momentarily around his. She'd seen and interpreted the expression on the surgeon's face, too.

"Give me the bad news, Doc," he told her.

Ribas placed her hand on his shoulder and patted it gently. She brought up her iPad and tapped it. "A little bit of anatomy here for you, Logan. You've fractured your tibia here." She pointed toward the ankle area. "I'm going to have to put screws in because it's a clean break. You're lucky the way you fell didn't make it an open fracture, the bone sticking out of your flesh. Now, the nail is easy enough to take out, but it's rusty and I'm concerned about infection. You're going to be loaded up on antibiotics and it will probably make you feel exhausted, Logan."

"Okay," he said slowly. "Can I still heal up in six weeks?"

"It may be a little slower than that," she cautioned. "Jody was telling me that you have a housekeeper who comes in daily, but leaves at night. For the first four weeks, you're going to need someone else in that house at night with you. You're not going to be able to do a lot of things you used to do, like dressing and undressing yourself without some help, especially the first two or three weeks."

"I live there," Lea said. And then she saw the two nurses look at her. "I mean, I'm his employee. I work for him on a special project. He's given me a bedroom and his wood shop. I'll be there and available should he need help."

Ribas looked pointedly at their held hands. "That sounds good to me. You'll be more in caregiver mode for a while. He also is going to need to be driven in to our physical therapy unit, because during the six to eight weeks he's going to lose a lot of muscle mass and that leg will be weak. I'll outline a regimen for him later on and we'll send it out to you."

Logan looked up at her. "You sure about this?"

"Positive."

"Do me a favor, Lea? Don't call my folks yet. My mother is a worrywart and I don't want them thinking they've got to leave Phoenix to fly up here to be with me. Wait until I get out of surgery and hear what Dr. Ribas says. And once I get settled enough, I'll call them and let them know what happened. I want to downplay this."

"Don't you think your parents will find out sooner or later that you didn't call them right away? How will they take that?" she asked.

"My dad will understand. My mother will be furious," he said, shaking his head, "but the other side of that coin is her amping up her worry. She has high blood pressure. I don't want to contribute to it rising more."

His reasoning made sense to Lea. "Dr. Ribas said this was an in-and-out surgery, and it's only a couple of hours."

"That's true," Logan agreed. "These meds are really screwing up my thought processes."

"I do want to text Barry and keep him updated, though."

"That's fine. Barry knows not to call my parents on something like this."

"Okay, I'll wait until you come out of surgery."

Inwardly, Logan felt like the only good thing to come out of this was they were being drawn closer to one another. He searched her darkening green eyes, the soft tendrils of red hair near her temples making him want to lift his hand and smooth them into some order. She was a wild woman trapped inside the body of a woman who had found out that hiding was survival. He wanted Lea to do more than survive. He wanted to think that with his help, she could thrive and maybe, just maybe, he would see her blossom into the daredevil child she used to be. "Okay," he said. "Maddy could help."

"She'll be cooking and cleaning," Lea offered. "Between the two of us? We can take over and help you get back on your feet."

He grimaced. "An appropriate pun, eh?"

Ribas smiled a little. "Unconscious pun," she said, giving Lea a warm look.

Touching her cheek, Lea murmured, "Now I'm blushing like a schoolgirl, Logan."

"That's okay. On you, it's becoming." He turned to Dr. Ribas. "When do I get this surgery?"

"We're prepping the OR right now for you. I'm going to have Nurse Adams take you to our presurgery area. We'll give you an antianxiety IV drip, just to reduce the shock. You'll probably be very sleepy and feel very relaxed." She looked at her watch. "In about twenty minutes, we'll be wheeling you into the surgery theater."

Logan nodded. "Okay, Doc, sounds good. Thanks for everything."

Nodding, Dr. Ribas left the cubicle.

Lea stood aside as the nurse wheeled the gurney out and she followed, in turmoil. This was serious surgery. She kept telling herself that Logan was young, athletic, healthy, and that he would pass the surgery without difficulty. Or would he? She chewed on her lip, unsure.

* * *

"Hey, I'll be fine," Logan assured Lea, clasping her hand before he was wheeled out of the prep area, heading for the OR.

She squeezed his fingers. "I know you will. But I'll wait here."

"Are you sure? I'm going to be fine, Lea. This isn't a major surgery, it's just putting a couple of screws into my bone."

"You really are good at minimizing something when you want to," she teased, smiling a little and shaking her head. "I'll bet you drove your mother up a wall with these types of rationales?"

He chuckled a little. "Busted."

"At least you are honest." She leaned over him, her gaze locking on his cloudy one. They'd given him an antianxiety drug earlier through the IV and he was just this side of dropping off to sleep, boneless and not a worry in the world. He seemed scattered, which wasn't like him at all. What felt so darned good were his fingers tightly holding hers. If Logan was afraid, he wasn't showing it. She would be, for sure. "I'll be waiting out here. Dr. Ribas said it shouldn't take more than two hours. It's one thirty p.m. right now. When they bring you out of surgery, I'll talk to Dr. Ribas and then I'll call Barry and he'll let everyone else know how you're doing."

He licked his lower lip, which felt dry. "Sounds good," he said, sinking against the pillow and closing his eyes. "I'm suddenly so tired, Lea . . ." His voice trailed off into an unintelligible whisper.

"It's the drug," the nurse said quietly to her. "He's fine. Go to the visitors' surgery lounge on the second floor and wait. As soon as Dr. Ribas is finished, she'll come and see you."

Giving the young blond-haired nurse a nod, Lea said, "Good enough. Thank you." She felt Logan's fingers slip from hers; he appeared to be fully asleep. On an impulse, she leaned down, pressing her lips to his smooth brow. She doubted he would remember it. But she would. Her hand tingled in memory of his larger hand, those calluses on his palms and fingers reminding her he was the owner of a ranch and worked just as hard as any of his wranglers.

Lea went first to the small cafeteria before going up the elevator. She wanted some coffee, and although her stomach was tight with nerves and worry, she knew she had to eat something. Luckily, they had a fresh fruit salad that appealed to her. Not wanting anything heavy in her stomach, the fruit was the perfect choice. Taking the elevator, she found the lounge. It had inviting apricot-colored sofas and chairs, calming light blue walls, plus coffee tables and lamps, looking more like a home décor instead of a hospital one. Soft classical music played unobtrusively in the background. Taking out her cell phone, she texted Barry to let him know that Logan was going into surgery and the potential time it would take to care for his broken ankle.

What a day! She sat alone in the large, roomy lounge, glad that it was quiet. There was a huge TV panel on the wall, but she never watched much, so didn't have a desire to turn it on. The classical music was soothing and she finished off her fruit salad. She also texted her parents to let them know what was going on. Leaning back, closing her eyes, Lea felt as if her world had suddenly canted into a new direction. She had held Logan's hand. She had kissed him. She'd *wanted* to. And if she were honest with herself? Lea wanted much, much more with this man. No one had inspired her to dream like Logan did. Ever. In some ways, Lea felt as if she were a fairy-tale princess like Snow White, who had eaten the apple and fallen into a deep sleep. And when she awakened, there was Logan staring down at her.

Her thoughts waffled between what it might be like to take more risks, to tell Logan the whole truth of how she felt about him. Now she knew that whatever was going on between them was mutual. But how much so? Was he like so many other men who strung a woman along just to get her in bed and have sex with her? Or was it something rarer, something that every woman yearned for but didn't always get in a male partner? A long-term, equal, serious relationship. That is what Logan was stirring up in her, causing her to want him, causing her to dream of something she felt was impossible to reach.

It was true her parents were deeply in love with one another and always had been. She'd grown up seeing the best that a relationship could become. But after all that had happened to her, she bitterly realized that it was one percent of the population who had what her parents had achieved with one another. So many marriages and live-in situations crumbled easily within five years, eroding before the couples' eyes.

That was not what she wanted. Her parents were dinosaurs from a bygone era compared to today's generations. Was it too much to want that now, in today's throw-away world? Was she more dreamer than realist? Above all, she'd watched her parents communicate, and as she grew older and more mature, realized that was the glue that kept their marriage going. That and being the best of friends. They truly enjoyed doing things together and appreciated the other person.

Why wasn't that possible in today's world? What had happened to make a lasting marriage such a rare commodity? Frustrated, she stood up, slowly pacing around the room, hands behind her back, head down, pondering the blossoming relationship with Logan.

Wouldn't this time with him after his surgery be a good yardstick for measuring their budding relationship? Yes, it might be. She'd never taken care of someone who was injured before, however. Would her ignorance put Logan in jeopardy? Her mind went to nooks and crannies as she asked herself a lot of questions and didn't get any good answers in return.

Maddy would be there to cook for them, and for that, Lea was grateful. She was older and couldn't be expected to care for Logan, especially the first three weeks of his recuperation. That pining away that would come and go in her heart, came back strongly right then. Unconsciously, she rubbed that region. She wanted to talk to her mother about this odd reaction she was having toward Logan. Was it real? Was it her creative, wishful side tricking reality? She wondered how Jessica and Mike Anderson, Logan's parents, would take not being alerted immediately that he'd been operated on. She was sure her parents would be upset to no end about it. But she'd never met Logan's parents, and had to rely on him to do what he thought was right. Intuitively, Lea felt his mother would be stripping gears over not being told right away. Shrugging, she knew she could be wrong about that, too. At least Logan said he'd call them after he became fully alert after the surgery.

Her cell phone rang. Frowning, she pulled it out of her jeans pocket.

"Hello?"

"This is Barry, Lea. Listen, it seems like things are gonna go in threes on bad luck today. Maddy's husband, Alvin? He just suffered a heart attack. They're takin' him by ambulance to the hospital where you're at."

"Oh," Lea whispered, "no! Oh, this is awful, Barry! Is he going to make it?"

"Dunno. Maddy was away in Thermopolis for the day, visiting her relatives when it happened. Alvin was out on a job at the end of town. He said he wasn't feeling good, broke out in a sweat, and then the attack came and he lost consciousness out in his truck. The woman he'd done the electrical work for in her home, called in the emergency."

"Have you called Maddy?" she asked, her voice urgent.

"Yes, but she's an hour away. I told her you were at the hospital already and she has your phone number. She doesn't text, Lea, so expect a phone call. Maddy's coming straight to the hospital. You have her cell number?"

"Yes, yes I do."

"I'm going to stay here at the ranch because this is where I need to be, but I'd like you to keep me in the loop on Logan's surgery and let me know how Alvin's doing?"

"Of course," she said, her own heart pounding with anxiety and fear for Alvin. "I'll go down to the ER desk and tell the supervisor what's going on. I'll give them Maddy's cell number so they can be in touch directly with her, because I don't think they will tell me a thing about Alvin's condition. I'm not family."

"I agree. Okay, this is two. Lordy, I hope there's not gonna be a number three."

Her mouth thinned. "I hope not either, Barry. I'll be in touch."

For the next fifteen minutes, Lea was busy at the main ER desk with the supervisor, Nurse Pamela Dutton, who was close to retirement age. Lea gave her Maddy's phone number, and the nurse thanked her profusely. She saw Alvin brought in, but in a matter of less than a minute, they had powered him through the ER area and out another door and she didn't know where it led.

"Can you stay in touch with me on Alvin's condition?" Lea asked.

"Maddy will be here in probably thirty minutes," Pamela said, rising from behind her desk in the small office. "I'll tell her you are up on the surgery floor visitors' lounge. I'm sure she'll find you. Right now, the cardiac doctor is assessing Mr. Long's condition. We don't know anything yet. I did receive a call from the ambulance driver, who said that he was semiconscious, so that's a good sign. Just keep your fingers crossed."

"For sure," Lea murmured. "Gosh, two of our people going down within hours of one another is so shocking," she whispered, touching her brow.

"Things come in threes," Pamela warned her grimly, moving around the walnut desk that had neat stacks of reports on it. "Best thing you can do is be up there and wait for Logan to get out of surgery. Dr. Ribas is the best, and I know she'll be a terrific surgeon for Logan." She patted Lea's shoulder. "Just keep taking some deep breaths and this, too, shall pass."

It was good advice. Looking at her watch, she knew Maddy would be at the hospital in half an hour. She was probably breaking every speed limit to get here to Silver Creek, and Lea didn't blame her. Pamela promised to call

Maddy, as soon as she went and checked on Alvin's condition so she had something concrete to tell her. More than anything, Lea hoped it would be good news. People died of heart attacks all the time. Not wanting to go there, Lea stepped out of the elevator doors after they slid open.

It would be an hour at the earliest before Dr. Ribas had finished her surgery on Logan's tibia. Feeling like she'd just been slammed into a concrete wall, Lea sat down in the surgery lounge. Her mind spun. With Alvin surviving this cardiac event, that meant he would probably need some caretaking himself. And that meant she would have to take over the cooking duties for Maddy at Logan's home. Lea resisted asking *What else could go wrong?* and grabbed a magazine, and tried to concentrate on it instead of people's lives being suddenly upended at the Wild Goose Ranch.

Chapter Nine

June 2

A groan awoke Logan. At first, he didn't know where he was. Unable to open his eyes simply because he was a lifeless ragdoll, he could sense that he was moving. It felt as if there were jigsaw puzzle pieces inside his skull, slowly oscillating, none attached to one another. He heard voices, muted, unable to understand what they were whispering about. The movement halted. It sounded like a door was opening and closing. The gurney moved again. He was vaguely aware of an ache in the ankle region of his right leg. What had happened? Fleeting bits of conversations filtered off and on through his consciousness.

Finally, the movement stopped and he sank back into a nether world of soft, white cotton once again, pain-free.

The next time he came up from wherever he had been, Logan no longer felt movement. It took all his strength to try and open his eyes, but the lids were simply too heavy. He felt long, warm fingers close over his hand that lay across his blanketed belly.

"Logan?"

His heart leaped. He knew that voice! His mind refused

to work and name the woman who was nearby, and frustration curdled deep within him. He opened his mouth to speak, but it felt dry, like the desert. What was her name? He should know it! He compressed his lips, focusing his meager consciousness to force his eyelids upward. It felt as if he were lifting three hundred pounds of weight. His focus wandered. He felt her fingers wrapping gently around his icy-cold hand, sliding lightly, sharing her warmth with him.

"It's all right, Logan. It's Lea Ryan. You're okay and you're out of surgery. Don't struggle. Try to relax . . ."

Just the soothing huskiness of her voice was like sweet honey pouring through his cartwheeling mind. He focused instead on forcing his fingers to squeeze hers in return. It wasn't much, a very weak response, in fact, but he was able to communicate with her in that way.

He felt her fingers gently remove a few strands of his dark hair off his brow, pushing them back into place. His lids refused to move. What the hell! He'd never felt as vulnerable and weak as he did right now.

"Dr. Ribas said you are still coming out from under the anesthesia from your operation, Logan. She wants you to know that it will gradually wear off. Don't fight it. You're here in the Silver Creek hospital. She just finished pinning your ankle bones back together, and said it was a success. All you have to do is let the healing take over and not fight it like it was an adversary." She laughed softly, curling her fingers around his once more and letting him know so much without a word passing between them.

"Do you understand what I just told you? If you do, squeeze my fingers?"

He squeezed them.

"Good," she said, "that's wonderful. It was Dr. Ribas

who suggested hand-holding as a way to talk with one another until that stuff gets out of your system. She's going to return in a couple of hours and check in on you. She said by that time your eyes will be easy to open and you'll be able to talk again."

More stress dissolved within Logan. Just listening to the humor in Lea's voice . . . there . . . he remembered her name! Finally! That was a huge step forward to Logan. And then, along came her face, her body, and that she was a master wood-carver. Everything about Lea downloaded from his anesthesia-soaked, wobbling brain, and joy filled him. Now he remembered that she came into the barn shortly after he'd fallen. She'd been with him ever since. That flooded him with unimaginable happiness. Her loyalty, her care, and the powerful affection he held in his heart for this woman, flowed through him in the best of ways. All his impatience and frustration dissolved beneath her fingers, trailing slowly up and down his forearm, to his hand, and then enclosing his fingers once more. Nothing had ever felt so good.

And then, he sank back into the white light once more.

The next time he came to the surface, Logan's first awareness was of Lea's hand around his. How much time had passed? How long had he been out?

"You're back, Logan."

He heard the smile in her low voice, absorbing it like it was life itself trickling back into him. And he was even more surprised when he could barely lift his lids. At first, everything he saw looked blurred and distorted.

"Good, you can open your eyes," Lea said.

"Not . . . much . . . ," he managed. She squeezed his hand gently.

"It takes time. Who knew you were such an impatient

person, Logan. You've been fooling me." She laughed a little.

Turning his head slightly, he wanted so desperately to see Lea's face. At first, she too was distorted-looking, but then, as he held his focus, which was much easier this time, her visage changed, sharpened, and he drowned in the deep green gaze that was fastened on him. Her red hair was tousled, giving her a winsome look. Noticing shadows beneath her eyes, he looked beyond her, seeing the blinds were open, the sunlight less.

"What—time?" he managed.

Lea raised her wrist, looking at her watch. "It's five p.m. You've been out of surgery for about an hour and a half. Are you in pain at all?"

He barely rolled his head from side to side, realizing speaking was a huge drain on his resources. "No . . . no pain."

"Good. You went away for about twenty minutes and now you've resurfaced again. Dr. Ribas said it would happen. Can I get you anything? Are you thirsty?"

"Mouth feels like . . . a desert . . ." Logan hated sounding like a three-year-old child who couldn't string a coherent sentence together. Now he understood it was the drug they used on him during surgery. He had another download: falling off the ladder after the wood cracked and broke beneath his booted foot. His ankle. All his meager attention went to his right ankle. He couldn't feel anything. He tried wriggling his toes and he felt them move.

"Do you want some water?" Lea asked.

"Y-yes, please . . ."

She released his hand and walked around his bed, pulling the tray on wheels over to the side of it. "I'm going to slip this straw into your mouth," she said, picking up a glass and filling it half full of water. Leaning over, Lea gently slid the straw between his parted lips. Holding the glass in place, she said, "Try sucking and see if that water comes into your mouth."

Logan groaned as the tepid water filled his mouth. It tasted so good! In no time, he'd finished off that glass and Lea poured him another one. He drank all of that, too. Just to have Lea this close, he could smell the scent of her hair, which reminded him of lilacs. There was a tightness to her face, stress he thought, as she slid the straw between his lips and he drank. When he finished, she placed the empty glass on the bedside tray.

"Thanks," he uttered, exhausted. "I feel so damned tired, Lea . . ."

She turned to him. "Don't fight it. Close your eyes. Go to sleep. When you wake up, you'll feel better than before. I'll be here."

He barely turned his head, catching her gaze. Lea looked strained and tired. "What about you? You have to be falling over."

"Don't worry about me. Close your eyes, now . . ."

And he did, slipping back into that warm, white light cocoon that just seemed to be there, waiting for him.

Lea decided to call Logan's parents. She could barely live with herself if she didn't. They had no idea what had happened to him. Going outside to get fresh air and some late, western-horizon sunshine on the hot June day, she went around the building to the parking lot, finding her vehicle. Starting up the engine, the air-conditioning cooling her, she called Jessie and Mike Anderson. She had talked to them a couple of times when she had answered the phone in the wood shop. They were nice people as far as she was concerned.

"Hello," Jessie sang out.

"Hi, Jessie, it's Lea."

"So good to hear from you! It's not like you to call us. Is everything all right?"

Lea sat back in the seat, and told her what had happened, making it succinct and without any drama.

"And Logan is all right? You said he's in the hospital coming out of the anesthesia?"

"Yes. He's in and out, exhausted, as you would expect after an operation. But his vitals are normal and Dr. Ribas will see him in about an hour. Once I talk to her, I'll call you again, if that's okay?"

"Of course it is. Hold on, I want Mike to hear what's going on . . ."

Lea waited, hearing the sudden stress in Jessica's voice. She heard Mike in the background and waited. When he came on the phone, she repeated Logan's injury and present condition.

"Well," Mike drawled, "do you need us to fly up there and help out?"

"Logan said no. Barry, whom you know, is going to be running the ranch for the next week or so until Logan can get back in the saddle, so to speak."

"I see. Are you sure, Lea?"

"Logan is positive about that, Mike. He was afraid to call you earlier because he knew you would be really upset and he saw no reason for you to leave Phoenix to fly up here. He intends to run the ranch like he always has, except that he won't be out on the front lines every day."

"That's true, Jess is a big worrywart. And I'm glad to

hear he's not gonna try and get out there, hobble around on crutches and try to work. Barry's a fine foreman and he'll take the reins of running the ranch. What will you be doing, Lea?"

"Well, things are a bit upside-down right now. Maddy's husband, Alvin, just suffered a heart attack a few hours ago. He's here at the hospital and they have him stabilized. Maddy just got here because she was in Thermopolis visiting friends."

"Is Alvin gonna live?"

Lea could hear shock and concern in Mike's gravelly voice. "He's awake and conscious, and they're running all kinds of tests on him right now. I sort of drift between Logan's room and Alvin's. Maddy is just so torn up over this."

"That's really bad," Mike muttered. "Do you think we should come up? Who's gonna do the cooking and house-cleaning? I'm sure Maddy will want to be at home to care for Alvin. I know I would."

"Yes, I talked to her just a bit ago and she's definitely staying home to help Alvin. And according to one of his cardiologists, he's going to need a lot of help the first couple of months. I guess the heart attack was pretty bad, and did damage, so he'll need Maddy's help."

"Should we come up?"

"I've yet to tell Logan about this, Mike. He's still coming out from under that drug haze everyone gets after surgery. As soon as he's awake and alert, I'm going to let him know. I'll ask him what he wants to do."

"Can you cook?" Mike asked, chuckling.

"What woman doesn't know how to cook?" she parried, laughing with him. "If Logan wants, I can pinch hit for

Maddy being gone several months until Alvin is stable and starting his recovery."

"But what about all your woodworking?"

"I can do that, too. Just not as much, but I'll ask Logan what he'd like to do in this situation. I want to tell him about this as soon as he's back with us and not dropping off to sleep due to the drugs."

"Of course," Mike said. "Have him call us once this is all settled? We wouldn't mind flying up there to be of help to Logan and Maddy and Alvin. They are good friends of ours, more than just employees."

"I understand," Lea said softly. "It's so refreshing to see people like yourself, and Logan, too, who treat the people who work for them like they were family. It's very touching."

"It's the smart thing to do," Mike added. "When people know they are appreciated, that they are part of a team, not just an employee picking up two checks a month from their employer, they work harder. They're loyal. And they get good raises yearly. Did Logan tell you that when he returned from the military, the first thing he did was get a preschool built in Silver Creek for the parents of those who worked for us? That way, they got free childcare while they were on the ranch."

"No, he didn't tell me that. What a wonderful thing to do."

"We're proud of him," Mike said. "He's turned out to be a fine young man."

"Well, let me hang up here and I'll go check in on that son of yours. I hope this time when he comes awake, that he'll be alert."

Laughing, Mike said, "Go ahead. In the meantime, can you tell Maddy that when she gets a chance if she could call us and keep us up on Alvin's condition, we'd appreciate it. And tell Logan we love him."

"I'm sure Maddy will call you once all this craziness is over with here," Lea said. "And I'll tell Logan you're sending him your love."

Logan looked up as the door to his room opened. His heart leaped and it wasn't from this damned anesthesia. It was Lea. She looked worried. "Hey, I'm awake and I'm alive," he told her, his voice rough, his throat sore.

She halted, surprised, brows rising, hand on the door. "Wow, what a difference! You're back, Logan. That's good news." She closed the door and walked around his bed to a nearby chair. She pushed back a few tendrils from her brow. "Your eyes look clear. You really are here."

He reached out, touching her hand that rested on the arm of the chair. "And you've been my guardian angel throughout. One of the nurses was just in and she told me that you've rarely left my side. Thank you . . ." He lifted his hand away, still having memories of her holding his hand off and on when he resurfaced from the anesthesia. Lea was more than tired. He could see the strain at the corners of her eyes, the way her mouth was set. Even though she sat in the chair, she was tense.

"How long have you been awake?"

"About twenty minutes." He motioned to the water glass and pitcher sitting alongside the bed. "I drank two glasses of water. I was really thirsty. The nurse said she was going to get Dr. Ribas, that either my IV had to be adjusted and drip faster to stop me feeling so thirsty, or be taken out of my arm."

"I'd have it taken out of my arm."

He managed a slight, one-cornered grin, giving his left arm a glance. "I'm with you."

Just then, Dr. Ribas popped in. When Logan had seen her before, she wore her blue scrubs and cap. Now she was in a starched white coat, the stethoscope hanging around her neck, a pink blouse, and navy-blue slacks. "I just heard you've arrived back from the land of Oz," she teased, giving him a smile as she entered. "Hi, Lea."

"Hi, Dr. Ribas."

She came to the right side of his bed. "Logan, you look pretty chipper." She removed her stethoscope, listened to his heart, looked at the latest readings on the instruments, and nodded. "Good. You not only look good, but all your stats are normal. Excellent." She looped the stethoscope back around her neck, turned and lifted the sheet and blue bedspread. Beneath it was an aluminum contraption, and Logan's broken ankle was beneath it. She touched the lightweight cast. "Any pain or discomfort?"

"No, not really," he admitted.

"Good," Ribas murmured, straightening and carefully pulling the bedding over the contraption again. She picked up the chart from the footboard. "I'm going to get you off the IV. I'll have the nurse bring you a pain med and you can drink all the water you want. It will continue to flush that anesthesia out of your system."

"That's what I wanted to hear. So? Can I go home tonight?" It was six p.m.

"No. I want you to stay overnight. I'll release you tomorrow morning." She glanced over at Lea. "There's things Lea needs to know about, look out for, and I want my nurse to sit down with her and give her that information. The first four weeks you're going into a wheelchair.

Those screws have to have time to begin the healing before you can start walking."

"I don't like that prescription," he muttered, shaking his head.

"I knew you wouldn't. Lucky for you, Lea is here and she's going to be shouldering a lot of different responsibilities while you recoup." She smiled down at him. "You'll survive, my friend."

Logan reached out, shaking her long, thin hand. "Thanks for saving my hide, Doc. I really am grateful."

"I know you are," she said, looking over at Lea. "I'm sure everyone at the ranch would love a call from you. Let Barry know his boss came through with flying colors."

"I'll do that," she promised.

"Gotta run, Logan," she said, lifting her hand. "I'll check up on you before I release you at nine a.m. tomorrow."

"Thanks," he called to her. Once she left, he turned toward Lea. "I don't even know where my cell phone is. I need to call my parents."

Squirming a bit in the chair, Lea said, "Before you do, I need to fill you in on something that happened while you were in surgery, Logan." She sat up. "Alvin had a heart attack, and he's survived it. He's here in the hospital. Maddy is with him. When it happened, he was on an electrical job here in Silver Creek, so they were able to get him over here right away."

"What?" The word came out low and urgent. "Alvin?"

"Yes," she whispered. "He's only forty-five. He seemed indestructible."

"And he's okay?"

"He's in ICU right now. Maddy's with him."

"Damn, I'm sorry to hear this. I wish—" He looked

around the bed. "Can I see him? See Maddy? I'm sure she's just beside herself."

Giving him a sympathetic look, Lea said, "No . . . not right now. You are bed bound until they release you, Logan."

He wanted to curse, but thought better of it. His mind still had fuzzy moments and he couldn't think on his feet like he usually did. "How bad was the heart attack?"

"Bad, but I'm not a doctor and I've only spoken to Maddy once since Alvin was brought in. He's going to live, and for me, that's what I hoped to hear."

Frustration curdled through Logan. He felt helpless in ways that he hated, and pulled at the spread, holding it in his fist and then releasing it. "At least Alvin is alive, that's the good news here."

"Yes," she sighed, "it is. Maddy is devastated, and if I were in her shoes, I would be, too. They remind me of my parents. They love each other so much. I hate when bad things happen to good people. Anyway, I told Dr. Ribas that I'd be taking care of you and cooking your meals. Maddy has her hands full, Logan. She's not going to be able to work for you until Alvin is better, and no one knows when that will be."

"Understood." He gave her a sympathetic look. "That explains why I saw the stress in your face, that you couldn't relax even sitting here. I thought it might have been worry about your job or something . . ."

She managed a shake of her head. "Nothing like that, Logan. I was worried about *you*. I wasn't worried about my job."

He gave her a sad look. "Now you're going to cook,

clean, and take care of me? Is that what you want to do, Lea?"

"Of course, it is. I can't cook like Maddy, but you won't die of food poisoning, either." She gave him a teasing look. "And I can still do my wood carving on the cabinets for you. So, don't worry about that."

He studied her for a moment, feeling overwhelming emotions. Maybe it was the anesthesia wearing off. He wasn't usually so emotionally volatile. Clearing his throat, he rasped, "Whatever you do? Don't leave. I like what we have, even if we don't call it anything, Lea." He reached out, touching her hand again. "I remember you holding my hand. I would surface and then I would go down again, and I always felt the warmth and strength of your fingers around my hand. You have no idea how comforted that made me feel . . . how much I needed that . . . you . . ." He held her green gaze, seeing her face soften, the stress dissolving.

"I'm not sure what we have, but I like it. Just know that. Right now"—she took in a long, deep breath—"I just feel torn up. First you, and then Alvin goes down. It feels like a one-two gut punch to me. Bad news on top of bad news."

"Yes, but I'm going to live, Lea. And it sounds like Alvin is going to make it, too. His medical emergency is far worse than mine, for sure."

"True, but it makes me feel raw inside, if you want the truth," Lea admitted quietly.

"Bad times are something that happens to all of us," he agreed darkly. "I guess it was my and Alvin's turn, and you and Maddy are on the receiving end of it. We'll get through this together, one way or another."

"This is when you find out if you have real, internal

strength to walk through these times," she agreed. Pulling up her purse, she handed him his cell phone. "I'm sure your parents could use some good news by you calling them. Do you feel up to it?"

He liked touching the tips of her fingers. They were warmer now than before. A bit of blush touched her cheeks, making her look less frail, her color off. But she'd suffered two events in a period of one day and both had been devastating to Lea in different ways. "Yes, I feel up to it," he assured her.

Standing, she said, "I called your parents before, Logan. I didn't know when your anesthesia would wear off, and I felt pressure to let them know."

"You made the right decision."

"I told them that when you surfaced from the anesthesia, you would call, and they were relieved. They said to tell you that they love you."

"Thanks for doing that," he murmured, grateful.

"Can I get you anything before they take you off these IVs?"

"A cup of strong, hot coffee sounds good to me."

She grinned. "I'll be back."

Logan wanted her to stay, but he could see that she was giving him space to be alone to speak to his parents. She didn't have to do that, but whatever they had, this unnamed quasi-relationship, he wasn't going to ask her to stay if she felt uncomfortable about it. Logan had never seen Lea as an outsider to his family, anyway. He needed to emphasize that to her another time. Punching the cell phone keypad, he knew he had to calm his mother's worry about him.

By the time he got done speaking to them, almost as if on cue, the nurse came in. She was quick and efficient in ridding him of the IVs. Another person, a man in blue scrubs, came in with a fresh pitcher of cold water for him, along with some orange juice, which the nurse told him to drink, at least a glass. It would give him a needed shot of sugar, and sure enough, it did just that. He'd had to take a pain pill, too, since the IV had been disconnected.

Lea entered with two cups in her hands just after the nurses left. She looked better, her face was more the color it should be. Logan didn't realize how stressed she had been until that moment. He reached out and thanked her after she placed a cup on his tray and pulled it around so he could have it across his bed.

Taking off the lid, he inhaled the scent deeply. "This smells good," he told her, giving her a look of thanks before she walked around his bed and sat down in the chair.

"They make good coffee here." Lea took a sip and said, "I made a detour to the ICU. I told Maddy you are awake and doing fine. She almost cried, so happy to hear some good news."

"And Alvin? How is he?" Logan asked, sipping the coffee.

"Marginally better. He's sleeping right now and the nurses told Maddy that was a good thing. He's out of pain and that's hopeful."

"Does Maddy know if he's got to have surgery?"

"I don't know. I wanted to be there for her. We talked outside of the ICU for about five minutes. I think it has helped her immensely to hear you're recovering. She told me that she couldn't come to work for you, and I told her about our conversation. I think she felt relieved. I was teasing her about me not being able to cook like her, but that I wouldn't poison you."

Chuckling, Logan said, "Come on, you've made sandwiches for us before when Maddy wasn't there and had to run errands."

"I know, but I wanted to make her feel good about herself, because her whole life just got destroyed in a matter of minutes."

"Is there any chance I can see her tomorrow? I'd really like to be able to go to the ICU lounge and speak to her. I know I can't see Alvin, but I'd very much like to see her."

"I talked to her about that. I hope you didn't mind me making an executive decision before talking to you about it. Maddy wants to see you as badly as you want to see her. But she remains in the ICU, holding Alvin's hand, at his bedside."

"You did the right thing, thank you," he said, grateful to her for doing just that. "Maddy is like family to me, Lea."

"I could tell that from the very beginning." She gave him a warm look. "It's lovely to have a place where you work and you're treated like family, not an employee. But I see that with everyone you've hired, Logan. It's you. And I guess that is what touched me the most when I first came to the Wild Goose, was your love of the people around you. It was real and genuine. I've just never seen a place of employment like yours."

"My parents were like that, and so I grew up in that kind of environment. And speaking of my mom and dad, they were relieved to hear from me. I downplayed everything, making less of the break than it is, because my mother will worry herself to death over it."

"Are they going to fly up to see you? They asked me about that and I couldn't give them an answer. I didn't want to make that kind of decision for you."

"I told them the same thing you did: Stay there. My mother is very happy that you're taking over babysitting me, feeding me, and wheeling me around, as well as being my taxi service when I need it," he joked, giving her an appreciative glance.

"I'm happy to do it. It will be a new rhythm for me and you, but I intend to carve out time to still do my wood-working for those kitchen cabinets."

He held up his hand. "Listen, things are going to be un-settled until I can get back in the saddle and pick up the reins of the day-to-day operations. Until then, I have every belief you can do it all, and Barry certainly can. It's just that our normal, daily rut is blown up."

"I can handle it," she assured him dryly. "Did your mom tell you that she was more than willing to come up and cook and clean for you?"

"Yes, she did." He shook his head. "She has given so much to this ranch that I didn't want her taking on that kind of task again. Retirement should be just that, not doing what you did for fifty years of your life. I assured her that you were perfectly capable, no problem."

"I talked to Maddy just now and she asked for their phone number. She wanted to talk with them, so I did."

"Good. Maddy and my mother are the best of friends. They're just as devastated by Alvin's heart attack as we are."

"We're lucky to have Jody there at the ranch in case Alvin needs anything after he's allowed to come home."

"I was thinking the same thing. I'm going to miss her paramedic expertise when she leaves. I know she's going on to fulfill her dream, but I hope she never forgets that the Wild Goose is another one of her homes, either."

"I'm sure Jody will come around when she can," Lea said.

He relished the coffee, drinking most of it quickly. It tasted good and he felt fortified, more alert in every way. "It's almost eight p.m.," he said. "Why don't you go home? I'll be fine here. I'll see you at nine tomorrow morning?"

Lea capped her coffee and stood. "I'll be here."

"I'll make a few calls," he said, holding up his cell phone, "to Barry and Jody. I have them on speed dial and I'll catch them up with all the news. Go home, take a good, hot soak in that tub you love so much, and then sleep."

"Okay, I will."

He reached out and captured her hand. "Thank you, Lea. You've been incredible. I don't know what I'd do if you weren't here right now." Then, he reluctantly let go. Just the look on her face, the softness coming to her green eyes, made his heart balloon powerfully with the need to have her in his life.

"I'm just glad I was there when it happened, Logan. Good night . . ."

Chapter Ten

June 3

"Hey, how are you doing?" Lea asked, entering Logan's room the next morning at 8:45, wanting to hear what Dr. Ribas had to say about Logan's condition. In Lea's left hand was a brown paper sack with a fresh set of clothing.

Logan was finishing off breakfast from his tray. His skin color looked closer to normal; she was sure shock was still a part of the issue with why he still didn't look like his chipper self. At her voice, he looked up.

"You're a sight for sore eyes," he muttered, pushing away the half-eaten tray of food. "Nine a.m. can't come soon enough."

She left the door ajar and came around the bed, sitting down in a nearby chair. "Wanting to escape, huh?" she teased, smiling over at him.

"Hardly slept. The nurses kept coming in all night long. I'm pretty grumpy."

"I couldn't tell," she deadpanned, hanging her purse over the chair. "Jody and a couple of wranglers are getting your bedroom set up for your healing ankle," she said, motioning toward the contraption beneath the blankets. "And Barry said everything's fine. Nothing going on. Just routine stuff, so don't start worrying about it. Okay?"

"Good to know. I'll be glad to get home."

"No place like home," Lea agreed. She saw how the hospital gown stretched across his broad shoulders. He hadn't shaved and the darkness gave him, in her opinion, a sexy look that pulled at her. No longer fighting the idea that she was truly drawn to him, man to woman, she hadn't slept well last night, worrying over this ongoing discovery. What was she going to do? The job he'd given her meant so much to her; a way to show the world that she was capable of the same artistry as her father, and therefore, employable. A part of her felt tugged in that direction, to take care of herself fully, on her own, to prove to herself, to her parents, that she no longer needed to lean on them and their resources. No, this was a make-or-break situation for her and Lea knew it. And she wasn't about to go home without accomplishing what she set out to do here in Wyoming.

"Good morning," Dr. Ribas said, opening the door. With her were two nurses. "How are you doing, Logan?" She opened her iPad and tapped it, bringing up all his patient information from the night before.

"Hi, Doc. I'm grumpy. I didn't sleep much last night."

"Understandable." She quickly went over his record and then looked up. "Any pain in your ankle?"

"No, that medication seems to stop it pretty good."

"Well, you get five days on it, and then I'm transferring you to something else."

"That's fine," Logan said. "So? When can I get out of here? Not that I'm not grateful to you and your staff for putting my ankle back together."

She grinned. "How about right now?" She nodded to the head nurse and they went to his bed. An orderly brought in a wheelchair.

"Sounds good to me," he said, relieved.

"I'll have the nurses get you unplugged from all these monitors and ask that Lea get your clean clothes out of that sack she brought with her. She'll help you get them on. Or? Or, do you want Chuck, our orderly here, to help you instead?"

Lea gulped inwardly. And then she told herself she had to do it. "No problem, Dr. Ribas. I'll get him dressed. I need practice since I'll be helping him for the next month."

"Right you are," Ribas agreed. "Chuck will wait outside until you're ready to leave. According to hospital regulations, he has to wheel you out to the curb, Logan. Lea, if you want, after you're done dressing him, go to the parking lot and bring your car or truck up to the front of the hospital."

"Good idea," Lea said, rising.

"The nurse will give you a bunch of instructions to take home with you, Logan. I expect to see you at my office in seven days and we'll check on your ankle and how you're doing."

"Music to my ears," he teased.

"Jody already has that aluminum metal frame, which she picked up at the medical supply business in town for you, yesterday," she added. "I don't want any weight or pressure on that ankle for a month. You'll get used to having it be your best friend for a bit." She grinned.

"That's nice of Jody to do that," Logan said.

"She's special," the doctor agreed. "I'll see you in a week, Logan." She raised her hand and left.

They were alone, the door shut. Lea forced herself around the bed. She saw Logan perk up, relief in his expression. She understood what home meant to him. "Let me get the bed covers pulled away and then I need to remove that metal frame."

"Right." He gave her a worried look. "Are you okay with this?"

"Well," she said in jest, "I need to be. Don't you think? You aren't going to be able to pull up your jeans by yourself. The material has to be carefully worked up and over that cast. Dr. Ribas doesn't want any pressure on your ankle while it's healing for the first four weeks." She saw he was concerned. Maybe he hadn't thought his ankle would be a deterrent to hauling on his clothing over it. The best way to get through this was to pretend it didn't bother her. Would she see him naked? That made her run hot and cold. More to the hot range, if she were honest with herself.

"Let me know if this gets too embarrassing for you, okay?"

She walked over and pulled the bedsheets down to the footboard. Logan smoothed his gown over his knees and she appreciated him being circumspect about it. "Okay," she murmured, taking the frame away. His cast was mobile and waterproof, according to the nurse. But it was bulky, even though it wasn't very heavy. The cast encased the lower half of his foot and went half way up his leg. It was removable, and that was good news to Lea.

"Can you sit up, turn, and put your legs over the edge of the bed?" she asked.

"I hope so," he muttered. "This lying around isn't my idea of fun." He slowly lifted his legs, turning his large body, able to drape his long legs over the edge of the mattress.

Lea saw him grimace as he slowly lowered his legs to the floor. "Are you in pain?"

"Just a lot of pressure in the foot," he said, frowning. "Blood flowing downward into it. Gravity at work."

Lea brought the skivvies and Levi's around and laid them on the bed.

"I can do the skivvies," he protested. "You won't have to help me with that. Just the jeans . . ."

"Dr. Ribas was sure you would need help, Logan. So? Let me?"

"No," he said, and grabbed the skivvies. "I can do this." He started to lean forward, but didn't stop.

If Lea hadn't been beside him, he'd have crashed to the floor. Probably injuring his newly fixed ankle once again. "Whoa," she murmured, gripping his shoulder, feeling the play of muscles beneath his gown. "Did you get dizzy?"

"Yes," he growled, gripping the edge of the bed with his hands. "I didn't expect that . . ."

"I think Dr. Ribas did. Okay if I let you go, or do you still feel dizzy?"

"No," he said unhappily, "it went away. I'll just sit here for a moment . . ."

She knelt at his feet. Her heart was pounding because he was embarrassed and so was she, but Lea wasn't about to show her shakiness. "Lift your left foot and I'll slide your skivvies on," she coaxed quietly.

Logan obeyed. "That was the easy one. Is that other opening big enough to get over this cast?"

She studied it. "I think so. We'll see. Lift your right leg?"

He did, but not very far off the floor because it was such an effort for him. Gently, she slid the other side up his foot, being very careful to widen the opening so it wouldn't hit the cast. Once past that point, she slid them to his knees. His hands immediately closed over hers.

"Okay, I got this. Why don't you stand and turn around? I'll get these up the rest of the way."

She grinned. "Good idea." She stood.

"This might take some time," he warned.

"I have all day, Logan." She stepped well out of his way in case he wanted to stretch out his legs.

He managed a tight chuckle. "This isn't funny."

"No, I'm laughing because of nerves," she admitted, facing the door. "I've never dressed a man before."

"And I've never had a woman dress me either. But I guess my mother sure did when I was a baby."

"But you have no memories of that, so this is new to both of us."

"You doing all right?" he wondered.

She could hear him moving around the bed, the bed groaning now and then.

"This is tougher than I thought," he griped.

"Take your time," she soothed. And then she laughed a little. "You could go commando, you know?"

Logan snorted. "No way. You can't ride in a saddle that way, that's for sure."

"I can imagine. Not a sight for sore eyes . . ."

He managed a short laugh. "You have a deadly sense of humor in serious situations."

"Black humor," she informed him archly. "How are you doing? I hear you breathing hard."

"Not from lust, believe me."

Cracking up, she laughed heartily. "But things are moving along, Logan? Right?"

"They're moving, just not as quickly as I want."

"Do you feel like a flounder out of water?"

"Better believe it . . . okay . . . I got them on. Turn around. Let's try those jeans next."

When Lea turned, she saw he was sitting upright, the hem of the gown draped over his knees. There were beads of sweat on his wrinkled brow. "You're going to get your exercise, no question," she commented, picking up the Levi's and kneeling in front of him once more.

"I'd rather do this than just be lying in this damned bed. I can hardly wait to get out of here."

For the next ten minutes, they both struggled with his jeans. His cast was snug in the jeans, but still had a bit of wiggle room, which was good as far as Lea was concerned. "Lucky thing you don't wear those narrow stovepipe type of jeans," she told him, pulling up the last of the fabric so it bunched at his knees. Standing, she said, "This time, I think you need to lie on your back, Logan, and stretch out. Then, use your left foot, draw the fabric up to your butt, lift your right leg and pull the jeans upward."

"Turn around," he said gruffly.

"You don't have to ask me twice," she said, trying to sound light about the situation that had her heart beating rapidly. And it sure wasn't from anxiety! Just touching the hard, warm flesh of his left leg, the dark hair upon it, was doing something to her lower body, making it clench. Turning her back to him, she gulped several times, trying to subdue her escaping primal feelings, wants, and needs. She wrapped her arms across her chest and she heard the bed creak and groan as he wrestled with the jeans.

"Okay," he huffed, "they're on. You can turn around. Can you hand me that white T-shirt?"

A quick glance told Lea that he indeed had his clean

Levi's on, although the right lower leg was puffed out with the cast. "Are you in any pain?" She sure was! His gown was bunched around his lap, hiding his powerful upper body.

"Just griping, that's all. No big deal." He opened his hand to receive the T-shirt. "Can you get those ties in back? Someone knotted them and I can't reach them."

"Sure," she said, coming around to the opposite side of the bed. Her hands shook and she forcefully willed them to stop. Indeed, those three ties were knotted, not just tied for easy release. Her fingertips accidentally brushed his warm, firm flesh and it was a silent pleasure for Lea. He didn't react to the grazing touches as she undid all three of the ties. "There," she said, a little breathlessly, "you're free," and she slid her hands beneath the gown, easing it across his broad, capable shoulders and onto his upper arms.

"Thanks," he grunted, grabbing the gown and pulling it off, as if it was vermin he had to wear, dropping it onto his pillow. On went the white T-shirt.

Lea handed him a blue chambray cowboy shirt that had pearl snaps on the front of it, and then stood back, watching him. This man worked hard, daily. There was no doubt. In moments, he had the shirt on and was snapping it shut.

Taking a deep breath, Lea hoped she didn't look rattled or wanton and he couldn't read her mind as she walked around in front of him. "Now for the tough part," she warned him. "Your boots."

"The doc only wanted me to wear the left one," he muttered, shaking his head. "My right foot isn't swollen, is it, Lea? Can you check it out?"

"You see that one sock in the seat of your wheelchair?" she asked, pointing to it.

His brows dipped and he glared at it. "Looks like an Energizer Bunny. It's pink, of all colors. And it looks like a blimp."

Chuckling, she went over and picked it up. "I brought you a pair of dark blue socks from home, and you can wear them, but the pink bunny gets put on your right foot. Dr. Ribas said she wants all the circulation your body can muster in that foot, not a tight-fitting sock over your foot." She tried not to smile as she picked up the thick, fuzzy pink thing. "I'll ask the orderly if they have any other colors available, okay?"

"Yeah, I'm not wearing pink."

She couldn't help laughing as she gently eased the dark blue sock on Logan's right foot. "Your toes are cold," she noted, easing the sock on.

"Not from lack of circulation," he corrected, giving her a scowl.

"Okay, if you say so." She put the other blue sock on and then rose. "The orderly is outside, waiting for us." Picking up the pink sock, she said lightly, "I'll go out and ask him if he has any other color."

Opening and closing the door, she found the young man waiting. Holding up the pink sock, he grinned.

"Hey," he said, shrugging, "it's the only color left."

"No one wanted to wear a pink sock?" she teased, smiling.

"No, ma'am. The guys all made me take them back. We had some black ones, but they're on back order. I'm sorry, that's all that's left. The order's supposed to be in, two weeks from now."

"Oh, Logan's going to love this explanation," she said.

"I wouldn't wear it either," the orderly admitted wryly, grinning.

"Well, he's going to have to. Doctor's orders. I'll be bringing him out in about ten minutes."

Reentering the room, the pink sock in hand, she saw Logan stare at it.

"You know, I have this awful, sinking feeling that I'm gonna have to wear that monstrosity."

Giggling, she turned and shut the door. "Yep, you are, cowboy. Doctor's orders, too. The orderly said there's a black one on backorder."

"Did he say when it was coming in?"

She knelt down and carefully eased the pink sock onto his foot. "Two weeks."

"This is embarrassing. What will my wranglers say when they see me with this fuzzy pink damned thing?" He jabbed an index finger down at it.

Lea enjoyed touching him. A lot. Keeping it to herself, she tried to remain lighthearted about the pink abomination. "The Energizer Bunny is male. He's all pink."

Snorting, he muttered, "I'm not a rabbit."

Rising, she brought the wheelchair over and put the brake on each wheel so it wouldn't move. "Let's see what we can do about it when we get home. Okay?"

"Do you have any fuzzy socks that aren't pink?" he asked hopefully.

"I don't. All my winter gear is in Brookings at my parents' home. I was planning on staying through the summer, possibly. So," she said, tapping the chair, "all I have is summer clothing. Come on, try to stand on your left leg and slowly rise. Dr. Ribas said you could be a bit dizzy upon standing, so let me get around, and you put your arm across my shoulders when I sit next to you.

Then, we'll slowly rise together and you can maneuver yourself into the wheelchair."

Nodding, he patted the bed next to him. "Come on. I want to get out of here."

"Roger that," she agreed, coming to sit down. Her body molded against his right side and she took silent pleasure in his arm hooking around her smaller shoulders. "Ready?" she asked him, trying to steady her feminine, yearning side.

"Better believe it," he murmured.

"Okay, let's do this," she urged, taking his weight, and all two hundred pounds of Logan slowly began to rise. He had all his weight on his left leg, his right foot held off the floor. In moments, he had maneuvered himself with her help into the chair, sitting down carefully and trying not to jar himself in the process. Lea missed his arm as he lifted it away from her shoulders.

"Good job," she praised, coming around and bringing down the paddles so he could rest both feet on them.

"Thanks. This is harder than I expected. I'm feeling pretty shaky physically."

"Dr. Ribas told you that you might feel weak, muscle-wise, for the rest of today. By tomorrow," she said, rising and walking around behind him and placing her hands on each brake and releasing them, "you should feel a little better."

"The anesthesia?" he growled unhappily.

"Yes. She said to drink lots of liquids when you get home and flush it out of your system."

"I'll do that."

Opening the door, Lea pushed Logan out to the hall, where the orderly took over. Hospital rules said an orderly had to wheel him to the front door. "I'll go get the truck, Logan. I'll meet you in front of the hospital."

"Thanks," he said, reaching out, touching her hand as she walked past him.

The unexpected contact sent heat and more wanting deep into Lea's body. She tried to pretend it didn't affect her. "I'll see you downstairs," she promised, taking the exit door to the stairs to the first floor.

Logan curdled in his frustration as the orderly maneuvered him from his wheelchair and into the cab of the truck. His broken ankle throbbed, but it couldn't be helped. As the door shut, he said, "Cabs aren't meant for long legs and a broken one, at that."

Lea gave him a sympathetic look, waved thanks to the orderly, and slowly drove away from the entrance to the hospital. "It's your fault," she teased, trying to get him out of his dark funk over his condition. "If you weren't so tall and didn't have such long legs, you might fit in this cavity."

Drawing in a deep inhale, he released it and wished he had his cowboy hat, but it was back at the ranch. "You're right. I miss my hat."

"Feel naked on top of your head without it?" She stopped and then, looking both ways, made a left turn that would lead them through town and out the other end of it, heading for the Wild Goose.

He pushed his fingers through his dark hair. "Do I ever."

"You weren't born with one on your head," she said, giving him a quick grin, seeing that her teasing was lifting some of his obvious frustration.

"Feels like I was," he teased back, one corner of his mouth quirking upward.

"At least you're out of prison, that hospital. Look on the bright side, huh?"

"I'm trying to. I've broken bones before. I wish it had been an arm. At least I could have gotten around on two good legs and continued my daily work on the ranch."

"It's only six weeks, Logan, not a lifetime sentence."

He chuckled and slid her a glance. "I didn't realize you had this testy side to you. I like it."

"Well," Lea said, slowing for a stoplight, "I get this way when things are going south. Like you, I tend to go to a dark place and swirl around in it instead of looking at the other side of it for hope."

"Yes, and it could be a lot worse. Look at Alvin." He scowled. "Have you heard anything this morning about how he's doing?"

"Still in the ICU."

"Did you talk to Maddy? Did you see her?"

"I ran into her at the cafeteria when I drove in today. She's frazzled, stressed, and exhausted. The doctors say Alvin is slowly recuperating. The good news is that if this continues in a positive direction, he'll be in a hospital room, out of the ICU, within a few days."

"When that happens, I want to come and see him, broken ankle or not."

"I'll bring you," Lea promised, hearing the sudden emotion in his growly tone. She drove slowly through the busy morning traffic. There were plenty of trucks and a lot of out-of-state licenses on cars. "Lots of tourists in town, Logan."

"This is the season for them. They bring fresh money

into a lot of businesses. And they're also coming for the fair."

"How are you going to handle the fair? Who's taking over some of what you do?"

He sighed and sat back, mouth pursed. "I'm going to ask Jody to leave her wrangling position and be my right hand in the administration of the fair. I usually do this by myself and have for many years. She knows how it runs and flows, and she can step in and do a lot of the checking on pens, corrals, the arenas, and other areas where I can't walk to right now. I'll rely on her eyes and ears, boots on the ground, and she'll do a good job of it."

"Trading a horse and saddle for a desk and paperwork," Lea agreed. "I think I'd much rather be in the saddle." She gave him a quick smile.

Logan nodded. "I've always had a head for numbers and organizing things. I take after my mother in that area. My father is like you: He needs to throw a leg over a good horse, be outside in the elements, damn the weather."

"I don't think I'd like riding a horse in a blizzard or a thunderstorm, but I've heard the wranglers talk among themselves, and they always have stories about your dad being out in the worst of weather conditions."

"A ranch doesn't stop working when the snow flies or a storm blows through," Logan agreed.

"Do you enjoy being outside like your dad? Or are you happy being a supervisor and administrator in an office?"

Snorting, Logan said, "I have my dad's love of the outdoors. Sometimes, depending upon the geography, I might take an ATV in the back of my pickup to get to places that are pretty inhospitable. Other times, me and some wranglers will haul our horses, already saddled and in the trailer, to other areas and use them instead."

"I've come to realize you wear a lot of hats, Logan. I'm not sure I'd be capable of such a thing."

"Didn't have a choice. My mom and dad had a huge ranch with a rich history behind it, to run. They raised me to honor our family generations and to carry on what we're well-known for."

"Did you ever want to be something else growing up, though? A different dream for yourself?" she wondered, driving past the town. Now, it was a four-mile drive on a nearly empty highway to the Wild Goose, and she stepped down on the accelerator.

"I wanted to see the world," he said, leaning back, relaxing. "That's why I went into the military for four years." He raised his hand. "Looking back on that time at my age now? It was a fantasy I was chasing."

"What kind of fantasy?"

"Being a hero, rescuing good people from bad people." Shaking his head, he muttered, "I found out good people are capable of murder, and bad people are capable of humanity. Nothing over in Afghanistan was black and white. It was all some color of gray, with good and bad, living and dying, all mixed together. I was a software mechanic on the Apache gunships, and we were in Helmand Province, which is the worst one to be in, in that country. Even though we had a base behind high walls of fence and concertina wire, it didn't stop the Taliban or ISIS attacks, lobbing grenades or rockets at us from time to time. On my days off I'd work with the only charity that was left and hadn't run back to the safety of their own country. I'd drive them into the surrounding villages and we'd deliver shoes for the children, clothing, and sometimes I'd bring in a Delos medical team to help everyone who was sick in the village. That was the only part of my time spent over there for three years that made me feel good. The rest was ugly and is still with me, I think, for the rest of my life." He glanced at her. "Sorry for becoming maudlin."

"Don't be," she whispered, touched by his sudden and unexpected personal admission. "There are times when I feel like I'm an oyster that was born without a protective shell to cover and shield myself, from people and this world that's always at war. I can't handle watching television or being on social media on the internet. There's just too much bad news, and I find myself getting so upset about it that I can't sleep at night. There's such inhumanity and heartlessness in our world. It scares and saddens me as nothing else ever could. Where are the decent people with good hearts? Who have morals and know right from wrong?"

"There is that," he agreed quietly. "I was glad to come home after my four-year obligation. I decided at that time that life shouldn't be wasted. And I'm sure my dream and immaturity at eighteen when I joined the army, taught me a lot of sobering lessons. Leaving the Sandbox behind and coming back here"—he waved his hand around at the green, fenced pastures on either side of the highway— "was like coming back to heaven. We might have problems, but nothing like a war-torn country has. People of all colors have helped make Silver Creek what it is today. There's no hatred, no racism, nothing against immigrants. The people here live in their hearts, and that's what makes this place so special. We help one another. We don't care what color your skin is, or what your gender is. We treat everyone with respect and as our equals. Believe me, I kissed the ground once I got back to the ranch, back to my parents, to those men and women who have worked on our ranch for twenty, thirty, or even forty years. We're all one big family. My dad and I had a lot of talks about my time in the Sandbox. He had never gone into the military, and it helped me to put into words some of the terrible things I saw. I never told my mom because she's a lot like you: sensitive. I didn't want her to remember some of these things and not be able to forget them."

"But you don't forget them, do you?"

"No, and we had enough other young sons in the valley here who, like me, volunteered for the military. They're all out now, back on their ranches, free of war, but will never be free of the memories that will haunt us, I'm sure, for the rest of our lives."

"Is that why you do so much for others? I've been here long enough to see all that you do for the school children, for this huge fair coming up, and so many other little things that you do on a weekly basis for people in need."

"I came back from Afghanistan swearing that I would not allow anyone to live in the squalor I saw over there. Women are treated like animals. They are seen as less than a camel or a donkey. That's why my dad helped me draw up blueprints for the homeless, having a place where battered women and children could live and feel safe, as well. The medical clinic meant a lot to me, personally, because I'd seen the Delos teams fly in and then spend weeks in a village giving medical help to those people. We take for granted getting a pair of glasses, going to the dentist, and having our ailment fixed by a doctor or hospital. They had nothing. We have people in America who have nothing, and I was damned if it was going to happen in our valley. When I got home, we called all the ranchers together and we hammered out plans to help those who need it. We created a safety net. We brought in a vocational school for those who didn't want to go to college. We helped them to help themselves. And over the years, I've seen it pay off magnificently. And maybe that's why we're such a melting pot of immigrants, all colors, so diverse and yet knitted together by our common humanity. Afghanistan may have changed me, but I sure as hell came home knowing that our valley was *not* going to be like it was. Not ever."

"Then," she said gently, giving him a proud look, "you saw something that needed to be fixed. You might not be able to do it in Afghanistan, but look at what your family has put into action here in Silver Creek. I was dumbfounded when you drove me around, introducing me to the town, by how many supportive places you have for the people who can't afford to buy or rent, or who need a helping hand."

"That was all the ranchers getting together. Our blueprint plans to make Silver Creek a place of hospitality, togetherness, and networking, makes me feel good," Logan admitted. "There's other ranchers who have helped these dreams turn into reality, too. It wasn't just our Wild Goose family. We all know, by living in such a rural area of America, that no one is coming to help us in moments of crisis. We've all put our heads, hearts, money, and time into building these needs into reality for another type of safety net for everyone who lives here. That's why we have one of the best rural hospitals in the state. We have been able to talk physicians and surgeons from around the country, into traveling here."

"And Dr. Ribas is one of them," Lea said. "I was surprised for such a small community that you would have an orthopedic surgeon on the staff. That blew me away, Logan, but I was also relieved, for your sake."

"Yes, and if our hospital hadn't been built and we hadn't gone out to sell Silver Creek to professionals like

Dr. Ribas, we would have to drive or fly to Cheyenne, our capital, which is hundreds of miles away, to get that kind of top medical help."

"And today, that safety net paid off for you," she said softly.

"Yes, it did. That hospital was built five years ago. Every big ranch pitched in, the families, the citizens of the valley, contributed and we got it done. Rural people know if they don't work and stick together, nothing is going to happen at the federal level or in Congress to have money flow out to us, instead of the big cities or the growing population centers. We are taxpayers, but our money goes elsewhere. My dad was key in educating the population here on that fact. He was the one that went to the state legislators, to the governor and other administrators at the state level. In the end, he'd bring in twenty of the biggest ranchers in our valley and they'd meet with these men and women. We got a lot more money flowing to us as a result, because we stood as one, spoke as one, and didn't back down."

"Sort of a lobby?"

"We didn't pay any lobbyist any money," he growled. "We decided *not* to put our hard-earned ranch money into that dark hole that had no end of greed to it. No, we combatted that with the fact that we have so many registered voters in our county, and that it *does* make a difference as to whether a candidate gets voted in or not. That is what changed the equation for us: voting numbers. We have a ninety-percent turnout for voting here. When you consider the rest of America has around forty-five percent, politicians snap their heads up and listen to us because our people do vote."

"Wise strategy," she congratulated, slowing down, glancing in the rearview mirror. Since being hit from behind by that unknown assailant, Lea was always looking for a truck barreling down upon them. It was her own brand of PTSD. She braked and turned into the dirt roadway that would lead to the ranch proper. There was no vehicle behind her, either. She always found herself giving a relieved sigh when turning into the ranch. Who knew if that man who plowed into her was still around? And was he hired by the fracking billionaire, Polcyn? Lea knew that Logan suspected it, but couldn't prove it. And that meant, since that was a possibility, even the sheriff, Dan Seabert, wouldn't take it off the board because they'd never found the culprit. It was important that she remain watchful.

"Hey," Logan said, "I like our deep, searching discussions like this. Can we continue them for the next four weeks while I recover? I like exploring your ideas, hearing of your experiences, and how you see things, Lea. It's refreshing."

"Oh"—she laughed, slowly moving down the road toward the main ranch house complex—"me? My world is very narrow compared to yours, Logan. I'm happy in my dad's woodworking shop or yours, and I love being here at your ranch."

He nodded, giving her a long, studied look. "I like seeing you happy, Lea."

"Well," she teased, "I'm hoping this six weeks of incarceration here at the ranch doesn't turn you into a sour, grumpy wrangler."

"I'm gonna have to work on that on a daily basis," he promised. "I'll try not to be a royal pain in the ass to you."

Laughing, Lea slowed and the gravel crunched under the tires as she swung the vehicle around the oval and toward the white picket-fence gate. "You'll never be a pain in the ass to me, Logan. Really. Look, there's Barry coming out of your house. He's glowing. I'll bet he's happy you're back, too."

Logan watched his foreman lift his hand and wave to them as he came down the steps of the porch to meet them at the gate. How he wished he had two legs to walk on and not one! Lea had had the orderly fold up the wheelchair and place it in the rear of the truck. Giving the stairs a renewed look, he realized he was going to have to get up them in the chair. *Great. Just great.*

Chapter Eleven

June 4

The soft knock on Logan's bedroom door the next morning, roused him. For a moment, he didn't realize where he was, but then, as he lifted his head, he realized he was home, not in the hospital. Even the smells were different. Familiar. Comforting.

"Come in," he rasped, struggling to sit up, the bed covers falling away to his waist. He wasn't one to wear pajamas, but Lea had found a pair of pale blue striped cotton bottoms. Last night had been embarrassing to him and, he was sure, to her, also.

The door cracked open and Lea stuck her head in. "Hey, it's nine a.m. I wanted to make sure you are all right."

"Yes, I'm okay. Come in," he said thickly, sitting upright.

Lea pushed the door open and stepped inside. "I woke you."

"Nine is late for me," he muttered, wiping his face with his hand. "It's way past time I was up." He saw the sunlight outside the room, slanting out into the hallway. Lea was wearing a pale green tee, jeans, and her work boots. She had a canvas apron around her waist and he could smell the scent of wood around her. "Been working out in the shop?" His ankle throbbed a little and he knew the pain pill had worn off.

"Yes, I'm choosing the different types of wood for the next two cabinet doors." She smiled, coming to the end of his large king-size bed, pulling the bedclothes up and off the frame that protected the cast on his lower leg. "Are you in pain?"

Hungrily, he absorbed her quiet demeanor, glad to see her. "Yes, but it's not killing me. Can you help me so I can lift my legs, turn, and put them on the floor?"

"Sure can."

"How long have you been up?"

"Since five a.m."

"You look rested." And she did. And beautiful in her own, natural way.

"As soon as I tucked you in last night after we got home? I took a shower and fell into my bed and slept. That must have been around nine p.m."

"I think I'm still sleeping off that drug they used in my surgery," he groused, watching her lift the frame away and set it on the footboard. Lifting his legs, he soon had his left foot on the coolness of the cedar floor. He was careful to put his pink-sock-enclosed right foot down very carefully. He wore nothing above his waist and for a split second, he thought he saw something in Lea's eyes, like a woman appreciating him. It could have been his groggy, shorting-out brain, however, and he tried not to put too much stock into it.

"Hand me my bathrobe?" he asked. "I need to get to the bathroom."

In no time, she had the blue striped robe on him. Every time her fingers brushed his flesh, a soft ache began deep within Logan. Startled by it, he said nothing. Lea brought over the pair of crutches. She knelt down and added one sheepskin moccasin to his left foot, and then he tucked the crutches beneath his armpits and slowly rose, her hand on his upper arm to steady him.

"I can manage the rest," he said.

"Sure? Because last night you needed a little steadying."

"There's only enough room in that bathroom for one person," he countered.

"Okay," she said, her hand still hovering over his upper arm, frowning, watching him.

"I'm not dizzy, and that's good news," he said, placing his weight on the crutches and taking a small step forward. "I feel stronger this morning, Lea. Seriously, I'll be okay in the bathroom by myself."

She stepped back and nodded. "I'll walk you to the door, just in case."

The bathroom was across the hallway. He was bound and determined to do this on his own. Lea had enough on her plate for the next month without babysitting him to go to the bathroom. Taking it slow but sure, he was able to do just that.

"Have you heard from Maddy yet?"

"Yes, she just called. They're moving Alvin out of intensive care and into a private room. He's improving."

"Phew," Logan whispered, "that's such good news."

"Maddy sounds so tired. I want to go to the hospital this afternoon to visit them. There's some wildflowers

I want to pick and put in a vase for Alvin. At least it will remind him of home and the nature surrounding their place while he's stuck in there."

"I should go."

"No," she countered firmly, "you stay here, Logan. You're not ready to be driving all over the county yet."

He halted and she opened the bathroom door for him. He gave her a crooked grin. "My, my, you are a feisty one this morning." He watched her cheeks grow pink, but she didn't avoid his gaze.

"I can get that way upon occasion. I'm no milquetoast, even though I appear to be one."

He grunted and swung into the bathroom. "I've never seen you like that. Can you bring me a set of clean clothes? I'm going to take a shower by myself, and then I'm going to dress myself. You shouldn't have to do this stuff."

"After I hear the shower running, I'll put a clean set on top of the wash basin counter. Okay?"

"Yes, that's fine, Lea. Thank you."

"I'll be out in the kitchen," Lea said. "If you get into trouble, call me?"

"I will," he promised. Looking down the hall, the sunshine lifted his spirits. Earlier, he'd seen one of his wranglers on a bay horse, and that lifted his spirits even more. "Day one," he told her, nudging the door to the bathroom closed with the tip of the crutch.

"Day one. Are you hungry?"

"I am. I'd like something to eat after I get showered and changed."

"Don't get too frisky too soon," she warned, worry in her tone.

"As long as I can swing around on these crutches? I'll

feel more like I'm in charge of my own life and not some hapless appendage in a wheelchair."

She smiled a little, halting at the end of the hallway that led into the living room. "What do you want to eat, Logan?"

"I usually have a big bowl of steel-cut oats, toast, and bacon for breakfast."

"While you do your thing, I'll do mine," she said.

Logan nodded and edged carefully into the large bathroom. It was really big enough for two people, but he didn't want to be an invalid, either.

The nutty scent of the steel-cut oats drifted into Logan's nostrils after he'd been seated at the table. Lea had brought him a big bowl, just as he'd asked for earlier. "Hey, what's this?" he asked, pointing to several small dishes nearby.

"I love oats, too, but my mother always added dried cranberries, a bit of brown sugar, and pecans. You have a great pantry and I think Maddy bought these items and put them in there. You sprinkle what you want on top of your oats." She smiled to herself, watching him mull over the suggestions. "My mom is always on the side of nutrition," she added. "Brown sugar is sweeter and you would use less of it than white sugar." She pointed to the bowl on the table. "Or"—she pointed to the honey jar—"this is best of all. It has B vitamins in it and is the sweetest of all, and you'll find yourself using less of it. And I see it comes from Chase Bishop's ranch."

"Yes, he's trying to diversify his forty-thousand-acre ranch, wants more environmental things in it. He just hired a beekeeper a year ago and this is the first honey from that business he's trying to get off the ground." He reached for the honey.

"That's great. I really like Chase. He reminds me some-what of you. Maddy was saying that he's got plans this year to hire a master gardener. He wants to put in about a hundred acres of certain vegetables and then sell them locally and to regional grocery stores, if it takes off."

"Hmmmm, Maddy is plotting against me," he mumbled, eyeing the possibilities.

"Maddy and I are pretty much on the same page. You mean to tell me she never gave you options to go with your oats?" Lea teased.

"Oh," he muttered, "maybe a long time ago . . . years ago . . ."

"And you turned all these better choices down for white sugar?" She swept her hand across them before she sat down opposite him with her own bowl of oats. Not wait-ing, she took some cranberries and pecans and sprinkled them on her oats, and then drizzled some honey on top of the concoction. She could feel him watching her. She stirred all of it up.

"Here, take a taste." She picked up his large spoon and took a dollop from her bowl, handing it back to him. "Quit looking at this like it's going to poison you or some-thing, Logan." She squelched a laugh over his puzzled expression.

"I guess I'm pretty plain and set in my ways, in com-parison to you ladies," he admitted, taking the spoon and placing it in his mouth.

Logan had a wonderfully shaped mouth, no question. Lea tried to not think about how many times she'd thought about what his lips would be like against hers. All forbid-den thoughts for now. Still, it was a secret pleasure and she warmed inwardly over his tasting, crunching, and chewing the oats with the goodies in it. "Well?" she asked archly. "Do you like it?"

He swallowed. "It's different. But good." He smiled a little. "What? You think I'm one of those intractable males who never changes?" Picking up the spoon from the cranberries, he dumped some into his bowl. He did the same with the pecans and poured a couple of teaspoons of honey over it.

Chuckling, she added a bit of half-and-half, maybe three tablespoons, to her own bowl, stirring it into the mixture. "You kinda come across like that, Logan. I'm sure I'm not telling you anything you don't know or that Maddy probably hasn't scolded you about over the years."

He had the good grace to blush as he finished stirring up his oats. "Maddy and my mother, who is a health food nut, are on your side," he informed her lightly. "She's a nutrition nut like you."

"Probably why you've grown into such a big, tall dude, huh?"

Chuckling with her, Logan gave her an amused glance as he began to hungrily eat his breakfast. "I just need convincing from time to time. Did Maddy tell you at the hospital to spring these things on me with my morning oatmeal?"

"No. I did it all on my own recognizance."

"Are you gonna tell her?"

"Why? Because if she comes back, you're afraid she'll insist you put these on your oatmeal?"

"Well," he said between bites, "I was wondering about that. She'll probably crow when she hears that you bush-whacked me."

"I did no such thing!"

It was his turn to laugh deeply.

Feeling her face turn red hot, Lea shot back, "Maybe you need to be blindsided from time to time for your own good?"

"Is that what Maddy told you?"

"She has never spoken an ill word about you to me, Logan. No, this is me talking to you. I don't use other people's words to make a point."

"Well said," he praised. Raising his brows, he said, "Maybe breaking my ankle wasn't for naught. I kept wondering about you, the personal you, not just the great wood artist that you are."

"All you had to do was ask, for gosh sakes."

"I didn't want to make you feel uneasy, Lea. When you first came here, you were pretty closed up, and I could feel that wall between us. I didn't want to scare you off with my nosy and personal twenty questions."

"You can ask me anything you want, Logan. If I feel it's way off base, I'll let you know. Fair enough?"

He gave her a little-boy grin. "Oh, you've just opened up Pandora's box to me."

"Be careful what you ask for, pardner."

"With you? That's true. I'll try to think before I blurt out another question."

"I don't mean to make you feel walled out, Logan."

He frowned. "I think it comes from that time and event when you were a teen? Am I right?"

"Yes," she answered hesitantly. "You're good for me because you are so open in comparison. You're a good role model for me."

He added more pecans, stirring what was left of the oats in his bowl. "Well, I have a big confession to share with you."

She finished her oats, setting the bowl aside. "Want to share it over coffee? It's fresh. I just made it."

"That would be nice," he rumbled, giving her a look of thanks. "Normally, I'm the one making coffee while Maddy works in the kitchen, but with this ankle?"

"It's only for six weeks, Logan, and then you'll be back to your normal kitchen duties," she teased gently. He handed her his empty bowl and she took it and hers to the counter, rinsing them out and setting them in the dishwasher. Picking up two mugs that had an owl painted on one side of each of them, she poured the coffee. She knew Logan liked half-and-half, and there was white sugar nearby. She sat down after giving him his mug. Picking up the honey, she put some into her coffee, stirring it. He saw what she did, and followed suit. That pleased her. He was trying to make some good changes for himself.

"That's true—well, five weeks and six days now."

"You're going to count each day until then?" She grinned over at him, liking the openness in his features. The darkness of the beard only enhanced the curves of his high cheekbones and square jaw.

"Better believe it," he mused, sipping his coffee with relish. "I actually think your coffee is better than Maddy's. Did you do something to it?"

"Oops, caught red-handed. I have a particular love for Peet's coffee. There's a strong one called Major Dickason's. I need a very strong cup of coffee to wake up in the morning and this does it for me. Do you like it?"

"Yeah, it really packs a punch, but it's hearty and not bitter tasting. I don't like bitter coffee, do you?"

"Is that question one?" She giggled, seeing his brows rise, laughter shining in his eyes, his mouth following suit.

"Can be, sure."

"I hate bitter coffee. I don't like burned-tasting coffee, either. Yuk."

"So, a way to your heart is buy you a bag of Major Dickason's from the store and you'll swoon into my arms?"

Now, it was her turn to laugh uproariously. "Oh, what a wicked, devious sense of humor you have, Logan! I'd never thought that of you!"

"Well," he murmured, looking down at his leg with the cast on it, "maybe breaking my ankle will result in some good things happening between us, huh?"

Lea bit back the question, *What do you want to happen between us?* Instead, she gave him a nebulous look and murmured, "It will take a lot more than a bag of ground coffee beans, pardner."

"Thought so, but I had to find out."

"Nothing of value comes fast or cheaply."

"You know," he said, raising his eyes to the ceiling, "Maddy and my mother have both said the same thing."

"Women know. And women who value themselves is a good thing. We haven't always been that way."

"That's true," he agreed, becoming serious and sipping his coffee. "Thanks to us men and how we saw women in general throughout history."

"Not all history suppressed women like the male patriarchy has for the last ten thousand years, Logan. If you go deep into ancient history, you find women were equals and held at the same level of respect as men. They were leaders, philosophers, poets, and artists and just as good as any man."

"Well, your gift of artistry is off the charts," he said, meaning it. "I've never seen anyone work with wood, its grains, its colors, like you do. It's just sort of magical what you do, Lea."

She warmed to his sincere praise, seeing awe in his expression. "That's nice to know. Not everyone thinks of woodworking in that vein or light. But then, your family has grown so many groves of different trees, that I think the men in your family are all special and aren't like most of the men in the world today. They were visionaries."

"They listened to their wives, that's why," he told her. "I have several photographic scrapbooks from my family first coming to this area. It was the women, the wives and daughters, whose idea it was to plant these massive groves of trees. They were out on these areas of the ranch, planting them right alongside their husbands and fathers. But it was the women of the family whose vision it really was. They saw that the miners needed hardwood to build the adits and frame the tunnels, so they wouldn't cave in and kill the miners."

"But the husbands listened to their wives."

"Absolutely. I grew up in a household where women were seen to be just as capable as any man. My own mother has put so much of her own vision into the Wild Goose Ranch, that it's incredible and it's a far better place, as a result."

"I hope I get to meet your parents," she said, meaning it. "Do they come back here very often?"

"About every two years they'll come up during the summer to escape the hot, dry desert heat of Phoenix," he told her. "Next year, they'll be up here for about five months. We have a house near Barry's that they live in while they're visiting."

"I won't be here," she said sadly, shrugging. "My job will be done by this fall."

"Well," he said, looking around the place, "that might change. You just never know." He pointed to his broken ankle. "Just like me breaking a bone. That was not expected either. But I like the conversations we're having right now even if it means I'm hogtied for the next six weeks or so. Sometimes things happen and the life that we thought was going to run a certain way goes another."

"Yes," Lea agreed.

"Would you like to stay on here if I have more work for you, Lea? We've never talked about your schedule or maybe other job commitments you might have elsewhere this year."

She slid her hands around her cup and frowned, looking down at the half-gone contents in it. Lifting her chin, she held his softened gaze. There was such a swirling, comforting sense surrounding her and him at that moment. "Truth be known, Logan? This is my first real job where I'm on my own, not in my dad's workshop or helping him with all his orders from around the world." She took a deep breath and whispered, "I've hidden all my life and my parents have allowed me to do it. I don't know how or why that event when I was a teen made me such a scaredy-cat, but I became one. I didn't want to date boys because I was afraid of them, of what they might do to me. And of course, you grow up at school thinking some boy is going to come in and shoot the place up and murder a bunch of us. I just felt scared and wary all the time."

"All that's understandable," he agreed quietly. "By working with your father, you learned your craft sort of like in the Middle Ages. Back then, a young man would work as an apprentice for many years with a master craftsman before striking out on his own. You've done the same thing. Nothing wrong with it and everything right about it. Have you been taking photos and sending them to your parents so they can see the progress of your work?"

"Yes, I have. And I hadn't thought of it in that way, but you're right about being an apprentice to my dad, who is absolutely the best, a real master of woodcraft."

"You've paid your dues. So? You don't have a job lined up after mine?" he asked hopefully, not hiding the fact he wanted to keep her here on the Wild Goose.

"No . . . not really." She saw the look in his eyes, a sharpness and a glint that made her smile a little. "What do you have up your sleeve, Logan? I can see it in your eyes."

"You're worse than Maddy and my mother. You can read me a mile away," he grumped.

"You aren't exactly shy about what you'd like to see happen here."

"Okay, question two: Would you like to stay here past your first assignment and remain at the Wild Goose a while longer?"

"Sure, I'd love that. I just thought . . . well . . . once the cabinets were finished, I'd be leaving."

"Hang around. Partly because I didn't know the level of quality in your craftsmanship, but now that I do? I want you to, for sure, finish that new door that I know you have sketches of. But there's other things around here I'd like your touch on, too."

"Such as?"

"You can see that almost everything in this ranch house is a hundred years old or more." He pointed to a buffet in the living room that had once been a sideboard in another time and era. "All of them need care, some replacement of wood, or other touches that absolutely require a master craftsman's experience and expertise. They've never been repaired and I think you're the person to do just that. There are twelve rooms in this place and every one of them has wood antiques in them. The wood that they were made from is probably growing here on ranch property. You could match it up when it needs replacement or partial replacement."

"Wow," she murmured, looking around at several pieces of furniture in the living room, "that is a long-term kind of assignment, Logan. Are you sure?" and she drilled a look into his eyes.

"Dead positive. Your work is incredible, Lea. I'll never find anyone close to your quality or knowledge of wood craftsmanship. I know. I tried for years to find someone, but never did. And now that I know the quality of your work, I made up my mind a couple of weeks ago to sit down with you and discuss these other projects."

"And then, you broke your ankle."

"Yes. We'll survive this together. And it's actually given us a chance to honestly get to know one another. I'll be underfoot for six weeks. You're more or less tied here with me, under the circumstance."

"It's not an imposition. I'm sure, at some point, if Alvin continues to get better, Maddy will return to her job."

"I sure hope she does," he said, shaking his head. "I've been spoiled rotten with my mother and then Maddy, cooking and taking care of the house while I work keeping the ranch going. I was always grateful for them being there when I needed them. And now, you're filling that vacancy."

"Well," she warned, "I'm no housewife, Logan. My time, my talent, is spent on better things that I love to do. I don't mind stepping in now because it fits with my assignments here in your home. If your wood shop wasn't down that hall"—she pointed to it—"I would have second thoughts about being caretaker, housekeeper, and cook."

"I got it," he said. "And if it ever becomes too much or you don't want to do it? I'll hire outside help until Maddy can come back."

"If she can," Lea warned.

"Yes," he agreed, "none of us know the extent of harm that heart attack did to Alvin."

"For now," Lea said, "I can do all of this and still do my work. It's temporary and we both know that."

"Guaranteed, it is. But you're still a good cook." He gave her a teasing look. "I liked that stuff you found to put into my oatmeal."

She smiled. "Good thing."

"Listen, I do want to talk to you about something serious for a moment, about me . . . my earlier life."

"Sure." Lea wondered why, but remained silent because she saw Logan struggling with a lot of things, his eyes murky looking, his mouth a slash, as if to stop a barrage of emotion from overwhelming him.

"When I came back from my military obligation, I married my school sweetheart, Elizabeth, when I was twenty-two. I'd met her in the first grade and I fell in love with her, even though at six years old, I didn't understand what I was feeling toward her. We became best friends for the first ten years of school, and then when we were juniors, our friendship turned into something serious and we knew we were in love with one another. I promised to come home and marry her when I left the service, and I did. It was the happiest day of my life. She became pregnant three months later and I was on top of the world. Life seemed so perfect. I was learning the ropes of running the ranch with my father, to take over when my parents retired and left it in my hands." He stopped, scowled, and looked away, his mouth working once more. Clasping his hands, he turned and held Lea's gaze. "Elizabeth was twenty-three when she died in an auto crash. She was days away from having our daughter. The baby died, too." He wiped his jaw.

"I'm so sorry, Logan." Her voice shook with emotion. "When I stopped in and visited Poppy after arriving in Silver Creek, she told me you had lost your wife and daughter. She said you are a widower. I had asked about you because I was on my way out to meet you for the first time. I was hoping Poppy could give me some information about who you are."

"The whole town knew what had happened," he told her, his voice roughened. "I'm glad Poppy was able to give you some perspective on me. It's not something I talk about often, but I did want to share more about it with you."

Nodding, Lea was afraid to ask why. His eyes were shadowed and she could feel the grief and loss around him. What she wanted to do was get up, walk over to him, and slide her arms around his shoulders and rest her head against his, comforting him from that terrible moment in his life. "I hope I'll always deserve your trust, Logan. This is something so . . . painful . . . to talk about to anyone."

"Well, it's not a big secret to the folks in the valley," he said heavily, shrugging his shoulders as if to get rid of the sudden weight of that loss and experience. "And you deserved to hear it directly from me. There's been times, especially the first three years, when I'd fall into depression. Maddy, Alvin, Jody, and Barry were always surrounding me more often at those times, because they were here when I lost Elizabeth and my baby girl. They helped me through those times."

"And now? Does it still hit you?" she asked softly.

"This past few years it has been different. It's as if I've gone through most of the feeling of loss with them being gone. I'll never forget them, Lea. They own a piece of my heart, but now, I guess I've come to terms with it. I don't know. Maybe I'm older, thirty now, and I've matured? Whatever it is, I have a different outlook on life than before."

"Grief has its way with us all, Logan. Maybe not the kind of terrible tragedy you lived through, but other things that impact us. My parents told me a long time ago that grief is not one year long and then it suddenly goes away. I've seen with my friends and their families when something terrible happens, that grief can be three, five, or ten years long."

"I guess it just depends upon the individual," he acknowledged quietly. "The heart has its own time, I guess."

"It does," she whispered. She saw his hand was curled into a fist on the table. Reaching out, she slid her fingers across it. "Thank you for such incredible trust with your personal life, Logan. I didn't expect this of you."

He turned his hand over, their fingers interlacing. "Something's happened to me, Lea, and it has to do with you. I can't explain it. It makes no sense to me, but my heart is open to you, and it was from the moment I spotted you in that wreck of your truck at the entrance to my ranch." He searched her eyes. "I just needed to let you know. I don't expect anything from you and this certainly is not me chasing you. I won't make the move on whatever it is that's happening to me . . . maybe to us. More than anything, I want your trust in me. I want you to know that whatever is going on between us, because I saw it before I went into surgery, that it's good, clean, wonderful, and just amazing to me. I need to know if you feel the same way or if it's just me. And if it is just me, I promise not to ever burden you with a talk like this again. I respect your artistry and what beauty you're bringing to this ranch. I do want you to stay and finish your work."

Her fingers curled deeper into his. "I think I told you earlier that it's mutual, Logan. There's a part of me that accepts this relationship that seems to be blossoming between us, without any fear. But another part of me, the scared woman, is frightened."

"I could feel that," he admitted. "And I don't know how to fix that."

She gave him a sad smile, liking the monitored strength of his callused fingers around hers. "I need to learn how to heal my own wounds. There's no one outside myself that can do it for me. I can tell you that since coming here, I've felt safe. And the only other place I did was at my parents' home. *You* make me feel safe, if that means something to you. It's not that you're overprotective of me or anything like that. It's something else, something beautiful and full of possibilities. I just have to jump over my own inner-fear hurdle and reach out to you and trust fully."

"I kind of felt it was something like that," he said, squeezing her fingers. "I like what we have. What we have reminds me so much of what Elizabeth and I had: a strong bond of friendship. My parents will tell you that before they ever fell in love, they were friends for a long time, too. I'm convinced the best relationships, the ones that will last over time, are made of friendship first. Friendship means that we basically like the same things, that we share a commonality of curiosity, exploration, and experiencing life with one another. I feel like that toward you, your incredibly beautiful work, and I relish the passion that you put into it."

"That's so good to hear," Lea admitted. She slowly withdrew her fingers from his. "And I'm so glad we've had this deep, searching talk. It helps me know you better, where you're at, and how you see me."

"I'd like to have more deep talks with you," he said. "Whenever you want. I'm forever mesmerized by your qualities, how you see the world, and how the world comes alive in your hands, in your vision when you work with wood. You make me hungry to know everything about you."

"And I'm no less interested in you," she said, feeling her heart explode with such joy that it nearly overwhelmed her.

Chapter Twelve

June 10

"Your break is healing just fine, Logan," Dr. Ribas said from behind her desk.

"Seven days in this cast sucks, Doc," Logan protested.

"I know, I know. You type A cowboys don't like being out of the saddle." She smiled, typing in some information on her desktop computer.

"When can I get this cast off?"

"Another five weeks."

Frowning, he slid a glance in Lea's direction. There were two chairs in front of the doctor's large, wide walnut desk. The morning sun was making the summer day beautiful, and he ached to either be driving his truck or throwing his leg over a horse. "I'm really getting tired of being stuck in the house either on a radio with my foreman, or him having to drive all the way to the house to speak to me about something."

"Sorry, Logan, but you want full use of that ankle for the rest of your life? You have to pay your dues, just like everyone else, and be patient."

SILVER CREEK FIRE 213

"You're a tough one, Doc."

"But fair," Ribas reminded him archly, finishing off her notes. "How's the pain level?"

"I'm on aspirin now. Lea took me off the heavy drugs at four days."

"Good," she praised, giving Lea a pleased look.

"So? Continued incarceration is my prescription?"

"'Fraid so, Logan."

"Can I start driving him around in the pickup so long as he's in the passenger seat?" Lea asked, giving him a quick look to see if he approved. He did, his eyes lighting up.

"So long as he doesn't start banging that leg and ankle around by accident, yes. But he can't stay in the cab too long because his circulation isn't as good as it will be after the swelling reduces. He could throw a blood clot, which is very dangerous."

"How long can I stay in the cab?" Logan wanted to know, excitement in his tone.

"Fifteen minutes at the most, and then you'll have to haul yourself out on your crutches and get that foot on the ground to increase circulation, as well as with movement. You can't keep that leg immobile for too long. Not right now."

Giving Lea an amused look, he said, "Okay, so fifteen minutes away from the main ranch area. My tether just got loosened a little bit. I feel like a man that just got out of prison."

Lea laughed and shook her head. "What you don't realize, Logan, is if you'll do as Dr. Ribas tells you, you'll be out of the cast sooner, not later."

"Smart cookie," Ribas congratulated Lea. "Why is it men are so thickheaded sometimes?"

Shrugging, Lea saw Logan grin sourly and nod in agreement. "I don't know, Dr. Ribas. Wish I did."

Placing his hands on the arms of the chair, Logan slowly stood up, leaned over to where his crutches were propped up against the desk. "I feel good, Dr. Ribas. I have fifteen minutes I didn't have before."

"Be grateful for baby steps," she warned, giving him a scowl. "And I want you on at least one aspirin a day, even though there won't be more pain. That reduces the chances of a blood clot."

Lea wrote it down in her small notebook. "Got it."

Placing the crutches beneath his arms, he said to Lea, "The fairgrounds are only five minutes away. I'd like to go over there, go to the main office and see how Jody is doing."

Smiling to herself, Lea nodded, said nothing, gathered up her purse and her canvas tote bag that held her pen and notepad.

"I have a feeling," Ribas muttered warningly, "that you're the kind that if we give you an inch, Logan, you'll take a mile."

"Not while I'm around," Lea promised. "He's been the perfect patient for the last week."

"Yes, well the antsy disease sets in about now." Ribas chuckled, shaking her head. "So, time him on that fifteen minutes, because it's very important."

"I will," Lea promised, heading for the door before Logan could get to it on his crutches.

"We need to go to the fairgrounds office," Logan said, standing. "I need to start catching up with Jody, who's spearheading this in my absence. The opening of the fair is August fifth through the tenth, this year."

"We'll go there," Lea promised.

* * *

Lea drove toward the fairgrounds from the clinic. She'd learned quickly that Logan was going to do things on his own—or else. She was relieved of having to help him dress by the third day. He'd gotten the hang of it and although awkward, he'd managed fully on his own so long as she brought him clean clothes and left them on the dresser, near his bed. And he'd also started shaving the same day, grumbling that he did not want to grow a beard. He was tough-minded and focused. It didn't hurt that he was adaptable, either, making the crutches friends instead of enemies. There were many things he tried to do to help relieve her of kitchen duty.

Maddy had come over for a visit, giving them an update on Alvin's condition. He would have to have open-heart surgery within the next six months, but the doctors wanted him to recuperate as much as possible before that. Age was a factor in his present condition and it was a plus. He was an outdoors guy, an athlete of sorts, running two to three miles every other day. The doctors couldn't wish for a better patient. Plus, Alvin did not smoke or drink alcohol. Two more pluses.

Lea had seen Maddy circumspectly looking around the place with her keen housekeeper's eyes. Luckily, Lea'd cleaned the house! As for making dinners, she wasn't the best, but Logan was pitching in, giving her recipes he knew from memory, and they were beginning a cookbook that they put on his office Apple desktop computer. Maddy also dug out a cookbook from the pantry, nearly sixty years old, belonging to his mother, and that was helpful to Lea, too. If Logan was bummed out that Maddy wouldn't return for probably nine months to a year, he didn't show it.

Instead, he asked how he could support her and Alvin during this time. That made Lea feel joyful. But she'd seen this care from Logan toward everyone, not just them. It was a pleasant surprise to see a man being thoughtful toward others, just as her father was.

"We're here," she told Logan as she eased the pickup through the front gate, which had a sentry, one of their wranglers, at the entrance.

"Good to get back to work of some kind," Logan said. "I'm not a good patient."

"No, and you never will be." Lea laughed, parking the truck in front of the office.

"Hey! Logan!" Jody called, rising from her desk behind the long, wooden counter in the fair office. "You're alive!" She laughed, walking quickly up to him, grinning and giving him a careful squeeze of hello.

"Barely," he teased. He looked around. The counter was busy with five lines of people coming in to sign up for various classes, contests, and prizes that would be handed out during the fair itself. There were five women behind the counter, doing the paperwork. "Looks like you're busy."

"Well, it's crunch time organization-wise. It might look early to get started, but most of the signing-up happens now," she agreed, reaching out and touching Lea's shoulder, telling her hello. "Want to come around the counter? I've got some chairs at the desk where you can sit down and take some stress off that foot."

"Yeah," Logan grumbled, giving Lea an amused look, "Lea's gonna time me on everything. Dr. Ribas said I could ride in the passenger side of the truck on the ranch but it couldn't be more than fifteen minutes at a time. Blood clot scare or something."

Opening the swinging counter door, Jody said, "Dr. Ribas is right. Blood clots form where circulation isn't good. And with that swelling around the surgery on your ankle, it can happen. So, stop moaning and groaning. Come on around." She gestured toward the end of the counter.

"Is everything under control?" he asked, heading for the desk that he usually occupied during the fair.

Jody pulled out one of the chairs, placing it at one corner of the desk for him. "Yes. Hank and your wranglers are getting the bleachers up in all contest areas, cleaning them off and painting them right now. Anything having to do with the classroom lectures is already done. The contests for different flowers, baked goods, sewing, quilting, jams, jellies, pies and such, are underway and we're ahead of schedule." She turned to Lea. "Here in our valley, garden veggies and flowers are ripe and the flowers at full bloom in early August. We set our fair opening based upon our climatic conditions."

"I was wondering about that. Out in Brookings, we have our fair in late July."

"Yes, and in Arizona they have a fair, mid-May, but their growing season is a lot earlier than ours is, too," she said, smiling.

Logan sat down, placing the crutches against one side of his chair. "What about livestock contest arenas?"

"Barry pulled another four wranglers off the Wild Goose this morning and they're busy making sure all are painted. They just finished putting down a nice sand mixture in the riding arena for horse events. Everything is either on schedule or about half a day ahead of it." She sat down and crossed her fingers. "That is, if everything goes as planned."

"Do you like doing this kind of work better than on the Wild Goose?" Lea asked.

Wrinkling her nose, Jody said, "It's okay for a change of pace, but I'm kinda like Logan: I like being on the move, not stuck or rope-tied to a desk." She pointed down at it and laughed, giving him a wink.

"Any security issues?" he asked.

Jody frowned and clasped her hands on the desk. "We noticed that someone has shot out four of our ten cameras that we have up in certain areas, Logan. We don't know when this happened, but I have cameras on order to replace them, and they'll be installed before the fair opens."

"That's never happened before," Logan growled.

"Want my guess? It's the frackers. The places where the cameras were knocked out are at different points around the fairgrounds. We have the ten-foot-high cyclone fences that your dad installed decades ago, around the whole outer perimeter. That's where those cameras were shot up and destroyed."

Logan looked over at Lea. "My dad wanted a secure fairgrounds so that teens couldn't drive sprint cars in there and race them on the track anytime they wanted. He worried about insurance issues, so he spent nearly a quarter of a million dollars to erect this fence."

Lea gave a low whistle. "That's a lot of money."

"It was worth it," he said, frowning. Turning, he looked at Jody. "Where, specifically, were these cameras knocked out?"

Becoming grim, she said, "At every entrance/exit point, Logan. Don't worry, on the first day when my team and I were inspecting the outer perimeter, we made notes, took photos, and called in the sheriff, as well as the insurance company. The sheriff came out, took the report, took our photos, and he also brought out his forensics unit. They dusted for fingerprints and took DNA swabs on the posts where the cameras were located, and they found some boot treads in the dirt around them. They made plaster casts of them."

"That's good. I think you're right: It's the frackers."

"Why do you think they're doing this?" Lea asked.

"Cause damage of all kinds. The fair closes at ten p.m. We have a lot of lighting around it, but if someone wanted to come in and damage, let's say, an arena where livestock is being judged? That is a big deal. All kinds of things can happen and go wrong." Logan rubbed his chin. "You said you contacted our insurance about this damage?"

"Yep, they sent out a claims agent yesterday to assess the damage. We should hear something from them shortly," Jody said. "I didn't want to tell you anything about it until now, Logan. You were recovering from the surgery and I knew I could handle the situation."

"Well, from now on, if anything else happens or looks out of place? I want you to call me right away." He pointed down at the crutches. "I may be gimpy right now, but I can get around. This burglary act concerns me."

"Sheriff Seabert is concerned, too. You'll probably get a call from him today. I guess the plaster casts on the shoe treads is a match from a prior burglary attempt out on the Wild Goose."

"Oh?" Logan's scowl deepened.

"Remember when the frackers cut our barbed-wire fencing and the cattle got out?"

"Yes."

"Dan told me one of the treads in the dirt matched the one at that fence cutting."

"We didn't have video cameras around at that time," Logan muttered, shaking his head.

"The cameras I've just purchased," Jody said, "have a second camera which is attached down below it, so if someone hits the main one, the video is stored in the second one, which is hidden behind the pole, and it keeps on videotaping. You'd have to be inside the grounds to see it, Logan."

"That's a great idea," he praised.

She grimaced. "Based on that, I put in an order to replace all the cameras everywhere on the outside fence. It cost four thousand dollars, and it's within the fair budget, so I ordered them. They will be here tomorrow, and Barry has two wranglers who will set them up for us. Under the circumstances, I don't trust the frackers won't come in and try to do some damage while the fair is going on. They are after you to sell the ranch to them, Logan, and I think this is just another way for them to make your life miserable so you'll sell and leave the area."

Logan whispered a curse under his breath, giving them both a look of apology. "That will never happen." Normally, if he cursed, it was away from everyone else. His hand clenched and then he forced himself to relax in the chair. "We need a security crew who drives around that outer fence for the duration of the fair, Jody."

She grinned. "Already done, Boss! Barry has been helping me a lot. He called several of the ranches around the valley, asking if they had wranglers who would volunteer to drive the trucks around that perimeter from dusk to dawn." She picked up a clipboard on her desk. "Here," she said, getting up, leaning across the desk and handing it to Logan. "The men and women who are volunteering their time to do this for us. They don't want pay. But they all ask if they could come into the fair for free with their families, instead."

"Of course, they can," Logan said, looking at the ten ranches, all owned by friends of his. There were plenty of volunteer wranglers to help them out. "This is nice, Jody. You've been busier than a one-armed paper-hanger. You know that?" He grinned tightly, giving her a look of admiration.

"Just part of this job. Remember? The last five years you've been running this fair, I've always been your assistant. I know where all the bodies are buried." She giggled.

Logan laughed and nodded. "That you do, Jody." He handed the clipboard to Lea. "If you want to see how well the people of this valley work together to support one another? Look at this list of ranches."

Taking the clipboard, Lea recognized the names of six out of the ten ranches. She didn't know them personally, but she knew how tight the people of this valley were now, as never before. "I think this is incredibly generous of them to all volunteer to help you out like this. The sheriff's department doesn't have that kind of person power to pull it off."

"Which is why the ranchers stick like glue to one another," Logan said. "And a number of the wranglers are part-time deputies with the sheriff's department, which is even better."

"Maybe another way to thank them would be for you to hold one of your world famous summer barbecues sometime this early fall?" Lea asked him, handing the clipboard to Jody.

"Wow! That's a great idea, Lea!" Jody beamed at her.

"What about it, Logan? Are you up for that? Sometime after your ankle is healed? That would be so much fun! And the kids just love swimming in your small lake. Early September is warm and the water will be just right. That would be a really fun day for everyone."

"I like the idea," he told them. "Maybe Labor Day in September, when it's the hottest. The local kids do enjoy coming to swim in the lake."

Rubbing her hands together, Jody said, "This is a wonderful idea! I'll let the ranches know, get their feedback on it, and I'm sure they'll be up for it. This valley loves celebrations of any kind."

"Maybe hold a September barn dance as well?" Logan wondered out loud.

"Ohhhhh," Jody sighed wistfully. "I love barn dances! Everyone in the valley does, too."

Logan said to Lea, "During the summer, all the ranches get together and put money in a pot to hire a band. Normally, three or four of the ranches in a given year, open up their barns for a dance. We've already got four planned, and this would be the fifth one."

"The people of the valley will love it!" Jody said. "A huge barbecue, children swimming in the lake, and dancing in the barn is always a good time out for everyone."

Lea saw the pleasure come to Logan's eyes over Jody's unvarnished enthusiasm, and she smiled. She liked that not only did he think of others, he looked for ways to compensate in a way that also rewarded everyone's volunteering efforts. What was there not to like about Logan? Every day, there was something new she was discovering about him. Didn't the guy have warts like the rest of them did? She was sure he did. Otherwise, he was like the dream cowboy for her, and that still scared her, although not half as much as before. Maybe she was getting used to having Logan in her life in many different ways. Was this what her parents had in their marriage? That seamless ability to be like water moving around the rocks or challenges in their lives? It was sure beginning to look like that.

"Catch me up on anything else, Jody? I need to get back to the ranch and take a rest, although I hate admitting that to you."

Snorting, Jody said, "That's normal, Logan. You're only a week out after a huge trauma, a broken bone and then surgery. Of course, you're going to get tired a lot quicker. Shock is the number-one killer of people, and very few know that. You're still wearing off that shock around your stellar event," she said, gently teasing him. "I know you think you're invincible, but no one is." Shaking a finger in his direction, she said, "Go home. From now on, anything that comes up that you should know about, I'll call you or text you. Fair enough?"

"Music to my ears," he said, picking up his crutches. "Thank you."

June 17

"The swelling has gone down quite a bit," Dr. Ribas told Logan on their two-week checkup. "Are you able to get around more comfortably on the crutches?"

Logan gave Lea an amused look and then turned to the doctor. "She's got a fifteen-minute stopwatch she uses on me when I ask her to take me out to the fields by truck."

The morning sun at nine a.m. was leaking through the stained-glass window behind the doctor's desk. It featured a beautiful pink lotus floating on water, something very serene-looking to him. He wondered if Dr. Ribas had chosen that particular stained-glass art for the reason that it would be soothing or calming to the patients she took care of. He thought she might have.

Dr. Ribas said, "You need that kind of watching over, Logan."

"But my ankle is fine," he said. "You had to change my removable cast. The swelling has gone way down."

"Your bones are just starting to knit in week two," she warned him. "Size of the cast doesn't matter. Keep using your crutches."

"Is he allowed more than fifteen minutes in the truck?" Lea asked.

Leaning back in her black leather chair, Ribas said, "Half an hour. There, does that satisfy you, Logan?"

"Sure, that sounds really good, Doc. Is it because the swelling has gone down?"

"Yes, because that means better circulation flow through that area now and less chance of a blood clot. I still want you on one aspirin a day for the next week, however."

He perked up. "When do I start my exercises?"

"Not until the bones have fully knitted together," she warned. "Minimum of six weeks, and usually eight or ten weeks. Just depends upon the individual and their body's healing schedule."

Grunting, Logan sat back. "Can I trade my crutches in at some point for a cane or something else?"

"Maybe, we'll have to wait and see. Just depends upon your body."

"But, I'm young, in great shape and good-looking. Doesn't that account for something?"

Both women burst out laughing, trading a look women knew all too well.

"No," Ribas deadpanned, "to all the above."

"Shucks," he muttered. And then he gave her a silly grin. "I had to try."

"Men are very trying," Ribas shot back good-naturedly.

"Glad I'm not standing between the two of you," Lea laughed. "This is getting to be lots of fun standing on the sidelines watching these battles."

Ribas rolled her eyes. "I have patients just like Logan. They're all male. And I don't give them an inch, because, frankly, they'll take a mile in a heartbeat if you don't rope and hogtie them first."

"Guilty as charged," Logan admitted drily. "Okay, I'll be a good boy for next week, Doc."

"Use your crutches. Continue to keep the weight off that leg."

He rose after scooping up his crutches. "Yes, ma'am."

"Do you deliberately bait poor Dr. Ribas on purpose?" Lea asked as they drove out of the clinic's parking lot.

"Oh," Logan said, slanting her an amused look, "probably so."

"Why do you do it?"

"Because she enjoys our repartee as much as I do, I suspect."

"I think you're right." She looked out the window of the truck and then turned to head back toward the Wild Goose Ranch.

"But I like what we're discovering with one another, too," he murmured, holding her gaze momentarily.

"I've not been available very much," she apologized. "I'm at a critical point with those two cabinet doors."

"I know you are, and that's fine. I like being able to pop in and watch you work."

"That has to be boring," she said, chuckling.

"Not really." He settled back, enjoying the early morning of the day that stretched in front of them. "The way a person works? It tells you a lot about them. Have you ever thought of that, Lea?"

"No . . . not really. I'm finding you're a lot more observant about people than I am."

"Surviving Afghanistan demands that of a person, Lea. You learn to watch the little things, things that give someone away, and whether they can be trusted or not."

"You can trust me, Logan. But I think you know that by now."

"I do. I like the way you work. You're organized and you're disciplined. Not everyone in life is. I especially like to watch you with the boxes of different varieties of wood, how you'll pick up a piece, feel it, run your fingers over it. I know you're looking for just the right piece, but there seems to be more going on than that."

"Oh, there is," she said, giving him an enigmatic look.

"Tell me about it?"

Shrugging, she said, "Not much to tell, really. My dad, when I started showing an interest in wood carving, would take me out in the field with him when he was looking for a particular piece of wood. I'd watch him touch the trunk of a tree, he'd close his eyes and I would wait. Then, afterward, he'd walk slowly around, beneath the tree, looking at fallen branches, big and small. One by one, he would pick a piece up, hold it, and then either choose it or set it back where it had been."

"You do the same thing." He gave her a searching look. "What is going on?"

"Funny. I asked my dad the same thing: *What are you*

*doing? Why do you hold them and run your fingers lightly
over them?* And promise you won't laugh."

"Me? No, I wouldn't laugh."

She waved her hand for a moment and then rested it on
the steering wheel once more. "It's about energy. How a
piece of wood feels to me. My dad explained how alive
everything is, and that includes rocks, twigs, blades of
grass, or a flower. Mother Earth is alive. My dad sees all
of life as her children, including humans, of course. I
guess I inherited his talent or whatever you want to call it,
for picking up energy."

"How does that feel? Is it like a shock?" he wondered.

"Not a shock. It's fainter than that. More like a subtle
tingling sensation."

"Fascinating. And does every type of tree limb have the
same feeling to you?"

"No. My dad would feel a branch and as he did, he told
me he was feeling for any cracks or weakness in it. He
said he could tell the different frequency of energy in the
wood, and if it was cracked or weakened in a particular
spot, the sensation was different. I guess you could say, he
could 'read' the wood."

"And you can do the same thing?"

"Yes." She smiled a little. "My mother says I inherited
my dad's gift of what the Irish call the Sight, only he could
'see' into wood. When I lightly run my fingertips over the
surface of a piece of wood, I'm feeling that sensation of
conflicting tingling. Where it's different, it means there is
a crack in that area. Or, there's a weakness to the limb."

"That's rather amazing," he murmured, giving her a look
of respect.

"I've never talked to anyone about it before," she

confessed, "because I didn't want to be seen as strange or odd."

Nodding, he shifted his foot a bit on the floorboard. "Do you have that feeling when you touch, say, a horse? Or pet a dog?"

"No. It's really weird, Logan. And my father doesn't, either. I guess it's the gift of the trees speaking to us. I don't have any other explanation. It's certainly not scientific or logical."

"Did wood sculpture run in your family?"

"Yes, through my father's side. Wood, at one time, was plentiful in Ireland, but then, as the trees were cut down for firewood, the island was deforested over thousands of years. Later, in the seventeenth century, the Irish discovered that coal could be used to keep a hut warm and to cook with it, instead. I remember my dad telling me that only one percent of the native woodland is left on the island today. And that is sad."

"Back in that day, furniture was made from trees on the land," Logan said. "On top of that, Ireland is an island. They couldn't go elsewhere to get wood or coal."

"Right you are. Today, Ireland gets its coal from Colombia. There are no longer any mines on the island itself. The coal veins were all used up and are gone."

"I think my great-great-grandparents realized that using wood to burn for heat and cooking would eventually deplete our area here," he said, gesturing out the window. "And that's another reason why they planted seedlings and created these huge groves that would restore trees to our area."

She gave him a quick look, keeping her focus on driving. "Don't you find it rather mystical that we've met and both our families, in some sense, have trees and wood in common?"

"Hmmm," he murmured, "no, I hadn't, but you're right. Is that a good sign?" He gave her a grin along with a teasing look.

She laughed. "Maybe it is. Who knows?"

Logan looked out the window, appreciating the green, rolling pastures bracketed with fencing. "It was wood that brought us together," he said, thinking more deeply. "Maybe wood is magical?"

The corners of her mouth curved slightly. "Wood has always been magical to me, Logan. When I'm working in your shop, I just sort of lose myself to the process, to the different scents of the wood, the different texture each one has. Never mind the energy sensations I pick up from it."

"I wondered about that, because you sometimes have two or three pieces of wood and you study them. One morning, I almost asked you if you were talking to them." He gave her a silly look.

"Well, there are worse things than talking with a tree." She laughed. "I don't know. I've never looked at or questioned how I work the way I do. Sometimes it's the color of the piece, whether it's the correct color, tone, or shade to go next to the one I've chosen on the door of the cabinet. I'm not communicating with them telepathically, if that's what you're asking. I'm just weighing in my mind the right color, right texture. My father does talk to the tree's spirit, and he's always told me that."

"Poppy doesn't make any bones about talking to trees, you know?"

"Really. I didn't know that."

"People think she's magical. Children love to be around her."

"Remember? I told you that she read my tarot cards for me," Lea admitted slowly. She slowed the truck, getting ready to make that turn, her gaze flicking to the rearview mirror. There was no one behind her. She wondered if she'd ever not look to see if a pickup was barreling down upon her as it had the day she'd arrived.

"I do remember."

"I know she read the tarot cards for you," Lea told him. Up ahead, she could see several wranglers on horses, moving a large group of cows and calves to another, richer pasture.

"As a matter of fact, she did," he said.

"Did you ask her to do it? Or did she volunteer?"

"She volunteered to do it because I was in there one morning for one of her donuts, and things were slow at the restaurant."

"How long ago?"

"About a month before you arrived." He grinned. "Okay, I'll tell all. I can see you're dying to ask me what she said. Poppy told me a woman of the trees was going to come to the ranch."

Her mouth about dropped open. "No! Seriously?" She turned into the driveway, parking the truck.

"Yes," he said, watching her reaction, "she did."

"Am I that woman?"

"The woman of the trees? Yes, I think so," he murmured, pushing the door open and picking up his crutches from where they leaned against the console, resting them on the gravel below.

"Well," Lea pressed eagerly, "what else did she say?"

Her heart pounded a little harder in her chest. Poppy's card-reading had been accurate so far for her, so she was dying to know what Logan's card-reading was all about.

"Oh, no," he said, sliding carefully out of the cab, "I can't tell you the rest."

Flustered, she climbed out. Coming around the front of the truck, she saw him swinging on his crutches toward the fence gate. She hurried past him and got there in time to open it for him. "Well," she said, squinting against the sunlight, "why can't you tell me?"

He grinned and shook his head. "Maybe someday. Okay?"

Giving him a dark look, she stood aside. "Well, was it good or bad?"

"Oh," he said lightly, "all good . . ."

Whatever that meant! "You are exasperating, Logan Anderson!"

His laughter was deep, and Lea grinned belatedly, locking the gate. He was a man with many secrets!

Chapter Thirteen

June 30

Logan stood back, amazed at the beauty of the cabinets that Lea had installed earlier. It was ten a.m., the last day of June. She'd made him promise to stay in his office down the hall earlier in the morning, until the workman had come and put them into position. She stood off to one side, looking worried, as if he wouldn't like the loving artistry she'd given each set of doors.

"They are incredible," he said, turning, holding her wary gaze. The ranch house had been built so that the front door faced east and the bedrooms were opposite, in the west. The morning light poured in through the L-shaped bank of windows that followed the outline of the massive kitchen, illuminating them until they were radiant.

"You really like them?"

"Who wouldn't?" he asked, moving forward on his crutches. It had been nearly four weeks now, and he could hardly wait to see Dr. Ribas tomorrow, the first day of July, to examine his healing ankle. Halting at the counter, he set the crutches to one side, staring up at the cabinets, lifting his hand, trailing his fingers along the colorful seams. "You make them come alive," he rasped, emotion in his voice, turning his head, smiling at her. "Unbelievable, Lea. How did you make them so lifelike?"

She slowly approached, her arms falling to her sides. "It's just a matter of finding the right grain, the right color."

"And a lot of patience. You've spent untold hours out in those groves hunting for just one piece to set into one of these dioramas."

Nodding, she whispered, "When I work with wood? I'm so in-the-moment with the energy of that living being." She looked up. "Are you giving me that woo-woo look, Logan?"

"Well," he said lightly, "my mother, who read me many, many fairy tales, always told me that there were humans who were really fairies in disguise, that they were special and supersensitive to the world around them." He liked the gleam coming to her eyes.

Since breaking his ankle, he could have said that it was the best thing that had ever happened to him. Why? Because Lea was with him 24/7, and he liked it a lot. Logan wasn't fessing up to it—yet. But it was coming. He'd seen Lea, slowly but surely, shedding that armor she wore around herself, that feeling that she was always holding him at arm's length. *Not anymore.* How he looked forward to each night with her. Since Dr. Ribas had given him an hour to ride around in the truck, in thirty minutes or so he could be anywhere on the ranch, should he be needed. He tried to stay out from underfoot where Lea was concerned. She was an artist. She needed long stretches of time alone, undistracted, off into her own beautiful world of creativity. He wanted to give that to her, not bending to his own selfish need of her in his life.

Leaning her hips against the counter, she said wryly, "I don't know about being special, but I am supersensitive to a lot of things."

"In my book? Fairies rock. Real or not." The fact that her lips rose an inch told him she thought that was a funny statement. Logan wanted to make her laugh. So much of the serious demeanor that Lea had come to the ranch with, had dissolved and was gone. He liked her even more now than before, realizing that she was honestly becoming relaxed on the ranch, especially around him. He gloried in those stolen moments when she'd reach out and touch his arm or hand. He lived for her grazing touch.

"Oh," Lea murmured, "I think fairies are very real. We call them the *little people*, and they're magical."

"Well, we share that in common, then. My mother, who is a professional genealogist, traced our family roots clear back to the Scottish Highlands in the fourteen hundreds. My relatives raised Scottish cattle in the Highlands and still do to this day. We have all kinds of fairy tales about the *wee folk*, as we called them. For instance, we believe that having a good relationship with the fairy folk will yield us a good crop. And a good crop meant the cattle were not starving, nor were my relatives."

"Did your relatives bring that belief over here to the U.S. with them?" Lea wondered.

"Absolutely. That's in part why we have these huge groves of different types of trees. They have huge groves of trees where they live to this day."

"Do you see them, Logan? The fairies?"

"No . . . I don't see them, but I believe they are real. When my parents and I traveled to Scotland to meet the rest of our family, who had remained behind to raise the cattle, they would always take us out on the Highlands. They were dead serious about how to get along in a good way with the fairy folk. There were places they took us, for example, where we saw a white flowering heather bush that was adorned with ribbons holding small hand-knit or crocheted pouches filled with food by the women of our family. They explained to us that this particular area was an entrance/exit point between humans and the fairy folk. My relatives would always come up to this area, put shiny new colorful ribbons on that bush, sit down and meditate, although they didn't call it that, and ask the fairy folk to be kind to their crop during the coming year. They asked for good rain, but not too much rain. They asked for a good crop so they could feed the animals and humans."

"I thought all heather was purple?"

"No, that's a different kind. The white variety has grown in Scotland forever. Later, the purple and pink were introduced. One of the important things heather does in the Highlands where my relatives raise the cattle, is that it is found in poor, acid soils. It's akin to peat soil. No grass will grow in that, but the heather does. Down in the valley where my kin have their cattle farm, they have enriched the soil over hundreds of years with compost from the cattle, so grass grows thickly, richly and very well there."

"I'm glad you keep in contact with your relations from Scotland. That's wonderful."

"Next year my parents are going for another visit, and they've asked me to come along. It will be during March, so I can leave the ranch to travel with them. Maybe, if you're around, you might like to come with us?"

"I've done very little traveling," Lea mused. "And

I've always wanted to visit our family roots in Ireland. Scotland isn't that far away."

"As a matter of fact, my mother found out that three hundred or so years ago there was a huge migration of Scottish families to Ireland. I'm wondering if you don't have some Scot blood in you, after all?"

She raised her brows. "I don't know. My dad has some of our genealogy, but he's not got all of it. Next time I'm on the phone with him, I'll ask him."

"Wouldn't it be interesting if you had Scot blood in you, after all?" He grinned.

She laughed. "Like draws like?"

"Well," he said, giving her a sly look, "stranger things have happened. I mean, look at you taking after your dad's woodworking talents and love of wood." He lifted his hand. "And look at my family's love of trees and wood. Don't you find that kind of fascinating? That intersection that we share between us?"

"That is something to ponder," she agreed, curious.

"We have a lot of overlap," he teased. "I like discovering what they are."

"I'm kind of interested in it, myself," Lea admitted. She saw him beam and it made her feel good.

"I like hearing that. Let's keep it up, shall we?"

"In each grove that I've gone to on your property, I've found one tree that has a lot of ribbons hanging all over the lowest branches. I meant to ask you about that, but I forgot. Is this your way of working with the fairy folk on this land, bringing your family's belief in them from Scotland?"

"My relatives started that ceremony when they first came here to the U.S. and planted these massive groves of trees. In each one, as you've seen, there is one tree that is always hung with ribbons, or other items, to honor the fairy folk here, on this continent."

"Fairies live everywhere?"

He shrugged. "I think so. It's just that in Ireland and Scotland, they are seen to be very, very real and a part of everyday lives. They are like an invisible, but still very powerful and necessary part of our relationship with the land."

"And how many people do you admit this to?"

He chuckled. "Very, very few." He pulled his crutches over, settling them beneath his armpits. "They'd think we were crazy, I suppose."

"I think it's wonderful. I grew up believing that we see only half the world with our two eyes. That there's another half, an invisible one that we can connect with intuitively, through our hearts, and have a relationship with it."

"Ah, but you have to believe in fairy folk to do that. Most people here on this continent don't believe in them, at all."

She walked slowly with him toward the living room. "To their detriment. I would rather be a part of the whole web of life, not half of it."

"My mother would say that you are 'awake' and not 'asleep' with that belief," he murmured, pleased.

"Would you mind if I spent some time in the groves with your decorated trees? Would they mind if I sat and meditated with them from time to time?"

He smiled, heading for his office down the hall. "Ask the tree. You said your dad talks to trees, but you can't?"

"Yes, he says it's telepathy between him and them. All I do is I feel them. It's hard to explain. When I go into one of your groves looking for a particular piece of wood, I always mentally ask the tree if I may have that piece of branch that fell. I ask permission, but that's something my dad taught me to do when I was very young."

"And what happens when you do that, Lea?"

She halted and opened the door to his office for him. "Well, I always get a warm, fuzzy feeling suddenly surrounding me. And when I get that wonderful feeling, I know the tree is giving its permission for me to pick up that branch. It's not mental telepathy, but I believe it is the tree letting me know that I can have it."

"Maybe we're more alike than we ever knew," he murmured, holding her gaze.

"It's beginning to look that way more and more," she answered, a bit of wonder in her tone.

He turned just before entering his office. "Even across the living room, your beautiful work is so powerful and moving to look at and appreciate."

"Thanks," Lea said, pressing her hand against her heart. "That truly makes me feel good in ways you can't possibly know."

"And I'll get to look at them for the rest of my life. That's not a bad thing, that's a good thing."

"I'm going to work on the front door commission now that my cabinet art is finished," she said. "I'll be out in the wood shop, finalizing some drawings that will be the actual size on the door, so you can see it in about a week and let me know if that's what you want."

"I can hardly wait," he said.

"Call me if you need me?" They had set up an intercom phone system from the office he'd cobbled together in his makeshift bedroom. The newly installed line went to the wood shop where she worked.

"Roger that," he said. "I'm going to take photos of the

finished cabinets after lunch and send them to my parents. They are going to be blown away by what you've done for us. I know they will love them as much as I do." He wanted to say, *I'm falling in love with you, Lea,* but bit back the admission. Every day, it was getting tougher for him to remain quiet about how he really felt toward her. And she was giving all the indications that she liked him as much as he liked her. Was it love? Was it too early to talk to her about his feelings? What would she say? Do? Logan was unsure, trying to tame his need to share that with her. He watched her walk away, her shoulders back, her proud carriage, and he smiled, turned, and hobbled into his office.

July 1

Lea made her way to the oldest oak tree in the grove. It was a venerable oak, which split into three main branches, reminding her of a triangle between the thick, massive main branches above her. It was the lower branches, however, that were adorned with many, many ribbons, knitted pouches, necklaces, and pieces of paper wrapped in ribbon and then wrapped around a branch. She knew from her parents' descriptions of a *ribbon tree* or *fairy tree,* that this was a place women and men and children came to ask a favor of the fairy folk. Not all requests were one-sided. Some had notes that Lea would bet were thank-yous to the fairy folk for helping them or answering their need. Others, she was sure, were just heart-to-heart thank-yous for them being around and a part of a greater web of life.

There were hundreds of them as she walked the full circumference of the healthy oak that towered over sixty feet tall. It was nearly noon, and the sunlight drifted through the quiet of the grove. She heard a blue jay squawking somewhere far away, warning those who lived in the grove to be alert, that a trespasser was nearby.

Pulling off her knapsack, she opened it up. In a plastic bag were two ribbons, one gold and one silver. As she straightened, the silver one in her fingers, she found a spot to wrap it gently around a branch. As she did so, she thanked the fairy folk for being in this grove and tending it with their love and energy. Leaning over, she picked up the gold metallic ribbon. Finding another spot on the limb, she placed it there, adding a bow, thinking about Logan, and asking the fairy folk to support him during his healing.

She took out her cell phone and took a number of pictures from different angles. The tree felt light and joyous to her. Why not? It was being adorned, acknowledged as a thread in the life that surrounded her. She would feel good about it, too. As she walked the perimeter of the mighty tree that towered above all the rest in the grove, Lea smiled softly. She, too, was happy here. And she knew that Logan was the main person who made her feel that way. Silver Creek and the surrounding valley made her feel at home. Welcoming. Wanting her to stay here.

As she took more photos, sometimes standing far enough away to shoot the entire tree, some much closer, Lea admitted quietly to herself that she'd like to spend the rest of her life here. She'd loved the forests surrounding Brookings, taking advantage of long and short hikes among the pines. But here? Depending upon her mood, she had groves of different types of trees, including the pines, to walk among, to dream within, and that was so enriching to her soul. It was like going from one dimension to another; each very unique from the other. There were different colors to the leaves, different shapes, different ways the trunks and limbs of the trees grew. The way a leaf was shaped, how large or small, the bark's color, how rugged or smooth it felt beneath her exploring hand, fed her soul.

As she walked and took the photos, she thought deeply about her most recent conversation with Logan. He, like herself, was letting down his own private shield, allowing her to see who he really was. The discovery of sharing fairy folk this morning was exhilarating to her because she had always felt trees and it always made her feel so happy. Being in trees was salve to her soul. And so it was with Logan, too.

That was a wonderful discovery, one that sent her creative imagination into overdrive. She pictured little children running amongst these mighty brethren who tolerated and loved them. How much fun to race around, to play tag, or other games! It brought to life a new level of need within her. Suddenly, her life was no longer like before, when she lived with her parents in Brookings. Being out in the world, walking in it, no longer avoiding it, brought new and positive awareness to Lea. The world wasn't the ogre she thought it was. The world, depending upon the circumstances, could be filled to the brim with life, joy, pleasure, smiles and laughter, too.

She came to the trunk of the oak, asking the spirit if she could sit and lean her back against its trunk. Would it mind? The sweet answer that came was like an invisible hand wrapping gently around her heart, drawing her toward the trunk. Putting her cell phone away in her pocket, she sat down and nestled between two huge roots that had grown deeply into the Earth. Leaning back, she whispered her thank-you to the tree for allowing her to sit with it. Closing her eyes, her creativity sprang to life as she re-ran the photos she'd taken of the tree. It was almost a Christmas tree, but it was summer, not winter. And just as beautiful, and perhaps even more poignant, with each visitor tying a ribbon, asking a favor, or thanking the fairy folk for their kindness and support.

The day was perfect.

August 5

Logan felt deep pride as the county fair was opened up earlier in the morning, when it was cooler. An excited crowd of over a thousand people, adults and children anxious to get inside, charged into the huge area. At one end was a carnival, which the children made a beeline for. Older adults were going to the classes, or looking to see if their plant or goods had won a prize in one of the large, air-conditioned buildings. Through it all, Lea had been an invaluable helper.

He was now rid of his removable cast. A strong Ace-type bandage had taken its place around the knitted bone. And it wasn't visible beneath his pant leg. The only good thing to come out of this was that he and Lea had the ranch house to themselves, and daily, they were growing closer and closer.

Logan could smell cotton candy in the air, barbecue being grilled, and the sweet smell of funnel cakes being baked. His foreman, Barry, had suggested he take a golf cart and use it to get around, but Logan nixed the idea. Over at the livestock arenas there were plenty of horses, and 4-H children with their cows, sheep, or goats who were going into their particular class to be judged. The music from the carnival, the merry-go-round, added to the sounds he enjoyed.

"Ready?" Lea asked. She was leading two horses from the ranch, saddled, over to where he stood off to one side of the main traffic area.

He nodded and reached out, taking the reins to his horse. "Yes. You?"

Giving him a grin, she mounted up. "I would much rather have four legs under me than four wheels on a golf cart. How about you?"

Laughing, he slid his left boot into the stirrup and easily mounted. Dr. Ribas had approved of him riding a horse around. Luckily he was able to wear a size larger sneaker to fit over the bandage, since the swelling had disappeared and his foot size had returned to normal. His cowboy boot was too narrow and his doctor wanted to wait a bit longer, so he now had two different-size shoes on his feet. Logan never wanted to break another bone in his body after this experience. It had really crippled him and forced him to slow down.

"I'm more than ready." It had been a good idea to use the horses in the fair rather than a vehicle. Everyone was used to having horses around in this county, no question. Plus, Logan didn't want to stick out like a sore thumb. Lea looked beautiful to him in her pale pink cowgirl shirt, her white straw Stetson that he'd bought for her when Dr. Ribas had given him permission to start riding again. Her hair was short, the sunlight striking the coppery strands around her ears. The Levi's fit her nicely, not too tight or too loose, but definitely showing off her long, streamlined form. The red bandanna around her throat made her look like she'd always been a cowgirl.

"Let's mosey on down the main street here," he said, keeping his horse off to the side, flowing with the traffic. Children, especially younger ones, darted around like happy puppies frolicking after being boxed up for too long without exercise. Ranch horses were especially good around people—patient, not tending to spook or jump if someone bumped into them. A lot of horses unused to this type of crowded activity might sidle, or worse, kick out and harm someone in the process. He ran his hand down the neck of his buckskin horse, the animal's ears twitching, showing him that he liked the attention.

"Gosh," Lea said, riding at his side, her right leg occasionally brushing against his left one, "this is one busy fair! It's so alive."

"You have them in Brookings, don't you?"

"Oh, yes. I entered my woodwork for years."

"Bet you won blue ribbons."

"A few," she admitted.

"You're always humble, Lea."

She rested her hand on the saddle horn, reins between her fingers. "Just me, I guess."

"So?" he prodded, giving her a teasing look as they rode slowly with the traffic past the many stalls and trucks. "What have you so diligently been working on and not letting me see in the wood shop?"

Chuckling, she said, "A surprise . . . well, of sorts."

"Ever since you came back from the oak grove about a week ago, carrying a bunch of wood in your truck, I've seen a lot less of you."

"It is your birthday coming up on August twenty-sixth," she reminded him archly.

"Ah, so it's a birthday present for me?"

Shaking her head, Lea laughed and said, "You're like a little kid at Christmas, Logan. Really."

"Well," he said, pleased that he'd discovered what she was secretly working on, "I do like gifts. I drove my parents crazy at Christmastime. I had this way of waiting until they were out of the house, then I'd go and secretly ease the tape off one end of the present, and slowly open it so I could see what it might be, without tearing any Christmas wrap."

"Ohhhh, you are *really* sneaky!" Lea hooted. "The more I hear about you growing up, Logan, the more I can see why your mother moved to Phoenix to retire."

They laughed together, approaching the fenced area where people stood in line to buy tickets for their favorite carnival rides. Giving her a merry look, he grumped, "Hey, they never knew I did that!"

"Not to this day?"

"No, and you're not going to say anything to them. I don't want to hurt my mother's feelings. She was very proud of her package wrapping. It would hurt her to know what I'd done. It's a secret that goes to the grave with me." He gave her a grin.

"Okay"—she sighed—"cross my heart, I won't say a peep even though you're guilty as sin."

"Didn't you ever do that?" he prodded gleefully.

"Gosh, no! *Never*, Logan!"

"Weren't you curious about what was in those presents under the tree?"

"Of course, I was." Her brows knitted as she studied

him as they came to a halt near the ticket booth. "I didn't have a deviant mind like you do and decide to be a burglar and break into them to see what was there. I liked being surprised."

"You're no fun."

She tittered and lifted the hat off her hair, smoothing away some strands off her brow before settling it back on her head. "Obviously, you have a much more refined, intense kind of curiosity than I do." She shook her finger in his direction. "I'm warning you: Do *not* go to the wood shop. I will be really hurt if you try to see what gift I'm making you for your birthday, Logan. I mean it."

He had the good grace to lay his hand across his chest. "Cross my heart. I won't. It will kill me now that I know you're making me something special for my birthday, though. I'll lose sleep over it," he said, giving her what he thought was his sad puppy-dog look. It didn't work.

"Boundaries, Anderson. Put 'em up, because if I find out you sneaked in there to see, I'll be very, very hurt."

"No, I don't want to hurt you," he agreed, becoming serious, holding her blazing green eyes filled with honest indignation. Red-haired women were said to be temperamental, but that was okay in his book of life. He liked Lea's sensitivity to everything. In part, that is what made her the incredible artist that she was. "I promise," he said somberly. "I'll be tortured, but I'll not peek."

"Ohhhh, you are such a manipulator when you want to be!"

"Me?" He shifted in the saddle, always liking the creak of the leather when he did so. They had stopped in the shade, the heat of the August day building rapidly. Many people came to the fair early or in the evening after supper.

The kids usually dragged their tired parents along, wanting to go on all the rides.

"I watch you deal with your employees all the time, Logan," she said, becoming serious. "You're very skillful."

"But I'm always honest," he said, raising his index finger.

"That you are, and that is one of the many things I like about you."

"Good," he gloated. He dismounted, being careful to gently add weight to his right leg. There was some residual tenderness to his ankle, which Dr. Ribas said would happen. Over time, it would lose that sensitivity and he wouldn't even know he'd broken a bone in his leg at all. How he looked forward to that day! "I know it's only ten a.m., but would you like some cotton candy?" He pointed to the truck with the red and white striped awning over where people stood in line to get their pink cotton candy.

"No, but if you want some? Go ahead." He picked up the reins he'd pulled over his gelding's head and handed them to her. Not that his horse would go anywhere. It was ground-tied trained.

"Sure?" he asked, his smile widening.

"Very sure." She pointed to her waist where her slender cowboy belt was. "I don't want to gain weight."

"Oh . . . okay, but you were too skinny when you came here, anyway, Lea. It wouldn't hurt you to put a little more meat on your bones."

"I'm fine the way I am, Logan. Go grab your brunch dessert."

He liked her pluckiness. He liked everything about Lea. No longer was that mask in place where she hid who she really was. Since breaking his leg, they had taken a step toward each other. How symbolic. How perfect. If he'd realized from the outset that breaking his leg would cause a wonderful breakthrough? Logan would have done it sooner.

As he walked up to the truck, he noticed a Hispanic family off to one side. There were three children, probably ages four through six, and the mother cradled a newborn in her arms. Logan noticed that the father, who was behind his family, was looking through his pockets. The three children were around their mother, one hand on her long ankle-length red skirt and their small hands pointed up at the man who was making the pink cotton candy. He saw the frustration in the father's face as he came up empty for money to pay for his kids' treat.

Stepping up to the counter, Logan ordered enough for the entire family and for himself. The family was out of earshot and he turned his head, smiling at the mother and children. The husband looked depressed, speaking to them in Spanish, trying to get them to leave the vicinity of the truck. The children stubbornly stood their ground. Logan grinned at them, liking their spunk, but also understanding the humiliation of the father, who clearly showed his disappointment that he couldn't buy cotton candy for his children.

"Here you go," the man behind the counter said, handing him the first two.

"Thanks, keep making them," Logan said, taking them and walking over to where the family stood. He nodded and spoke in Spanish to the mother and father while at the same time, going down on one knee in front of the children. He spoke to them in English.

"Girls first," he told the oldest, the son. They all nodded, excitement and surprise in their small faces. He gave the two to the two girls, stood and walked back to the counter to fetch two more. The son got one, and so did the mother. She smiled gratefully up at him, telling him thank you. The last two were given to him and Logan took one over to the father.

"I want you to enjoy the fair," he told the thunderstruck man, pressing the cotton candy into his hand. "Kids, especially, love them." He tipped the brim of his hat to the mother, who had tears of gratitude in her eyes, waved at the three children who surrounded her, eating voraciously, enjoying every bite. Turning, he walked away from the truck and realized Lea was watching him with the intensity of a hawk. As he drew near, he saw her eyes were watery-looking, a softened expression coming to her face.

"Sure you don't want any?" he teased her, holding the cotton candy up in her direction.

"No, thank you, Logan. Let me hold it while you mount up?" She held out her hand.

"Thanks." He took the reins from her, looping them over the buckskin. In moments, he was back in the saddle. Lea handed it to him and he thanked her.

"We're not going inside the fair," he said, turning his gelding and heading in the direction of the livestock show arenas.

Lea came up beside him on the dirt road that led in that direction. "What you just did back there? It was so wonderful, Logan."

"The guy looked distraught," he admitted. "I wanted to do something to help him out."

She gave him a long, warm look. "You did. I was so touched by your thoughtfulness."

He avoided her gaze. "I think people should be helpful to those who don't have as much, that's all."

She watched him eat the cotton candy with gusto. "In my book? You rock."

Chapter Fourteen

August 10

Logan took a deep breath. This was *it*. Finally. He'd plotted, planned, hoped, prayed—and tasted the fear of rejection—every time he thought about doing *it*.

Standing in the kitchen at six a.m., the morning sunlight shooting through the bank of kitchen windows to the right of him, he was whipping up an omelet with anything he found in the fridge earlier. Glancing across the living room, down the hall where Lea had her bedroom, he waited impatiently for her to wake up. He needed to get this off his chest, and let her know. What would she do? What would she say?

Fear clenched his stomach and he forced in another deep breath to steady his frayed nerves. He hated not knowing. He'd lived with it since Lea had come here. At ten a.m., the fair opened for the last day. Logan knew it would be the heaviest day people-wise. Today the grand prizes were to be awarded. Many contenders had put their favorite animal, plant, quilt, jelly, or jam, into competition with everyone else in the valley. It was a day of celebration and he smiled faintly, whipping in the last of the fresh tomatoes that grew out in the large, enclosed garden. He'd found some leftover baked potato, some sharp cheddar cheese, steamed broccoli, and fried bacon. Together, they'd make a tasty morning fare for both of them.

The door to Lea's room opened and he looked up. Her short red hair was mussed and she was dressed in a knee-length cotton robe covered with bright flowers, and carried a towel, washcloth, and her favorite soap, Herbaria, as she walked across the hall to the bathroom. Logan knew better than to holler out a *good morning* to her. Lea didn't wake up easily and needed two or three cups of very strong coffee to be coherent, much less conversational. He grinned, said nothing, and set the bowl aside, reaching for some freshly baked sourdough bread he'd bought at the fair late yesterday afternoon.

His heart expanded with a quiet joy that threaded around it like soft yarn. Having Lea here, in his house, was something he looked forward to every morning. His parents had always taught him to be grateful for little and big things, and sometimes he didn't understand the depth of this simple thing called gratitude. But during the weeks since he'd busted his ankle, Logan finally understood his mother's valuing of gratitude. He was grateful Lea was in his life, as no other woman. His wife, Elizabeth, would always own a piece of his heart. Until Lea unexpectedly dropped into his life, Logan hadn't realized how lonely he'd become. He missed the kinship, the friendship, of having the right woman sharing his life, his home, and his heart. He missed having a partner, a woman of equal strength, someone he respected mightily, to share the days and nights with him.

As he dropped the sourdough bread into the toaster,

ready to be browned later after Lea emerged from her shower and got dressed, he set to making a new pot of coffee for them. Outside the window he saw several wranglers on horseback as well as two of the white employee trucks leaving for different parts of the ranch. Daybreak meant a hearty breakfast and then working hard until sunset every day. Barry, his foreman, was the best. He could easily run this ranch without Logan, for sure, and he grinned a little.

Getting busy, he pulled plates down from the cupboard, absorbing the beauty of Lea's woodworking talent. The animals on these doors breathed, so filled with life. She was an amazing, gifted person.

Half an hour later, Logan saw her emerge from her bedroom, dressed in a pair of Levi's, a pale green short-sleeved tank top, cowboy boots, with her damp hair combed into place. Now, she looked awake and he poured her coffee, handing it to her as she approached him.

"You're a godsend," she muttered, giving him a nod as she sipped the coffee.

"Gotta feed the grouchy bear after she wakes up."

Chuckling, she turned and saw that the kitchen table was set. "What time did you get up?"

"Five," he answered, bringing the heated omelet out of the skillet and dividing it on two awaiting plates.

"You've been up about that time since the fair began," she noted. "Can I help? Need an extra pair of hands?"

"Nope," he said, handing her a plate. "Just go sit down. I'll have the toast ready in a moment and then I'll join you."

She lifted the plate, inhaling the scent of the omelet. "Smells good."

"We're going to be busy today. Everything comes to a head. I figured we'd need a hefty breakfast."

She smiled. "You and your parents have really put out

and helped Silver Creek folks in general," she said, moving to the table and pulling out a chair.

Logan sat opposite her. He never used the end chairs, always feeling like it was an unspoken symbol. People in charge, parents and elders, sat in such chairs to honor who they were. He preferred to sit across from someone where it felt equal. Not one rising above another person.

"So? Are you going to tag along today? A glutton for punishment?" Because Lea had been with him every day. She didn't have to be, but made it clear she'd like to pal around with him on his various check-ins with his people who were responsible for the fair being as successful as it was. He liked her company, hoping she would come along today. Mentally, he crossed his fingers.

"I'd love to. I want to see who wins the grand championships. I enjoy seeing kids' faces light up with surprise."

"It's a long day," he warned.

Shrugging, she dug into the fragrant omelet. "I'm used to long days." She lifted her head and gave him a teasing look. "Like someone else I know."

"Guilty and caught red-handed," he said, matching her smile. "Then? Are you up to come to the dance at the close of the fair?" His stomach tightened. He stared hard at her and knew it broadcast how badly he wanted her to say yes. But he didn't care about that. He cared about Lea. He'd dreamed too often of what it would be like to hold her close, to feel her beneath his exploring hands. Her brows dipped and he could see her thinking about it. Had he pushed too hard on their slowly evolving relationship that was opening up for both of them? Chastising himself for his own impatience, he pretended to pay attention to the food on his plate; the farthest thing from his mind right now.

"Well," she began tentatively, "I don't have a dress with me, Logan. I'm sure people are going to get gussied up for this once-a-year celebration dance." She tilted her head, giving him a concerned look.

"The ladies wear whatever they want. Some come all duded up in cowboy clothes, some in pantsuits, others in Levi's. There's no one at the door being the fashion police."

Her lips drew away from her teeth. "Well, I do have one skirt and a blouse. I could wear my low heels, which I brought for special occasions. They don't look good out in a wood shop."

His heart leaped. "That sounds fine." Frankly, he couldn't care less what she wore. He wanted her close to him. He ached for that kind of human contact that only one woman, a very special woman, could share with him. And that was Lea.

"What about you? Are you going to dress up?"

"No. The dance starts at eight p.m., after the fair closes. We could come home, take a quick shower and change into some fresh clothes and go back to the dance?"

"Yes, because being in all those arenas, as nice as they are with wood shavings and all, I'm a dust ball by the end of the day." She picked up some strands of her drying hair. "And my scalp feels gritty."

"Okay, that sounds like a plan," he said, trying not to look too eager. Logan kept a tight rein on himself. "The band that we always hire plays all sorts of music. Some of it is square dancing, but there's also some nice down-home music you can slow dance to."

"I'm not great on my toes," she warned. "In fact, I can't remember the last time I went to a dance."

"That's okay, I'll be careful and try not to step on your

toes. I'm not exactly great at dancing, either." He laughed quietly. "We could help one another out on the dance floor, then, since we both have two left feet. Right?" Her lilting laughter sent an ache through him. One of sexual hunger, but Logan was clear about that line of demarcation, too. There were times in the last month when he'd catch Lea staring at him, and what he thought he saw in her eyes was a woman desiring her man. Always careful to shield his expression at times when he found himself wanting her too much, Logan wondered if she felt similarly: hiding in plain sight, never mentioning how much she meant to him, how much he wanted to hold her, kiss her, and then make delicious love with her. All these fantasies had been hovering around him, especially in his dreams, which was rough because it woke him up, and sometimes he had to quietly pad down the hall and take a cold shower at three in the morning.

"Two left feet is right," she agreed, slathering the toast with butter and then opening up a jar of apricot jam that sat between them. "That sounds good, Logan. I'm really looking forward to it."

The softness in her green eyes punched him in the heart and he felt an incredible heat shimmering through him. "Great," he said, clearing his throat. "I think we'll have a good time. Everyone is pretty happy and ready to celebrate the fair."

"Not to put a damper on things, but did you hear the latest?"

"About what?"

"Chase Bishop ran into me the other day at the fair," Lea said. "You were in one of the livestock arenas at the time and I was getting some lunch at one of the trucks. I forgot to tell you about this last night because we were so tired." She gave him an apologetic look.

"What did Chase tell you?"

"He said that someone had set fire to the farthest area of his ranch. He has a barn out in that area, and someone set fire to it."

"Yes, I heard that from one of my wranglers last evening before dinner. Barry had called Chase, who happened to be home at that time, right at dusk, and asked if he needed people power to help put out the fire. Chase said that by the time his wranglers drove out to the area, because they saw the plume of smoke, it was too far gone. So, they let it burn to the ground. The only good thing is that there were no animals in the barn; just hay and straw bales that he stores in there for winter use."

"Oh, good, then you did know."

"Some of it. What did he tell you? I haven't had time to call him."

"He just said that he thought it was arson; that it was probably some of Polcyn's hired thugs doing the dirty work for him." She paused. "Do you think Polcyn is behind it?"

Heavily, he muttered, "I have no doubt. The man is so filthy rich that he can afford to hire men to do this to us and never have it traced back to him. Plus, he's hiring men who are professionals, and they know not to leave prints or anything else that might get them identified by the sheriff."

"Is Chase's ranch over some rich fracking areas?" Lea wondered.

"Yes, just as ours is." Logan realized his slip of using *ours* instead of *mine*, and decided not to correct it. In his mind and heart, Lea was already a partner, if she wanted, and he always thought of things as *ours*. "The threats, which is what they are, seem to be escalating," he said, shrugging. "I know when you got rear-ended and your truck tossed into the ditch, that was Polcyn's work."

"And yet, no one has been arrested. And he can't be indicted if the act doesn't follow to his doorstep."

"Right," Logan said, finishing off the omelet. "That's how it's gone. Sheriff Seabert went to another county, where he knows the sheriff, to ask him if stuff like what we're experiencing went on in their region. Dan found out that in every county Polcyn has been in, where he can snatch the mineral rights so he can frack the area, those farmers, ranchers, or land owners have had similar unexplained attacks, just as we have. So, we know who it is behind the scenes." Shaking his head, he pushed the chair back and stood. "No one likes it."

"Has the sheriff thought about asking the FBI to get involved? To get some help at the federal level?" Lea wondered, scooting back and standing.

"Yes. But so far, the FBI isn't invested in it." He picked up his plate and flatware, walking through the kitchen and rinsing them off in the sink.

Lea stood nearby. "Does someone have to die in order to get their attention?"

He gave her a dark look, taking her plate from her hand. "God, I hope not. Dan has only so much manpower, and our county is big. He's stretched thin. I've talked to him about that and he wants to hire more deputies, but there's got to be federal money being released to the county before he can do it. Politics, you know?"

She leaned against the counter, watching him work, his motions economical. "You've put up a lot of motion sensors in all the groves and I think that's a good idea."

"Yes, and I need to put more video on the buildings around here," he grumbled. "Barry's had a long-term plan to mount them and I really don't know where he's at with doing it. Dan said if we could get video on the perp, that would go a long way in identifying the guy and hopefully, arresting him."

"That could be a break in this county-wide assault," she agreed, seeing the worry in his eyes as he dried his hands on a towel.

"Well, hey," he said, "let's get ready to go. We've got some happy times ahead of us today."

She pushed away from the counter. "I'm going to get my only skirt and blouse out, hang them up so that I can get to them easily later today," she said.

"Yes, I'll lay out some clean clothes myself."

"Sounds like a plan," she offered.

Logan followed her down into the living room, feeling heady about the coming dance tonight. The day wasn't going to pass soon enough for him. Trying to rein in his expectations, capturing his heated desire, he watched her disappear into her bedroom. She was going to the dance with him! He almost couldn't believe it, yet, it was real. It was really going to happen. Trying to hogtie his dreams and separate them from reality, Logan felt as if he was walking two feet off the ground. There was a lot to be done today. This would be the busiest day and night, a celebratory end to a wonderful time for all people who lived in this valley. That made him feel good, carrying on his family's work and seeing it come to fruition.

Now he could turn to personal dreams and needs. What would happen tonight? Lea was in charge, that was for sure, no matter how hot his dreams were. Would dreams and reality meet? Or not?

* * *

Lea tried to quell her excitement over the dance, where the doors were now opening and people were streaming in. The stars were sparkling, winking lights overhead in an ebony sky, the wind warm, the day cooling off. As she walked at Logan's side, their hands sometimes brushed against one another in the line as they waited to enter the huge arena that was now turned into an oval dance floor.

Earlier in the day, sheets of plywood had been put down after the arena's soil had been smoothed and flattened. Long ago, Logan had told her, his family had made up squares that were hinged together so that when they were laid out in order, it would present a smooth, polished dance floor. And sure enough, as she craned her neck, she saw the shining surface beneath the lights high above on the rafters that arched across the arena. There was a band up on a large dais, warming up. Microphones were nearby. She could feel the electricity in the air, and how the people of the valley were looking forward to this shindig, as Logan referred to it.

Glancing discreetly, she thought Logan was terribly handsome, just recently shaved, the scent of lime mixing with his own male fragrance. He wore a white cowboy shirt, a thin black tie around the collar and pearl buttons down the front, and a clean set of Levi's; his leather boots that he kept for special occasions were polished and on his feet. His hair was recently washed, still damp beneath his Stetson straw hat.

She had on a pink ankle-length cotton skirt, with wildflowers around the bottom of it. The blouse had a boat neckline, puffed sleeves, and a soft pink grosgrain ribbon woven around the neck. She felt very feminine, very pretty, and she saw that many of the people were dressed down, not up, to her relief. They fit right into the talkative crowd, laughter rippling continuously through the group.

Finally, they were in the arena. On one side, small round tables had been set up, with folding chairs around each of them. The fire marshal would allow only so many people into the area, and once that cut-off number happened, the people still in line outside would have to wait patiently until someone left. That was why Logan hurried them through grabbing a quick bite to eat, a fast shower, and got out to the fairgrounds long before the actual time of the dance. Even better? Almost everyone from the ranch was here and got in under the quota set by the fire marshal. Lea estimated at least two hundred people had gotten lucky and could dance the night away.

Logan leaned over and said, "The people who didn't make the cut? They'll dance outside the arena and still have a good time. We set up a second dance floor for them."

"I'm so glad. This dance seems like the perfect end to a wonderful fair week."

As the crowd began to move, Logan placed his hand lightly against the small of her back. "We have some tables reserved up there." He pointed. "We try to get everyone from the ranch in the same area if we can."

"Sounds good." She warmed to his large hand against the small of her back, easing her forward and making an opening so they could get on the dance floor. She tried to squelch her disappointment that as the crowd dissipated, he dropped his hand from her back.

Becoming bold, she slipped her hand into his. For a moment, there was surprise in his expression, and then satisfaction. His fingers curled gently around hers as he led her forward and they wove between the groups of

people. It felt good to Lea to take charge, to let Logan
know she wanted his touch. This was a nonverbal way to
do it; the message, she hoped, was loud and clear to him.
By the look in his eyes after his initial surprise wore off,
he liked it every bit as much as she did.

Lea no longer tried to fool herself. She was falling in
love with this cowboy from Wyoming. What did that
mean? Where would this growing need for him go? She
wasn't sure and that's what made her uneasy, but her heart
was not. Her heart had Logan squarely pegged, and she
had blossomed these last weeks with only the two of them
in the house full-time. What did Logan want from her?
What were his expectations? How did he see her? As a
bedmate only? Something more? He'd never broadcasted
any signal for her to decipher, frustrated by the situation.
Was tonight the night to find out?

Lea recognized everyone at the six tables that were in
a semicircle. Almost all were ranch hands with their girlfriends or wives, and they shook hands with her. After a
while, she'd forgotten some of the names, much to her
chagrin. There were at least thirty people from the Wild
Goose Ranch here! And best of all, some were dressed up,
but many in more everyday clothing like the skirt and
blouse she wore. That made her breathe a second sigh of
relief, that she wouldn't stick out, and was in sync with
the ranch group as a whole. Even Barry was here, alone,
and she felt bad for the foreman because she'd found out
earlier that his wife, Beth, had died two years earlier from
a "silent" heart attack. He didn't have a woman on his arm,
sitting with several couples at one table.

The band struck up the first song of the night, a square
dance. Something she knew nothing about. Logan sat
down next to her, explaining it to her, urging her to watch

because if she felt up to it, he'd like to square dance with her on a later song. Tapping her toe, she drank some of the bright red punch that Logan had earlier brought over for them. Plus, a plate of homemade cookies on a paper plate. He was like a little boy, scarfing those cookies like there was no tomorrow, and she grinned.

"I like that you can be a kid when there's the time for it," she said, leaning against him, her lips near his ear so he could hear her above the toe-tapping music and the caller of the square dance.

"I'd better slow down," he joked, pushing several cookies to one side for her.

She picked up one and it was mouthwateringly delicious. Now, Lea could see why he was gobbling them down. "I like seeing you like this," she admitted.

He wiped his mouth with a paper napkin. "Like what?"

"Being relaxed, being at ease."

"You mean I'm not like this all the time?" He picked up another cookie, giving her a glinting look.

Shaking her head, she laughed. "The fair seems to bring out the little boy in you. I think that's wonderful." She saw the gleam in his eyes change, felt a powerful sensation that he wanted to kiss her! That was so startling that she raised her brows and sat up. Where had *that* thought come from? Logan had not touched her. Had not suggested such a thing. But that look in his eyes? It was indisputable, and Lea didn't try to talk herself out of what she saw in that millisecond.

"I like being a kid when I can," he said, becoming serious. "And you look beautiful, Lea."

She chuckled. It was her turn to give him an evil look of teasing. Picking up the fabric of the skirt, she said, "What? That I'm wearing a skirt instead of my Levi's?"

"Well," he said, leaning back, cookie in hand, "the color really brings out the blush in your cheeks. It reminds me of that little girl you hide so well from the world. I like seeing her come out here tonight, too."

"Maybe we both needed this time out to relax a bit," she said, absorbing the softness she saw in his gaze meant for her alone. Her whole body took off like a five-alarm siren with just that wistful, wanting desire that came to his expression. She wanted what he wanted. Allowing the skirt fabric to drop, she reached out, sliding her arm across the back of his chair, making contact with his strong, powerful back beneath that shirt he wore. Leaning forward, she said, "If I told you I wanted to kiss you sometime tonight? What would be your reaction?" and she held his startled look that came and went in a split second. His strong mouth curved at the corners and that gleam came back in his eyes.

"Am I hearing you right? Did you just say you wanted to kiss me?"

"You heard right. I want to know how you feel about it. Is it something you want to share with me or not?" Lea was stunned at her own brazenness. She tried to understand why and knew instantly that Logan made her feel respected.

That glint turned feral and a shiver of excitement went down her spine, warming her lower body, heat suddenly beginning to uncurl, making her feel sexually ready to find out what they did or didn't have with one another. Nothing like laying it on the line, but Lea understood from being raised by her parents, that communication was everything. They'd taught her that over and over again in the way they conversed with one another on deadly serious topics to silly ones and everything in between. She watched him become serious. And she wasn't about to drop her arm from around his chair unless his answer wasn't what she hoped it would be.

The square dance ended. The next one was a slow dance.

"Dance with me?" he asked, holding her gaze.

"Even though we both have two left feet?" Her voice was a little breathy. She was scared and thrilled all at the same time, if that was possible. He still hadn't answered her question.

He rose from the chair, smiling, holding out his hand to her. "Even people with two left feet can make it across the dance floor. Come on . . ."

It was so easy to slide her hand into his. The calluses on his fingers made her whole hand tingle with possibility. "Let's go," she said, standing.

The dance floor became very crowded, but Logan chose a corner and laid claim to it by taking her into his arms. His hand rested lightly on the small of her back, his other hand enclosing hers. He kept about six inches away from her, but she could feel the strength and heat from his body stirring her lower regions into a bubbling cauldron of need. He was a head taller than herself; the breadth of his shoulders, this close, made her understand why she felt safe. It wasn't anything Logan did; he was just being himself. Unlike the teen boys in high school who were always flaunting their muscles, their size and height, their power over girls, he did not.

"So," he began lightly, holding her upward gaze, "let's talk about that kiss you mentioned earlier."

Her lower body quivered inwardly. Never had a man ever made her feel like this, much less physically! "I believe in being honest, Logan. I saw my parents always talk things out with one another. It wasn't easy for me to ask you that, but it's how I feel. I want to know how you feel about it." She drilled a look into his thoughtful gaze. His hand squeezed hers a little, as if to reassure her. At least, that's what it felt like to Lea.

"I've been wanting to kiss you for a long time, Lea," he admitted, his voice thick with emotion. "I was worried it was only one way. You don't give off a lot of signals and I just wasn't sure how you felt about me. How I feel about you? I was realizing the other day how happy I was and I began to root around and ask myself why that was." He glanced down at his healed ankle and then lifted his chin, meeting her gaze once more. "If it wasn't for me breaking a bone and these weeks under the same roof with you? Being in the ranch house alone, with you, was the difference. I liked having you around me more often. I like sharing meals with you because we talk about a lot of things, and I got to know you on a deeper and more intimate level." His voice lowered. "I like what I discovered about you. I'd always liked you from the beginning, but I needed to be patient and see if you felt anything toward me. I was thinking it was all on me, that it was my wanting you. Not the other way around."

A quiver of joy raced through her over his admission. "I was drawn to you from the first. When you came riding up, that dark, intense look on your face, worried about me, I knew I was going to be okay no matter if I was injured or not. There was just something about you, Logan. And luckily, I wasn't injured, just bruised and shook up, worried that my job was over before it ever got started." She saw laughter come to his eyes.

"Too funny. I was thinking that whatever had happened, this would scare you off and you wouldn't take the job."

They both laughed, shaking their heads over their reaction to that accident.

"So," Logan said in a low, gritty tone, "where are we now with one another? You've been with us for some time now, you know the ranch rhythm and, yes, we've had some attacks by Polcyn, even though I can't prove it yet. Aside from that? I need to know what your future plans look like."

Now it was her turn to become somber. "That's not an easy one for me to answer, Logan. I didn't come here looking to, well, be drawn to a man. I was happy just being commissioned to do the job you hired me for." She gave him a gentle look. "I tried not to fall for you, but every time I had myself convinced that it was me, that you weren't interested, you would do something else that made me just fall for you even more. For instance, that Hispanic family where the father didn't have enough money to pay for his family's cotton candy at the fair. I was so touched by your compassion for others." She pulled her hand from his and pressed it against her heart for a moment. "You touch me so deeply, more so than anyone ever has, when you do things like that."

The music ended. He nodded and reluctantly released her, but picked up her hand, holding it as they began to wind their way back to the table. "Tell you what," he said, slowing their walk, "let's use tonight, the slow dances, to talk and share. Would you like that, Lea?"

Her heart pounded once to underscore how far she had fallen for Logan. "More than you know," she said, holding his intent gaze.

"Maybe, in the next three hours, we can solve the world's problems, too?" He grinned, lightening the moment.

Her laugh was somewhat nervous. "With two people with two left feet?"

He chuckled and pulled out her chair to sit down. "Hey, I think we did pretty good out there, pardner. We didn't step on each other's toes. That's a high five in my world."

She liked that he sat near her, although he didn't make physical contact with her. Most likely because all his employees were nearby. Lea understood. "It's a high five in mine, too."

He glanced at his watch. "They usually do a fast one and then a slow one. I'm looking forward to sharing some more with you."

Heartened by his sincerity, she whispered, "I am, too."

Chapter Fifteen

Logan kept himself in tight check as he squired Lea on the dance floor. He kept his hand lightly against the small of her back, still able to feel the natural heat of her body beneath the clothing. In the last hour, so many barriers had melted away between them. The woman in his arms who he wanted to crush against him and hold forever, but didn't, was so much more relaxed than he'd ever seen her before. Hell, so was he. His heart wouldn't stop beating harder in his chest as he heard from her own lips that she was as drawn to him as he was to her. Joy replaced dread. It was so easy to drown in her dark green eyes, those red lashes a beautiful frame for them. Only when they danced together, was he able to speak to her. Knowing everyone in the valley, people dropped by their table to say hello and spend a few minutes with them. One part of him was frustrated because he'd waited months for this opportunity to speak openly, from his heart, to Lea. The other part of him was fine with people talking to him and everyone catching up on the latest about other folks in the valley.

"Are you working on the front door?" he wondered. He saw her lips quirk.

"Sort of . . . I have, well, a special project I've been working on. I intend to get to the door by the end of August, if that's okay with you."

"Sure. I'll never question your artistic moods," he teased. She laughed.

"My father is a lot like you," she said suddenly.

"What's your mother like?"

"She's very assertive, speaks her mind, holds her own space and is a strong believer in communicating. I picked up the importance of talking from her."

"Is your father like that, too?"

"No . . . he's more introverted, like me. But Mom draws him out of his shell and gets him to fess up and talk eyeball to eyeball with her. I watched it as I grew up."

"That's good," he said, nodding. And then he grew somber. "When I met Elizabeth in the first grade, she was like a magical being in my life. She was the one who poked and prodded me into talking. I hadn't been much on communication until then. By the time we married, she'd really crafted serious talks between us into an art form. I always appreciated that about her. She had to draw me out, like your mother does your dad."

"Talking isn't the first thing that comes to men's minds," she said darkly. "Or at least, my experience with them, it wasn't. I mean, if you can't talk about how you really feel, or you have something of weight and importance to talk to the man about, why be around that kind of guy? What is it about your gender that likes to hide your feelings and real thoughts from us women?" She tilted her head, digging into his gaze, demanding an answer.

"I honestly don't know. Maybe we're all missing the

communication gene in our DNA?" He saw her smile and then snort, giving him a chastising look.

"You got a set of vocal cords in your neck just like women do. That isn't going to wash, Logan. You also have a tongue to form words with, just as we do."

He liked her feistiness. "You're right on all accounts. Maybe it's just the way society brainwashed men into being the strong, silent types?"

"This patriarchal, male-dominated world is the reason. It's the way parents raise their sons. Women have always been told to shut up and be seen, not heard. My mother is a bra-burning feminist and she did a lot of protesting for women's rights when she was younger."

"And so, she raised you to be a totally confident, secure woman who knew she could pursue her dreams, unlike a lot of other women who are trapped to this day." He liked the thoughtful expression that came to her eyes. Logan had to force himself to hold her gaze, not allow it to slip down to those wonderful, soft lips of hers. How many torrid dreams had he had about kissing her? Loving her? Imagining what it would be like to be skin against skin, mouths clinging to one another, their breath moist and mingling together as one? Way too many. Logan was sure if Lea knew, she'd probably run away from him, heading back to Brookings. There were a lot of dark corners in a man's mind, and with all the women he'd ever known, he kept himself out of those garbage pits, as his mother referred to them.

"Your mother and my mother sound like they came out of the same pea pod," he teased.

"Really?"

"Yes."

"Is she a feminist?"

"Absolutely. I think most of the baby-boomer girls grew up with mothers who never got to chase their dreams and they taught their daughters to do just that. It's a good thing."

"When I first came to your ranch, I was amazed that about one-third of your employee work force are women."

"I found out a long time ago, through my father, that women pay a lot closer attention to details than most men. And even though ranch work is physically demanding, which they can deal with, it's the small things that make the ranch work well. If you don't set posts properly, or put barbed-wire strands on just so, you're spending a lot of time and money to fix the original sloppiness."

"My mother being an art quilter, knows all about teeny, tiny details," Lea said.

"Why didn't you become a quilter? I usually see quilting as a family generational thing."

"I like quilting with wood, not fabric. I'm just as detail oriented as my mother, but in a different medium, is all."

Chuckling, he whirled her around on the dance floor as the music ended. "Well put." He released her and then held out his hand in her direction. She took it, walking close to him as they threaded their way between the many couples. Just the slightest touch of her arm against his, sent a frisson of pure happiness rippling through him. Logan knew this was more than about a man wanting sex with a woman. This was love blossoming between them. Did Lea think about them in the same way? As in falling in love? Another thing he didn't know, and he wasn't about to ask it tonight out on this dance floor because it was such a serious topic with him. No, he needed privacy. A one-on-one with her. Logan had no doubt that Lea would be open and honest with him. Some women he'd met were coy, withholding their honesty about themselves or a possible relationship with him. That had disappointed him deeply because Elizabeth had been exactly like Lea: painfully and sometimes brutally honest with him. Truth always took them to a better place even if it hurt to talk about certain subjects. And now? Lea was no different. That was good in his book.

"Last dance of the night," Logan warned her, leading her to the dance floor.

"It has been a wonderful night," Lea agreed softly, liking the strength and warmth of his fingers around hers. How badly she wanted to kiss him! This was not the place to do it. Lea didn't want the world to know how they felt toward one another. At least, not yet.

She went into his awaiting arms, her fingers curving around his, luxuriating in his hand against her back. Leaning upward, her lips near his ear, she whispered, "I'm going to kiss you once we get to the truck. Are you okay with that?" She pulled away, watching his eyes, smiling inwardly. Oh, yes, he liked that suggestion.

His hand tightened around hers, his palm firmly against the small of her back. The glint in his eyes was unmistakable. "Well?" she nudged. "Communicate with me. Are you on board with my idea? Or do you want to take a different tack?"

"I almost tripped over your feet."

She laughed and they moved apart for a moment, both looking down at their feet. "You're still standing, Logan."

"And so are you."

She tilted her head, holding his amused gaze. "Well?"

"I like the idea."

"It's dark out in the parking lot. No one will see us, if that has you concerned."

Shrugging his shoulders, he said, "I think everyone knows that we sort of like one another, after tonight. Me holding your hand? That kind of thing?"

"I didn't want to be brazen about it and kiss you silly here on the dance floor."

"Oh, save my reputation?"

They both laughed deeply.

"When I kiss you," he said, his mouth near her ear, "I don't want to be hurried about it . . ."

Later, as they walked to the gravel parking lot with many other couples after the dance was over, Lea felt hot and cold inside. This was a new chapter in her life. It was one she never thought would happen, but it had. When Logan dropped her hand and slid his arm around her shoulders, it was so easy to lean against him, feeling his strength, but also his gentleness with her. Sensing he was just as awed by tonight, by their frank conversation with one another, a lot of her worry and anxiety drifted away.

Climbing into the truck, he turned it on, the air-conditioning cooling in the hot summer evening. Placing her purse on the floor, she scooted over toward where he sat. There was a big console in the center between them, but she wasn't going to let it stop her. He had just placed his cowboy hat on the rear rack and turned toward her when she placed her hand on his left shoulder, guiding him toward her.

In the semidarkness, the few streetlights here and there, she could see the glitter in his eyes and it thrilled her. Leaning forward, she placed her hands on either side of his jaw, guiding Logan's mouth toward hers. Eyes closing, she barely glided her lips across his parting ones. The scent of him made her groan inwardly, the strength of his mouth sliding against hers increased her yearning for him. She felt his hands settle firmly on her shoulders, holding her in place, positioning her and yet allowing her to be comfortable, with that console between them. How she wished it wasn't there! Lea wanted to sidle forward and press her body against his.

Lost in the heat and wetness shared between them, she relished the power he held in check. Her own power as a woman soared as she deepened the kiss between them. He groaned, his hands gripping her momentarily, and then loosening. That told her he liked it as much as she did, and that thrilled her. Heart beating wildly, she gripped his shoulders, letting him know that he was hers, no mistake about it. He released her, threading his fingers through her hair, her scalp tingling with pleasure over his caress. There was nothing to dislike about Logan. Her mind melted as he kissed her hard and she returned his fervor, hungry and starving for him, as a man, in all ways.

Gradually, unwillingly, they separated because of the barrier between them. They sat, breathing raggedly, staring at one another. Gulping, Lea whispered unsteadily, "That . . . was nice . . ."

He nodded and sat back, his arm resting on the steering wheel. "Better than nice," he rumbled. And then, in a low tone, he asked, "Where do you want this to go? How far do you want to go, Lea? This is up to you, not me."

"I'm not in this for one night, Logan. That isn't me."

"I'm not either."

She drew in a shaky breath. Opening her hands, she said, "I don't know where this will go, Logan, I really don't."

"You control where it goes."

She gave him an owl-eyed look. "My past keeps inter-fering with the present."

"The boys beating up on you?"

Giving a jerky nod, she gripped her hands together. "Yes. I've been trying to get past it. Let it go."

"You can have all the time you want regarding us, Lea," he rasped. "I'm not going to push you, take anything away from you. I want you to come to me like you did tonight. You initiated this kiss, not me, and I was fine with it."

"I'm just . . . scared . . . I want this to work out to be something forever, not just for a week, month, or year," she whispered, holding his softening gaze.

"That's what I want, too. Look"—he reached out, placing his hand over hers, squeezing them gently—"let's sleep on this. We'll keep this where it's at and go no further unless you're ready to go that next step."

"And you're fine with it?" she demanded.

"I consider having you in my life every day, a blessing I thought would never, ever happen to me again. I never dreamed that I could fall for any woman other than Eliz-abeth." He grimaced, looked out at the emptying parking lot, and then turned his attention back on her. "I always thought there was one woman in a man's life or vice versa. I didn't think love could strike again, Lea. I honestly didn't. But ever since you literally crashed into my life? I've slowly realized that what I feel for you is far more than sexual. I like waking up every morning knowing you're going to be out there when I leave my bedroom. I like sharing and talking with you over breakfast, lunch, and dinner. There isn't a time that I'm not grateful you are here, with me. I have crazy dreams of us being together. I'm not the kind of man that wants anything more than a partner who loves me as much as I love her. Maybe I've said too much. I don't know. But that's how I really feel about you."

"How long have you felt this way, Logan?" She searched his eyes.

"It started from the moment I met you. It didn't hit me over the head at first, but as time went on, I began to realize how much more my outlook on life was changing, with you in it. I didn't realize how far down I was until you came into my life." He slowly released her hands, his index finger tracing the side of her cheek. "You breathed life back into me by you just being you. I know you didn't know that, but it's the truth. My outlook, my mood, has done nothing but change for the better since you've arrived. I honestly don't want you to leave. I know I'm blurring the lines between us on an employee level, but I don't care anymore. I just like having you around, having you close. Everyone on the ranch loves you and I know why. You're just a wonderful person with a beautiful heart." He caressed her hair and then sat up, watching her. "How am I doing for communication?"

"Pretty darned good," she admitted throatily, watching the self-deprecating humor gleam in his shadowed eyes. "It takes guts to admit what you just said. I've thought the same, Logan, but I was too cowardly to say it. At least . . . until now."

"Look, a solid relationship doesn't spring up overnight. It takes time, patience, and work. I'm glad how we feel about one another is out between us. A lot has happened tonight. Let's go to our respective corners and feel our way through it?"

"Yes, I need some time to absorb it all," she admitted wryly. "I didn't realize my asking for a kiss was going to produce something this serious. I'm shocked in a good way by it, but I just need time to digest it all, Logan."

"You have all the time in the world, sweet woman." He started the truck and belted up. "Let's go home?"

"That sounds good," she quavered, deluged by so many wonderful, happy emotions. "Home is where the heart is . . ."

August 11

Lea had a tough time going to sleep after the dance. Logan's kiss was like eating the sweetest of desserts. She'd never been kissed quite like that by a man. And she liked it a lot. He was tender with her, and that was something she'd never experienced with a male. The sexual chemistry between her and Logan was explosive, and even now there was a gnawing ache deep within her lower body that wanted to consummate what they'd started with that hot, searing kiss. There was nothing tame about herself, that was for sure, and Logan seemed to appreciate her assertiveness when it came to their personal relationship.

Finally, around midnight, she dropped off to sleep, dreaming of that torrid, exploratory kiss they shared with one another.

Something, a sense of danger, pulled her from her sleep. Drowsily, Lea turned over, not quite awake, looking at the clock on the nightstand. It was three a.m.

What was wrong? She suddenly sat up, sniffing the air.

Smoke? Was that smoke she smelled? Urgency thrummed through her as she grabbed her cotton robe, yanked it on, and slipped into her sheepskin moccasins. She opened the door so as not to make noise. Logan's room was opposite her bedroom, down the hall. As she stepped out into the poorly lit hall, the strong odor of smoke assailed her nostrils.

Where was it coming from? She knew that Logan had just had new batteries installed in all the smoke detectors. He had done it only three weeks earlier. If that was smoke, and she was sure it was, why hadn't a smoke detector gone off?

Worried, she hurried quietly down the hall, unsure of everything. What if the smoke was outside? Had one of the groves been set on fire again by Polcyn's thugs? God, she hoped not, hurrying out into the darkened living room.

Her heart banged in her throat. She saw flames licking hungrily outside the ranch house. It was the wood shop! It was on fire! With a gasp, Lea whirled around, running down the hall.

"Logan! Logan!" she yelled, skidding to a halt at his door. She beat on it. "The wood shop is on fire!" She raced down the hall to the phone in the kitchen. With shaking hands, she called 911 and reported the fire.

Just as she hung up, Logan came barreling out of the bedroom, half dressed. He'd hauled on a pair of Levi's, his upper body naked.

"What?" he called from the hall. "What's wrong?"

"Fire!" she cried, pointing. "Fire in the wood shop! I called the fire department. They're on their way out." Her voice cracked. Logan slid to a halt, staring openmouthed out the window of the living room. The wood shop was attached to the garage and to the ranch house.

"I'm getting dressed," she called, racing past him and skidding into her bedroom.

Logan raced for the phone. He made an urgent call to Barry, his foreman, who lived a mile away. In moments, Barry would get the male wranglers who were single and lived in a bunkhouse, out of bed. They had to fight this fire or it would consume the home itself!

Lea came running back out, wearing her hiking boots, Levi's, and a shirt. "What can I do, Logan?"

"Let's get out of here," he said. "I'm going to get my shirt and then I'm going to the office to take the important papers out. I've called Barry. We'll have six men here in a tanker water truck with hoses in the next ten minutes. Get out of here. I want you safe. Stand back from the buildings."

"Like hell," she growled. "I'm coming with you. I'll help you gather those papers."

He started to say something and then snapped his mouth shut. "The safe is open," he instructed. "Grab everything you can out of there and get it outdoors and away from the house."

"Right!" The smoke was stronger now. Why hadn't the alarms worked? It made no sense. She flipped on a light. There was none. Cursing under her breath, she raced down the hall right on Logan's heels until he turned into his bedroom. In the office, she pulled open the curtains, and there was enough moonlight to see where the safe was located. Logan always kept it open, but it wasn't now. Kneeling down, with trembling fingers, Lea pushed the door wide open. Luckily, all the papers were in three stacked plastic boxes. There was no lid on the top one, but it didn't matter. She easily slid all of them into her awaiting arms. Rising, she raced out of the office and almost collided with Logan as he burst out of his room, fully clothed.

"Take them to the truck," he told her, running ahead, unlocking the front door. He threw it open and stepped out on the wraparound porch. He could see the orange and yellow flames now, rising higher and higher. Forcing himself to act, he quickly ran to the yard gate, opening it for Lea.

Someone had set this fire! He was damned well sure of it! Polcyn! Trying to drive him and his family out of his homestead. *Like hell!* They ran to the truck, Logan clicked the fob and opened the door so that Lea could dump the most important papers into it. He peered into the dark night, looking for strangers or a truck. There was nothing he could see.

Slamming the truck door shut, he locked it, hearing the water tanker truck rumbling up the road from where Barry lived. He gripped Lea's arm. "Come on, I want you well away from this area. Barry's here with a water truck with hoses up from the bunkhouse area. We can start putting water on the wood shop before the fire department arrives. I want you safe." He gave her a pleading look not to fight him on this.

"Give me the keys to the truck," she said. "I'll get it out of here so the fire trucks can get in and out of here without any problems."

"Good idea," he said. "I'm going to check out the fire. Stay back!"

Lea opened the driver's side of the truck, hopping in. She was breathing raggedly, her heart feeling as if it would leap out of her chest. Logan's beloved family home was on fire! What had started it? Why hadn't the fire alarms screamed out a warning to them?

She sobbed, wiping away tears with the back of her hand, and drove out of the oval graveled area. She took the truck around the circling road. To her right, she could see a huge tanker truck lumbering up the road, dust clouds in its wake. Every month, Barry drilled his wranglers on using the water tank truck. They were a team of cowboys trained to fight ranch fires. She'd been told by Jody one time, that the water truck had come in handy on several other fires that had started over the years, saving structures, animals in their barns, and so much more. Thank God they had this truck!

The darkness was complete, the lights of the truck stabbing forward on the dirt road as she swung it into a lower parking lot area a good quarter mile away from the house. A gravel path led from the parking area back to the main ranch house area and she would use it.

Something caught her attention. Frowning, she squinted against the darkness. What was she seeing? There was a truck, indefinable in color, racing away on the same road she was on. Was this the arsonist who had set the fire? Gripping the wheel hard, she scrambled to find the truck cell phone that was always plugged into the console. Jamming her foot down on the accelerator, she blew past the turnoff for the parking lot, through the rising cloud of dust made by the other vehicle racing at high speed away from the area.

She fumbled with the cell phone, pressing one key to call Logan's cell phone. Did he have the phone on him? *Oh, God, please let him have it on him!* She waited, driving with one hand over the gravel road, bouncing violently over the ruts. She had to be careful how fast she was going or her truck could spin, tumble, and possibly crash.

"Answer me!" she yelled, holding the phone to her ear. "Logan!"

For another five seconds, there was no answer.

"Logan here."

"Logan, it's me, Lea! There's a truck racing as fast as it can go on the main road, heading toward the groves at the other end of the ranch. I can't tell what color it is. Would any of your wranglers be out at this time of night?"

"Hell no!" he exploded. "Where are you at?"

"About a mile past the lower parking lot. I'm following him as fast as I can. He's going at least sixty or faster."

"It's the arsonist! Dammit, stop, Lea! Stop! I don't want you to get near them!"

"No way!" she yelled back. "Just get someone to follow me! We can't lose them!"

Cursing, Logan yelled something to Barry that she couldn't make out. He came back on the phone. "Me and Jody are grabbing the other company truck. We'll be on your tail pronto. Under *no* circumstances are you to get too close to them, Lea. They'll have weapons. Military grade. They can fire at you and kill you. Keep your distance and stay in touch with us."

"Okay," she rasped, breathing hard. "I'll lay this cell down on the seat, on speaker. I need two hands to drive!"

Lea was damned if this person or persons was going to get away with this! She was going fifty. *Screw it.* She pushed the truck to sixty-five miles an hour. Luckily, she knew this road well. The dust was getting thicker. It was harder to see where she was going, all her attention on the side of the road. Luckily, she had the seat belt on. The truck was screaming along, jolting her every moment, fingers wrapped hard around the wheel, keeping it steady and on the road. Her mind raced. Who was it that had set that fire? She wished it wasn't so dark; the milky moonlight didn't help at all because she was completely absorbed by the huge rooster tail of dust raised by the racing truck ahead of her. She knew she was in danger because she couldn't see two feet in front of her.

There was only one road to the groves and this was it.

This road led between two groves and then stopped at a gate in the barbed wire fence at the property line. She was sure that whoever was in that truck, had either cut the padlock and chain on that gate and opened it, or took wire cutters and cut through the five strands of barbed wire to get access to Logan's property. *The bastards!* Was it Polcyn's men? Had he bought off one or two of them to start this fire? Another way to harass Logan and try to force him to sell off his property and leave? There was no way Logan would *ever* leave his family's homestead. He'd die protecting it.

"Lea!"

The cell phone squawked with Logan's yell. She scooped it up, her eyes never leaving the side of the road. "Yes, I'm here!"

"Do you know where you are?"

"No, it's thick dust. I can't see anything beyond two feet in front of me."

"How fast are you going?"

She grimaced, knowing he was going to be upset. "Sixty-five. I'm trying to catch up with them!"

"SLOW DOWN!"

"No!" she snapped. "I'm okay. I know this road. I'm thinking that there's probably two men in that truck, Logan. They either cut the chain on the gate to get in or they cut the barbed wire. Next to the gate."

"Doesn't matter," he growled. "There's only one way for them to go once they leave the property and that's to the left. That road is dirt, too, and kept by the county. It's not smooth like ours, it's rutted as hell. You could flip on it. It's really rough driving. Why don't you pull back a little? It will be easy to follow their dust. We want to catch up with you and pass you. We have military grade weapons on us and Jody and I both know how to use them. I don't want you in the line of fire, Lea. Please, slow down a little. I'm already in your dust, so I know you're not that far from us. Find a place to pull over and let us pass. Put your foot on the brake so I see your red brake lights and don't hit you."

She hesitated, but realized she had absolutely no way to protect herself if the thugs in the truck started firing at her. "Okay," she rattled. "I'm slowing and pulling over to the right, onto the berm."

"Good," Logan praised, relief in his harsh tone laced with fear and danger.

"I still want to follow you!" she insisted.

"That's fine," Logan said. "Jody's on the other cell and talking to Barry. The fire department has arrived. They've got hoses spread. They're fighting the fire. We can do this. Jody called the sheriff's department and told him that we're pursuing the arsonists."

Taking her foot off the accelerator, she saw the road widen on the right and she pulled off, keeping her foot on the brake. "I've pulled over. I've got my brake lights on, Logan."

"That's good. We'll be there in just a minute. You follow us at a safe distance. I want to catch these bastards once and for all."

Grinning hard, she whispered harshly, "So do I."

"We'll need your backup. Jody just told me the sheriff is sending all three cruisers out to the highway where that other dirt road intersects the main road. We can catch them in a pincers movement, if we're lucky. You hang back and if we need you to call anyone, you can do that?"

"Yes," she said, looking through the dust in the rearview

mirror, seeing headlights coming her way. "I see you, Logan . . ."

"Jody saw the red brake lights. We're coming past you at Mach three with our hair on fire!"

And he wasn't kidding at all! Her truck shook as Logan and Jody flew by her parked vehicle, as if they were lifting off like a plane, throttles to the firewall. She stomped the accelerator, tires spinning, gravel flying. Damn, she wanted to catch these guys! Her heart raced with fear. Even though Jody and Logan had military rifles, they could still get killed or injured. Danger sizzled through her. Fingers so tight on the steering wheel that they ached, she was up to sixty-five miles an hour in a matter of ten seconds, now following Logan and Jody. God, let them live through this night! She loved Logan! There was no way she wanted to lose him! Not now! Not ever! There were no guarantees. Her mouth was dry as cotton balls. The cell phone bounced next to her hip. She'd never done anything as dangerous as this! Would they survive it or not?

Chapter Sixteen

Logan gripped the wheel hard as they approached the end of his property. The dust was thick and blinding. Jody had her M4 locked and loaded with a large clip in it. He trusted her with his life. She had been a medic who carried a weapon just like this in Afghanistan and was an expert shooter. His M4 was strapped to a rifle rack at the back of the truck window. Jody was on the phone with the sheriff.

"They're just now getting to that turnoff from the highway," she informed Logan with satisfaction.

"Good. I think they've made that left turn . . ." He slowed, knowing that turn was coming up. As they came to a crawl, he saw through the flash of headlights that the gate had been broken into and was wide open. The rooster tail of dust went to the left. "They're now on that side road," he growled, wheeling around the corner and slamming his foot down on the accelerator. "Tell Lea to back off and stay behind at this gate until and if we tell her to come forward. I don't trust these guys. Once they see flashing lights at their escape point—that highway—they're gonna do something, and I don't know what that might be."

Jody nodded, getting in touch with Lea, relaying Logan's orders. "I'm going to connect with the sheriff again," she said, ending the call with Lea. "We need to know if they've put their cruisers in a position to stop them or not."

"These dudes don't have any other place to go," Logan grunted. "There's barbed wire fence along both sides of this road. There's a six-foot culvert and cow grate at the other end. They either crash into those cruisers, or stop and surrender, or it will turn into a firefight."

"Roger that," Jody said grimly, connecting with the sheriff, who was now on the scene. After some back and forth, she said, "Two cruisers are pointed nose forward like a wedge. The third cruiser is behind them, as a buttress. Those dudes will either try to break through them or they're gonna stop and fight."

Mouth slashing, Logan muttered, "No telling what they'll do. Get on the horn to Lea and then Barry. I want to know if they've been able to stop that fire from going into my home."

"Roger that."

Logan focused as never before. He didn't dare let his emotions get the better of him. The road was rough and he was forced to slow to fifty miles an hour, for fear of arcing the truck out of one of these nasty ruts and going airborne. The dust was just as thick in front of him, telling him that the arsonists had slowed down as well. His mind switched to Lea. He wanted her to remain at the gate. An M4 bullet had a long reach. He wanted her *out of danger*. Damn! He loved her! And he didn't want to lose her.

"Barry says the fire is bad. The woodshed and garage

are gone. They're working to stop it from entering the main house."

Grimly, he nodded. "Did Lea say she'd stay at the gate?"

"Yes."

Relief flowed through his tight gut. "Good."

"Logan, there's only a mile left until we hit that T-intersection," Jody warned in a low voice.

"Yeah, I know it. Call the sheriff again. Let him know our position. I'm sure they can see their headlights by now . . ." He gripped the wheel, feeling danger swirling around them, like a bolt of lightning being thrown into their midst.

"Your M4 is locked and loaded, large mag, safety off," she reported, contacting the sheriff.

"Thanks," he grunted. He'd only had time to grab his black baseball cap, the bill somewhat shielding his eyes as the dust reflected back on the high beams of the roaring truck shaking and shuddering around them. The ruts were getting really bad! He didn't want to slow, but he had to or else.

"They're ready for them. The SWAT team just arrived and they are in place, as well."

"That's good," he growled.

Suddenly, dirt clods and rocks flew at them.

Logan slammed on the brakes. His truck skidded sideways and he fought for control.

"They've crashed!" Jody yelled. "I just saw their truck fly off for a second!"

"Which side?" he snapped.

"To the right!" She grabbed at the cell as it flew across her and hit the passenger door. Leaning down, she groped until she found it, the truck still skidding, Logan trying to stop it from crashing or sliding off the road.

Logan straightened out the nose of his truck, skidding to an abrupt halt.

"Where are they?" he yelled, putting the truck in park, twisting around, grabbing the M4 off the rack.

"To the right. I see lights about three hundred feet ahead of us, one o'clock, Logan."

"Bail!" he ordered, grabbing his M4 and shoving open the door, hunkering down, keeping his body out of the line of fire in case they had weapons.

It was dark. All he could see in the wall of dust now slowly moving away from the road, was headlights piercing the night to the right at one o'clock from their position. He heard Jody telling the sheriff what happened, giving him the GPS coordinates.

Before he could do anything, the *chut-chut-chut* of gunfire rippled through the night, putting holes, literally, through the dust clouds that rose ten feet in the air between them and their enemy.

"Stay down," Logan ordered Jody, who was kneeling at the passenger-side end of the truck bed. She had her M4 up, ready to fire.

He came up behind her, breathing hard, his eyes slitted. The arsonists' overturned truck was less than three hundred feet away from them. The driver had lost control and the vehicle had flipped into the five-strand barbed-wire fence, tearing the fence open for a good thirty feet, posts scattered around it like toothpicks. The dust cleared.

"Body-heat lens," he ordered Jody, flipping one scope down and bringing the other up. The beauty of the M4 was that it could carry three different types of scopes. The infrared scope would show body heat as well as the human form of whoever he had drawn a bead on. In this darkness, it was the only thing they could use. Lifting the M4, he remained below the truck top. "Four of 'em," he rasped. "Tell the sheriff. We're going to keep them pinned down until SWAT can arrive."

"Roger," Jody rasped, cell phone to ear.

More bullets poured into the truck. Metal popped. The screech of a bullet being fired, tearing through it, filled the air.

"Sheriff says do not return fire unless necessary," Jody called over her shoulder.

"Roger that," he said, watching the red-orange blobs that reminded him of Gumby, the clay figure, scattering around from one side of the arsonists' overturned truck. "I still count four."

"I'll let them know," Jody said, relaying the intel.

"Moving to the other side and to the front left fender," he told her. "You hold this position."

"Roger."

Sweat dribbled down his hard features as he crouched and ran forward. Up ahead, once he knelt one knee on the ground, he could see headlights coming toward them. The SWAT van would be first. He knew the men and women on that team. They were well trained and more than prepared for something like this. He felt naked because neither he nor Jody were wearing a protective Kevlar vest that could save their lives. He made a mental check to buy some if they got out of this alive.

"LOOK OUT!" Jody yelled.

Gunfire erupted everywhere around him. Logan cursed, seeing the four men rushing forward, toward them.

They obviously didn't know that Logan and Jody had weapons, too.

"Shoot to injure if you can," he yelled at Jody.

Damn it! Raising his M4, he sighted on the closest man, at least six feet tall, racing toward them. They must have thought that they were going to take this truck and still try to escape! Like hell they were! Squeezing the trigger, he aimed for the man's leg.

There was a scream, and the enemy flew three feet into the air, jerked backwards, the rifle he was carrying, flying out of his hands.

A second shot, this time Jody firing.

Logan hoped that they would stop trying to steal this truck.

A second man flew into the air.

The other two stopped, hesitated, looked toward their truck, and then at Logan's, once more.

"Don't try it!" Logan bellowed loud enough for them to hear. They were less than two hundred feet away from them.

Without warning, one man pulled something from his vest, tossing it their way.

"Grenade!" Logan yelled to Jody, throwing himself on the ground, hitting the dirt hard, mouth open.

No one could throw something two hundred feet, and Logan knew it as he jammed his eyes shut as he hit the earth. But a grenade could do major damage. Dammit! He hadn't counted on that type of weapon at all.

He saw Jody slam to the earth, too, her M4 in her hand, her other hand over her head. They had no body armor on, no helmets to protect themselves from this fierce and lethal firefight.

The only thing Logan thought about in those seconds before the grenade exploded, was that Lea was far enough behind and safe.

"Logan!" Jody yelled.

The grenade went off.

The concussion wave threw Logan into the air. He rolled, keeping a grip on his rifle. How was Jody? He got to his knees, shaking his head, his ears ringing so badly he could hardly hear anything. He gripped the M4, waiting for the two men to show up.

Jody appeared around the rear of the truck.

"Logan! They're running away! Down the road, back toward the ranch!" She jerked her hand to indicate behind where they were parked.

No! He straightened, keeping his rifle ready, joining Jody. He couldn't see the men, so he lifted his rifle, sighting their fleeing bodies as they hotfooted it down the road. Right toward a truck that was coming up rapidly. What the hell! It had to be Lea! His heart sank. She hadn't stayed at the gate!

"Get the sheriff!!" he told Jody.

"The cell is dead. It doesn't work." She wiped away blood from her nostrils with her hand. "They're heading to take that truck comin' up behind us!"

"It's got to be Lea," he snarled. "I told her to stay behind!"

Jody cursed. "It has to be her. No one else is that close to where we're at."

"We've got to stop them! There's no way for us to get ahold of her!" Logan muttered.

Logan took off running, Jody on his heels. They stayed far enough apart so if one was shot, the other wouldn't be.

Both had been well trained in combat. Lea was less than half a mile away! Well within the enemy's rifle range.

"Take 'em down!" he yelled at Jody. Because if they didn't? The arsonists would capture Lea, possibly killing her and stealing her truck.

Jody halted, took a stance, and fired. So did he.

They both missed, puffs of dust shooting into the air.

Again! He was shaking with adrenaline and he wasn't accurate. They fired again.

Missed!

Wanting to scream in frustration, Logan saw Lea braking. He saw the two men firing across the hood on either side of the truck, warning her to stop. The two men were close enough that Logan and Jody couldn't fire now, for fear of hitting Lea. *Sonofabitch!* Breath tore out of his open mouth as they dug the toes of their boots into the dry, hardpacked earth and started running.

"She's bailing!" Jody yelled.

Logan didn't stop running hard. If Lea could escape, it meant they had a shot at those two bastards. He watched as she flung the door open and then ran into the darkness, into the nearby field. There were shots fired at her.

He couldn't see anything! If he fired, the M4's bullets could find Lea. Helplessly, he watched as the two men climbed into the truck. They made a three point turn, jammed down on the accelerator and headed back toward the ranch!

Where was Lea? Anxiously, Logan searched for her. Had the thugs shot her? He slowed, looking around in the darkness, swinging his rifle around, looking through the scope, trying to locate her via the body-heat scope.

There! He saw someone kneeling down in the tall grass next to the barbed wire fence. It had to be Lea!

"Over here, three o'clock," he yelled to Jody. "I found her!"

They both ran hard, sliding off the road and stumbling into the rocky dirt and weeds.

"*Lea!*" he cried out, dropping to his knees, releasing the rifle, his arm going around her shoulders.

"I-I'm okay, okay," she sobbed, straightening, looking at the fleeing truck.

"Are you hurt?" he rasped.

"N-no. I'm so sorry," she choked out to Logan. "I couldn't stand waiting at the gate. I-I heard all the guns being fired. I had to come. I-I never thought they'd come after me. They hit the windshield and it shattered in on me. That's when I braked and bailed."

He hugged her tightly. "It's okay, okay," he breathed raggedly.

Jody joined them. "Logan, here comes SWAT! I'll flag them down. They have to know these dudes are trying to escape through your ranch."

"I'll be okay," Lea said, breathing raggedly. "Go . . . go help the sheriff . . ."

"Come with us," he growled, and he hauled her to her feet. She gripped his hand in a death grip. "Ready to run?" he demanded.

"I'll keep up," she managed, still breathing hard.

By the time they came back to the vehicle, Jody was out in the center of the road, waving the SWAT truck to a halt. She was giving the commander of the SWAT team the intel, to warn Barry to get everyone, including the firefighters, out of the immediate area to protect them. He ran back to the nearest cruiser behind the black truck. Sheriff Dan Seabert rolled down his window. Logan rapidly told him what had happened.

"Then, your men fighting the fire and our firefighters are in jeopardy because those arsonists will drive right by the ranch house complex in order to get to the main highway."

"Yes," Logan said, his voice unsteady. "We have no cell phone left."

"We'll call Barry. We'll try to apprehend them before they get there, but it's gonna be dicey. Follow us in your truck. Is it still working? We saw the grenade go off."

"Yeah, they hit the side of the road." Logan breathed rapidly. "It should work. We'll follow you."

"Here," Seabert said, thrusting another cell phone into his hand. "Use ours. We got radios."

"Thanks," he said, still trying to catch his breath. He straightened and saw Jody running toward him, weapon in hand.

"Go!" Logan urged the sheriff. "Be safe!"

Seabert gave him a grimace. "We'll do our best. Follow close, okay? We're gonna put pedal to the metal. I'd like to stop these dudes before they reach your ranch."

Logan nodded and patted Seabert's shoulder. "Thanks, Dan . . ."

The SWAT truck was hightailing it at a speed Logan wouldn't even want to think about. A truck like that, filled with six well-armed members, was weaving unsteadily over this rugged road. They had no choice but to go as fast as they dared.

At least Barry knew what was happening. The house could burn down. Everything would be lost, but at least their lives would be intact. That's all Logan cared about at this point. He gripped Lea's dusty hand. She looked like she was in shock. Who wasn't? Jody ran for the truck after he gave her the keys. He hoped the engine would start.

"You all right?" he asked, placing his arm around her shoulders. She sagged against him.

"Y-yes, okay . . . let's just catch these guys . . ."

"We will," he promised her grimly. "One way or another."

One cruiser had pulled over because two of the men were wounded in their legs. Logan saw that the deputies had taken their weapons away and searched them, giving first aid after that. He was sure ambulances had been called and would arrive in minutes.

"Truck's operational," Jody called, scooting out of the driver's seat.

"Good! Lea? You sit in the middle. Jody is going to ride shotgun, in case she has to fire."

"Right," she answered, running around the front of the truck. She saw the entire side of the truck had bullet holes in the rear panels, and a lot of dents. Jody motioned for her to climb in.

"They threw a grenade at us," she explained. "Belt up, Lea, we're in for one helluva ride."

"Got it," Lea answered, swiftly climbing in. By the time she was in, both of them were belted in and Logan was turning the truck around. She was pressed against the seat by the speed of the vehicle as Logan jammed his foot down on the accelerator. The engine was screaming like a banshee on the warpath! Glad that the safety belt was tight, Logan was fighting to keep the truck on the road as they roared down it, following the rooster tails of dust kicked up by law enforcement ahead of them.

"Can they catch them?" she asked, her voice quavering.

"Maybe," Logan said grimly.

"The Commander of the SWAT team, Hunter Grant, is a sprint-car race driver in the off season," Jody told Lea. "If anyone can catch them, it's gonna be him at the wheel. Hunter'll drive to hell and not bat an eyelash."

"Wow," Lea whispered, her eyes huge as she saw the truck turning at the gate. "At least the dirt road on the ranch property is a lot smoother to drive on."

"Oh, yeah," Jody said, grit in her tone. "It means SWAT might be able to make up the distance." She was sitting up, the butt of the M4 between her legs, hand near the trigger mechanism.

"If he can't—" Lea turned, asking Logan, "What will happen?"

"Everything's up in the air," he growled unhappily, his eyes on the road, hands gripping the wheel hard.

"And they're armed," Lea said, terror mounting in her tone. "They might have more hand grenades on them, or worse."

"Yeah," Logan said, "and they don't mind throwing them, either."

They had another mile to go. By the time they made the turn, the SWAT truck was a mile ahead of them. Hunter was flying! Logan would bet he was going close to eighty miles an hour with that beast of a truck. And he'd bet money that van had probably never gone that fast in its life. But lives were on the line and he felt the urgency eating through him. He didn't want his wranglers hurt, or the volunteer fire department firefighters, either. It was an ugly, escalating situation and he didn't know how the hell it was going to end.

"What if that truck gets to the house first?" Lea asked tautly.

Jody shook her head. "All bets are off. I've been running the scenario in my head. Those guys, if they know the area, their best bet is to go speeding by the ranch house and make a beeline for the main highway."

"I agree with you," Logan said. "I don't think they want to spend time shooting up firefighters fighting a fire. They got SWAT on their ass."

"Not just any SWAT," Jody said proudly. She looked over at Lea. "All SWAT members, three men and three women, are led by Hunter. And believe me, he lives up to his last name. He was a U.S. Navy SEAL for nine years and saw it all. When he returned home, he went to SWAT academy and got credentialed. Then he came here and settled down. He's fierce. I've seen some really great soldiers and marines, but Hunter kicks ass and takes names."

"And he doesn't ask first," Logan put in, giving her a tight smile. "He's all business and so is his team, who all happen to be military vets, too."

"I'm just glad we're behind them. I'm scared spitless," Lea admitted hollowly.

"Look, you can see your house up on the hill," Jody told Logan. "It looks like they're beating back the fire!"

Relief sped through Logan. "That's good." Now he could see, as they broke out of the groves of trees, the straight-ahead mile run to the homestead. Up ahead of him was the black SWAT van going like a bat out of hell, and two more sheriff's cruisers with their headlights cutting like beams through the night, not far behind it, lights flashing.

The cab fell quiet. Logan felt so damned tight with

tension and it hung in the truck like a heavy blanket. He was grateful Lea was all right. She was clearly shaken up, but who wouldn't be? Jody, as usual, was cool, calm, and collected. She was a warrior. Like him. Funny, in a sick sort of way, how easily their days in the military had come back to them, how if someone scratched their skin, the warrior came out and all that training was right there, right on the surface and ready to tap into. It had saved their lives tonight. *So far.*

"I see the headlights of the lead truck," Jody said as they crested the last hill. Now, all the vehicles, their headlights like knives stabbing through the darkness, were racing ahead of them.

"And Barry has everyone out of harm's way?" Logan demanded. He saw little flames at the ranch house, wondering if they had been successful in saving his home. He couldn't bear to think what his parents would feel if it had been destroyed. So many of his relatives had lived there, loved there, had children there, the stories within those walls, vital to him. It could all have been destroyed. He just didn't know how this was going to end.

"Wait," Jody said, pointing out the cracked window of the truck, "look over there. Headlights of a number of vehicles on the other road that goes around the house."

"It's probably the fire department and our water truck taking cover," Logan said.

Jody quickly dialed into Seabert's cruiser and talked with him. She finished the conversation. "Logan, you were right. They've pulled out and are taking cover down below the hill. They're going to park there and wait it out."

"They don't have any way to protect themselves, either, do they?" Lea asked, worried.

"Just a stream of water," Logan growled.

"Dan is hoping these guys in our truck will just race straight out of the ranch and either go north or south on the highway. He's already setting up a trap for them, either way. His other deputies are out with gear to blow the tires on the truck. And the highway patrol is involved, as well. We have plenty of law enforcement and that's a relief."

"If they go south, that would be better for the deputies and highway patrol," Logan said. "That takes them out in a lot of country with no people or houses around. If they go north? They will be racing down through the center of Silver Creek. A lot of people could get injured or killed." His mouth slashed. "Damn, I hope Hunter can drop them here, on our property."

"He's driving that van like hell was after him," Jody said, "barely a hundred feet between it and the escaping truck. They must be moving at seventy or eighty miles an hour. That's crazy speed."

Lea clasped her dusty hands together, lips tightening.

"Something's gotta give," Logan muttered darkly. "Hunter will *not* allow them to make it to the highway. I know him too well."

"Oh!" Jody cried. "They're firing out of the SWAT van down at the tires on the truck! Wow! Look at that!"

All Logan could see was two SWAT people firing out of the two front windows and down toward the earth.

Lea gave a gasp. The truck carrying the arsonists suddenly went airborne as it slid and then hit the side of the road. It bounced and then shot off into the air. She couldn't see if it rolled or flipped, out of sight in the darkness.

"Whoa!" Jody yelled excitedly. "The truck's turned over! Hunter has jammed on the brakes! Holy moley! He's raising a huge dust cloud!" She lifted her rifle, sighting through the infrared. "Oh, yeah, Logan! The two guys in the pickup truck have just been apprehended by SWAT! They got 'em on the ground! They're putting ties on their wrists!"

Logan took his foot off the accelerator. "Jody, call Dan. Ask if the fire department and water tanker can go back now and put out the fire at the house."

Jody nodded, setting her rifle butt on the floorboards between her booted feet, and made that call.

"Dan's already called the fire chief. They're on their way back up to your home."

"Good," he whispered, giving Lea a glance. Her face was etched with exhaustion, and he couldn't see much else. He loved her. And he'd almost lost her tonight. That shook him more deeply than anything else. He'd already lost one woman he'd loved. He wasn't about to lose the second one. "We're going to drive up to the house. We'll meet the firefighters and the chief there. Hunter knows what he's doing. He doesn't need us there."

Trying to control his emotions, Logan parked at the house. The fire department had returned, putting up huge floodlights aimed at the home, and the smoldering ruins of the wood shop and garage were easy to see. Inwardly, he winced. He claimed Lea's hand once she climbed shakily out of the truck. Instinctively, his arm went around her waist and she leaned heavily against him, her arm going around his waist. All the adrenaline would soon leave, he realized as they walked toward the one end of the home. The smell of smoke was heavy in the air. The firefighters were putting a lot of water on the end of the house that had been attached to the wood shop. All of Lea's tools had been in that shop, and were now destroyed. He knew she had been working on preliminary drawings for the door. That too, was gone. Glancing over at the house, most of it appeared to be unburned. Rounding the corner where all the water was being used, he tried to gird himself. Had the fire reached into the house?

His stomach curled in a knot as the glare of the flood-lights revealed that, yes, a portion of the house, the living room area, had been fully breached by flames. Two hoses sprayed water up on the cedar roof, as well. He heard Lea give a little cry, as she stood there staring at the damage.

"Oh, Logan . . ." She sobbed, pressing both hands to her mouth.

"It's okay, Lea," he whispered, leaning over, kissing her dusty hair. "We got lucky," he told her, his voice gritty with barely held emotion. "Maybe a third of the living room area is gone. We can rebuild that. The rest of the house has been saved. It's all right. We'll get through this together." She looked up at him, her eyes welling up with tears. He tried to smile, but failed. Turning her so she was pressed against the front of him, he groaned as her slender arms wound around his torso and she buried her head against his chest. Gently, he placed his hand across the strands of her hair, smoothing them back into place, kiss-ing her temple, and holding her tightly because he never, ever wanted to let this brave woman go again. She was his. He was hers. And he wanted to spend the rest of his life proving it to her.

The noise of the fire engines, the pumping sounds, the water spraying, hitting the roof and side of the house, dimmed as he focused in on Lea. How brave she'd been! How many women, in the dark of night, would go after a dangerous group of men like that? She'd been so coura-geous in unknown circumstances. No one in their right mind would have gone after the arsonists if they had known they had military weapons and grenades. She didn't even think in those terms, and Logan knew that. Still, her desire to catch them showed him the fierce woman warrior who lay beneath the soft, artistic, gentle part of her he knew so well.

Holding her tightly, he pressed his cheek against her hair, closing his eyes, allowing the waves of tension to ripple through and out of him. He knew what was coming with the adrenaline crash, and he was sure Lea would experience it as well. Getting shot at was not something, he was sure, she was expecting. Life becomes very precious when one stares down the barrel of a rifle that is spitting bullets at them. He felt her quiver. And then felt the wetness of her tears being absorbed into his sweaty, dirty shirtfront. Murmuring soft words of comfort, kissing her ear and temple, his hand moving slowly up and down her strong spine, he felt her slowly begin to relax. And then she sagged against him, as if surrendering fully to him, wanting and needing his protection, the safety of his arms around her.

Swallowing hard, he lifted his head, looking up at the inky sky, the stars twinkling above them, some of them blotted out every now and again by the smoke still curling heavenward. Another breeze from a different direction drifted by them and he could smell the clean scent of pine, inhaling it deeply into his lungs.

"Hey," he murmured near her ear, "let's see where we stand with this fire and then we're going into town tonight to get a hotel room. We're both exhausted."

Lea gave a shaky nod and slowly eased her grip around him and pulled away enough to look up at him. "That sounds good."

"Most of the house is still standing," he reassured her,

motioning toward it and the powerful lighting flaring across the roof. "There's going to be a little water damage and probably a lot of smoke damage, but we can deal with that," he promised her quietly, caressing her wet cheek, drowning in her haunted and darkened eyes. "We'll get through this together. Let's go talk to the fire chief . . ."

Chapter Seventeen

August 12

Dawn came, looking like bloodshot eyes on the horizon to Lea. She had remained at Logan's side throughout the night as the water was poured on the hot, smoldering remains of the wood shop and garage. The garish, blinding floodlights had shown clearly that the fire had eaten into the home, destroyed about five feet of the living room. In the darkness, she could let her tears fall and no one would see her cry for Logan's family's loss.

The firefighters continued to work hard, pulling the burnt lumber and wooden beams apart and hosing them down to ensure no embers were going to be around to start another fire later. She worked with Jody in giving the firefighters water to drink. This kind of brutal, physical work that went on for hours afterward, made them susceptible to heat exhaustion, Jody had explained. They did what they could when extra hands were needed.

Lea was too hyped up on adrenaline to do anything but keep moving and find tasks she could tackle. Logan had gone into the house with the fire chief to assess the damage to that end of his home. Her protective gloves were blackened by charred wood that she and Jody had helped to pull out of the debris of where each building had eventually collapsed. Her muscles hurt, she was filthy dirty, smelling of smoke and longing for a hot, cleansing shower. The electricity was out, due to the fire. As dawn grew brighter, she saw the extent of the destruction. Logan had already called his parents, letting them know what had happened. He told them he would call later today about the damage to the family house and send them photos via email.

She saw Dan Seabert drive up in his cruiser. Behind him parked the forensic team's white truck with the county logo painted on the side of it. Mind numb, she kept wondering who had done this to them. Why hadn't the fire alarms worked?

Yesterday they had been gone all day, for the most part, for the last day of the fair and the dance. The ranch had stood empty with the exception of a couple of skeleton-crew wranglers who kept an eye on things in Logan's absence.

She saw the fire chief and Logan emerge from the house, heading toward Dan, who was standing next to his cruiser. Everyone looked exhausted. And why not? Lea saw Logan lift his chin, searching for her. When he spotted her, he gestured for her to come and join him.

Lea stood next to him as Dan approached the three of them, his face expressionless. He was only twenty-nine years old, but had been an officer in the military police in the army for eight years previous. His law enforcement background was similar to that of Commander Hunter

Grant, an ex–U.S. Navy SEAL who had also entered law enforcement after he left the service. She was glad they were around after tonight's clash with the unnamed men who had tried to kill them.

"I wanted to give you an update," he told them. "The two perps we apprehended are in jail and being processed. They've already lawyered up. The other two are in the hospital. Both are undergoing surgery, one for a calf wound and the other, a thigh wound. They'll live. We've gone through their wallets and anything else they had on them. All four are in our database with long rap sheets. Our county prosecutor, Jenny Hatcher, is waiting for our reports. I'm sure they're going to be nailed with a number of crimes, not to mention trying to kill you two." He gave them a sympathetic glance. He flipped the notebook paper. "Right now, I've got my detectives doing the paperwork on all four of them. It's obvious to us that they are hired guns sent to set your house on fire, Logan."

"Yeah," he muttered. "The fire chief and I checked all our fire alarms and someone had taken out the batteries so they wouldn't work. I'd just replaced those batteries in all of them about a month ago. They meant to kill us."

Grimacing, Dan looked past them to the ranch house. "That means one of them, maybe more, were in the house, prior to setting this fire. It appears they took out the batteries while everyone was at the fair, and few eyes were on the place so they could drive in, do the dirty work, and leave without being spotted. They knew what they were doing."

"My two wranglers who were left here at the ranch while everyone went to the fair," Logan said heavily, "were stationed at the two barns below the main house. We have horses in stalls and a lot of hay, feed, and straw in them. When it gets hot like it's been, I always have a wrangler at each barn in case of spontaneous combustion of one of our hay bales, which could burn the barn down."

"Because you're bailing alfalfa right now in one of your fields," Dan said, "and it can get hot, smolder, and start a fire after it's baled and in a barn."

"Right. More than one barn has gone up just like that, so I always have one wrangler at each of our barns during this time frame." He hefted a thumb across his shoulder. "Both barns are down below the hill. My people would not have seen anyone coming in our entrance road or going into the ranch house."

Nodding, Dan made notes. "That makes a lot of sense."

"So why did they wait until we got home?" Lea demanded.

"Well," Dan drawled, "that's the missing piece to this puzzle. Whoever did this wanted you home. And taking out the batteries in the fire alarms and setting this ablaze at three a.m., would guarantee you were asleep."

Lea rubbed her face tiredly. "They wanted to murder us."

Logan placed his arm around her shoulder, drawing her protectively against him. "First degree attempted murder, Dan," Logan growled. "And my gut tells me Polcyn is behind this attack on us."

"Proving it is the hard part," Dan said sympathetically, taking off his sheriff's black baseball cap and scratching his head. "I don't disagree with you at all on who's behind it."

"Won't one of those men talk? Tell the truth?" Lea asked hoarsely, feeling the terror of almost dying in a house fire hitting her. Getting shot at wasn't good, either. She could have died twice tonight. Logan had put himself in the line of fire as well, not to mention, he and Jody having a hand grenade thrown at them! As if Logan were reading her thoughts, he gently squeezed her shoulders, as if to reassure her that the worst was over. But was it?

Dan gave her a searching look. "I wish I could say that they will talk, but I can't, Lea. Maybe if we can flip one of these four, we can find out more. Jenny's good at getting a perp to turn state's evidence, but she's got to have those reports first in order to fully evaluate this situation."

"I'd really like to catch Polcyn," Logan growled unhappily. "I *know* he's behind it. My gut is screaming at me that he's responsible for this."

"Makes a bunch of us," Dan agreed with a sigh. "Look, you two need to get some rest. We want you, Lea, and Jody, to come in and fill out a report of your experience. Right now, you're emotionally and physically exhausted. If I were you? I'd get a room at the Regency Hotel in town, Logan. Get cleaned up, go to bed, and sleep for as long as you want. Then, come over to the office and I want each of you to write up your report."

"We're exhausted," Logan agreed, giving Lea a concerned look. "And we'll get over there. I know you want the info as soon after the incident as possible."

"Yes," Dan said, closing the notebook and stuffing it into a pocket of his shirt. "You'll remember details that will go away within forty-eight hours of the incident."

Logan held out his hand. "Thanks, Dan. We'll leave here shortly. We have to pack some clothes, and Barry, my foreman, will be here at all times. The fire chief said the piles of rubble are pretty well soaked and won't start a fire, but they have to cool down completely before I can get someone in here to haul it all away. I've asked Barry to get a backhoe in here twenty-four hours from now, after everything has cooled down, and start the cleanup."

"I'm glad they saved your family home," Dan murmured, giving the place a glance. "My forensics team is going to work. We'll see what we find. I'll be in touch."

"Well," Logan said, holding Lea for a moment, "ready to go in, and we'll get some overnight clothes and get to that hotel?" He kissed the top of her head, smelling the smoke in the stiff strands.

"Am I ever," she murmured tiredly, turning and sliding her arm around his waist as they walked toward the house.

He opened the gate for them. "Do you want me to get you a separate room, Lea? I don't mind."

She shook her head. "Right now, Logan, I need you. I'm feeling shocky. I hate to admit it, but that's where I'm really at."

He gave her a concerned look, taking her hand, leading her up the walk to the covered porch. "There's only king beds in that hotel, not a second bed in the room. I can sleep on the sofa."

It was her turn to give him a look of disbelief. "What I need is to have you close. I need to be held for a little bit, Logan. I'm not up for sex."

"Makes two of us," he said, taking the steps with her. "Let's get some clothes packed. I need to call my parents and let them know what's going on. I know they're worried."

The hot shower at the hotel multiplied her exhaustion. Lea scrubbed her hair, the smoky smell replaced with the scent of fresh lemon. The room was large, plush, and Lea felt like she'd stepped from hell into heaven. Logan had told her to shower first, that he had phone calls to make in the office of the suite. Wrapping herself in the light-weight cotton knee-length pink nightgown with red roses across it, she absently ran her fingers through her hair and then combed it into a semblance of order. She looked shell-shocked in the reflection of the misty mirror. She padded out in plush slippers that the hotel had provided for them.

"I'm done," she called, sticking her head around the partly open office door.

"Oh," Logan said, "good timing. I'm next. In the meantime? Hit the rack." And then he slowly rose, giving her a dry look. "That's mil-speak, military speak, for a bed. I drop into my military lingo when I'm dog-tired."

"No worries."

"See you when you wake up," he murmured, unable to tear his gaze from her. Lea reminded him of an old-time Raggedy Ann doll, her hair mussed, those copper-colored freckles across her nose and cheeks giving her a look more like a little girl in that moment than the strong, brave woman he knew. "I'd kiss you goodnight, but I smell and I'm dirty."

"I don't care . . . I'd rather have your kiss . . ."

Logan slowly rose, moving toward her, holding her luminous gaze that clearly showed exhaustion, but also showed something else: desire for him and him alone. The knowledge flowed through him like heat cracking the glacier of grief that had been immovable in his heart since Elizabeth's sudden and unexpected death. Lea moved toward him. Wanted him. And he wanted her. Slowing, he reached out, opening his hands, sliding them against her flushed cheeks, still gazing into those huge black pupils surrounded with forest green, fearless and resolute.

Leaning down, he caressed her parting lips, inhaling the lemony scent surrounding her, the dampness of her copper-colored hair feeling good against his fingers. Logan became lost in the heat and desire glittering in her eyes. She pressed herself to him, her clean cotton gown against his filthy clothes that smelled of sour sweat, fear, dirt, and smoke. Her clean limbs curved like cool liquid around his shoulders, her long fingers moving into the hair at the nape of his neck, caressing the strands, her mouth opening, a soft moan rising into her throat as he caressed her lips. Out of the hell they'd just gone through, heaven burst through his chest like cooling calm and peace, and he felt the nudge of her hips and belly against his narrow hips, silently letting him know just how much she loved him. Her internal strength humbled him.

If Logan didn't stop, he was going to pick Lea up, place her on the bed and love her with everything he had. Reluctantly, he eased from her lips, which glistened and beckoned him to come back, to continue his exploration of her.

"I've got to get that shower," he muttered against her lips. He felt her smile, her arms sliding free of his shoulders. He already missed her closeness.

"I know . . ." Lea stepped out of his embrace, staring up at him. "And I'm not going to sleep until we can hold one another in bed, Logan. And forget what I said about no sex. I've changed my mind." She gave him a shy, mischievous smile.

"You're allowed to change your mind anytime you want." Running his hand down his filthy clothing, he growled,

"I've got to clean up, Lea. I'll be there as soon as I can," and he planted a quick, hard kiss on her mouth to back up that promise.

Logan didn't know what to expect when he emerged from the bathroom, wearing a pair of pajama bottoms. The early morning sun was making a bright rectangle around the closed, heavy dark blue drapes. It was six a.m. And any exhaustion he felt, was gone. As he approached the bed, he saw that Lea was sitting up, back against the padded headboard, the gown covering her upper legs and knees, waiting for him. She still had that rose flush to her cheeks, making those small freckles endearing to him. There was shyness to her, and yet she looked resolute at the same time.

He sat down on her side of the bed, placing his hand on the bed near her thigh. "Are you still feeling the same as before?"

"Yes." She had her hands clasped in her lap. "I had twenty minutes to think about a lot of things, Logan." Reaching out, Lea allowed her hand to slide from his well-muscled upper arm to his hand that lay flat on the mattress beside her thigh. "Every time I think that I could have died twice out there last night, it scares the hell out of me." She tucked her lower lip between her teeth for a moment. "I've never been close to death before. And twice, within an hour, it happened." She looked around and then held his sympathetic gaze. "I'm reeling from it. All I could think of, when this was all happening, was you, Logan. What we'd just confessed to one another earlier in the day, our hopes . . . our dreams . . . and they could have literally gone up in smoke like part of your home just did. Life is"—her voice lowered with emotion—"so precious . . . so fragile." She sighed and whispered, "Now? I know what you went through with losing Elizabeth . . ."

He dragged in a breath and sat up, enclosing her hands between his. "Yes, I know that every minute of the day is important. Losing Elizabeth forced me to reorder how I looked at life, how I lived my life after she passed. It taught me to be grateful for so many things I'd taken for granted. I learned everything could be gone in the snap of one's fingers." He cocked his head, looking at her. "We're going to find out over the coming weeks and months what that one hour we survived has done to us, and how, in large and small ways, it's reordered our lives. And it's not all bad." He opened his hand and took hers, lightly outlining each long finger with his. "Like your hands, Lea . . . you work so hard and it's damned demanding physical work. Your hands are beautiful. You aren't afraid to be who you are."

"I became that way as a teen, and I've come out of my shell over the years. I'm comfortable with who I am now, Logan. And last night . . . well . . . it really focused me on what was the most important thing in my life: You."

He held her liquid gaze and caressed her fingers. "I never thought I'd love again, but here you are and you hold my heart in your hands, sweet woman."

"And you hold my scared little heart in yours," she managed, shaking her head. "For whatever reason, Logan, with you, I'm bold, fearless . . . well . . . almost reckless."

"Does that scare you?"

Her lips twitched. "Not at all. I feel as though being bold and up front about how I feel toward you is worth the risk. Every woman you employ on your ranch is super confident, and I like that. I want to be like them. I guess I had it in me all the time and I just didn't realize it." She slid her fingers slowly up and down his hairy forearm. "I just needed the right person in my life to bring it out in me, is all."

Lifting his hand, Logan cupped her smooth, flushed cheek. "I love you, Lea. That was the one thing I was sorry about—not telling you sooner. Last night, I was regretting it more than anything else. What if I died? You'd never have known." His mouth tightened and he looked away for a moment. "From now on"—he turned, locking on to her gaze—"I won't hold back anything from you. I don't want any regrets. I don't ever want to wish I'd told you something that was important, and not have said it when it happened."

"Funny," she murmured, "I was thinking the same things you were. Do you know how long I've wanted to touch you? Kiss you? Wonder what it would be like to love you?"

"Same here," he said, shaking his head. "Well, here we are. I wish it hadn't been last night that forced our hand with one another, but I'm not sorry about it, either."

"Listen, before we make love? You need to know I've only had sex once and that was a long time ago."

"We'll go at the pace that you feel comfortable with. All right?"

"Yes . . ."

"Are you protected?"

"No."

"I can wear a condom. I don't have any sexual diseases, either."

She shrugged. "I just got off my period six days ago. I'm in my safe zone, Logan. And I'm clean, too."

"As we go along and explore one another," he said gently, "talk to me, tell me what you like or don't like. Okay? I'm not a mind reader. I need feedback."

"It should work both ways."

"I'll let you know," he said, smiling a little. "I just want you to be comfortable. This is our first time together and I want it to be good for both of us, not just one of us."

"Now I'm not so nervous . . ." she admitted in a low voice.

"Tell you what," he said, getting up and turning a light switch off, the room darkening, "I want you to touch me like you touch the wood you create such magic with."

Lea's eyes adjusted to the dimness in the room and she watched him pull off his pajama bottoms, placing them over a chair. She stood and pulled the gown over her head, dropping it to the floor. She knew Logan could see her and she could see his outline, his shadowed expression, intense. A shiver of anticipation arced through her as he came and lifted her into his arms, her limbs curving around his shoulders. Their flesh met, rubbing pleasantly against one another, soft against hard, smooth against hairy, and she smiled and closed her eyes, her brow pressed against his head as he walked around the end of their bed. Drawing in his male scent simply made her sigh with pleasure, her one hand sliding down across his broad, heavily muscled shoulder, his prominent collarbone, drifting to that soft, dark hair across his chest.

Logan deposited her in the center of the bed. She gripped his arm, silently guiding him down so that he lay on his right side, facing her as she lay on her left side. His hand slid across her waist, coming to a halt against the small of her back. The gesture was one of capturing her, letting her know that he wanted her, that she was his.

The heat built between them, their bodies less than eight inches away from one another. "I want to touch you," she whispered, "memorize you, your body, how you feel to me . . ."

"Same here . . . ," he rasped.

The moment his hard, callused palm slid from her shoulder, slowly moving down her side, across her ribs, her skin prickled and tingled in the wake of his exploring fingers. Her nipples instantly puckered with anticipation. There was such sensuality to Logan. It surprised but pleased her. Lea had always thought love could be gentle. It didn't have to be rough or hurtful, and she'd experienced both, unfortunately. Pushing those memories away, wanting to make new and healthier ones, she slid her hand along the same route as he'd done with her. Her fingertips were supersensitive as she felt the hard muscle beneath his heated flesh, which grew taut wherever she caressed him.

Her lashes dropped as she continued to memorize his body. She slid her hand across his hip, his long, hard, hairy thigh. All that masculine power, and yet Logan held it in check until he needed it. So many men tried to use their physical power against women; she'd seen it too often, but here she was with someone who was not like that at all. Something cold within her melted and then dissolved, trust replacing the unknown about him. Logan was an incredibly even-handed man, quiet spoken, a good listener, never interrupting anyone, especially her.

A soft moan rose in her as he caressed the side of her breast, brushing the nipple with his thumb. A jolt of electric-like sensations felt like a bolt of lightning coursing down through her, congealing between her legs, the wetness immediate. Hips twisting, she wanted contact with him, his hard erection telling her just how much he wanted her. It was a euphoric moment of discovery.

Logan's hands slid around her hips and he rolled onto his back, bringing her on top of him, her long thighs settling on either side of his powerful ones. The moment he slid her against him, she gave a little cry of raw pleasure, the heat bursting throughout her lower body, destroying her mind and all thoughts, everything focused on the scent of him, the raw power being shared between them, his hands guiding her, sliding her against him, teasing her, making her moan with need of him.

Enveloped within his maleness, the softness of the hair on his chest tantalizing her breasts that hungered for more contact with him, she sank into a heated cauldron of molten desire. Nothing else mattered except to love him, show him her love and become one with one another. Rocking, entering her wetness, she arched, her fingers digging into his chest as she did so. The teasing sensation of him moving slowly back and forth into her throbbing entrance, made her groan. She had orgasmed once in her life, but now it was a volcanic eruption taking place deep within her body, red-hot streams of rippling heat spreading ever outward until she was consumed by it. If not for the strength of Logan's hands against her hips, she would probably have fallen off him, light-headed and ungrounded by the surprise explosion now moving through her entire lower body like a tsunami of pleasure. She heard a cry, more like a shout of raw satiation, spill from her throat, frozen and consumed by it all at the same time. Never had she felt such ecstasy!

Dizzied, she gasped for air, clutching at his shoulders, feeling as if the sun shone fiercely through her entire lower region, the pleasure ongoing, like tidal waves, demolishing her mind so that only primal gratification, fulfilled, was within her. And it wasn't over. Logan brought her to a second, and then a third orgasm. Completely exhausted by the power of her own body to devour so much satisfaction, he seemed to know she was ready to collapse, her limbs feeling like so much jelly.

Gently, he lifted her off him and settled her back against the mattress, taking her lips, cherishing her until she understood for the first time in her life what it was like to be truly loved by a man. It felt as if she were floating, that clouds were around her, the light bright but not blinding behind her closed lids. The only awareness she felt was of Logan easing her thighs apart and slowly entering her once more.

Wanting to be a partner, not just a recipient of his skills, she focused on her hips and thrust upward, hearing him give a low growl of satisfaction. Yes! She placed her hands around his waist, sliding her lower legs around his massive thighs, entrapping him so all he could do was be held by her body and give him the same level of satisfaction he'd just given her. He'd placed his hands on either side of her head, holding her as he arched into her, a groan tearing out of him as she pushed her hips upward, taking him, making him give everything he had to her. As he froze above her, his breathing shallow, his hands holding her head tightly, she felt him tremble, felt that powerful release within her. It made her feel strong and good as a woman. Love has many aspects to it, and this was the physical one. At some point, Lea felt herself capitulate as he sank heavily against her, pushing up on his elbows to avoid crushing her. The last, wonderful thing she remembered was him

easing off her, drawing her against him, her head resting
on his shoulder as he pulled up a cooling cotton sheet
across their waists.

Logan watched Lea sleep deeply. He'd awakened at
three p.m. And he didn't have the heart to disturb her.
Her hand was curled near her hair, which was soft and
shone in the midafternoon light leaking around the window.
Wanting to touch her but knowing it might disturb her, he
was content to simply watch the shallow rise and fall of
her chest. He lay on his side, facing her, the sheet draped
languidly across her hips. Love suffused him and made
him almost want to cry because he never thought it could
happen twice. But it had. And for that, he was deeply,
forever grateful.

At the same time, his dark brows dipped. It was never
far from his mind that the arsonists were caught, but the
real killer behind the scenes, had not been. More than anything, he wanted Lea to be safe, and blossom beneath his
care and love, just as he would with hers. Having been
married, he understood that two people under the same
roof meant compromise. But that had been easy for him
because love trumped anything else, every time. He
knew it would happen with Lea, also. Happiness collided
directly with fear of losing her to the killer. Knowing it
was Polcyn, he had no way of stopping him. At least, not
yet. He wrestled with his rage over what had happened.
Lea was a strong woman despite how she might see herself. Last night had proven that without any doubt. He loved
her with his life. He'd willingly give up his life so that
she could live. And last night, that had almost happened.

They'd walked away from a potential nightmare with only bruises and scratches, but emotionally, it had been devastating to both of them and he knew it.

His phone was on vibrate and he heard it in the drawer of the nightstand. Rolling over, he slid the drawer open, picking it up so it would stop making that slight sound. Looking over his shoulder, he saw Lea continued to sleep deeply. Slipping out of bed, he went to the office and shut the door in order to answer the call.

"Logan?"

"Yeah, what's up, Dan?" He slid his fingers through his mussed hair.

"We caught a break. One of the perps' cell phones yielded out big-time. There are calls to Polcyn. I want you to know that a judge just approved our request for an arrest warrant and the sheriff from Cheyenne, Wyoming, is going to his house as we speak."

Relief poured through Logan. "Thank God," he rasped. "What does this mean?"

"He'll be arrested. The phone calls were subpoenaed and there is no doubt that Polcyn ordered these four men to burn your house down around you."

"I can't believe it. This is good news. Phone calls and texts stand up in court."

"Yes," Dan said, "they do. But Polcyn will hire the best damned defense lawyers this country has. Jenny, our county attorney, is already on it. What we have to do now is get him locked up and denied bail. He's a flight risk as far as I'm concerned. The sheriff in Cheyenne, Cortney Horner, will keep him in jail. Forty-eight hours after that, Polcyn goes before a judge. His defense attorneys are going to argue to give him bail, that he's not a flight risk or a danger to the public."

Snorting, Logan snarled, "Like hell he isn't! He tried to kill me and Lea. He *is* a danger to the public."

"Jenny is flying down there tomorrow morning to meet with the county attorney for the city of Cheyenne. They'll pool their resources and be there for that meeting with the judge. Right now, are you and Lea awake? Up for writing up your reports?"

"She's still sleeping, Dan. She was totaled by almost dying twice last night. I didn't have the heart to wake her."

"I understand. Well, I'll be here until eighteen hundred, er . . . six p.m. If you make it in by that time, I'll be around and we can talk further."

"Ever the military," Logan teased. All military people spoke in Zulu, or twenty-four-hour clock time, not a.m. or p.m., like civilians did. He smiled a little. "That's okay, I'm sure she'll be awake in an hour or so."

"Hey, on a personal note? I didn't know you had a relationship with Lea. When did this happen?"

"I think it started the day her vehicle got hit at the entrance to our ranch," he uttered. "I wasn't looking for a woman to be in my life, believe me, but she just grew on me over the weeks and months."

"I like her a lot," Dan said, congratulating him. "And given you lost Elizabeth? It's past time you found a woman, pardner."

Logan closed his eyes. "Yeah, I'm one lucky bastard. I just want Lea safe from the likes of Polcyn, that's all. That has scared me more than anything, Dan. I knew he was behind this, but I felt damned helpless trying to protect Lea from another attack."

"I hear you," the sheriff said quietly. "We caught a break. The perp didn't lock his phone, so it was easy enough to open up and get all his texts and emails. It proved to be a treasure trove of evidence. Listen, I have to go. Tell Lea the good news when she gets up and maybe I'll see the two of you before I go home tonight."

Chapter Eighteen

August 25

Logan lifted his straw hat off his head and wiped his brow with the back of his gloved hand. Lea had just entered the ranch house, picking her way through new lumber lying around and the many hired people who had come to help rebuild their home. He smiled as she entered.

"Hey, where have you been?" he called, settling the hat back on his head.

"Oh . . . places," she said coyly, holding a large brown sack in one hand. "I saw the lunch van coming to feed the folks who are here helping us. It's going to be time for everyone to eat and find shade." So many people volunteered to help rebuild that Logan, in turn, had called the local food truck to come and feed everyone a hefty breakfast and lunch.

It was eighty degrees Fahrenheit and that was far hotter than this valley normally saw. It was climate change. Lea looked around, pleased. The entire area that had been burned was being rebuilt. New lumber, new logs were trucked in, drywall put up and painted, and the fireplace cared for, as well. Even the smoky smell was finally going away. They had spent their first week in their own bed at the ranch house and it felt good to be home. "Let's take the swing on the porch. I have some lunch for us."

He grinned. "Sounds good. So, you said you were visiting Poppy this morning? Did you get lunch from her restaurant?"

"Sure did. Your favorite: vegetarian lasagna with all the trimmings."

"She and her husband, Brad, have been life savers," he said, coming over and walking her out to the shady side of the porch. "And both of them are pretty darned good cooks," he added, his hand coming to rest on her back.

As they rounded the corner, he spotted a big, wrapped present sitting at one end of the swing. "Hey, what's that?"

She smiled. "Happy birthday, Logan. You do know that today is your birthday? The townspeople have come together to help us get the wood shop and garage rebuilt. I think you lost track of time." She laughed.

"You shouldn't have," he said, leaning down, kissing her temple.

"Let's eat while the food's hot," she said, sitting down and patting the cushion next to her. "We'll let you open your gift afterwards."

He sat, took off his hat, and placed it on the small table at the end of the swing. They opened the cardboard boxes that contained the food. "Mmmm, smells good," he murmured, handing her a huge salad with all the fixings. Even the cutlery was made of stout cardboard, everything recyclable and healthy for the Earth. No plastic, that was for sure. She sat back after opening a packet of ranch dressing, drizzling it over her salad.

"We're almost done with the remodel," he said between bites of the spicy lasagna and the thick French bread slathered with butter and garlic.

"Today should be the last day," Lea agreed. "And then? We can have our lives back, sort of."

"Dan Seabert called a little while ago," Logan told her. "The judge has thrown Polcyn back into jail."

"Good. He put him on an ankle monitor and he was free to roam his house," Lea grouched, frowning.

"Well, no more. Polcyn defied the judge's limits on where he could go. Now he's going to spend a year or more in jail, waiting for his trial." Logan's voice dropped to a growl. "Couldn't happen to a better person."

"I'm just glad we had the phone records and that Jenny got one of those four guys to flip. If she hadn't, Polcyn would be free to come after us again. I was so worried about that."

"Anyone would be." He reached over, caressing her cheek. "Now we can sleep soundly again."

"Dan has been a blessing to us," Lea acknowledged. "He's really pushed to get Polcyn behind bars. He and Jenny worked together like the good team they are, and fortunately, the judge in Cheyenne took seriously what they had to say about Polcyn attacking the ranch. Some judges might not have." She shook her head.

"The law is the law," Logan said. "There's not supposed to be any politics in the law. It's blind, as it should be."

"Chase was just over at Poppy's," she said, changing topics. "Do you know what he's going to do?"

"No. What?"

"Well, he's run a big organic cattle ranch for nearly as

long as your family put down roots here," Lea said. "Chase came in like a kid who found a frog in a pond."

Chuckling, Logan said, "What's he all excited about?"

"Apparently, Poppy has been doing a lot of work behind-the-scenes with Chase. He was wanting to get out of the business of cattle, and was looking for something more Mother Earth friendly to raise on his ranch."

"I'd heard rumors that he was wanting out of the cattle business for some time now," Logan said. "So? Is he going to do it?"

"Well"—she hesitated—"maybe . . . it all depends on him finding the right person, a master gardener he can hire, who will stay at the ranch and help him with this new vision."

"What is his vision?"

"I guess he's been working on a concept for a couple of years with Poppy's input. He feels that with the loss of honeybees happening at such a horrendous level, thanks to pesticides, that he wants to put in more hives, sell the honey, but also sell the hives and bees to farms and ranches anywhere in the country. He wants to enlarge everything."

"That isn't going to keep him monetarily solvent," Logan said, finishing off the lasagna, wiping up the last of the marinara sauce with his final piece of garlic bread.

"He knows that. But I give him credit for going green. It has to be our future because fossil fuels are killing the Earth."

"I won't disagree with you. Funny, I was thinking about bringing bees to our ranch." He gave her a searching look. "We could put them on the edges of our alfalfa pastures. I wonder if he's got a honeybee wrangler yet?" He grinned. "How do you feel about that?"

"I'm all for sustainable living, Logan. I was raised to be environmentally conscious."

"I like that we've built compost bins and put them in each grove, as well."

"We've always had a compost bin at my parents' home. That, and we have a recycling center, too."

He gave her a sly look. "For the past couple of years, and, I admit, after hashing over different ideas with Chase and some of the other ranchers, I've been considering some changes, too." He looked up at the house. "I held off talking to you about them, with Polcyn's attacks on us. I was afraid I'd lose you before I could convince you to stay with me."

Giving him a thoughtful look, she placed her empty salad box on the end table at the other end of the swing. "I know we haven't said much since we admitted our love for one another. Things have been crazy ever since that night."

"It has been hectic," Logan agreed. He placed his arm around her shoulders, drawing her next to him. "And out of all this bad, came something good." He looked into her eyes, which had a new luster in them since they'd made love to one another. His heart expanded with joy. "I have you. And you have me. It doesn't get any better than this, Lea."

She leaned up, kissing him for a long, long time. When their mouths parted, she saw that gleam in his eyes: He wanted her. She wanted him. "Now's not the time, Logan."

"No," he said unhappily, "but I can dream . . ."

She relaxed against him, looking out beyond the porch. "Things are getting back to normal."

"For us, yes," he agreed, frowning. "For Maddy and Alvin? It's a different story. He's going to always need her around to help him from now on. She won't be coming back as our housekeeper."

"We can hire someone to do that for us on a weekly basis," Lea said. "Pay them a good salary, too."

"I was thinking along those lines," he admitted. "With the wood shop almost done, and you buying a new set of woodworking tools, you're going to be back to work, doing what you love to do."

"I know we haven't talked a lot about it, but yes. I like working and will continue to do what I want. With my parents coming out in mid-September for a visit, I'm looking forward to my dad helping make the wood shop even better. He called me earlier today and told me he had sent a lot of his extra wood-shop tools via carrier, for me. I can hardly wait to get started on that front door I promised you." She grinned.

Logan absorbed her happiness. "The door got destroyed in the fire."

"Only the wood I'd chosen for it, and the pattern. Both are easy enough to replicate." She eased out from beneath his arm and stood up, going to fetch the gift from the end of the swing. "Speaking of which? Happy birthday, Logan."

He took the large gift, which was a lot heavier than he first realized. "This must weigh twenty pounds," he said, gesturing for her to sit down next to him.

Laughing, she nodded. "It's actually twenty-one pounds. Go ahead, open it up."

"I wasn't expecting anything," he admitted, placing the gift, wrapped in silver and gold paper, on his thighs. There was a bright red ribbon around it.

"I know. It's been so busy around here . . ."

"How did you find time to do this?" he wondered, pulling off the ribbon and handing it to her.

She looked up at the sky, her smile deepening. "I'll tell you in a minute. Open it up!"

Logan did so. What he saw took his breath away. He ran his fingertips over the wood sculpture of the oldest tree in the oak grove. He'd recognize it anywhere, especially because it was the fairy tree where people came to make their requests and prayers to the little people. Only, the ribbons were delicately carved and painted to make the oak look like a year-around Christmas tree. And even more touching, an eight-year-old boy sat against the oak's mighty trunk, reading a book. Giving her a look of awe, he croaked, "This . . . this is beyond beautiful, Lea. When did you do this?"

"I took photos of it and then started working on it. Luckily"—she sighed—"I had it all done, except for painting the ribbons. I'd taken it over to Poppy and Brad's bookstore to use her brushes and paints. It was over there in her art studio when the fire hit us and destroyed everything in the wood shop. I got really lucky. I was so glad that this piece had been saved, because of all the stories you'd told me about it as a kid growing up, how you used to love coming out to this old oak, sitting beneath it and reading your books." She smiled a little. "At that time, there was no WiFi out there, and all you had were good ole books."

Shaking his head, he couldn't stop touching the huge wooden carving. "And I'll bet you've used fallen limbs from that same oak to create it here?"

"Oh, yes. That was a week-long scrounge, believe me. I knew what I wanted, and put a lot of the downed branches in the back of my pickup. But some were newer and still had dampness in them, so I couldn't use them. I needed very, very old branches that had fully dried. That way, they wouldn't crack or possibly fall out of the sculpture as they shrunk."

"This deserves to go somewhere special," he rasped, his voice filled with emotion as he stared down at it.

"Since the fireplace was affected by the fire, why couldn't we hang it up above the mantel? I think it would look beautiful there. Don't you?"

Nodding, he placed the sculpture on the floor of the porch. "I like it," he said, standing and pulling something out of his front pocket. "Now," he said, "close your eyes and hold out one of your hands. I have something for you."

She smiled. "It's not my birthday, Logan."

"That's okay." He approached her. "Close your eyes and hold out your hand."

Her smile grew. "Okay, just because it's *your* birthday." She did as he asked.

Logan gently placed a bright red velvet pouch, half the size of her palm, into her hand. "Open your eyes," he whispered, kneeling down on one knee, his other hand on her thigh.

Lea did so and looked at the pouch. She glanced over at him and saw the love shining in his eyes. "You've been busy, too, I see," she teased. Every time he smiled, that sculpted mouth of his simply turned her into yearning heat. The man did not recognize his own sensuality, and she silently promised him that she would show him how wonderful a lover he truly was.

"A little," he chuckled, lightly running his hand on the top of her jean-clad thigh. "This is for you . . ." He watched her open the red cord on the pouch. She peeked inside.

"You'll have to turn it upside down," he suggested.

Lea nodded and did so. A wedding ring and engagement ring fell into her cupped palm. She gasped, jerked her head up, staring at him in shock.

"Logan!"

"I know it's a little soon," he apologized, "but I'm not sorry I did it."

Pressing her hand to her heart for a moment, emotion flooded her as she stared down at them. "They're so beautiful." She picked up the gold wedding ring that had a channel-set group of five rectangular green stones that flashed like fire. "What kind of stones are they?" she asked in a hushed voice, turning the ring, watching the light play through the faceted gemstones.

"My father is a rock hound," Logan explained. "He found sapphires in the Montana mountains a long time ago. He found several green ones. They come in all colors, not just the blue ones that most people are familiar with. He'd held on to them for a long time. I called him a month ago and asked if he was willing to make channel facets of those green sapphires he found, and he did it. My dad is a serious jeweler, too."

She nodded, setting it down and picking up the flat, gold engagement ring. There was a tree carved around the entire circumference of it. "This is so beautiful," she whispered. "Who did the etching of this?"

"Me," he said humbly. "I know it's not artistic like what you create, Lea, but my heart was in it. I know how much trees mean to you and it's more than just because you use their wood to make your magical pieces of art."

Closing her fingers, holding the rings, she leaned down, her other palm against his cheek, kissing him softly, with all her heart and soul. Lifting her mouth away, she drowned in his darkened eyes, felt his fingers brush strands of hair away from her temple.

"Marry me when the time is right, Lea. No pressure here. I want you in my life for the rest of my life. I never thought anyone could fit me like you do. We love the same things: Nature, trees, and the land. We care about one another, but we also care about the Earth, and that's important to me. Family is important to both of us. And so are the people who work here on the ranch. They're my second family and I wouldn't want it any other way."

She straightened and placed the wedding ring into the pouch and handed him the engagement ring. "If we hadn't almost died that night of the fire, I might have said that I did want to wait, to mull it over, think about my life and what I thought was important," she whispered. "That night taught me that time is precious. That I could be gone in a blink of an eye."

She handed him the ring. "Put this on my finger, Logan. I want the world to know that we love one another. Do you think your parents might be able to fly up here and be here at the same time my mother and dad will be here? I'd like to invite them to be a part of our journey together. I'd like to hear from them when they think is the best time for a wedding." She saw his eyes widen, and then they filled with tears. Logan had lost so much when Elizabeth suddenly died. And she wanted, in some small way, to give back all those lost years of grief and loneliness, because this man was made for a partner: someone who was as strong as he was, who shared the love of the land, and treated people with kindness and generosity.

He eased to his feet and pulled her to hers. "Come here," he rasped thickly, sliding his hand beneath her left one. Holding her stare, her own eyes glistening with unshed tears, he slipped the ring on her finger. "There," he choked. "The rest of our lives are tied to one another, Lea, and I can't think of a better way to live. Can you?"

She solemnly shook her head, moving into the circle of his arms, leaning fully against him, relishing the contact, his strength and his love for her alone. "No, I can't think of a better way to live. I want to share my life, my heart, with you. Forever."

We hope you enjoyed the first novel in the
SILVER CREEK series.
Don't miss

COURAGE UNDER FIRE

by
Lindsay McKenna
Coming to your favorite bookstores and e-retailers in
March 2021!

Turn the page and enjoy a quick peek!

Chapter One

"No . . . no, don't murder the bees!" Cari Taylor turned in her sleep, reliving a moment in her life when she was five years old. Moaning, she cried out, "Don't hurt them! They won't sting us!"

Mrs. Johnson, their kindergarten teacher, was horrified. There, near the rear gate of their playground out in back of the house, was a huge ball of honeybees, the size of a basketball, in the apple tree.

Frantic, Cari saw her teacher's face go from shock to horror. Her own heart bounced in fear. Fear for her friends, the bees. Her father and uncle had beehives and she had grown up with the beekeepers and dearly loved her little friends. "No!" she cried. "They're harmless, Mrs. Johnson!" she squeaked, putting herself between the twenty other children who surrounded the teacher, who were all staring at the ball of bees in the fruit tree, fear in their faces.

"All of you," Mrs. Johnson said, her voice hoarse with

near hysteria, "in the house! Get in the house! These bees will sting you!"

Tears jammed into Cari's eyes as she stubbornly stood her ground between her teacher and the fruit tree. She could hear the soft, gentle buzzing of twenty thousand honeybees all in a ball, protecting the queen in the center of it, who had flown from someone's beehive to find a new home due to overcrowding. The hive had become populated with too many bees and the queen had taken half of her female worker bees and perhaps some of her drones who attended her, on a flight from the hive in order to find a new place, less crowded, to start a new hive. Cari knew this, but it was obvious blond-haired Mrs. Johnson, who was only twenty-two years old, did not. She was frantically gathering all her five- and six-year-old charges to her, pushing them gently toward the rear door of the house.

"I'll call the fire department," she told the kids, continuing to herd them inside. "They'll kill the bees and you'll be safe. Then, you can go outside and play on the swings, slides, and monkey bars."

Cari followed dejectedly, hearing the teacher's words. *Oh, no!* She turned on her small heel, looking longingly at the ball of bees. They wouldn't hurt anyone. How could she get the teacher to believe her?

"Cari! Get in here!" Mrs. Johnson ordered, gesturing frantically. "Hurry up! The bees could come and sting you to death! Run!"

Grudgingly, she came, a pout on her lips. She shook her head as she approached her teacher. "They won't hurt anyone!" she cried out. "Don't kill them! They'll leave in a bit. They're just resting. They're trying to find a new home, is all!"

Frustration appeared on Lucy Johnson's face. She

grabbed Cari's pink T-shirt by the shoulder, pulling her forward. "Get in the house! You must be kept safe!"

Cari grudgingly entered the house. All the kids were in the large sleeping area where they took naps, looking at one another, some afraid, some upset, some curious, and others stressed. A few were crying. Mrs. Johnson had never been in such a dramatic and emotional state like this before and it scared all of them. She was afraid of bees. Dodging to the right, Cari ran out of the room, down the hall, and into another room that led to the rear door to the backyard playground. As she quietly, like a shadow, edged toward that hallway, she saw Mrs. Johnson pick up the phone, dial 911, her voice cracking with fear as she told the dispatcher at the fire department they had to get over here right now. They had to kill the bees in order to protect her children.

Cari slipped away when Mrs. Johnson turned her back on the nap room. On tiptoes, she ran to the rear door exit. Heart pumping with terror for her bee friends, she leaped down the steps, ran across the yard to the fruit tree. Just above her, the basketball-size group of bees were surrounding a Y in a large branch. Terror filled her as she looked back at the door, making sure Mrs. Johnson didn't discover her out here.

Pursing her small mouth, Cari closed her eyes and sent a mental message to the queen bee she knew was at the center of this swarm of honeybees. She had been taught that she could "talk" to the bees with her mind. "Let me find you, queen. Guide me to you. I need to carry you out of here or they will come and murder all of you! I'll take you down the alley. There's a nice fruit tree orchard at the other end. I'll find a safe place for all of you!" She opened her eyes, struggled up the trunk, grabbing branches to hoist herself up to the mass of bees.

Without hesitation, Cari gently placed her small fingers into the mass. The bees were humming, but were not upset by her nearness. They felt like warm, living, soft velvet enclosing her as she eased her fingers down, down, down toward the center. The edge of the bee swarm was almost up to her armpit as she slowly, gently, felt around for the large queen. There! She'd found her!

The bees continued to hum, not at all perturbed by Cari's arm stuck into their swarm ball.

Mentally, Cari told the queen that she would ease her into her palm, close her fingers carefully around her and slowly draw her out of the center. She felt the queen, who had a much larger, longer body, and cupped her palm beneath her. In a moment, she had the queen and began to ease her hand back, bringing her out of the swarm.

Once her hand drew free, Cari struggled down to the ground, carefully holding the queen, ensuring she would not accidentally squeeze her and kill her. Running for the gate, she unlatched it, moved outside of it, closed it, turned right and dug her toes into the dirt of the alleyway, running as hard as she could. The wind tore past her, her mouth open, gasping for air as she passed through the alleyway and headed into the huge stand of apple trees in the nearby farm orchard. Spotting an easy-to-climb fruit tree, Cari raced over to it, nearly tripping on a small rise of dirt in her path.

Climbing awkwardly, with one hand only, she wriggled up into the tree, spotting a low hanging Y-shaped branch. Cari was sobbing for breath, tired and worried. If Mrs. Johnson did a head count and found her missing? That would be very, very bad for Cari. But she had to rescue her bees! They couldn't be murdered by the firefighters! And the fire department was not that far away from the kindergarten.

Gasping, lungs burning with exertion from her run, she twisted a look over her shoulder. There, behind her, was a dark cloud of honeybees flying toward her, following the pheromone scent of their queen, heading directly for where Cari was standing.

She told the queen that she'd be safe here with her family, that no one would find or hurt them. Gently placing the queen on the Y of the branch, Cari pushed off and fell to the ground, landing on her hands and knees. Quickly leaping up, brushing off her knees of her jeans, she raced toward the alley, opened the gate and slipped back in, latching it once more behind her. Her small hands shook as she placed the latch on it once again, turned, and ran for that rear exit door.

Once inside, Cari hurriedly tiptoed through the supply room, cracked the door to the hall and peered out. She could hear the teacher talking loudly to the firefighters who had just arrived. Her heart feeling like it was going to burst out of her chest, Cari walked quietly down the hall, edging silently toward the nap room. All the children were gathered there, frightened, some clinging to Mrs. Johnson's slacks. There were three firefighters standing there, listening to her.

Cari tried to slow down her heart, still breathing through her mouth, trying to remain undetected and quiet and not wanting anyone to discover her. She had pressed her back to the hall wall and listened intently.

"Well," the lieutenant was saying, "we have foam, Mrs. Johnson. We can use that to get rid of the bees. We'll go look at that fruit tree and assess the situation. We could also call a beekeeper to come and get them, too. That way, they wouldn't be killed."

"I want them killed!" Mrs. Johnson said, her voice high pitched with fear. Her arms weren't long enough to hold all the children who were now fully frightened and who surrounded her navy blue slacks, watching the firefighters with trepidation.

Cari knew the bees would be gone. They followed the queen, no matter where she flew. Leaning down, she made sure her knees weren't dusty looking, or sharp-eyed Mrs. Johnson would see the patches on her jeans and ask a lot of questions that Cari didn't want to answer.

She straightened and saw the children dispersing from around the teacher, wandering around, wondering what to do. Mrs. Johnson had left them and went to the back door to watch the firefighters as they tramped through the house and out the rear door. It was then that Cari silently slipped back among them, no one having missed her presence under the circumstances.

Just as Cari got comfortable on her little bed in the corner of the nap room, she heard the door open and close, the clomping of heavy boots, the firefighters moving back near the front door and the nap room.

"Well?" Mrs. Johnson demanded. "Did you see them?"

"No, ma'am," the lieutenant said. "They're gone."

"What? No! That's impossible!" she said, hurrying past them, disappearing as she headed for the rear door.

Cari held her breath for a moment. The bees were gone! Relief made her sag, her small back against the corner of the two walls. She heard the click-clack of Mrs. Johnson's low-heeled shoes echoing and coming closer and closer.

"They are gone!" she exclaimed to the firefighters.

"Where did they go? Are they hanging around? Will they come back?"

"No, ma'am, they're gone and we don't know where they flew. That's a swarm. In the spring, honeybees will swarm if their hive is too crowded. They're harmless, really. When they're swarming, they don't sting anyone. They're following their queen to a new home, is all."

"So? They won't return to harm the children?"

"They would never harm anyone," the lieutenant said. "Now, it's safe to let the kids out into the playground."

"Heck," one of the other firefighters said, "you might even use this as a teachable moment for the kids, ma'am. Let the children learn about bee swarms and why they happen."

Mrs. Johnson curled her lip, glaring at the younger man. "Never! This was a dangerous situation for my children! I'm charged with their safety and welfare. I hate insects!"

The lieutenant shrugged and lifted his hand. "Come on," he told his team, "we're done here. You and your children are safe now, Mrs. Johnson."

And so were her bees, Cari thought, keeping silent, remaining the shadow that she was. When she got home this afternoon? She'd tell her parents what happened. They'd be proud of her for helping the queen and her worker bees to safety. But she could never tell the kindergarten teacher what really happened. Not ever. Mrs. Johnson would not be happy and Cari knew she'd get five minutes of detention staring at a corner, if she was found out. Secrets were good.

When the dream ended, Cari opened her eyes, suddenly awake in the darkness of her bedroom in her San

Francisco loft. Looking at a digital clock, the red numbers read 3:13 a.m. *Ugh.* Why did she have such a rich dream life? Most nights, she had happy dreams. Flights of fancy. But tonight? This one was different. Pushing herself up in her bed, she rubbed her face, pushing back strands of black hair from her face.

At twenty-nine years old, her life was like a dream come true. She was a beekeeping consultant with an MBA and worked with countries around the world, showing them how to make beekeeping, and the honey the bees made in their hives, a commercial venture.

Because the bee populations around the world were nosediving, thanks to pesticides, hive collapses, and loss of rural land for the bees to gather pollen from local flowers, they were in a crisis. A global one. She worked for the state of California as their bee expert and was always busy with the farmers from the Imperial Valley, where so many crops grew. The many almond orchards thrived and all were dependent upon bee pollinators. That was where she came in, giving them sound, healthy advice on what beehives needed in order to pollinate the crops successfully. No cutting corners, no use of bee-killing pesticides, trying to get farmers to work with more organized and sustainable ways to grow their crops, as well as to protect the sagging honeybee population.

She saw herself as a Don Quixote tilting at windmills at times, because big agriculture wanted to use pesticides. Now, there was a global clash on using them, and billions of bees were dying off at such a swift rate, it was taking a toll on food production. Crops would not be pollinated. No pollination? No food. Food shortages could occur. Combine that with a horrifying loss of billions of birds every year, another pollinator, Mother Earth was in a real crisis, thanks to man. She felt like a frontline warrior trying to help both types not only to survive, but thrive. There were many raptor rehabilitator activists fighting right alongside of her to protect all bird species just as she was fighting to save bees around the world.

Sighing, she got up, knowing that she'd never go back to sleep.

The phone rang. Frowning, she picked it up.

"Hello?" Who would be calling at this time in the morning?

"This is the sheriff, ma'am. Am I speaking to Ms. Cari Taylor?"

"Yes?" A frown creased her brow as she sat down on the edge of her bed. "Why are you calling me? What's wrong?"

"Ma'am, your stepbrother, Dirk Bannock, just escaped from the prison. The officials from that prison called us about it. We've already contacted your parents, and now we're letting you know about it."

Gasping, Cari shot to her feet. "What? Dirk broke out? He's on the loose?" Instantly her heart thundered in her chest, and she felt dizzy, abruptly sitting down, her one hand wrapping into the quilt cover across her bed. Was she still dreaming? This was a nightmare! It couldn't be true! Oh, God, what if it was?

Dirk had entered her life when her mother had married Blake Bannock, a civil engineer working for the city of San Francisco. He had a three-year-old son from his former marriage when he married her mother, Nalani, a professor of English at Stanford University.

Terror ripped through her. She suddenly felt faint from the shock. "B-but, he was in for twenty-five years for the murder!"

"Yes, ma'am, we know. We have an all-points bulletin out for all law enforcement and we're working with the prison directly to find and apprehend him."

Pressing her hand to her chest, feeling the pounding of her heart, adrenaline racing through her, she whispered frantically, "But he promised to come after me! He threatened me in open court. He'll kill me!"

"Yes, ma'am, we're very well aware of that. We are sending a police unit over to your home. They will be on watch twenty-four hours a day."

Her throat ached with unshed tears. She squeezed her eyes shut, hot tears streaming out of them. "H-he said he'd kill me. You have to find him!"

"We're doing our best."

"What about my parents?" Dirk hated Nalani and herself. He was competitive and wanted all the attention of his father. Dirk had hated Cari the moment he met her. He saw her as direct competition.

"They also have police protection."

"But for how long?" Dirk had threatened her mother as well, but his hatred was reserved for Cari alone. She'd seen him fire the handgun at his girlfriend, Denise, and murder her. He was a cold-blooded killer. In court, a psychiatrist had labeled him as sociopathic. His world consisted of his rules and regulations. He defied the laws of society at every turn. By age twelve, he was selling drugs at his school. And that was when he became an addict. By age fifteen, Dirk had amassed a group of boys who sold the drugs over an even larger area where they had lived. And by the time she was sixteen years old, and saw him murder Denise, he was a regional drug lord in the San Francisco area. And as much as law enforcement tried to indict him for drug running, Dirk was incredibly intelligent and was able to avoid being caught. *Until Denise.* She felt sorry for the girl then, as she did now. Dirk was a law unto himself.

Cari wondered during the trial if he'd murdered other kids. If so, it had never been found out. But her intuition, which was very strong in her, told her that Denise had not been his first victim. Or his last.

"How long can you give us protection?" she demanded.

"Ma'am, we can't do it forever, but we will make sure while we try and hunt him down, that you are protected twenty-four hours a day."

That wasn't much consolation because Cari knew just how smart Dirk was. He had set himself up as the dictatorial leader of a drug ring and it had grown in size and scope in the four years he was in high school. He hadn't graduated, either, disappearing into the massive suburbs around San Francisco with his gang. She'd seen it happen with her own eyes. She was never interested in taking drugs or selling them; he'd wanted her to do both. She'd told her parents about his illegal activities, and they had talked with law enforcement, spent tons of money with psychiatrists and social workers, to try and "save" Dirk.

But none of that type of support had worked. Dirk was an out-of-control patriarchal white male with a fierce, focused need to have his own "army," as he'd referred to his drug gang. And he hated women. Especially her. Dirk had created a tattoo when he was twelve to make the boys around him feel like they were part of something special. Anyone wearing the Nazi swastika on their left forearm, with the inscription WARRIOR below it, was one of his followers. Too often, Cari had seen him in school with his gang, bullying other boys and girls, as well as selling drugs anytime he could get away with it. He was always being sent to the principal's office, always getting his hand slapped, but he wouldn't stop. Adults didn't scare him in the least. In fact, Cari wondered if anything scared him. She was sure as hell afraid of him.

She wondered about her parents. Were they still up? It was near four a.m. Should she call them now or wait until a decent hour? And what about herself? She usually took the bus into work and left her car in the garage beneath the townhouse. Was she safe to go out now or not? Was Dirk nearby? Watching where she lived? Waiting to jump her and put a bullet in her head like he had through Denise's head?

A cold wash of terror, so deep and upsetting, flowed through her. Intuitively, Cari knew Dirk would go after her first. He hated her more than anyone else on earth.

Sitting on the bed, she heard herself say into the phone to the sheriff, "What if he jumps me on the way to work?"

"Ma'am, we don't have those kinds of resources. The best we can do is to watch your townhouse."

Her throat closed up with dread, her hand moving against her neck, her fingers tightening around the phone. "What can I do? How do I protect myself? Dirk hated me and he hates my mother. What if he goes to attack her?"

"We've already talked to your parents, ma'am. They know the realities of this. Maybe you should take a vacation and remove yourself from this area for a week or two? We hope to catch him by then."

That was little compensation for something that was life-or-death to Cari. "A vacation?" There was derision in her tone. Disbelief. "That's the best you can do to protect us?"

"We told your parents to hire a trained law enforcement individual who can provide them around-the-clock protection. You could do the same."

That blew her away. "I'm sure a personal bodyguard for hire would cost a lot of money."

"Yes, ma'am, it would be a lot of money."

Anger wound through her. "Will you keep me and my parents informed on your search for Dirk?"

"Yes, we will. And once he's caught? You'll be the first to know."

"Did he escape alone or with others?"

"No. He was alone."

"He had a huge drug ring. Wouldn't it be logical that someone helped him from the outside?"

"The prison is still trying to trace his steps to escape. I don't have those answers yet, but once we do? We'll be in touch with all of you."

Her voice drained. "Okay, thanks for letting me know." And she hung up, sitting there, staring at the window with the blinds drawn. A bit of light leaked in around the edges of it. Living in the city meant she couldn't see the stars at night, something she'd loved as a child. But now, having streetlights felt comforting, making her feel less unsafe.

What was she going to do? Her mind was a clash of questions and no answers. What if they didn't catch Dirk? Prisoners had escaped before and disappeared. Why couldn't he? And she knew he had the capability of a chameleon. He was scarily intelligent, crafty, and strategic in his thinking. She'd seen him grow his Warrior gang from six boys into nearly a hundred of them as the years progressed.

She wiped her cheeks dry. Tears of fear.

The phone rang.

Cari jumped. Her heart took off in a wild staccato beat.

"Hello . . ." She whispered, afraid of who might be on the other end.

"Thank goodness you're there."

Relief plunged through her. It was her mother.

"Mom? Are you and Dad okay?"

"We're fine, Cari. I just wanted to call you, to see if the sheriff had gotten in touch with you yet."

"I-I just got off the phone with them. What are we going to do?"

"Not much except wait," Nalani said, sadness in her tone.

"How is Blake taking this?" After all, Dirk was his son.

"Not well at all. He's torn between Dirk maybe getting killed if law enforcement corners him, to Dirk hunting you and me down like he promised he would once he got out."

That cold, icy hand gripped her heart again. "Yes," she whispered faintly, "I've never forgotten, Mom."

"Neither of us have. He's so smart," she said wearily. "A brilliant genius gone astray."

Cari snorted. "He's a cold-blooded murderer, Mom. I don't care how smart he is."

"You're right, of course. We need a plan, Cari. What if they don't capture him? I know in my soul he's going after you first, and I'm tied in knots over worry about it."

Her hand tightened on the phone. "Yes . . . he will. I feel so helpless. What can I do? I hate guns with a passion. I don't want to learn how to carry one or shoot one. I couldn't kill anything, you know that. God, I had such a wonderful life since graduating. I have a dream job, something I love. Everything was going so well . . ."

Nalani sighed loudly. "Blake and I were talking about that just now. If Dirk isn't caught in two weeks? We both think you need to leave the state, get another job where Dirk can't find you. That way, you can at least have some peace. I know how much this is going to affect you daily,

Cari. You're not the kind of person to deal with this type of situation long-term. If Dirk isn't caught, we don't have a hundred thousand dollars a year to pay for one bodyguard, much less, two of them, to protect you and me."

"Is that how much it costs?" she said, disbelief in her tone.

"Actually, most bodyguards get around a hundred and fifty thousand dollars and upward, a year. We don't have that kind of money, and if Dirk's still on the loose, you will be his target."

"And you, too," she whispered wearily.

"His hatred is aimed at you, darling girl, and we're sick over this. We'll be fine. Blake is a hunter and we have guns in the house. He also can get both of us a concealed carry permit to have a weapon on us, which would make me feel much safer. I know you would not go that route."

"No, never . . . I saw him fire his gun at Denise . . . it's something I'll never forget, Mom. I-I just can't . . ."

"Which is why we think you should look for another job, Cari. My sense tells me Dirk isn't going to be recaptured very soon, and we need to keep you safe. We need a long-range plan in case he isn't in custody in the next two weeks. Also? We'd like you to vacate your townhouse for now. Blake would like to see you put in for vacation with your office. Your boss will understand and should give you the time off under these extenuating circumstances. Dirk could wait for you when you leave to go to work, too."

"I've already thought of that . . ."

"Would you do that for us? You can let us know where you are. We don't trust anyone to know our whereabouts. Computer information gets hacked out of sheriffs' departments, too. We want to wipe your footprints clear of your job and where you live. Would you do that for us?"

"To tell you the truth, I hadn't thought of these things. Yes, I'm sure my boss would give me time off. I think what I'll do is take my car and drive. I want to be near Muir Woods and the redwoods. I can get a long-term motel room rental in nearby Mill Valley. I would feel safe there because I know the area well. I can do a lot of hiking. The redwoods always give me a profound sense of peace and it's so calming and healing an area for me."

"Plus, you didn't start going there until after Dirk was in prison. He doesn't know your haunts, where you love to go."

"That's what I was thinking. Did you ever mention my love of Muir Woods to him when you visited him in prison?"

"No, he never asked about you and we purposely didn't talk about anything regarding you."

"Dirk never liked Nature. He was a city person. He liked the night life, the excitement, noise and lights," Cari murmured, feeling her heart rate begin to slowly stop racing. The adrenaline in her bloodstream made her feel shaky right now, a reaction to the fight-or-flight response, she supposed.

"I can call the sheriff's department and tell them they don't need to watch your townhouse twenty-four hours a day, then. We aren't going to tell them where you're at, however."

"Good plan." She looked up at the clock. It was early May, a beautiful month to be in San Francisco, one of her favorite months of the year. "We'll know in two weeks," she said more to herself than her mother.

"I don't think they'll capture Dirk. He's elusive, like a wild animal."

Animal was right, but Cari wouldn't even want to

compare Dirk to any other living thing. "He's a monster without a heart. Soulless. I don't care what anyone says."

"He is all of that," her mother sadly agreed. "You need to get on the computer and look for another job, just in case, Cari. I hate saying that because I know how happy you are with this one."

"I know. But I'm so afraid of him. He will come after me." She rubbed her face, her whole world in a slow-motion tumble, being destroyed once more by her step-brother. "Everything Dirk touches, dies, Mom. You know that."

"Yes, and I'm afraid you're going to have to disappear until he's caught if we go past this two-week limit law enforcement has set to recapture him."

"If only they would!" She could have her life back!

"We'll see," her mother answered hesitantly. "Dirk's mother was a drug addict, as you know. That's why Blake divorced her. Sherry loved her drugs more than anything else and Blake was worried about Dirk as a baby. He's sure that she sexually abused him even though he couldn't prove it."

"It was proven by his behavior as he grew up, Mom. He was angry all the time. I've lost count how many times he flew into a rage if you looked at him wrong, or stood up and confronted him. He hates women in general. All he wanted to do was destroy you if you disagreed with him on anything."

"Then, let's move forward with this plan. Muir Woods has always been your healing place. Call your boss this morning, and then pack and get out of there. You call us when you find a suitable motel to hole up in. Take your hiking gear, knapsack, and boots?"

She smiled softly, resting her elbows on her knees,

phone in her left hand. "You know me so well, Mom. I'll worry about you two, also."

"We'll be fine. It's you we worry about. You have no protection against him."

"I can have it by disappearing. He doesn't know where I live, knows nothing of my life, my likes or dislikes, Mom. I'm going to give him a cold trail to follow. I'll use my degree in agriculture, move to my biology major and take my camera and photograph the creatures that live in Muir Woods. That will make me happy. I'm always at peace when I'm out in the wilds and in rural areas."

"I know you are. Who knows? You might run into a honeybee hive out in the woods," she said.

"Oh, wouldn't that be wonderful? I'd love that! To see a wild hive? Nirvana." She laughed, feeling better, feeling some hope in the darkness embracing her.

"I'll never forget when you came home when you were five years old and told us what you'd done to save the queen and her swarm at the kindergarten. That was just incredible. Blake and I knew then that you would one day work with the bee people."

Cari appreciated her Hawaiian mother. She had grown up on Oahu, outside of Honolulu, where their family had fifty beehives. Their honey was sold throughout the Hawaiian Islands. Nalani had grown up learning from her father how to become a beekeeper, too. Five generations of her family maintained hives. They were referred to fondly as the *bee people.* "Finding wild hives is hard unless you're deep in woods where few people go," Cari agreed.

"Well, let's get this plan in motion."

"It's not fair one person can upset all our lives," Cari muttered, frowning.

"Nothing in life is fair," Nalani said gently. "Women

are adaptable and we'll do just that with Dirk on the loose. If we're lucky? This will be over soon and you won't have to institute these other possibilities."

"I hope you're right, Mom," she said, no hope in her tone. "My gut tells me my whole life is about to change and I have no idea if that's good or bad . . ."

Connect with

Visit us online at
KensingtonBooks.com
to read more from your favorite authors, see books
by series, view reading group guides, and more.

Join us on social media

for sneak peeks, chances to win books and prize packs,
and to share your thoughts with other readers.

facebook.com/kensingtonpublishing
twitter.com/kensingtonbooks

Tell us what you think!

To share your thoughts, submit a review,
or sign up for our eNewsletters, please visit:
KensingtonBooks.com/TellUs.

Books by Bestselling Author
Fern Michaels